MIND LIKE A DIAMOND

AMANDA PAVLOV

sword
&silk
books

Sword and Silk Books
105 Viewpoint Circle Pell City, AL 35128
Visit our website at SwordandSilkBooks.com

To request permissions contact the publisher at
admin@swordandsilkbooks.com.

First Edition: October 2021

Ebook: 978-1-7364300-7-1

❀ Created with Vellum

This book is dedicated to the hustlers, the dream-chasers, and the skeptics still searching for magic.

February 2002

Keeping secrets was my superpower. I inherited the skill from my mother, Ruelle. I didn't know whether my father shared the same tight lips, because I didn't know my father. As a child I wrote him letters, rolled them up and tucked them inside my mother's empty liquor bottles. But at seventeen, I only imagined him—and all the pirate witches Ruelle claimed we came from—as I sat on the balcony outside my bedroom, watching parade floats decorated to resemble ships rolling through the dense February fog.

To the rest of the world, it was just another Tuesday, but in New Orleans, it was Mardi Gras. The costumed strangers waving, the Krewe's King and Queen by their matching gold robes, could be anyone. Why not pretend they were my family? Doesn't every girl dream of a world where she could be related to royalty?

The creak of the door opening behind me turned my head. Ruelle stepped out onto the balcony with two forks in her fist and a plastic plate with a single slice of strawberry-cream-cheese king cake balanced in the crook of her arm. "Hey Lisette, you hungry?" she asked.

"Always," I said, moving my heavy combat boots to cover

up the pile of trinkets a few riders had tossed up to me before she could tease me about being childish.

"Which Krewe is this?" Ruelle squinted against the mist. "Neptune? They should be ashamed of themselves. Ships don't look *anything* like that. The ship I grew up on had a mermaid carved into the bow—"

"Yeah, I know—a mermaid with flowing locks accented with pearls. So many sails billowing, you would've thought a whole fleet approached. I remember."

Ruelle frowned but said nothing.

I chewed my king cake, the icing warm and gooey, melted from a quick spin in the microwave if I knew my mother. "If the ship was so fantastic, why did you leave?"

Ruelle speared a bite of cake, ignoring me.

"What are you giving up for Lent?" I asked. "My guidance counselor, Miss Fenty, suggested I give up staying up all night —maybe you could give up breaking into houses?"

Another, bigger bite of cake. After a beat, she said, "I only steal things that are insured. It's a victimless crime."

"Couldn't you do something else?" I asked, carving a sliver of cake for myself. "You say you have magic. There must be a thousand ways to use it that are—"

"What? Honorable? No, there is no honor in magic." Ruelle claimed the last bite for herself. "There are only degrees of evil."

She spun on her heels, leaving me alone to wonder why we still played this game. Part of me wanted to believe her stories about buried treasure and supernatural intervention. But how could I be descended from seafarers when I didn't even know how to swim? More likely she'd spun a fish tale, a whopper of ridiculous proportions to cover up whatever embarrassing facts had really brought us to New Orleans.

The thud of a brass band marching bled into my thoughts. I tapped my feet, fidgety from the sugar rush of cake on an empty stomach. Ash Wednesday meant no school in the morning, so I decided to follow the music. Rather than risk another fight with Ruelle, I climbed over my balcony and dropped to the identical one below. One last jump put me in the alley in between our dilapidated old building and its neighbor. Two majestic mansions of a by-gone era carved up into apartments with crumbling plaster walls and nightmarish plumbing. Relics redeemed by their prized location.

The parade had moved farther up my street, and I debated following. From the corner of my eye, I noticed my neighbor, Miss Opal, unmistakable even from behind by her beehive of blue hair. She leaned against her mahogany cane as she bent down to shake dry food into plastic bowls for the stray cats. I stepped further into the alley to help her.

"Hello Lisette," she greeted me without turning around. "Bit chilly to be out here without a jacket, don't you think?"

I followed her gaze to a puddle of water, my reflection revealing wind-blown curls and bare arms, reminding me everything had a logical explanation. "The cold doesn't bother me; I'm hot-blooded. Need some help?"

"Please." Miss Opal extended the bag of food to me. "I'm not as young as I was when the colony started. But I've made good progress. Notice how most of them have a notch in their left ear? That means they've been vaccinated and neutered and can't contribute to the overpopulation problem with more kittens."

I nodded politely, resisting the urge to pet the fluffy crea-tures congregating around the bowls as I filled them. Ruelle told me we couldn't have pets, claimed I was allergic. Probably a lie since she lied about everything, and yet it made me cautious around the creatures.

"See that calico one in the shadows?" Miss Opal raised a bony finger toward the cans overflowing with tourist trash— plastic cups stained with beer froth, greasy paper bags from hastily eaten po'boys—and for a moment, golden eyes stared back at me from behind an orange and black mask. What was such a beautiful cat doing out on the street?

"I see her," I whispered. "She's very pretty."

"Showed up a few weeks ago. Won't eat unless I'm gone, but that's all right. I'll earn her trust—then I'll trap her and take her to the vet."

"But if you trap her, won't you lose her trust?"

"Never thought about it like that." Miss Opal tapped one finger to her wrinkly lips. "But I would rather do right by her and have her fear me than do wrong by her and have her be my friend."

A gust of wind blew through the alley, rolling strings of broken beads close to the gutters. I hugged the half-empty bag of cat food to my chest, rubbing the goosebumps that had broken out across my bare arms.

"You look awful thin, child," Miss Opal remarked.

I slouched a bit, embarrassed. "Hard to keep weight on when you're six feet tall."

"Why don't you come on upstairs with me? I've got a big pot of seafood gumbo on the stove."

"Oh, that's okay. I'm not hungry," I lied.

"C'mon," Miss Opal said, touching my hand as she hobbled out of the alley. "I insist. Anyway, food tastes better with a friend."

My pride said no, but my stomach grumbled yes. I followed Miss Opal up the stairs, my hand on her elbow to steady her. Her hospitality touched me. Most of our neighbors had hated us. And who could blame them? Where Ruelle and I went, trouble followed. For three years, since the start of my freshman year, we'd lived here without incident: a sure sign the other shoe was unstable, swinging like those I saw on telephone wires during tropical storms. Who would it hit when it finally dropped?

SURVIVORS ARE GUILTY UNTIL PROVEN INNOCENT

Six Months Later

I woke up clutching my teddy bear, Bebe, feeling more seven than seventeen. Bebe was so old; I had loved all her stuffing out. Still, squeezing that bear-shaped scrap of fabric brought me comfort as the sirens outside my window sent me back to when we lived on Tulane Avenue and heard wailing all night —ambulances, cop cars, babies—a steady *wooo* of urgency.

Rubbing my eyes, I followed the sound to the front door where Ruelle was coiled in a shadow like a snake, clutching a shiny black rock. Minerals, she called them, but they looked like rocks to me. Stones, if I were feeling generous. The power she claimed they possessed seemed suspect. If they really worked, why were we always scrambling to pay our bills?

"What's going on out there?" I asked.

Ruelle shrugged. "Nothing. Just some cops trouncing through Miss Opal's place."

"If it's nothing, why are you holding that stone like you're about to bash someone upside the head with it?" I gestured toward her fist. "And what happened to Miss Opal?"

"Someone killed her," Ruelle said, flat as an old bottle of Coke. "Go back to bed. If they know you're up, they'll want to question you."

I sucked in air but still struggled to breathe. No. Not Miss

Opal. Who could've hurt the one person patient enough to put up with me? And why? I tried to remember the last conversation we'd had, over Chinese takeout because she swore she'd accidentally ordered too much, but there'd been nothing strange about it. Unless, of course, you count someone being kind for no reason as strange.

The cops' laughter echoed across the hallway, interrupting my thoughts. What a bunch of apathetic assholes. I tightened my hands into fists like balls at the end of chains, ready to swing and smash. But I said nothing, did nothing. Arguing with Ruelle was like teaching a pig to dance—utterly pointless and destined to get you dirty.

"Why are you still standing here?" she asked, stepping closer. "Go back to bed!"

Maybe it was my imagination, but I could've sworn I smelled sassafras on her breath, the signature ingredient in Miss Opal's gumbo. A knot formed in my stomach; my gut knew what my mind couldn't grasp. "Why were you in Miss Opal's apartment?" I asked.

She stuttered nonsense, tightening her grip on the stone. "It doesn't matter. I'm just the one who found her, not the one who hurt her."

"Who killed her?" I demanded, fingers digging into Bebe's shabby fur. "You have to go talk to the cops. You have to tell them—"

She shook her head, the dark circles under her blue eyes wet with tears. "People like us don't talk to police."

Miss Opal was laid to rest a few blocks away at St. Louis Cathedral. Hardly anyone showed up. At one point, some tourists wandered into the church, snapping pictures of the carved marble altar and gilded pews. An usher advised them it was a private event, and they shuffled out, muttering curses like drunks being escorted from a party.

Some party. The priest who spoke hardly seemed to know her. After the service, her family rushed out of the church, eager to move on it appeared. Miss Opal would've been so disappointed. She deserved a second line, a full jazz band like the ones that played when important musicians passed. But there was no spectacle to send her into the next life.

Ruelle didn't go to the funeral. She was too busy making some changes to our apartment—arranging clusters of rocks along the windowsills and drawing strange symbols onto our floors in red ink. Appalled, I stared at our beautiful original wood floors. To keep from crying, I cracked a joke. "We are *so* not getting our deposit back."

Ruelle sprawled out on the saggy denim sofa that doubled as her bed. Her black curls pooled against the armrest. "A problem for another day. Can't you see I'm exhausted?" she huffed, the sickly sweet smell of Coke mixed with whiskey on her breath.

"Getting drunk in the middle of the day doesn't help," I said before I could stop myself.

Ruelle could be insensitive sober, but drunk she was downright cruel. She scowled at me in that foul, familiar way of hers. She was about to throw something back in my face, like a wall I colored on when I was two, but she noticed my expensive black dress and switched gears. "Where did *that* come from?"

"I borrowed it. From Xavier's mom."

"Go take it off. I don't have money to get it dry-cleaned if you get it dirty."

I winced. "Okay. But first, I want to ask you something."

"What?" She sat up wearily, looking much older than the thirty-five she claimed.

"Are we… are we responsible for what happened to Miss Opal?"

"What do you mean by that, Lisette?" She spat my name out like sour milk.

I took a step back. "I mean, don't you think it's kind of *weird* for someone to break into a third-floor apartment, and not even a *nice* apartment…"

Ruelle huffed. "I thought you loved this apartment."

"That's not the point! My point is… well… do you think it's *possible* the people who broke into her apartment… the people who killed her… were really after us?"

Ruelle stared at her hands. She wasn't wearing her lucky ring, probably so as not to get it dirty. I couldn't help imagining the red ink staining her fingertips was blood. Ruelle's silence confirmed her guilt and amplified mine. We had caused Miss Opal's death.

"You want to move?" Ruelle asked at last. "Maybe it would be better if—"

"No!" I shook my head for emphasis. I loved our apartment. Loved my balcony, loved walking to the levee to watch the boats roll by. I couldn't bear the thought of moving. Not again.

"If you want to stay here," Ruelle said, her voice clipped and cold as hail, "you must *never* say anything like that again. Not a word of people being after us or anything like that. To speak such evil is to invite it. Do you understand?"

"I understand," I said, choking back a sob.

"Good. Now go change your clothes. We have an errand to run at Lagniappe."

What errand could we have at Lagniappe Pawn? To my knowledge, she hadn't pulled a job this week. Work was always slow after Labor Day, when people stopped vacationing. Fewer empty houses meant fewer opportunities, which meant we lived lean until Thanksgiving.

"Be thinking about what color rug you want for your room." Ruelle's voice followed me into my bedroom—the sight of fresh graffiti on my floors making me gasp.

"Why do we need rugs?" I answered as I unzipped the dress and stepped out of it.

"So what happened to Miss Opal doesn't happen to us," Ruelle answered.

"Who killed Miss Opal? Why? How will rugs—"

"No more questions," Ruelle snapped. "Less you know, safer you are. And from now on, if anybody asks, we barely knew Miss Opal. You got that?"

I wanted to scream, to release the frustration bubbling up at the back of my throat. But maybe Ruelle had a reason to keep her secrets. Maybe I was safer in the dark.

"Lisette! You got that?"

"Got it," I grumbled, grabbing a faded purple Prince t-shirt off the floor. I straightened my shoulders, compressing all my nasty emotions—guilt, anxiety, and fear—into a tight little ball. Then I shoved the ball deep down inside of me where it could never bounce back up. I had to bury my emotions. Otherwise, they might bury me.

The bells from St. Louis Cathedral chimed, marking the quarter-hour. Usually, I absorbed their peal unconsciously, but on this particular night, the incessant clanging interrupted my eavesdropping.

I cracked my bedroom door open, so I could peer through and read Ruelle's lips whispering into the cheap plastic phone tethered to the pony-wall between the galley kitchen and our meager living room. "No, they didn't find it. What do you mean, how do I know? I just know."

Ruelle twisted her lucky ring—a silver horseshoe set off by four flawless half-carat diamonds—around her right index finger, a nervous tic so familiar it hardly registered.

"Tonight? Why does it have to be tonight? I would've appreciated some advance—" Ruelle's mouth hung open, but no sound escaped. The person on the other end must have been yelling because she rarely shut up otherwise.

"Fine. I will get it tonight. But this is it. After this, I owe you nothing. You got that? Nothing." The whispering must've worn through her restraint. She slammed the phone down so hard it bounced out of its cradle and hit the black-and-white-checkered tile floor with a *crack*.

I eased my door shut and tiptoed over to my twin mattress. Instead of a headboard, I had a bulletin board cluttered with ribbons from gymnastics competitions and group photos someone else's mom took in which I towered over the rest of my teammates. I was *whoa-that-girl-is-tall* in most situations, but when I hit the mat at gymnastics meets, I was a freak show with free admission.

There was only one memento of me and Ruelle, a caricature drawing from a day spent playing tourist in the Quarter. We had powdered sugar on our noses and exaggerated smiles on our faces. Maybe that's why I liked it so much; Ruelle never looked that happy in real life.

A Polaroid of my only real friend, Xavier Monroe, was tacked beside ticket stubs to concerts we'd attended. I never cared who we saw because it was always on his dime. In the picture, he leaned against his fully restored 1957 Thunderbird convertible with his vintage aviators perched on the bridge of his upturned nose. That was why I liked Xavi. He didn't chase trends. He appreciated the classics like me.

I moved my faded blue backpack aside, careful not to whack Bebe, and laid down on my stomach. The combination of the hard mattress and foreboding dread pressed against my abdomen, carrying fumes of the peanut butter sandwich I had for dinner up to my throat. Ruelle was hiding something big, maybe something to do with Miss Opal.

Rather than indulge my urge to squeeze Bebe, I unzipped the backpack and took my calculus textbook out—the only subject Ruelle wouldn't pretend to understand. I didn't have homework but couldn't let on that I'd been listening. I opened the book, but my mind wandered to more pressing problems. What did Ruelle need to do tonight? I couldn't rest until I knew.

The door swung open, and Ruelle barged in. Her forehead was damp, her dark hair a halo of frizz. "Oh good, you're studying."

"Yup." I stared at the textbook, afraid my eyes would betray me. "You work tonight?"

Ruelle nodded. "You know the drill. Don't go out and don't answer the door."

I slammed my textbook shut, rolled over, and sat on the edge of my bed. The stiff fibers of the faded wool rug Ruelle had put on my floor to cover her weird artwork pricked my toes through my socks. "You can't keep me in the dark forever. I want to come."

"Stay put, Lisette. This isn't one of your video games."

I ignored her, scanning the floor for my Doc Marten knockoffs. "Why is it okay for you to make money however you see fit, but when I want a piece of the action, you ice me out?"

Ruelle didn't speak, but I recognized her expression. She wore the same one when we met with the principal at St. Bernadette's to ask about scholarships for people with *financial hardships*. Same downcast eyes, same cheeks flushed with embarrassment. She fiddled incessantly with her stupid ring. It was probably worth a mint, but she'd never dream of selling it. Even the week we lived in a tent beneath the I-10 overpass, it stayed on her finger, the diamonds turned to her palm to avoid attention.

I reached out and touched her forearm. "You know what Miss Fenty says? She says it's okay to ask for help when you need it. Strong people ask for help, even when it's hard."

Ruelle withdrew her arm and rubbed the back of her neck. Then she picked her chin up, smiled, and said, "I got this, Lis. You keep studying. I'm gonna pull this one last job and then that's it, I swear."

I nodded, pretending to believe her. But how could I? She lied as easily as she walked out the front door without me.

The moment she was gone, I went back to looking for my boots. I spied them under my bed, dug them out, and pulled them on. As I laced them up, I wondered who would pull into the alley to pick Ruelle up. I didn't have the means to follow, but that wouldn't stop me from trying.

After several minutes of staring at the empty alley, it finally clicked into place—no one was coming to get her. She'd never left the building.

I don't know whose feet carried me out of our apartment and across the hall, though they wore my boots. It felt like watching a video of myself doing something out of character. Like the old home movie of me opening so many presents on Christmas morning when I was five. Ruelle had won enough money gambling at Harrah's Casino to buy a camcorder for herself and a new winter coat for me. I thought we'd finally gotten a lucky break, found a way to pay our bills on time. But the very next month, they banned her, and the camcorder went back to the pawnshop.

But no matter how bad things got, she tried to shield me. Drew the line at letting me be a lookout when she robbed houses. That's why I couldn't believe my fingers freed a bobby pin from my hair, releasing a wayward spray of curls. Had to be someone else; I didn't pick locks. I had only watched Ruelle enough times to guess how.

Surreal is the only word that comes close to describing it, the satisfaction I experienced wiggling that bobby pin around in the lock on Miss Opal's front door. It reminded me of cutting the tags off my new Christmas coat. And when the lock clicked and the door popped open, I thought about how I'd spun around the living room, the hem of that new winter coat whirling while Ruelle filmed me. I deserved this, needed this closure.

I expected the apartment to be empty, but apparently her family hadn't gotten around to it yet. The sight of Miss Opal's antique settee with a cozy quilt draped over the back made my eyes water. I sniffled, my eyes following the bright artificial beam of a streetlight shooting through the windowpane of her balcony door and landing on her old record player. I imagined the black blur of a record spinning, Etta James' raspy voice twisting my heartstrings into knots.

Miss Opal played it for me when I told her about my crush ignoring me at school. She made me pralines and promised my heart would heal. Who would bake me comfort food to ease the pain of losing her?

"What the hell is wrong with you?" my mother's voice broke through my bittersweet memory. "I told you to stay put. Close the door and go home."

I honored half of Ruelle's request, closing the door behind me after I stepped inside. Darkness pressed at my sides, so I kept my eyes forward, soaking up the dim light of the moon leaking through the lacy curtains hanging across the kitchen window. I saw her silhouette, back pressed against the fridge. She had something in her hand—something long like a cane, but metallic instead of wood.

"What are you doing here?" I asked. "Tell me right now, or I'll—I'll call the cops."

Ruelle snorted. "Go home, Lisette."

I stepped toward her. "Not until you tell me why you're here."

She raised her hand, moonbeams bouncing off the shiny blade and illuminating the ornate hilt of a sword so gorgeous I wanted to break it into pieces and clip them in my curls.

"Whoa," I said. "That sword is beautiful."

"Yeah, and it's dangerous. And so are the people who want it. That's why you need to go. They can't know you're here. They can't—"

The thud of footsteps on the stairs cut her off. All the color drained from her face. "Shit," Ruelle said. "Quick, go out on the balcony and hide. I'll come get you when it's safe."

She never cursed in front of me, so I didn't argue.

The layout of Miss Opal's apartment was completely different from ours, her balcony positioned off her living room. Once I stepped outside, I realized her balcony wasn't like mine at all either. The intricate ironwork had rusted out in places, and the bottom sloped so sharply I had to press my body against the building to keep from feeling like I might slide off. Jumping down occurred to me, but the balcony below hers had a giant crater in the middle. Besides, if I left now, I might never know who these people were—Miss Opal's murderers, possibly. I needed to hear their voices, see their faces. Had to know who they were so I could make them pay for what they had done.

I held my breath as the front door creaked open and clapped shut softly. Two voices—one polite if high-pitched and the other low and rough as sandpaper feels—exchanged greetings with Ruelle.

"We should go to my place next door," Ruelle said. "This place is practically a crime scene."

"Let's just get this over with," the rough voice said. "Is that it? Let me see it."

But Ruelle held her ground. "You got the money?"

"What money?" the rough voice growled. "We already paid you."

"You paid me half," Ruelle said. "Where's the other half?"

"Easy now, both of you," the polite voice said. "Rue, we'll give you the other half once the item's been verified. It's a simple process, shouldn't take more than two, three days tops."

When he referred to her by that nickname, I realized who he was—Mr. Amos, the grandfatherly gentleman who owned Lagniappe Pawn Shop. He always had a butterscotch and a genuine compliment ready for me, sometimes let me borrow rare books so long as I promised to take care of them and actually read them. It was hard to imagine him hurting Miss Opal, or anyone for that matter.

I inched my way closer to the door. Through the small pane near the top of the door, I could see their silhouettes. The moonlight glowed against the shorter man's bald head, definitely Mr. Amos. The man with the gruff voice was much taller. He wore a sleeveless shirt, his biceps accented in tattoos

I couldn't identify at this distance. He spoke first. "What I don't understand is that Freestar's *bragging* about it. Saying they stole the sword back."

Ruelle laughed. "They have a decoy. Now give me what I want, and I'll give you what you want. Or should I call Styg and let him know his minions murdered an old woman over a clever forgery? Surely he'd pay me the half you owe, or more."

"Now Rue," Mr. Amos said. "Don't go saying anything you don't mean."

The tall man stepped toward my mother, his shoulders taut, muscles tense. "Yeah, *Rue*. And don't go acting as if I can't just take it from you."

He moved as if to lunge, and I gasped. The tall man whirled around, and I dropped down, fast enough I hoped he hadn't seen me peering through the pane.

"What was that?" the tall man demanded.

Fear made me delirious, and every cartoon joke played in my head. Should I meow like a cat or tweet like a bird? Tell him there's no one here but us chickens?

"What was what?" Ruelle said, but her voice cracked on the second *what*.

"Someone's out there," the tall man said. "And if you won't say who, I'll just go over and see for myself."

Panic made my limbs twitchy from my unstable crouch. Then my feet began to slide, and from this angle I had nothing to grab. Gymnasts will do anything not to fall. It takes half a point off your score, and besides, it's embarrassing. So I didn't fall. I jumped.

BUSTED
NOT
BURIED

Flying through the air like a superhero felt amazing. I was my best self, a graceful gymnast defying gravity. In my mind, my hair was flowing, legs straight, perfect form. But it doesn't matter how good you look jumping if you don't stick the landing.

My back slammed into something rock hard, and the pain ripped a scream right out of my throat. Fear pushed my mind into dark places. Had I fallen on something sharp and cut myself open? Had I punctured a lung? No matter how much air I sucked in, I couldn't seem to satisfy the urge. A gruff voice called out in the distance. The man in Miss Opal's apartment—how long would he look for me?

I squeezed my eyes shut, lips trembling in prayer, begging God or whoever might be listening to give me a do-over. Restart the game, whisk me back to my bedroom and let me try this level again.

When I opened my eyes, I was still lying on my back in the alley. Fuzzy little dots swirled around my face, their bodies blinking gold. Lightning bugs? I swiped at them, but they disappeared inside my hands. I couldn't feel the weight of their bodies. They weren't real. Was any of this real?

Before I could decide, the world around me faded to black. When the color returned, I was lying on my bed, alone in my room. I tried to leap to my feet, eager to confirm it'd all been a horrible nightmare, but the movement triggered pain in my back so intense I couldn't breathe. I don't know how long I lay there in agony before the front door swung open so hard it banged into the wall.

Ruelle entered my bedroom, breathing so heavily she could hardly choke out my name. "Lisette, you're here. Oh, thank God, you're here."

"How, though?" I asked. "I fell. I couldn't move. I still can't move. How did I get here?"

"All that matters is you're here," Ruelle said, crouching beside me to brush the hair out of my face. "Don't worry, I'm going to take care of you. I'm going to fix it so nothing bad ever happens to you again."

The pain swelled again, knocking me down and pulling me under like a wave. Ah, hello again, Darkness. Back so soon?

When I awoke again, I was on a cold metal table wearing nothing but a thin, scratchy blanket. The room gave me major bunker vibes, and I wasn't sure if it was window-less to protect me from prying eyes or prevent me from escaping.

I tried to sit up, but the sudden explosion of pain in my spine stopped me in my tracks. I'm embarrassed to admit I cried out for my momma. Worse, she didn't answer.

Two white-gloved hands on my chest eased me back down. "Whoa there," said a deep but pleasant voice, like Mr. Rogers. "Take it easy, Catwoman. Don't need you passing out again."

"Catwoman?" I repeated, dazed. I squinted, trying to make out the speaker's face, but the bright light in my eyes made it so all I could see was his tall and stocky outline.

"Isn't that who you are? Who else would jump off a balcony expecting to land on her feet? Who else has nine lives to play around with?"

"Where am I?" I muttered. "How did I get here?"

"All right, enough," Ruelle cut in. "Can you help her or not?"

I bit my lip. So she was there. She was somewhere right outside my field of vision, and yet she hadn't made her presence known until now. Why?

"You only paid for a consultation," the stranger said, the politeness fading from his voice. "But yes, I can help her—if you can afford the fee."

"As soon as I get paid from this gig—"

"Right. And as soon as I get paid to help your kid…"

"Who said she was my kid?"

The stranger laughed. "I don't care who she is. I don't do *favors* for people like you who only deign to speak to the spiritual world when no one on earth listens."

I shielded my eyes, trying desperately to see the man Ruelle was speaking to, only to realize a glittering Mardi Gras mask obscured his entire face. In the right setting, the ceramic mask would have been comical with its purple sequins and flashy green feathers drizzled in gold glitter. But this was very much the *wrong* setting.

"Fine. I'll get you the money tonight," Ruelle said. "Let me call my boss."

"Phone is upstairs," the masked man said. "My secretary can help you set up a transfer. We take cards, but there's a three percent fee."

"Of course there is." Ruelle squeezed my hand so hard it hurt. "Hey kid, you all right? You look like dried-out dog shit."

I winced. Mothers were not supposed to casually insult their children. "I'm in a lot of pain. My back hurts so bad."

"You took a pretty nasty spill. Crushed two vertebrae. Spot you hit is too high up for a brace. You're gonna have to walk it off. Be tough. You understand?"

"I understand."

"Good girl. The doctor is gonna fix you up the best he can. I'm gonna go upstairs and handle the payment."

"Wait, before you go," my voice dropped to a whisper, "I need to know something."

Ruelle leaned in close and tilted her ear toward my lips. "Go ahead."

"Did they pay you for the sword?"

She nodded as she rose back to her feet. "It's all gonna be okay. Now try to relax."

Ruelle left me alone with the doctor. I could see the back of his head, dark silky curls pinned down by the bright purple ribbon holding his mask in place. He whistled as he moved around the space, readying his tools. The gentle clink of glass and the crunch of something being freed from its packaging sent shivers down my spine.

"Are you going to give me something for the pain?" I asked.

"No," the doctor said. "I'm going to take all the pain away."

Before I could ask him to clarify, a phone rang, and he answered. "Doctor Montgomery speaking. She did? Good. I'll wait for her then."

I gulped. "Doctor Montgomery?"

"I'm right here. Don't worry, Ruelle's coming back to hold your hand."

"What's going to happen to me?"

"You'll see."

I gritted my teeth, fighting through the pain, and managed to get my elbows underneath me. From this new angle, I caught sight of him fussing with something made from brown cloth. Was that... my teddy bear? I craned my neck, resulting in another wave of pain so intense I struggled to remain conscious. What was he doing with Bebe?

"Breaks my heart to see you so afraid of me." Dr. Montgomery snapped on a fresh pair of surgical gloves. "Your momma put some nasty ideas in your head about me, huh? But you aren't scared of me, are you?"

I bit my tongue, unsure of how to respond. Why was Ruelle pretending she wasn't my mother? Should I keep up the ruse? I already felt exposed, a scratchy blanket the only thing between me and a masked stranger. "Is that my bear?"

"Relax, girl, I ain't gonna hurt you. Your momma's a liar. Worse, she ain't got no sense. If you were my daughter, I'd let you learn from your injury," Dr. Montgomery said. "There's a price for taking away the pain. Price is you don't learn from it. Then one day you wake up and you just like your momma, grown-ass woman with no damn sense."

Before I could formulate a response, the door at the top of the stairs opened. Ruelle stomped down, her blue eyes cold and flinty. The fee must've been more than she'd anticipated.

Dr. Montgomery shot Ruelle a cursory glance. "Glad you decided to join us. I couldn't get ahold of my nurse at this hour, so I hope you won't mind acting as my assistant."

"Sure," Ruelle replied. "Do we get a three percent discount?"

Dr. Montgomery chuckled. "How about a free follow-up appointment?" He handed Ruelle something shiny.

"I only need her thumbnails to finish the poppet," Dr. Montgomery explained, which gave me approximately zero comfort.

I wiggled around on the table like a fresh-caught fish. Each movement made my back hurt worse, but I was too nervous to hold still.

"Close your eyes," Ruelle said. "You won't want to watch."

I had never liked being told what to do. My eyes bulged as Ruelle gingerly snipped one of my thumbnails and then the other. She handled the little crescent-shaped clippings as though they were priceless diamonds, cupping them in her palm. Dr. Montgomery picked them out with tweezers, moving with painstaking precision, as if dropping them would cause a nuclear explosion.

Dr. Montgomery set the clippings aside and handed Ruelle

another tool. Scissors! Why did she need scissors? "What's happening?" I whispered. But she only shook her head, unable or unwilling to tell me. My fingers gripped at the thin sheet, searching for comfort but finding none. "What's he doing with Bebe?" I asked.

"Sorry about this," Ruelle whispered, "but it's the only way."

Before I could beg for mercy, she gathered up my hair and hacked two inches off. Two inches, just a trim to most people, but my hair was my crowning glory, the only thing I liked about myself. Having it stolen reduced my essence from six feet to two.

Dr. Montgomery gathered up the springy ringlets and affixed them to my bear. My heart pounded like it might explode. I opened my mouth to demand he give Bebe back, but my voice escaped as an unintelligible squeak.

He sewed my hair to Bebe's head as if the needle were fused to his fingers, obeying his brain as any other appendage would. He used surgical glue to attach my thumbnails to her paws.

Then he set to work adorning Bebe in a little black dress. Her clothes reminded me of my own nakedness beneath the thin sheet, and I looked to my mother, searching for comfort she couldn't provide, as usual. Ruelle twisted her lucky ring around frantically, exposing the little white line where her finger never felt the sun.

"What's your name?" Dr. Montgomery asked, but before I could answer, Ruelle cut in, "I already told you—you don't need to know."

"The ritual needs her name."

"It's her bear, her hair, and her nails. The spirits will know who she is."

Poor Bebe. I could've sworn her button eyes were wide with fear.

"Fine, but don't blame me if it doesn't take." He held

Bebe high in the air and chanted, "Come spirits of war to drink your fuel, come spirits of peace to end this duel. Come healing spirits from every plane! Fill this vessel with her pain." He mumbled something beneath his breath I couldn't quite catch. It reminded me of the part during Mass where the priest blessed the Eucharist, holding it up toward heaven and speaking some magical nonsense that apparently only God could hear.

At last, Dr. Montgomery set Bebe aside and turned toward me. "Don't fight me," he warned. "If you do, I might hurt you. And I don't want to hurt you."

Before I could ask for an explanation, he slid his mask up, exposing his face for a moment so fleeting I couldn't make out any of his features—only the deep olive hue of his skin as his face flew toward me.

With his mouth pressed against mine, my instincts told me to push him away. He was violating my space, my choice. The worst part wasn't his weight, pressing down onto me, pinning me against the cold table. It wasn't the sickly-sweet flavor of the tobacco he must have recently inhaled. It was knowing my mother was right there, letting it happen.

I trembled. Helpless. Paralyzed with fear, wondering what he would do next. Then I realized he wasn't kissing me. He didn't pry my lips apart to push his tongue into my mouth as I expected he would. Rather, he was inhaling. Hard. Sucking the air out of my lungs so violently, I feared I might suffocate.

At last, he pulled away, leaving me gasping, my chest heaving, desperately working to replace the oxygen he'd stolen from me.

Then the real madness began.

He pressed his mouth against my teddy bear's mouth and blew.

I couldn't be sure I was still awake. It had to be a nightmare. This couldn't happen in the waking world. Bebe... she was... *screaming*.

She twisted her tiny body, struggling to escape from Dr. Montgomery's tight grip around her soft brown arms. The tenacious way she fought back reminded me of myself. But he didn't let go. He blew, blew, blew my pain into her.

My suffering wrapped itself around my dear old friend, choking her. She went limp, her tiny limbs still in defeat. Dr. Montgomery pulled his mouth away, his own chest shaking from the effort, slid his mask back in place, and seized up his needle and thread.

"No! No, no, no, no, no!" Bebe cried in a voice so chillingly similar to mine that for a moment, I thought I was the one screaming.

Dr. Montgomery stitched away at her gaping mouth, each scream a little softer than the last, until she couldn't make a sound. Until only her sad blue-button eyes expressed her torment.

"For the next three days, you must sleep with this poppet underneath your back." Dr. Montgomery handed me my bear. "It will continue to absorb your pain. After sunset on the third day, bury it. It will take your pain to its grave."

I stared at Bebe, unable to express my emotions. She had been the one constant in my turbulent life, and this was how I repaid her—by filling her with my pain and burying her.

"Thank you, Dr. Montgomery," Ruelle said. She shook his still-gloved hand. "Thank you for seeing us at this hour."

Dr. Montgomery nodded. He walked over to a little steel sink and turned on the water. He peeled his gloves off with a sickening pop. "You remember the best practices for burying the poppet?"

Ruelle nodded. "I will instruct her when the time comes."

"Very well. As I mentioned, the ritual may be impacted by omitting her name. You know how to reach me if any problems arise."

Ruelle reached out and squeezed my shoulder. "Come on. Let's go."

But I didn't move. I stared at my Bebe, limp in my hands yet thrumming with energy. Her little mouth sewn shut. Her black dress, the fabric I recognized as taken from my own black pants.

"What's the holdup? Let's go."

"I can't." My voice cracked. "I'm naked."

"Oh. Right." Ruelle shook her head as if admonishing herself. She turned to Dr. Montgomery. "Do you have an extra set of scrubs or something?"

"Sure. Tell you what—since you did such a great job assisting me—they're on the house."

I laughed. Not because it was a particularly good joke, but because I was so tightly wound up that any release was welcome. I laughed so hard my belly jiggled. Then suddenly I stopped. *Holy tamales*. My back didn't hurt anymore.

SPILLED
GUTS,
NO
GLORY

I woke up with Bebe wedged in between my shoulder blades. She seemed to cling to me, desperate to be consoled. How many times had I held her, found solace in her touch? Now she wanted me to hold her. But as I yanked her off, my face screwed up in disgust like I had plucked off a leech. The sight of my hair tacked onto her head made me want to throw her across the room. Guilt stung my heart like lemon juice in a paper cut as I set her down on the mattress across from me.

Stop it, I told myself. *Bebe is only a toy. Toys don't have feelings. You got a little sweaty in your sleep, and she stuck to your back. End. Of. Story.*

If I trusted my sleepy eyes, I would've said Bebe appeared to be waking up, too. She seemed to stretch her furry arms. The sight of my fingernail clippings attached to her paws like crescent-shaped claws made me shudder.

My memories of the previous night—the sword, Bebe screaming, the excruciating pain in my back vanishing after the ritual—were like wild animals hiding behind trees. I stayed very still in my bed, hoping to coax them out to the forefront of my mind, where I could see them clearly. But they remained nothing more than rustling sounds, too quiet to pinpoint their location but too loud to be the wind.

Ruelle tapped on the door, then swung it open before I could invite her in. Pretty polite for Ruelle. In one hand, she carried a white mug with a faded green Café du Monde logo advertising the restaurant where it was pilfered. Her other hand held a plate, but as she gave it to me, I lost my appetite. Dry toast. Gross.

"Breakfast in bed, how glamorous." I set the plate down and took a big swig from the mug. Dark roast with chicory. No sugar. No cream. This was how Ruelle took her coffee. I preferred a splash of espresso in my cup of milk and sugar. It was so bitter I nearly spit it out.

"Eat up. And drink every last drop," Ruelle said. "You need your strength. You'll have to keep your head up in the halls today. If anyone notices you're acting odd, it could draw attention to you. Someone could connect us with Miss Opal's murder."

"But we were in her apartment last night, weren't we? I fell somehow, didn't I?" I rubbed my temples, willing the details to return.

"We aren't discussing this anymore. You understand?"

I blinked at her, baffled. Why wouldn't she tell the police what really happened? Didn't she think Miss Opal deserved justice? Then again, Ruelle's selfishness was nothing new.

"You understand?" Ruelle repeated a little sharper.

I nodded to end the conversation. My hand holding the mug shook, and a little coffee sloshed over the side, splashing onto my purple velvet bedspread. The bedspread was a birthday present, so it was relatively new, and like all new things, Ruelle was annoyingly precious about it.

"Oh, now look what you've done." Ruelle snatched the mug away, which of course, spilled more coffee and left a big brown blotch in its wake. "I swear Lisette, right when I think you're starting to grow up, you do something so childish and make me feel like a fool for—"

"Hold up. What are you talking about right now? Because I get the feeling it isn't a little spilt coffee. Are you mad at me? Because I'm not the one who involved poor Miss Opal—"

"Enough," Ruelle snarled. "Eat your breakfast."

I tore into a piece of toast, chewing aggressively, wondering why we never had butter or jam. "Miss Opal had me eating much better than you ever—"

"ENOUGH! We're never going to talk about this again. Do you understand me? Never."

I rolled my eyes. "Well, what do I say when people notice this?" I lifted my arms. The cuts I sustained in the fall were small but numerous. A few scratches might have gone by without notice, but so many cuts would undoubtedly draw questions.

"You'll keep your school sweater on." Ruelle disappeared into the hallway and returned with a rag to mop up the spilled coffee.

"But what if that's not enough? What if someone notices I'm hurt?"

"Deny it."

"What do you mean? No way can I convince the whole school I'm fine. I can hardly stand up straight without doubling over in pain."

Ruelle blotted the coffee up little by little until it was like the spill never happened. "Fine. You were trying to sneak out through your balcony—yes, I know you do it—and I caught you, which scared you and made you fall."

"Gee, thanks for taking some of the blame here, Mom."

Ruelle reached over and stole a piece of toast. "Should I take some of the blame? Last I checked, I wasn't the one who decided to jump off a balcony like an idiot."

I blinked at her, hardly able to recall jumping, much less why. "Oh? I'm an idiot now? Well, guess what? You're a crappy mom. What kind of parent brings their kid to some sketchy doctor who doesn't even—"

"Lisette, stop."

"And another thing!" I slapped my mattress for emphasis, "Why were you pretending you weren't my mom? Are you too cool to give me a hug? Then you left me alone with—"

"That's enough! You have no idea what I did for you! Do you know what my mother would have done? She would have told me to suck it up! She would have told me to walk it off! She wouldn't have wasted *her* money taking *me* to *any* doctor! You think I wanted to pretend like I hardly knew you? You think that was fun for me? I was trying to protect you, Lisette. He knew me—they all know me—but I don't want them to know you. I want you to have something better than what I have. Be someone better than me."

"Too bad, because I'm not."

"You will be. Now finish your coffee and get dressed. I'm driving you to school."

"But Xavier drives me to school."

"I called him, let him know I was taking you. I'll be picking you up, too. You need to avoid him and anyone else who's comfortable enough to ask questions. Now go ahead and get ready."

"What about…" I trailed off, struggling to acknowledge the tiny button-eyed elephant in the room. "What about Bebe?"

"The poppet can come in the car, but you'll have to leave it with me during school. We can't risk someone seeing it."

Every hair on my arms stood up. "What exactly is a poppet? What did he do to her?"

"What do you think?"

"I don't know."

"That's a good place to be. If you believe in it too strongly, the wrong person can use it against you. If you don't believe at all, it won't heal you."

"What?" I yelped. "What does that mean?"

"Drink your coffee," she said, pressing the cup to my lips. "We'll talk more in the car."

But the conversation we had in the car left me more

confused.

"It's like the doctor told you, at night the poppet soaks up your pain. This can take a little time to work." Ruelle stared straight ahead as though the road might suddenly swerve in any direction. "In the meantime, you'll notice when you're away from it, the pain comes back. The farther away your poppet is, the worse you will hurt. There are sometimes other side eff—"

"You've got to be kidding me! I don't understand why I can't stay home. My back hurts just thinking about it." I wriggled in my seat, unable to get comfortable.

"I know it hurts, Lis. And it's going to get worse before it gets better. But I don't bust my ass paying for school so that you can stay home feeling sorry for yourself."

"Cut the crap. I know I have a scholarship."

"Partial scholarship," Ruelle corrected me. "I still pay tuition. Not to mention your uniform. And do you think those gymnastics classes you take are cheap? You are the most ungrateful—"

I rolled my eyes. "Right, I know. I never appreciate anything. You give me everything I could possibly want."

"Damn straight I do," Ruelle replied, missing my sarcasm. "You think I had hobbies when I was a teenager? I still don't have hobbies."

Ruelle turned into the drop-off zone in front of St. Bernadette's. The tasteful limestone steps looming in the background appeared as impassable as Mt. Everest in the dead of winter.

"Can't we say I have the flu? That should buy me three days. Please?"

Ruelle bit her lip. "Here." She dug into her purse and produced an emerald about the size of a pencil eraser. "Take this; it has powerful healing qualities if you—"

"Ugh," I huffed. "You know I don't believe in that crap."

I stared at her, waiting for her to take the bait, to explain what happened to me. But she just dropped the emerald back into her purse like it was medicine I'd refused instead of magic.

It hurt my back when I slammed the door. But it felt good, too. Like fighting back when you know you're outgunned.

Every step onto campus hurt more than the last. Even when I stood still, the pain swelled. It must have been because she was driving away with Bebe. I tried to relax, tried to play it cool. No one could find out. But hiding my hesitancy was hard when every step felt like easing into a frigid pool. I struggled to lift my backpack. My eyes darted down the hallway, looking for Xavier, but he wasn't around. The hallway was practically empty, save those few students too rich to worry about getting to class on time. Kids like Alison Smithers.

Alison with her silky platinum hair and gray eyes like a shark. And like a shark, she could smell blood in the water from a quarter of a mile away. She made a beeline for me, her plaid skirt swishing against her tanned thighs. Her skirt was shorter than the handbook dictated, but the teachers were too afraid of her, or rather her well-connected family, to write her a demerit for it.

"What's wrong with you, Lisette?" Alison moved closer. Her button nose twitched like a curious rabbit's.

I sighed and set my backpack down. "Nothing... my back's just a bit sore... from practice."

Alison's gray eyes narrowed. "Sore backs don't make people stutter. Something weird is going on with you. What is it?"

"Nothing. I just, fell off my balcony sneaking out, okay?"

"Sneaking out to go where?"

I rolled my eyes so hard I swear I felt my mascara flaking off. "Why do you care, Alison?"

"You're right. I don't care about you, Limp-ette," Alison sneered. "No one does."

The bell rang. Alison flitted away, gliding across the gray

stone floors wearing a smug little smile framed in glossy red lipstick.

I carried my heavy backpack to homeroom as fast as I could. I wouldn't see Xavier until third period, which gave me a little over two hours to figure out what to tell him. I certainly couldn't mention falling from my neighbor's balcony. Xavier would never look at me the same if he knew I had broken into Miss Opal's apartment.

We sat next to each other during AP Physics. The boys' soccer coach, who preferred if the seniors called him *Dave*, taught the class. He didn't pretend to care when we whispered to each other about things that wouldn't be on the exam.

"Your mom called me this morning," Xavier said out of the side of his mouth.

"Ugh, yeah, I know. Sorry about that."

He slid two sticks of gum from the pocket of his khakis, but I shook my head.

"Unless you think I need it?" I joked.

Xavier set the gum onto my desk, probably because of my lingering coffee breath. I palmed the gum while I unwrapped it. Xavi was the kind of kid teachers gave a chance to spit their gum out. I was the kind of kid who got written a demerit to go with the lecture.

"Why weren't you on AIM last night?" he whispered. "I need to talk to you about something important."

"Can it wait? I'm dealing with a lot right now."

Xavier pointed his pen at me and clicked it over and over, pretending to channel surf. "Of course you are. The Lisette show is always on."

"What's that supposed to mean?"

"Everyone's talking about it."

"About what?"

"Why won't you tell me what happened? I tell you everything."

I bristled. "What do you want to know?"

Xavi licked his lips as if anticipating juicy gossip. "Alison is telling people you snuck out. Sounds like the Lisette I know. But what I'm wondering is, where did you go?"

"What are you talking about? Since when do you talk to Alison Smithers?"

He tossed his pen down. "Don't do that."

"Do what?" I said. Okay, maybe I snapped a little. I'm not the queen of self-control.

"Keep me in the dark! Everyone keeps asking *me* where you were going, and *I* don't know. I'm pretending to keep a secret for you, but I don't even know what it is!" He sighed so dramatically it attracted the attention of the kids sitting in front of us.

I shot them death-stares until they turned back around. "Lower your voice, Xavi. Now, who keeps asking what?"

"Never mind, Lisette. I don't know why I expected anything different from you. I thought I was your best friend. I thought you trusted me with your secrets. You know all of mine."

"Being best friends isn't about spilling your guts to each other. It's about being there when the other one needs you. I'm always there for you, aren't I?"

Xavier suddenly switched gears and pretended to be fascinated by his notebook. He moved his pen across the page, but his elbow covered whatever he was writing.

I chewed on the inside of my cheek. Of course I wanted to tell him the truth. But he wouldn't have understood. He was born with a silver spoon in his mouth. Breaking into someone's home, even for a good reason, would have seemed wrong to him.

"Did you get your hair cut?" Xavier asked, his eyes still on his notebook.

"Yeah."

"I don't like it."

"Yeah, well, neither do I."

BALANCING
ACT

The following afternoon, I had gymnastics practice. I wasted my breath all through breakfast, begging Ruelle to drive me, to bring Bebe to give me some relief. But Ruelle had something more important to attend to. A job interview, but she wouldn't say where.

I perched on the edge of one of the two backless wooden barstools at the kitchen counter. "Come on, tell me what the job is! It can't be *that* bad. Fast food, or what?"

"I don't want to talk about it," Ruelle grumbled as she rinsed a coffee filter out in the sink; we always re-used them until the coffee tasted pulpy.

"Why are you getting a job, anyway?" I demanded. "Why can't we steal something?"

"Because *we* aren't doing that anymore. Especially not you. You're lucky you didn't get caught. Incredibly lucky."

I huffed. "Yeah, well, for someone who claims she can do magic, you sure seem to struggle with money."

Ruelle's pale blue eyes widened. "Are you seriously trying to lecture *me* about money right now? We would have plenty if your old pal Dr. Montgomery hadn't stuck us with a huge bill!"

"Not my fault. You could have taken me to a real doctor." I took a sip from the flavorless cup of coffee that had been forced on me. Ruelle had a weird way of showing she cared.

Her brow furrowed before she clenched her jaw. I didn't want to know what she almost said.

She fiddled with her ring. "You made the decision to follow me after I told you not to. I made the decision to take you to someone who wouldn't report your injuries. We all made difficult decisions. Today you have to go to school, and I have an interview for a job I don't want. We all do things we don't want to do. That's life."

I slurped down the last sip of my coffee. In the sugar-bomb drinks I preferred, the last sip was the sweetest, but every drop of the drink Ruelle served me was bitter. I wished instead of making me vile coffee, she would listen to what I actually needed.

*T*hat afternoon, Emma Johnson gave me a ride to gymnastics practice because Xavier had band. Emma was a wisp of a girl with a smattering of freckles and perfect teeth courtesy of her dad, the dentist. We didn't hang out outside of gymnastics, but my apartment was on her way home, so we formed an alliance of convenience.

"How come I don't know about your secret boyfriend?" Emma demanded as we slogged through traffic. "Everyone at school is talking about it."

I shrugged. "News to me, too."

"Is it Xavier Monroe?" Emma raised a brow suggestively. "You're so much taller than him. Most of the guys at school are shorter than you. That must be weird, huh?"

"Not as weird as this conversation."

Emma playfully punched my arm. "Talking to you is like pulling teeth. You know, that's why you hardly have any friends."

Her observation stung. I always thought I didn't have

friends because I was poor, not because I had a piss-poor personality.

"I did *not* know that," I said. "Thanks for the head's up?"

"Aw, come on, I'm teasing. Should we get ice cream after practice? I found this amazing little place off Canal—"

"Can't. Don't have any money."

"You never have any money," Emma sulked. "What do your parents do, anyway?"

"It's just me and my mom," I said.

I looked down at my bare arms, exposed in my practice leotard. I gently traced the little cuts from my fall. None of them were deep. Unbelievable how much blood came from such small wounds.

"My cousin's parents are divorced, too. She gets twice as many presents on Christmas, though. So it's not all bad, is it?"

I shrugged. I remembered nothing about my dad to know whether my situation might've been better if he were around. Of course, in my imagination, he was wonderful. I imagined he didn't know I existed. If he ever found me, he'd be elated, guilty but elated all the same. He'd whisk me away some place tropical where we'd spend a whole week getting to know each other. We'd do regular things normal families did on vacation, and it wouldn't be corny or boring because we'd be the ones doing it.

That daydream got me through the first grueling twenty minutes of practice, what Coach Karla called our *warmup*. We stretched for a few minutes, and then she ordered us to "run suicides until I say stop," which was basically a lot of running and bending down, two activities that made my back hurt so badly I almost quit. Almost.

"All right, good warmup, everyone," Coach Karla said. "Five minutes for water, then we'll get in our groups and work on our routines."

I was so eager to get to the fountain first that I didn't hear which section of my routine—vault, uneven bars, balance beam, or floor exercise—I was supposed to be working on. Truth be told, I was afraid to find out. I didn't feel up to doing a tumbleset.

Everyone else fell into their places, spotting their teammates or taking their turns, but I hung back on the outskirts of the gym. I dusted my hands with chalk over and over again, as if I could pretend to be almost ready forever.

I made the mistake of glancing toward the uneven bars. Emma waved me over. I took a deep, steadying breath. I looked down at my bare feet, toes wiggling with nervous energy, wishing I had chosen a sport with special shoes I could pretend to tie to buy a little time.

"Lisette? Come on! What's wrong with you today?" Emma shouted across the gym.

Great. Peachy freakin' keen.

I strolled over as fast as I dared. "Nothing's wrong. Why are you yelling at me? What's wrong with *you*?"

Emma glared at me. "Is it true what Alison said? Did you hurt your back?"

"It's not that bad."

"Prove it." Emma pointed to the balance beam.

I had never been afraid of the beam before. It had never mattered how many times I'd fallen off—often bashing my head into it on the way down. In my mind, the balance beam was my friend, a friend that enabled me to fly.

Under normal circumstances, this wouldn't have been a big deal. So I mounted the beam swiftly, like nothing was wrong. I'd been doing this for years, twelve of them to be exact, so in a way it was just muscle memory. I assumed a familiar position—standing tall with my feet elegantly pointed —but the spasms in my back caused me to double over, clutching my toes and biting my lip to suppress a howl.

"Get down," Emma said. "You aren't fooling anyone."

"I'm fine," I lied through gritted teeth, my crumpled body giving me away.

"Get down," another girl on the team, Clarissa Peters, shouted. "Our first meet is in four months, and we need you to be better by then."

I always hated being told what to do.

I stood back up. I took off on both feet, jumped backward onto my hands, then landed on my feet. A back handspring, nothing too fancy, but I hoped it would serve to show how fine I was. But my back handspring backfired. The pain shooting through my spine was so intense it transformed into nausea. I felt the contents of my stomach—tuna salad was a bad choice —rising up. With one hand over my mouth, I bolted.

Thank the Lord I made it to the bathroom, the sink to be specific, before I puked my guts up. The busted-battery taste on my tongue was eclipsed only by the near certainty that everyone had seen me hobbling across the gym with my hand pressed against my quivering lips.

When I finally finished, I calmly rinsed the chunks down the drain. Too bad the shame wouldn't go down as easily. I gargled and spit, gargled and spit, replacing the nasty bile flavor with neutral water. I splashed some water on my face and looked at my reflection in the mirror.

"Who are you?" I asked myself, staring at a girl with dark purple circles under her glassy blue eyes. "You're Lisette Starling Colbert. Get yourself together and act like it."

The door popped open, and Coach Karla called out, "You okay, Colbert?"

"Fine," I answered as boldly as I dared. It must not have sounded convincing because Coach Karla proceeded to walk in.

"Look, Colbert, I know now isn't a good time." Coach Karla rested a strong hand on my shoulder. "It's never a good time for these kinds of things. But I know you're hurt—everybody knows—so maybe it's best if you take some time off."

"No way!" I shook my head. "I'm fine. By the time competition—"

"It's not just your back, Colbert. Generally, I avoid financial discussions with students, but your mother hasn't called me back in months."

"We paid our fee. I gave you a check last week!"

"Check bounced, Colbert. There are girls on my waitlist whose parents can afford to pay me on time. And I need to get paid. You understand, right?"

"Yeah." I looked down sheepishly. Out of the corner of my eye, I saw a little bit of tuna that hadn't gone down the sink drain. My stomach lurched like I might throw up again.

"I really am sorry." She gave my shoulder a squeeze before taking her hand away. "But gymnastics is a sport for short girls, anyway. Maybe you could find a new sport at school? Like basketball?"

"Yeah, maybe." I ripped a paper towel off the roll and dried my hands. I needed to get out of there before Coach saw me crying.

"And, I know this is none of my business, but some of the girls are saying you got hurt while you were sneaking out."

"So what?"

"Well, I didn't think that sounded like you. I know you take school seriously. As well you should. You're smart as a whip, Lisette. There's so much more to life than gymnastics. Don't throw your talents away, okay?"

"Yeah, okay."

The bathroom door closed behind Coach Karla with a pathetic click. I crumbled up the paper towel and tossed it in the trash. I wasn't worried about what I might throw away. I *was* worried about what I had to bury.

*X*avier picked me up from the gym to save me the embarrassment of waiting for Emma to finish practice. I'd never been more grateful for his cell phone.

"Hurt too bad to practice, huh?" he inquired gently.

I still winced like he'd touched a bruise. "As much as I appreciate the ride, I'd rather not discuss practice if that's okay."

"Sure, no problem," Xavier answered. "I'm sorry about the other day in physics. I feel like a jackass for pestering you. Sometimes I feel like you don't tell me things because you don't trust me. But I know that's my problem, not yours. I should respect your boundaries."

I released a sigh so deep a jolt of pain zipped up my spine. "You don't have to apologize. It's not your fault my life is so chaotic right now. You're a good friend, dude. So don't worry about it, okay?"

Xavier frowned. I guess my acceptance speech wasn't good enough.

"What?" I asked. "I can tell by your face something's wrong."

"Nothing, it's just, I worry about you, Lisette. Bottling everything up isn't healthy."

"I got kicked off the gymnastics team," I blurted out.

"What? For real?" Xavier asked. "Because of your back?"

I nodded, far too ashamed to reveal the whole truth. Besides, a nod wasn't a lie. It wasn't *just* my back, but wouldn't Coach Karla have considered keeping me if I could help the team win championships? If I were just a little more important?

"But you'll heal, won't you? What did the doctors say— oh, wait, don't feel like you have to answer that. I'm prying again. I'm sorry, Lis, I really just, y'know, worry."

"It's okay," I said. "If you don't mind, I'd like to take some time to process it."

"Of course," Xavier said. "Here, I know just the thing." He fiddled with the fancy stereo on his Thunderbird—he had a GPS system too, the only modern parts of the classic car—

until the unmistakable intro of Prince's *I Would Die 4 U* spilled from the speakers.

I closed my eyes, soaking it up. Xavier liked to joke that it was our song. A sweet gesture, even though he was kidding.

We spent the rest of the ride to my apartment listening to *Purple Rain,* and gradually my stomach stopped churning. Xavi was kind enough to drop me off without asking any more embarrassing questions.

I started up the stairs, thinking at least I had feeding the cats to look forward to, trying not to wonder why Ruelle was writing bad checks again. But when I reached our front door, I had no choice but to confront our situation. There was no way to miss the bright orange paper plastered on our door.

An eviction notice.

7

FRESH
DIRT

Another morning, another black coffee, and another drive to school where Ruelle wouldn't talk to me about anything important. Especially not the notice on our door.

"I'll take care of it," she insisted. "Don't worry about it."

"Oh, okay," I replied with a sarcastic bite. "Don't worry about being homeless? Sure, no problem."

"Focus on the present," Ruelle said. "Tonight's the third night."

"Which means what exactly? You still haven't explained what a poppet is or how it works."

Ruelle chewed her lip but said nothing. She barely muttered goodbye once we arrived at school, and only after I said it first. The task of burying Bebe hung over our heads like a cluster of dark clouds, and school was no picnic either.

Miss Fenty stopped me in the hall before homeroom. Miss Fenty was in her 70's, but her big heart and delicate bone structure ensured she'd be beautiful forever. Her cataracts only added to her charm, giving her green eyes the appearance of milk glass.

"Why don't you come to my office for a chat?" Miss Fenty said with a thin-lipped smile.

I sighed as if annoyed, but secretly I was relieved. I desperately needed someone, *anyone*, to talk to about the derailed train I was paying a steep price to ride.

Miss Fenty's walls were free of inspirational posters. Instead, they featured framed diplomas from Ivy League schools, only the best for St. Bernadette's. I was more impressed by her artwork, a massive painting of wolves lurking around a swamp, their pointy ears and yellow eyes peeking out behind cypress trees.

Toys for stressed-out kids to tinker with occupied prime real estate on Miss Fenty's massive desk. Bobble-heads propped up on top of stacks of books with titles like *Every Mind Can Meditate* and *The Secret to Stress-Free Sleep* tempted my idle hands.

I fidgeted in my seat and waited for Miss Fenty to begin. Though her brows knitted with disapproval, her syrupy voice was a balm to my aching head. "I've been hearing some *odd* rumors about you, Miss Colbert. Care to share what's *really* been going on?"

"Not really." I flicked a bobble-headed pelican toy in the beak. "You hear anything from any of those scholarships you helped me apply for?"

Miss Fenty sighed. "Not yet. I promise I'll let you know as soon as I hear anything. Now, back to the matter at hand—"

Ugh. I hated being led through a conversation. For once, I needed someone to let me talk about what I wanted to talk about.

"Did I tell you about my neighbor, Miss Opal? Someone broke into her apartment and killed her a few weeks back. They still haven't caught the sicko, or sickos I guess."

Miss Fenty clutched her chest. "That's terrible, Lisette. Were you two close?"

I nodded, starting to tell her about the cats and the records and the hot meals, but the words died in my throat. If I started talking, would I be able to stop? What if I said something that got my mom in trouble? As bad as I wanted justice for Miss Opal, nothing I said would bring her back.

"Well, are you grieving in a way that honors her?" Miss Fenty asked.

I bristled. Strange how a question could feel like an accusation. "I'm doing what she'd want me to do. I'm feeding the alley cats for her."

"I see. And how are you managing that with all of your other responsibilities?"

"Fine, I guess. I don't have gymnastics to worry about anymore. Coach Karla said I was too tall for it. So it goes."

Miss Fenty frowned. "But you *love* gymnastics."

"Not anymore. Guess I outgrew it—literally. Funny, huh?"

Miss Fenty didn't laugh, but there was a twinkle of amusement in her milk glass eyes. "I'm glad you have a sense of humor about it."

"Can I go now? I don't wanna miss first period." I stood up without waiting to be dismissed.

"One last thing." Miss Fenty stood as well, as if her statement had to be delivered eye-to-eye. "Now, I don't know whether you snuck out like everybody's saying, but I know if you did, you made the choice yourself. You're a free-thinker, Lisette. I know you are. But you need to know this: even an independent woman like you needs to watch the crowd she's running with. You lay down with dogs; you get up with fleas. You understand?"

I nodded. "Don't worry, Miss Fenty, I won't get bit."

"So much her mother's child," Miss Fenty whispered so softly I pretended not to hear her. Had she ever met Ruelle? In passing at an open house maybe, but I couldn't recall. In any case, I resented the comparison too much to acknowledge it.

The cemeteries in New Orleans were as strange as the city itself. Things buried below sea level had a way of coming back up. Caskets were stored in mausoleums of crumbling stone and cracking plaster. Ruelle and I stepped lightly underneath a waning moon, our eyes trained on the manicured path between the graves.

Maybe it was the adrenaline, the strange cocktail of fear and exhilaration that hit my veins the moment I scaled the massive stone wall around St. Louis Cemetery, but my back didn't hurt at all. Not even a little bit.

Bebe was nestled inside my backpack along with three gold coins, the purpose of which Ruelle hadn't explained yet. That had been a running theme with us lately; Ruelle held all the cards and refused to show her hand.

"How do you know this is going to work?" I asked.

Ruelle waited for a beat, thinking. I knew that expression —the way her mouth twitched when she was holding back a secret.

"Have you done this before?" I probed.

Another twitch.

"Why? How did you get hurt?"

"It's complicated," she said in a tone that meant she wasn't in the mood to share.

But I was hungry for more. "I'm not an idiot," I said. "Explain it to me."

Ruelle didn't elaborate. I shouldn't have expected more than a scrap. My mother never let me get my fill.

She stopped in front of a white mausoleum that wasn't particularly elaborate or remarkable, except for a smattering of graffiti and an odd pile of mementos—candles, purple plastic doubloons, a rotting orange—that rested at its base.

I squinted at the scrawled messages, wondering who would defile a grave like this. Some artists had only drawn triple X's, as if they simply wanted to leave their mark. Some of the X's were circled. What did it all mean?

Ruelle rested a hand on the tombstone. In her other hand, she held a pale blue stone, angelite, perhaps. The less expensive ones were harder to identify. Ruelle's eyes closed, and her lips trembled as if reciting a prayer. At last, she looked up. "The coins."

"What?" I hitched my backpack up but didn't take it off. I knew what Ruelle wanted but didn't appreciate being ordered.

"The coins," Ruelle repeated. "Take them out of your bag."

"Why?" I cocked my hip and rested my hand on it. "When are you going to tell me what we're doing here?"

"I thought you knew—we're laying your poppet to rest."

"Okay, but at least tell me why!"

She tightened her grip on the angelite. "It's done the job—siphoned out what it was meant to. If you keep sleeping with it, something bad could happen."

"What, though?" I stamped my foot.

It was the wrong move. Ruelle recoiled. "You don't need to know. You need to trust me."

"Why tell me about magic if you aren't ever going to show me? How am I supposed to believe in it if you never explain it?"

"Take the coins out, Lisette," Ruelle said, ignoring my questions and infuriating me.

"No. Not until you tell me what they're for."

Ruelle sighed. "The coins are a gift—to the spirit who has dominion over the cemetery. Her name is Marie. This is her final resting place."

"Marie who? Why would she help us?"

"All that matters is, she was one of the most powerful women of all time," Ruelle explained. "Had God's ear some-how. We'll give Marie the coins and, in turn, ask that she sees to it no one digs up the bear."

"And what happens if they do?"

Ruelle frowned. She tinkered with her lucky ring. "Then you will have to muster up all the doubt you're feeling now, every last bit of it, and convince yourself magic isn't real. So they can't use your poppet against you."

I took the coins out. I started to hand them to Ruelle, but she shook her head and said, "Better that it come directly from you."

"How do I... what do I say? How do I say it?"

"Get close as you can, so she can hear. Say what comes from your heart. In my experience, it's better to give her the gift first. Catch her eye, and then you'll have her ear."

Seeming to sense my hesitation, she handed me the angelite, closing it in my palm. "Strengthens communication with the spirits," she explained.

"Thank you," I whispered, still not sure I believed but appreciative of the gesture.

The air around the tomb was hot, the water from an afternoon thundershower still evaporating off the earth and producing a mugginess I was accustomed to. I had no memory of living any place other than New Orleans, never been more than a hundred miles away to have any point of comparison to its subtropical climate. And yet, when I genuflected before Marie's grave, a suffocating heat came from that patch of earth unlike any I'd ever experienced before. Beads of sweat streamed down my face. A droplet rested in the divot above my lip, tickling my nose. I wiped my face with my sleeve, then set the coins down next to a vase with three droopy tulips.

"I brought this for you," I whispered. "All I ask is that you watch over my friend Bebe... see to it that no one digs her up. Please... and thank you."

As I rose to my feet, a little jab of discomfort radiated from my back. I squeezed the angelite with one hand, and my other rushed to soothe the wound. I looked at Ruelle, eyes pleading for reassurance. "I thought Bebe absorbed all my pain. Why does it still hurt?"

"The pain is in your mind," Ruelle answered curtly. "Come, we must find a suitable mausoleum for the poppet— this one is too prominent. Someone will notice if we enter it."

"A mausoleum? I thought we had to bury her." I raised an eyebrow. "In fact, I'm positive Dr. Montgomery said—"

"You need to be more flexible." Ruelle turned away, her gait so fast that I struggled to catch up with her. "Religion is, by its very nature, open to interpretation."

"I never knew you had a religion."

Ruelle chewed on her lower lip, taking a moment before she replied. "I'm like most people in that regard. I have no faith until I absolutely must."

"There are no atheists in foxholes."

She said nothing but snatched the angelite back. Then she hurried ahead, leaving me to wonder what I'd done to lose it.

After much consideration, Ruelle selected a mausoleum, white stone laced with ivy that hid the decay. It was the perfect one among rows and rows of others exactly like it—nowhere near new enough to have many visitors, but not so old that we couldn't read the inscription and mark its place. The family name *CHARBONNET* in all capital letters stuck out to me. Written beneath were the details of four family members: their full names, the day they were born, and the day they died. *Gerald Pierre. Dominique Nanette. Evangeline Rose. Germaine Francois.* I committed the details to memory in case I needed to find this tomb again.

Ruelle tapped on the wooden door, and it creaked open ever so slightly, like an invitation from fate herself.

"Go in as far as you can manage," Ruelle instructed. "Tuck the poppet in the deepest, darkest corner you can find."

I took the biggest inhale I could manage before entering the mausoleum, anticipating an awful odor. My heart thudded in my chest, begging me to run in and run back out, but I couldn't do that. This was a sacred place. To run would have been dishonorable, and I was in no position to taunt the dead.

The moonlight barely leaked into the space. I had to feel my way along, my hand dancing lightly across a casket like a guide rail. When I had gone in as deep inside as I dared, I gave Bebe one last hug before I set her down, squeezing her little body into a corner like Ruelle had instructed me. And then, thinking of my mother's words about flexibility and interpretations, I felt compelled to do something else—to put my own mark on the ritual.

I raked my fingernails through the dirt and collected a handful. It felt fresh, alive, nourished by the decaying matter around it. "I'm sorry, Bebe," I said, tears stinging my eyes as I flung the dirt at her.

The strangest thing happened—it was as if for a moment the dirt hit me too. I could feel it strike my face, taste its grit on my tongue. As if the bond between Bebe and me was so strong we shared everything. By walking away, the tie between us would stretch until it finally broke.

I swallowed.

The impulse to grab her, hide her under my hoodie, and hope Ruelle wouldn't notice overwhelmed me for a moment. But it flitted away, giving way to relief. In spite of myself, in spite of all I'd been through—the death of one of my only friends, getting kicked off the gymnastics team, losing my beloved teddy—I looked back on it all and smiled. I smiled, not because of what had happened, but because I thought it was over.

8

PUNCH
DRUNK

After the final bell, I transferred a few heavy textbooks from my locker to my backpack. I slung it across my shoulder and winced at the dull ache of pain the movement triggered at the top of my spine. I wondered why I hadn't fully recovered. Wondered if it had all been a bunch of hocus-pocus.

The thought made me so angry that my entire body tensed up like it was waiting for the next punch. It wasn't fair —I gave up so much, and for what? That day, my first day without Bebe, should have been painless, but it had been more hurtful than I could have imagined.

Speculation about my injury and my banishment from gymnastics spread around school faster than the time all the cheerleaders *and* the entire basketball team got mono. Every snippet of conversation I overheard seemed to be about me.

I did my best to ignore them. Though St. Bernadette was a small school, none of the students really *knew* me, so their opinions about me shouldn't have mattered. It wasn't like I was on their radars before I was *that girl who fell off a balcony.* What a boring story. Why couldn't we have come up with something better? I shook my head, internally chastising myself as my classmates hurried past, hoping to catch a glimpse of me to fan the flames of their hot gossip.

"Wonder where she was going?" A junior girl didn't bother to lower her voice.

"I heard she has a college boyfriend," her equally loud friend answered.

"Well, *I* heard she's a drug dealer," the first girl replied.

I slammed my locker as though I could close that chapter of my life.

"Hey, Gimpette," Alison Smithers called out. "What're you gonna be for Halloween? Tiny Tim? Quasimodo?"

I didn't answer her. Alison had bullied me a few times before the accident, but now she taunted me constantly, hovering like a vulture over a wounded animal.

"Gimpette!" Alison repeated a little louder. "Hey! I'm talking to you!"

Xavier jogged up beside me and threw an arm protectively around my shoulders. "You need a ride home?" he asked.

"Don't you have band practice?"

"It got canceled."

"Yeah, right. I can always tell when you're lying because your voice cracks."

He grinned sheepishly. "Okay, you caught me. I'm skipping. You wanna go to Funky Monkey and look for Halloween costumes?"

"I'm gonna make mine. No money to buy clothes I'm only gonna wear for one night."

"Maybe you could borrow something from my mom?"

"Hard pass."

"Why? You borrowed her black dress."

"That was for a funeral." I rolled my eyes, an attempt to appear nonchalant. Truly, I couldn't think about Miss Opal dying without wanting to cry. When it rained, it poured. It had been a soggy year.

"Anyway, I really need to talk to you." Xavier's voice dropped to a whisper. "It's Alison—I think she knows."

I clenched my jaw and unclenched it. "Knows what? How I hurt my back?"

"Ummm, no. Not everything is about you, Lisette."

We were halfway to Xavier's car in the back of the lot, where he always parked to keep his ride safe from dings, when Alison stepped directly in front of us. Her loyal cronies—Madison Graham and Emma Johnson—stood on either side of her to block our way.

Xavier and I called the three of them collectively "the sons." The little nickname used to make me laugh. But right then, I felt like if they had heard it, they would've liked it so much they would've adopted it themselves.

Emma Johnson, my old teammate, wouldn't look at me now without a sneer. I never held an illusion about us being close, but it still shocked me how fast she turned on me. Madison's dirty looks seemed out of place on her pretty face. But her glares didn't really sting. Madison was so rich she never had to form a personality; she just copied everything Alison did. And Alison was bullying me.

"Why are you avoiding me, Jolly Gimp Giant?" Alison demanded.

My hands reflexively balled into fists. "Get out of my way, Alison."

"Aw, don't be like that! I've got a proposition for you—a way for you to make some extra money. Which, if your beat-up old boots are any indication, you could use."

She laughed, and I resisted the impulse to smack her. My boots were awesome. How dare she. I looked over her shoulder, hoping the teacher on parking lot duty might wonder what was happening and intervene, but no such luck. No one cared what Alison did to me.

"Anyway," she continued, "I want your help with a Halloween prank. I'll pay you to hide in my brother's closet and jump out to scare him. Don't worry about wearing a mask—your skin is horrifying. In fact, you may wanna wear a little makeup, so you aren't *too* scary."

Madison and Emma cackled like hyenas, but I just

shrugged. "Yeah, I breakout when I'm stressed. Hormones are hilarious. Now move."

Alison frowned, clearly dissatisfied with my lack of reaction. She caught the smirk on Xavier's face and switched targets. "As for you," she said with an affected lisp, "Xa-vi, find a better beard, no one believes your psycho mom would let you date this gimpy piece of gutter trash."

Pop. My hand slipped. Okay, fine, I meant to do it. I punched Alison right in her obnoxious mouth. I didn't hit her full force, only hard enough to shock her into shutting up.

She wiped her mouth. Her red lipstick smeared across her perfect teeth. "You're gonna regret that, Limpette," she growled.

The parking lot was crowded, hundreds of students with only two teachers to monitor them. A magnetic frenzy drew them around Alison and me. Someone started chanting, "Fight! Fight! Fight!" Then the other kids picked it up.

Xavier was pushed to the side. I didn't see how; I was too busy fighting off Alison and her flying monkeys. Later Xavi told me he wished he had jumped into the fray, tried to defend me. He said if he could go back, he would have taken the beating for me.

But no one gets to go back. And only the lucky people get to move forward.

BLOWING
SMOKE

I stared out the open window as the streetcar clattered down St. Charles Avenue, past well-appointed mansions sheltered from the street by spiky iron fences. Strings of Mardi Gras beads decorated the posts; their vibrant hues faded from the sun.

The streetcar screeched to a stop at the edge of the French Quarter, and my oversized sunglasses slipped down the bridge of my swollen, purple nose. Vintage red and white headphones stuck out like stop signs in the overgrown landscape of my curls. My nose was probably broken; my headphones definitely were, but they served a purpose. They said *leave me alone; I'm not listening.* They lied.

In fact, I heard the soundtrack of the city clear as anyone. A madman on the median preached through a megaphone about the end of the world. A street vendor bellowed "big ass beers for two bucks" from behind the keg he pumped. A trio of musicians played *When the Saints Go Marching In* on brass instruments that had long ago lost their shine.

I slowed down to toss spare change into a velvet-lined case. The song revved up, the band energized by my gesture. The bassist smiled and tipped his hat. I smiled back, because I knew he would never tell anyone he saw me. People like him, people like me, we don't talk to the police.

Ruelle hated musicians. Never explained why. Maybe my

dad was a musician. Maybe Ruelle met him while he was passing through on tour. Maybe they had one wild night together and then never saw each other again.

I wove in and out of the costumed tourists. Halloween wasn't until tomorrow, but the revelry had long since begun. I wore a different kind of disguise, a slouch to hide my height. It bothered my back a bit, but anonymity was crucial as I stalked through the flocks of tourists singing and dancing in the streets. As they staggered from one unsteady foot to the other, I closed in for the kill. When they rose their arms to toast with their green plastic flutes shaped like hand-grenades, I slipped their wallets right out of their pockets.

The wobblier they walked and the louder they talked, the bolder it made me. If a mark looked particularly sloppy, I had no qualms about wiggling the rings right off their fingers. I never thought of it as stealing. It felt more like redistributing.

On the way home, I stopped at Jefferson Feed. While the clerk was distracted with helping some kid hold a rabbit, I dropped a few cans of fancy wet cat food into my old blue backpack.

I didn't feel bad about this either. Surely the owner was an animal lover. They would have let me have the food if I had explained why I needed it. I was saving us both from an awkward conversation. I paid for a bag of dry food, a trick Ruelle taught me. Always buy something when you steal; that way, if alarms go off, you could act like you forgot to pay for the rest of your items.

At least a dozen cats lived in the alley behind my apartment. I tried not to count them. I referred to them by their physical descriptions like the grey tabby, the orange-striped tom, or the old one with a scar where his right eye should be. This made it easier when thoughts crossed my mind like, *I haven't seen the fluffy white one in a while,* and I didn't have to waste energy inventing happy endings where some nice family took "Daisy" home. Because "Daisy" was a cat you took home and "the white fluffy one" could meet some untimely end without sending me down a spiral of shame. No matter how hard I tried to help them, I feared Miss Opal would look down and be disappointed.

A calico with alluring golden eyes and a round, protruding belly watched me from inside a blanketed cardboard box. She swished her tail expectantly but didn't make a sound. Clearly, no one had ever loved her enough to teach her about mushy greetings, but she was a queen among cats. She must've felt through some generational energy her way of life was superior. Freedom was worth the uncertainty.

"Hey there, Cali girl," I greeted her, then internally chastised myself. *Don't go naming the alley cats. You'll get attached.*

I extended an open can of food. "I brought you a treat."

The calico sniffed it, then dipped her pink tongue into the brown goop. She must have approved as she went in for a second, bigger bite.

"Atta girl," I said. "Eat up. You'll need your strength. Pretty soon, you're gonna do the hardest thing you've ever done."

A window squeaked open, drawing my attention up. A saggy face with a cotton-white poof of hair popped out. "Are you giving them water now, too? Food was one thing, but water?" When Miss Gayle scrunched her pale face up, she looked like a gargoyle, like part of the ancient building.

"Sorry, Miss Gayle." I tapped my headphones. "I can't hear you."

"They're strays!" the miserable old harpy shrieked. "They should drink from puddles like nature intended!"

Someone ought to get you a glass of water from a puddle. Maybe you can soak your dentures in it, I had enough sense not to say aloud.

I tamped down my anger and answered, "What's it to you if I give them water?"

"Mosquitoes breed in standing water."

"The water doesn't stand; the cats drink it."

"What about the water in the puddles then?" Miss Gayle said. "The water they should be drinking? You're disrupting the natural order of things."

I gestured to my headphones again. "Sorry, Miss Gayle, the volume's got a mind of its own."

Miss Gayle kept on ranting, but I tuned her out, and eventually she retreated.

I needed to start looking for homes for the kittens. Good, indoor homes where people wouldn't forget to feed them. It was the least I could do. If Miss Opal had been alive, she would've trapped the calico and brought her to a vet, but I didn't have money for that. I couldn't even take the calico inside to have her kittens; Ruelle had been adamant about my allergies.

The setting sun cast a rose gold glow across the top of my apartment building. My stomach rumbled, but I wasn't ready to leave. I sat down in the alley, cautiously petting the curious cats who rubbed their faces against my shins. I kept waiting to break out into hives, but it never happened.

Darkness crept in. Some of the surrounding streetlights flickered into action. Time to go, to end the only part of my day that made me feel less miserable. I shuddered as I stood. My back hurt—not intensely and not always. It was like a leaky roof you only remembered when it rained.

I brushed the gravel off my hands. I didn't notice the trio of teens, two guys and a girl about my age, maybe a couple of years older, ducking into the alley until I literally ran into one of them.

"Oh! Sorry!" the better-looking guy, taller with a broad chest, said. "Didn't see you there."

"It's okay. I'm used to being invisible," I muttered.

"You aren't invisible." The other guy had a fire in his russet brown eyes, which made him as handsome as his friend. He was more my type with his long, dark hair slicked back and sexy leather jacket. Like an archetype of teenage trouble.

"It was a joke," I lied, stretching up to my full height. "I'm six feet tall. No one misses me."

"Oh, I've definitely seen you around," leather jacket said. "You live in the building, right? I'm your neighbor—Tucker. And this is my girlfriend Kennedy and our friend Hal."

I eyed the girl warily. Girls who looked like her, so pretty and put together, made me squirm. I shifted back to Tucker. "My neighbor?" I repeated, confused. I'd never seen him before.

"Yeah. I live below you, with my grandma, Gayle."

"Oh, right. I'm Lisette. Gayle just got through yelling at me."

Tucker laughed. "For what? Standing too close to the building?"

"No, she doesn't want me to give the cats water."

"She's such a bitch," Tucker said. "Hey—let me make it up to you." He opened his palm to reveal a joint. "I'll smoke you out."

"Oh…" I looked from the joint to his face, uncertain whether the offer was sincere. I had only gotten high a few times before, and only with Xavier. He swore it helped with his anxiety, but it made me feel numb. At that moment, I *wanted* to feel numb.

"Come on," Hal goaded me. His dimples popped when he smiled, his handsome face framed by the collar of his preppy polo shirt. "You're not gonna run and tell on us, are you?"

I shook my head. "No, I'm cool. Let me get a hit."

"My girl," Tucker said brightly. He whipped out a neon green BIC lighter and took two puffs to get things started.

Kennedy took the joint next, then passed it to me when she finished. I took a quick drag then tried to hand the joint off to Hal, but he shook his head. "Puff puff pass—you only puffed once. We're gentlemen here. We follow proper etiquette."

"Gentlemen *and* ladies," Kennedy chimed in. Her beauty

seemed less threatening once she had relaxed. I took a second toke. I wanted to riff with Kennedy, but by the time I stopped coughing, the moment had passed.

I kept looking at the window, certain it would fly open at any minute. But if Miss Gayle noticed us getting high in the alley, she kept her observations to herself.

"You don't go to our school, do you?" Hal said.

My fuzzy brain took a moment to realize he was talking to me. The stuff they smoked tasted different from what Xavier had, sweeter. I smoked a lot more than I usually did.

"No," I answered at last. I shoved my hands in my pockets and rocked back on my heels. Everything felt so amazing; nothing hurt. The last thing I wanted to talk about was school, but I lacked the presence of mind to maneuver the conversation to something else.

"Where do you go?" Kennedy asked.

"As of right now, nowhere." I averted my gaze. "I got expelled for fighting."

"Really?" Tucker whistled. "Badass."

"You got in a fight? With who? Was it another girl? Is that what happened to your nose?" Hal raised an eyebrow. "What was the fight about? Some dude?"

Kennedy punched him in the arm, twice.

"Ow!" Hal rubbed the spot. "What was that for?"

"First one was for being nosey. Second one was for assuming dudes are the only thing women care enough about to fight for."

Hal giggled. He covered his mouth, trying to stop himself, but she had already noticed.

"What's so funny?" Kennedy demanded.

"Please don't hit me again!" Hal threw up his hands. "I thought it was funny you said I was being 'nosey' about her nose."

Kennedy shook her fist at him, and he flinched. She laughed. "You're such a douche canoe."

The unanswered question—*what was the fight about?*—hung in the air like a foul smell no one wanted to claim. Tucker offered me the joint again, and I took it; anything to keep from talking. I kept catching Kennedy staring at me, assessing me the way other girls always seemed to do. They always found something about me to dislike.

I studied her back, looking for something to compliment. "Your nails are cool."

Kennedy glanced at the flashy purple design offset with ten tiny crystals, as if such a bold choice had slipped her mind. "Thanks."

"How do you get them to look so nice?" I asked.

A smile spread across Kennedy's heart-shaped face. "My family owns a nail salon. I get a fresh set every week."

"Cool. They did a good job."

"Maybe next time I go, you can come with me," Kennedy said.

She made me nervous in a different way than the guys. I wanted to impress her. To prove Emma wrong when she said I was too difficult to talk to. Too hard to be friends with.

"Yeah, that would be cool," I said. "Since I'm not in school right now, it's not like I'm busy or anything. I spend most of my day robbing tourists in the Quarter."

Kennedy nodded her approval. Hal passed me the joint again. I took two drags this time, holding each inhalation of the sweet smoke in as long as I could. Hal beamed at me.

Once the joint was cashed, Hal tossed it into a trash can. He wiggled a phone out of his pocket and glanced at the display. "We gotta hustle if we're gonna make the eight o'clock show."

Kennedy turned to me. "We're going to see the Rocky Horror Picture Show over at Prytania Theatre. You should come."

"Oh... uhhh..." I tried to think of something besides the lame truth, that I didn't have any money. "I don't have a car."

"That's okay. I've got space in my van. And I gotta bring Tucker back here anyway," Kennedy said. "So? You in?"

"And don't say you have homework," Hal added. He laughed until Kennedy glared at him.

"I didn't realize it was so late." I stared at my boots. "I gotta cook dinner before my mom gets home. Some other time?"

"Yeah, sure," Kennedy said, though her voice dripped with disappointment.

I walked away first so I wouldn't have to watch them leave me behind. What crappy luck. I finally met some cool people who seemed to like me, and I didn't have the money to do something with them. I was sick of living like this.

The tantalizing smell of seafood gumbo lingered in the stairwell. A chill moved through me. It reminded me of Miss Opal, inviting me in for a hot meal. Still, it was nice to know someone in our building was eating like a king—or a queen, as Kennedy would note.

Maybe it was a happy side-effect of being stoned, but I was grateful for my microwaved hotdog dinner. I hovered over my plate, squeezing out little lines of ketchup and mustard from packets stolen from the mall's food court. If the people eating gumbo were royalty, guess I was the joker. I laughed a little too loud, a little too long, which caused Miss Gayle to hit the ceiling with a broom. But I didn't care. Nothing mattered. My back felt fine. Everything was fine.

LAGNIAPPE
PUPIL

I woke up at the same time as usual, courtesy of the alarm on my nightstand that I hadn't reprogrammed since my expulsion. I pulled my pillow over my ears and groaned. My brain was still fuzzy, but the familiar ache in my back, usually pronounced after a night on my hard mattress, was blissfully nonexistent. I chalked it up to the half-life of the weed in my system.

Ruelle was asleep on the sofa when I tiptoed out of the apartment, my hair still wet from the shower. If she heard me, she didn't stir to show it, and I wasn't about to wake her. I still hadn't told her I had no reason to wake up in the morning. No school for Xavier to drive me to. Another long day of nothing.

I went to the library, my favorite place to catch a nap. People with nothing better to do bothered me when I tried to sleep in parks, but in the library basement with a thick book propped up on my face, no one seemed to care. People who read must be more empathetic. They didn't judge me for trying to rest wherever I could. They got that some of us are more tired than others.

By the time I woke up, it was mid-afternoon. I wiped the drool off the side of my mouth and returned the book I'd borrowed. "Time to go make some money," I mumbled to no one.

It was only a five-minute walk to Lagniappe Pawn Shop,

but it felt longer. Cars whizzed by me, windows down, spilling their bouncy music into the street. The sun beat against my back so that by the time I reached my destination, I felt like going back to sleep. "Coffee! Of course!" I said as if I'd solved some ancient mystery. "As soon as I get the money, I'm splurging on some *good* coffee."

Advertisements covered nearly every inch of Lagniappe Pawn Shop's windows. I perused them, wondering how Xavier and I would celebrate Halloween. Bag of Donuts was playing at Tipitina's next Saturday night. There was an open mic comedy show every Thursday at the Howling Wolf Den. Razzoo's had two-for-one well drinks during happy hour.

I yanked on the door. It rattled in its rusty frame but didn't budge. Was Mr. Amos at lunch? I referred to one of the clunky men's watches on my wrist. Half-past two—kinda late for lunch.

Then I spied a makeshift cardboard sign taped up over the regular hours that read, "Closed Early for Halloween." I gasped. He couldn't close early! Not right before the first of the month!

I raised my sunglasses and pressed my busted nose against the glass, ignoring the familiar throb. I caught a glimpse of the old man hunched over behind the register. I flung my fists against the glass, pounding so hard my knuckles hurt. I didn't care if I broke the glass, as long as it made him look.

Mr. Amos hobbled over and opened the door a crack. A stream of cold air trickled out, but his face was flushed red from his second chin to his bald head, like a fire was burning within him. "What's the matter, Lisette?" He wagged a finger at the sign. "I thought you liked to read?"

"Is the sign fiction?" My eyes widened. "Because that's what I like to read."

"It's an excerpt from a memoir titled 'Amos Takes His Grandkids Trick-or-Treating.' If you'll excuse me, I've gotta go write it before they grow up and forget about me."

"Aw, c'mon, Mr. Amos. It'll only take a minute. Your grandkids can age one minute, can't they?" I fixed my aqua eyes on him, sucking him in like a surfer in a riptide. I latched onto the slightest quiver in his brow, the weakening of his resolve.

"Geez, Lisette, what happened to your nose?" he asked.

"Aw, I don't have time to worry with my nose—"

"You need to go see a doctor, get it reset. Otherwise, it'll heal crooked as a politician."

"See a doctor? Oh, sure. Then afterward, maybe I'll go buy a rocket and fly it to the moon."

"You could go to the free clinic. I'll take you tomorrow if you want."

"What I want is to do some business. Come on, let me in. Please? I promise it'll take less time than you already spent worrying about my nose."

"All right." He stepped aside. "One minute," he warned. We both knew he didn't mean it.

Lagniappe Pawn Shop smelled like the smoke from spiced apple candles recently extinguished and old things decaying until old people came in to buy them. The oriental rugs covering the bouncy floors were faded but thick, their mysterious stains mostly hidden by a hodgepodge of antique furniture.

I placed my offerings down on the glass counter, one by one, as though each was a treasured artifact. Mr. Amos flipped on the overhead light to get a better look. He clucked disapprovingly. "Where'd you get all of this?"

"You mean these priceless family heirlooms?" I picked up a gold watch and pretended to recognize the inscription on the back. "Ah, yes, this was Great Uncle So-and-So's favorite watch. He wore it practically everywhere." I set it down and moved on to a silver one. "And this was his other favorite watch—he wore it everywhere else."

"All right, enough with the wisecracks. I'm gonna give it to you straight Lisette, I can't do business with you."

"What? Why not?"

"Because your mother asked me not to. Said you were distracted with trying to make extra cash, need to focus on school."

"Where was this sage advice before I got expelled?"

"Expelled? Well… you can… go to a different school…"

"School can wait. Did my mother tell you we're about to get evicted?"

"I'm sure you'll find a way to get the money."

"Like how?"

"I have a buddy who owns a magic shop over on Maple. Maybe I could get you a job there."

"I need money now, not in two weeks."

"Here, take this." Mr. Amos extended a crisp twenty-dollar bill. "Go get yourself something good to eat. I gotta go count the register and bring the leftover costumes up to the attic."

"Up to the attic? I thought you had bad knees." I shoved the bill into my pocket. "Let me help."

Mr. Amos smiled. "Thank you." He gestured to three boxes on his left. "If you see something you like, take it."

I dug through the first two boxes looking for buried treasure but found nothing but trash. The final box was missing a flap. *Must be where the sign came from.* I rifled through the rejected accessories—masks missing half their glitter, a crooked cigarette holder, and a rainbow of nearly feather-bare boas—until I came across a black leather holster with two pistols tucked inside. I turned them over in my hands. *Nice weight. They look so realistic. If all else fails, I can rob a bank.* "Mind if I take this?" I held the holster up for inspection.

Amos didn't bother looking up. "Go right ahead. Happy Halloween, Lisette."

The strain on my back was worth my sense of satisfaction

when I got all three boxes up to the attic in one trip. "Happy Halloween, Mr. Amos," I called over my shoulder. "Have fun with your grandkids, they're real lucky to have you."

"Thanks. Oh, and Lisette? I wouldn't worry *too* much about the rent. My friend Neil says your mom is doing great dancing at the Gold Mine, got a couple of regulars and everything."

"Dancing? At the Gold Mine?" I commanded my jaw not to drop.

"Oh. She didn't tell you? Well, sorry. Didn't mean to let the cat out of the bag. Keep my slip-up between us, okay?"

"Sure, Mr. Amos," I mumbled.

I rushed out onto North Rampart Street. My cheeks burned, though I couldn't explain why. I was only a few steps from Lagniappe's door when I collided with my neighbor Tucker—again. He was alone this time, but wearing the same leather jacket and the same devious smile. "We've got to stop *running* into each other like this," he said.

"Sorry. Didn't see you there. Where's Kennedy?" I asked, studying my boots. Why was it so hard to look at him? His attention meant nothing. "And Hal," I added, downplaying my interest.

"We decided to split up and look for costumes," Tucker said.

I had allowed myself to get my hopes up when he uttered the phrase *split up*, and then I crashed back down to reality. "That's cool. Any luck?"

"Not yet. Lagniappe still open?" Tucker nodded toward the door I'd come out of.

I shook my head. "You just missed him."

"Damn."

"Yeah. So, uhhh, costumes, huh? Are y'all going to a party tonight or what?"

"Or what." His mischievous grin made me wonder what he was holding back.

I smiled and waited; usually that was enough. People wanted a chance to share their secrets; they just needed to know you wouldn't share them with anyone else.

Tucker stepped closer to me. He smelled like a bonfire, wild and magnetic. The supple leather of his jacket called to me, begged me to brush my fingers against it. "I really shouldn't be telling you—"

"I can keep a secret." I leaned in closer. My skin prickled with anticipation.

His lips nearly touched my ear. "If we see you there—you didn't get this from me."

When he took a step back, I swear my heart stopped. He reached into his jacket pocket and produced a crumpled-up flyer. I carefully smoothed it out and read:

Calling All Bold Souls to the Thirteenth Realm of Hell Haunted House
INSANE CASH PRIZES
$10,000 for anyone who makes it through on Halloween Night before the Witching Hour
The fun starts at 9pm
Visit our website for more details

I read the line about $10,000 again and again, my shock shrinking each time. Surely, they wouldn't print it on a flyer if it was a lie.

"Where did you get this?" I asked, my eyes on the flyer, memorizing the website address.

"Kennedy. She thinks only one person wins the grand prize, so she told me not to tell anyone. So uhhh, don't tell anyone, okay?"

"You think it's real?" I folded the flyer back up and handed it to him.

He nodded solemnly. "Kennedy knows people who've done it—and Kennedy never lies. Anyway, you should come.

Bring a friend though, so Kennedy doesn't figure out I told you. Cool?"

"Yeah, cool," I said. "Could really use the money."

Tucker's radiant smile broadened. "You and me both, baby."

It was a term of endearment that usually made me cringe. *Baby.* Why would anyone refer to another adult in such an infantilizing way? It didn't seem sexy or even flattering. But when Tucker said it, my brain turned to mush. Eventually, he said, "Hope to see you there," and I parroted the sentiment.

The second he was out of sight, I pinched myself. It hurt and felt heavenly all at the same time. I wasn't dreaming. A cute boy was really flirting with me—not that anything would come of it since he already had a girlfriend. I couldn't let myself care about Tucker. But I *did* care about the money. Ten grand to get through a haunted house? That seemed unbelievable. But if Kennedy was right and only one person won, it might be real. Maybe some kind of last-man-standing type of situation. My mouth felt full of cotton, but I built up enough saliva for a proper swallow. It didn't matter how scary this haunted house was; I had to make it through. Had to show my mother once and for all that I wasn't a little kid, always messing things up and needing to be bailed out. I was the one who would save us.

II

ON THE
LAM AND
OFF TO THE
SLAUGHTER

I called Xavier from the cracked plastic phone outside the kitchen. "Cancel your plans," I said as soon as he picked up. "I found the perfect thing for us to do tonight."

"Ooo, color me intrigued," Xavier squealed. "Is it a party? No, wait, is it a *costume* party? Please say it's a costume party! I have the *best* costume!"

"Yeah? What is it?"

"IT the killer clown."

"Very funny." I rubbed at the goosebumps that suddenly populated my arms.

"Naw, I would never do that to you. In all seriousness, you've never told me *why* you're so scared of clowns."

"I'm not scared of them; I *hate* them. Are they happy or sad? No one knows. What's funny about that? Anyway, it's much better than some lame party. It's a haunted house where —get this—if you make it all the way through, you get TEN thousand dollars."

"Ten thousand dollars?" Xavier whistled. "That ain't chump change. Must be one seriously terrifying haunted house. Are you sure it's ten grand and not ten bucks?"

I twisted the curly phone cord around my finger. "Actually, could you look up the details? Our internet's off again." I recited the website and waited for him to write it down.

"Why's your internet off? Is everything okay?"

"Yeah, we're fine. It's uhhh, a problem with the whole building, I think. Old wiring, I guess. The fun starts at 9, and I wanna be first in line. So pick me up in the alley, say 8:30?"

"Okay, but—"

"I gotta go! Gotta make my costume."

"Okay," Xavier said. "See ya tonight."

"Bye." I returned the phone to its cradle. My head hurt. I hated lying to Xavi, but he couldn't know how bad things were. I didn't want him forcing his pity on me. Or worse, his money.

I paced across the ugly rugs covering our once beautiful floors. My heavy boots thudded as I thought about all that money. How it could change my whole life.

Tap! Tap! Tap! I shook my head at the familiar bang of a broom striking the ceiling below.

"Yeah, I know, Miss Gayle, you can *hear* me. I hope you hear this: sometimes I hear you struggling to take a dump while I'm showering. It's called living in the city, you old kook. If you don't like it, go outside. Have a tall glass of puddle water."

I meandered over to my closet and pulled an old pair of black pants off a wire hanger. They fit snugly around my waist, the fabric tight across my thighs, but stopped short a few inches above my ankles. I stretched them out by lunging my way to the kitchen. I dug through our disorganized drawers until I came across a black Sharpie and a pair of scissors. I marked the spot for the new cuffs and peeled off the pants.

As I cut my old pants into shorts, I imagined the day I'd be rich enough to buy whatever I wanted without looking at the tag. I held my breath while buttoning the shorts. "Not bad. The frayed hems give them character."

In my bedroom, I found a black tank top on the floor and pulled it on over my head. I corralled my black curls into a messy French braid, sticking a few bobby pins in for good measure. I stood in front of the frameless mirror affixed to the back of my bedroom door. The corners were cloudy with age, but it beat applying makeup by memory. I pumped a nearly empty tube of mascara and wiggled the wand across my full lashes. Then I cracked open a fresh bottle of foundation. It blended seamlessly into my skin, a delightful discovery as I hadn't had time to swatch it before I stole it.

I frowned at the angry red bumps on my face, then caked on more makeup. It hurt to touch my nose, but I covered the bruising the best I could. I gave myself a little pep talk. "Don't worry. You look great. Well, you look okay. At least it'll be dark in the haunted house."

To make sure I had plenty of time to get through and win the prize, I tightened the smallest of my stolen watches around my wrist. For the final touch, I strapped on the holster from the pawnshop. Though the guns were fake, wearing them made me feel bulletproof.

Without warning, my bedroom door flew forward with such force I nearly fell, diving out of its trajectory. Ruelle's sickly sweet perfume crossed the threshold before she did. "What in God's name are you wearing, Lis?"

"A Halloween costume," I huffed. *How dare she police my clothes? I'm not the one with the secret stripping gig. Judge not lest ye be judged or whatever.*

Ruelle tried to tug the shorts down further on my thighs. "Too short and too tight. What are you supposed to be, anyway?"

I sighed. "I'm Lara Croft—from Tomb Raider."

"You know what you should be?" Ruelle waited for a beat, but I didn't take the bait. "In bed. It's a school night."

"There's no school tomorrow; it's All Saints Day." *And I got expelled. Which you'll figure out eventually, maybe when next semester's tuition is due.*

"I don't care, you're staying in. Why would you want to go out with your poor, busted nose? How did you get hit so hard playing dodgeball, anyway? I thought they weren't supposed to throw the ball at your face... I should call the school..."

"Seriously? First, I had to quit gymnastics because you couldn't keep up with the payments. Now you're threatening to call my school? As if I'm not enough of a pariah without my mommy complaining because her 'lil baby got a boo-boo."

Ruelle sucked in a deep breath and closed her eyes. "Yes, I admit I've become more protective since you got hurt, but I'm trying to do what's best for you."

"What's the big deal? I'm just going to a haunted house."

I knew Ruelle's face better than I knew my own, knew the meaning behind every wrinkle of her brow. But the face she made when I said we were going to a haunted house was completely new. Her mouth formed a little "o" of surprise, and her eyes went buggy.

"You are NOT going to a haunted house!" Ruelle declared. "Not tonight, not ever."

I crossed my arms. "Why not?"

"Because... because I said so." Ruelle rubbed her forehead, taking great efforts to compose herself, but it was too late. She was like a sweater with a loose thread, and I wouldn't stop tugging until she unraveled and revealed what was underneath.

"That's not good enough," I said. "Why can't I go to a haunted house?"

"For starters, we don't have money for something so... so frivolous."

"That's the beauty of it! There's a cash prize for finishing and I'm gonna win it. Then we won't get evicted."

Ruelle massaged her temples harder, like her fingers were trying to burrow into her brain. "Enough. You are NOT going! Besides, I already have a plan."

"This can be the backup plan."

"It's under control, Lisette. You aren't going out tonight. The car's been acting funny—"

"Xavier said he'd pick me up."

"No! I don't want you riding in cars with boys!"

"Since when? I ride with Xavi all the time. Besides, I've told you we're just friends."

"Teenage boys and girls can't be friends, they're too horny."

"Are you serious right now? We've ridden together a thousand times. To concerts, to school, to the mall. Why is this any different?"

Ruelle twisted her lucky ring frantically. The motion knocked a memory loose, but I couldn't quite pull it out. I wiggled it like a baby tooth, but it wasn't ready to break free. Something about another time when I could see the thin line of white where her skin never saw the sun.

"What's wrong?" I asked. "Did you... have a bad experience in a haunted house?"

"No," she said, but her head nodded yes. "I have just been rethinking the matter of you spending so much time with Xavier, unsupervised. I've only met him once or twice. Maybe he could come up and talk to me."

I rolled my eyes. Part of me wanted to tell her Xavier was gay. That might shut her up. But it wasn't my information to share. "Just because *you* got pregnant when *you* were a teenager—"

Ruelle tugged at the drawstring on her pink sweatpants. "This isn't about that. I don't want you going out. Bad things happen on Halloween night."

"Bad things happen every night. If you don't live your life because you're afraid of something bad happening—"

A booming knock shook the flimsy front door and echoed through our sparsely furnished apartment. *It's not Xavier,* I thought. *He rings the doorbell or waits in the alley. Trick-or-treaters? Naw, they'd see the eviction notice and know there's no free candy here. Must be the landlord.*

"Stay right here," Ruelle ordered me. She toyed with her

ring a moment, then wiggled it off and slammed it down on my dresser. "If I'm not back in ten minutes, take my ring and run."

"What? Why? Who's out there?" I asked in vain.

Ruelle locked my bedroom door before she shut it.

"Her paranoia has really gotten out of control," I grumbled under my breath.

The headlights of a car in the alleyway shot through my window, hitting the diamonds on Ruelle's ring and sending a dizzying array of colors bouncing around my room. I picked up the ring. Hadn't she practically told me to take it?

"Feels like it's been ten minutes," I reasoned, slipping the ring onto my right index finger. It fit snugly, as if it had been sized to my finger.

I lifted the broken blinds on my bedroom window and surveyed the street to make sure no one was watching. With the confident ease of an experienced delinquent, I slipped out onto the balcony and gave the iron railing a cursory shake. Flecks of rust followed as I climbed over it. Recalling the uneven bars, I relinquished my grip and dropped to the balcony below mine. My back spasmed in protest, but I swallowed back a yelp and kept my eyes on the prize. If only Coach Karla could've seen me. She wouldn't have been mad, she'd have been so impressed.

For my final trick, I lowered myself gingerly onto the decorative fence around the ground-floor apartment's patio. I hopped down, plodding through the soggy soil outside my neighbor's window and crushing her chrysanthemums.

"Those flowers are beautiful. Were beautiful, you klutz," I chided myself. I shook off my own rebuke. "Who cares?" I muttered. "They won't survive the winter, anyway."

As I walked toward Xavier's car, I twisted the ring so the diamonds were facing in toward my palm. I didn't need him asking where it came from or judging me for taking it without asking. Dollars to donuts Ruelle had stolen the ring, so could anyone *really* steal it from her? Besides, I was only borrowing it. I needed a little luck to win tonight.

"Groovy costume, baby!" Xavier greeted me as I slid into the front seat. The leather chilled my bare legs. "I can't believe your mom let you wear it! Remember when I tried to teach you how to swim, and she said you had to wear a t-shirt over your bikini?"

"Yeah, my mom's crazy." I leaned the seat back as far as it would go.

"Would it help if you told her I'm gay? You can if it would make things easier for you. I'm out to my mom, may as well be out to yours."

"Don't worry about her. She's the one making things hard on herself. Clearly, I don't need her permission to hang out with you."

Xavier chuckled. "Did you still wanna go to that haunted house? That website you sent me to was wild. These people that run it—covens of witches or whatever—seem really freaky."

"I don't care if Satan himself runs it; I gotta make it through. I need the money."

"What for?" he asked casually as he steered the car out onto the empty street.

"Because I don't have any."

"Ugh, I know the feeling."

I bit my tongue. To keep from snapping at him, I turned on the radio. *Monster Mash* flooded the car.

"Ooo! I love this song!" Xavier turned up the volume to drown out his off-key singing.

I shook my head and smiled at him. *He doesn't really get me. He wants to, but he can't.*

Xavier's GPS took us down a one-way road so bumpy it was hard to believe it was meant for cars. But potholes are as common as street signs in New Orleans, so I didn't overthink it.

"You have reached your destination," the GPS said as the headlights shone over a hand-painted wooden sign featuring a sloppy red arrow pointing simply to *Thirteenth Realm Parking.*

I grinned. "We're here."

Xavi didn't return my smile. He piloted past the mostly empty lot and parked in the back as usual. His hand hovered over the ignition, but then he withdrew without killing the engine. "It's not too late to leave," he said.

I unbuckled my seatbelt, opened my door, and stepped out into the lot. "Are you coming? Or are you gonna let some hokey props scare you?" I gestured to the giant oak tree shading the lot. A gigantic spider had been strung up in the upper branches, and bodies mummified with silky thread were stuck to its sprawling web. "You think that's real?"

Xavier sighed and followed me, dragging his feet. I slowed down to match his pace, my eyes wandering around the lot to keep from rushing him. *Poor kid. We're not even inside yet, and he's already terrified. I should tell him he doesn't have to do it, I can go by myself.*

A vintage teal van covered in Grateful Dead dancing bear bumper stickers stole my attention. I sniffed at the smoke wafting out of its cracked windows. My brain wanted it to be Tucker so badly, I thought I'd imagined seeing him in the passenger seat. A mirage in the desert of my love-starved mind.

But then I recognized Kennedy behind the wheel, and it felt like a dream come true. I couldn't believe how special I felt when she waved me over. "Hey! Look who it is! Howdy, Tucker's neighbor."

"Hi, Tucker's girlfriend," I said back. "Smells dank. Got space for two more?"

"Sure," Kennedy said. "Pile in the back with Hal."

Pile in with one of the hottest dudes I'd ever seen in my life? She didn't have to ask me twice. I hopped in without hesitation. Hal was dressed in all black, right down to his heavy eyeliner and studded leather collar. A goth kid costume? Boring, but I didn't care. He was still fine as hell. While I couldn't move fast enough, Xavier hung back.

He tugged at his white ruffled collar. "This Austin Powers costume is a rental. I shouldn't smoke in it."

"So take it to the dry cleaners." My laugh reverberated throughout the van and spurred everyone else to join me. Xavier shook his head and climbed into the backseat beside me.

What was his problem? He liked to smoke more than I did. I decided to ignore his attitude and used his presence as an excuse to move closer to Hal. Our knees brushed, and I felt —well, not much actually. It was kind of a disappointment, but he did smell nice, like Irish soap and sandalwood.

Kennedy passed me the thickest blunt I'd ever seen. "So," she said, "What do y'all know about the Thirteenth Realm of Hell?"

12

NO
PLAN IN
HELL

Twenty minutes later, all that remained of the blunt was a
soggy snippet so small it had to be held together by a clip.
Kennedy, the supreme authority of all things thirteenth realm,
talked while the rest of us listened. According to her, a nail
technician formerly employed at her parents' salon won last
year.

"He never came back to work—not even to pick up his last
check," Kennedy said wistfully. "But I saw him at Ampersands
a few months later—"

"Wait, how did *you* get into Ampersands?" Xavier interjected. "How old are you?"

Kennedy laughed. "Look, I know people. And if that
surprises you, then you really aren't gonna believe the rest."

"Maybe not," Xavier grumbled.

"Then what's the point in me telling you?" Kennedy
snipped. "Good luck or whatever."

"Hush Xavi, I want to hear." I shook my head at him. He
wasn't usually anywhere near this lame. He kept recoiling
whenever the blunt reached him, as if afraid of getting ash on
his outfit.

"Go on, Kennedy," I said. "What did he say happened in
the haunted house?"

Kennedy grinned. She wasn't wearing a costume as far as
I could tell, her all-black ensemble nondescript, but she

beamed like a queen presiding over court instead of a stoner in the driver's seat of an old van. "He said this place is like a bad acid trip, but worse. Something in the air creates a mass hallucination. It frees things, dark things, trapped deep in the recesses of your mind. But if you make it through, you get initiated into a secret society. And they're *rich*, so rich they can make your wildest dreams come true."

Xavier laughed derisively. "And you actually believe that?"

I punched Xavier in the arm, like I'd seen Kennedy do to Hal. But I must've hit him too hard because he looked at me as if I'd wrecked his precious car.

"It's okay, Lisette," Kennedy said. "He's got a right to be skeptical. I would've been, too. But I *knew* this dude before he went in, and then I saw him after with my own eyes. This dude's a first-generation immigrant. Came here with absolutely nothing. But when I saw him, he looked like old money. Tricked out Rolex, Armani suit, the works."

Tucker, who had been fairly quiet until this point, finally spoke. "When I win, I'm gonna open my own nightclub."

Xavier rolled his eyes so hard his glasses slipped. "Not with ten grand you're not. Opening a club takes—"

"Didn't you listen, Xavi?" I snapped at him. "The ten grand is only a start! Once you get in with these people, they set you up for life. Right, Kennedy?"

"Right," Kennedy said. "They own half the city as it is."

"I'll help you open your club, Tucker," Hal interjected. He rubbed his bloodshot eyes, smudging his eyeliner. "Ain't like I'm gonna win, but if I did, I'd help ya."

"Why are you gonna try if you don't think you'll win?" Xavier asked.

"For the experience." Hal shrugged, taking the blunt clip from Kennedy.

"Hal's got as good a chance as any of us," Kennedy said. "Well, maybe not as much as me, but the same as the rest of you."

"What gives you better odds?" Xavier demanded. "What's your strategy?"

Kennedy crossed her arms and grinned wickedly. "Wouldn't you like to know?"

"Here's *my* strategy!" Tucker, costumed as an old-school gangster in an ostentatious purple suit, grabbed a fake machine gun from the floorboard and mimed firing a few rounds. "Blast anybody who tries to take me out!"

"Try to take you out? Like out of the haunted house?" I asked.

Kennedy nodded gravely. "Heard *that* from someone who didn't win. She blacked out and woke up in the parking lot but doesn't remember how she got there."

"Yeah, and hasn't been the same since," Hal mumbled.

Kennedy shrugged. "If you say so. If you ask me, Jennifer's *always* been strange."

"Gee, this is making me really excited about going in," Xavier mumbled.

I glanced at my watch. It was nearly ten already. "We should get going," I said. I could see the parking lot filling up and imagined the line growing. "Y'all coming?"

"Naw, we're waiting for a few more friends," Kennedy answered.

"Bigger the group, the better," Hal added. He tried to hand me the clip, but I waved him away. "You sure? Y'all should wait, go in with us. It's like a school of fish or a flock of sheep or—"

"We get it; we're prey in there," Xavier cut him off. He got out of the van without telling anyone goodbye.

Though I was mortified, I managed to smile. "Well, it's been real. And it's been fun. But we gotta run. Guess we'll see y'all inside?"

"More importantly, hope to see you on the outside," Hal said with a wink.

"Don't be an ass, dude," Tucker scolded him. "It's a *rumor* that some people don't make it out. They're witches, not murderers."

I didn't engage with his remark. Refused to acknowledge anything challenging the narrative in my head: these people could make all my dreams come true. I just had to prove to them that I was worthy.

Xavier waited for me outside, his scowl incongruent with his goofy Austin Powers costume. "Who are those people anyway?" he asked.

"What do you mean?" I skipped through the parking lot, marveling at how being high made every movement lighter. Or maybe it was Ruelle's ring? I admired it flashing as I swung my arms.

Xavier shook his head and ran after me. "How do you know them?"

"Tucker's my neighbor. Kennedy's his girlfriend. Hal's their friend. They're all cool. What else do you need to know?"

"Oh, so you *don't* know them. I swear, Lisette, one day you're gonna get in the wrong van and get yourself killed."

I dismissed his concerns with a chuckle. "Spoken like someone who has never had to rely on the kindness of strangers."

"Or like someone who doesn't want to be called into the morgue to identify your body. Seriously, do you even *know* what you were smoking? It didn't smell right…"

"Since when are you such an authority on what pot smells like? There have to be like a hundred different varieties."

"I'm telling you, that wasn't *just* pot. It was laced with something. You're not acting like yourself. We're about to go into some Battle Royale-style haunted house and you're over here prancing like a lamb who doesn't know she's headed to the slaughterhouse."

That one made me laugh. "Stop being such a drama queen, Xavi. The hero never dies. At least not in the first act."

"You're the hero, huh? What's that make me?"

"My lovable sidekick, duh." I raised my hand to give him a playful nudge, but he flinched. I lowered my hand, ashamed. It didn't feel good having my best friend fear me.

Xavier frowned. "We should bail. Go back to my house, play some video games or something. I've got a weird feeling that—"

I whirled around and fixed him with my iciest glare. "You can chicken out if you want to, but I've got to do this. If I need to do it alone, fine. Nothing new."

"It's not like that." Xavier looked down. His glasses slipped to the bridge of his nose, and he pushed them back up. "You didn't see the weird-ass website. These people running it are like cultists or Satan-worshippers or something."

I ruffled his shaggy brown hair affectionately. "It's okay if you can't make it all the way through. You can just wait for me outside."

His scowl broke, and his jaw dropped. "I can make it through!" he protested. "How scary can a haunted house be, anyway?"

"As scary as the Satanists wanna make it, I guess."

"I don't believe in God, so why would I believe in Satan?"

"That's the spirit." I nodded toward the flow of people filing in ahead of us. "Let's go. I'd like to be safe inside before Ruelle realizes I'm gone."

"Safe inside the witches' haunted house." Xavier laughed. "You're crazy."

"You love it. Without me, you'd be at home wishing you were doing something this exciting." I hooked my arm through his and led him toward the line. Several sets of wide eyes ogled my skimpy costume. I didn't care. Everyone with taste was admiring what a fantastic Lara Croft I made, and everyone else could kick rocks barefoot.

"Whoa!" Xavier pointed up. I followed his finger to a

giant dilapidated warehouse. "How have I never seen *that* before?"

I shrugged. "We probably drive past it all the time and don't notice it."

"I would notice that."

"You two! Move along!" a chainsaw-wielding masked man shouted at us.

Xavier jumped out of his skin, but I calmed him down. "Relax, he's an actor. It's his job to scare us. He can't really hurt you."

"I know that," Xavier huffed. "I just don't like being yelled at."

Finally, we reached a card table where a vampire with a repulsive bite wound on her pale neck regarded us with something between disinterest and disdain. She shoved a pen and a five-page document in front of each of us. Xavier squinted at his copy. "This print is microscopic."

"Okay, but is your dick microscopic?" the vampire spat back. "Because if it's not, quit acting like a little titty-baby and sign."

Xavier pressed the pen against the signature line. "The actors can't touch us, right?"

The vampire barely lifted her skinny shoulders. "Dunno. Read the waiver."

"What?" Xavi gasped. "You work here! Shouldn't you know if the actors can touch us?"

"If you wanna go in, sign your name. If you're too scared, leave."

"Why aren't you answering my question? What's so damn scary—"

"Either sign or get out of the way! You're holding up the line," she hissed.

I gently laid a hand on Xavier's shoulder. "Come on, dude, it can't be that bad. And if you aren't feeling it, you can leave."

"I don't get it, every other haunted house I've ever been to tells you—"

"They'll probably tell us the rules once we're inside." I looked at the vampire for confirmation. "Right?"

Her bone-white fangs gleamed as she snarled, "Probably."

With an exasperated sigh, Xavier scribbled his name on the document. I pulled him along to the next table before he could change his mind. A werewolf wearing a red flannel shirt, slashed to expose his furry chest, guarded the cash box. "How many?"

"One, please." I held out the twenty Mr. Amos had given me.

"It's thirty bucks."

"I thought it was twenty." I pretended to search my pockets, praying he'd let me slide.

"We charge extra on Halloween to cover the prize money," the werewolf explained.

Xavier opened his wallet and tossed two twenties down. "Well, that's it, I'm out of cash. So if you were gonna beat me up and rob me in the final realm, you'll have to revise your plans."

Though the mask hid his mouth, I swore I heard a smile in the werewolf's voice when he said, "No problem, buddy. There's no plan in hell."

13

PRETTY
AS A
CAR
CRASH

"Whatever happens, we have to stick together," Xavier said as we were ushered into the first realm of the haunted house along with eleven other hopefuls.

I let him hold my hand, didn't mind when he squeezed it. I was riding a relaxed kind of high where nothing mattered and nothing hurt.

"See, Xavi, it's only a warehouse," I whispered as we walked in. My eyes shot up toward the ceiling and I shuddered, imagining monsters molded from shadows. "Nothing to be afraid of," I insisted.

"Not yet," Xavier replied.

We only made it a few steps when a police officer whose dull bronze badge read "Crash" corralled our group through an exit door. It didn't make sense for them to force us outside. Weren't haunted houses indoors? At least at the start? But I went along with it, trying to push what Hal said about sheep out of my mind.

Xavi tried to tell me something, but a clap of thunder cut him off. Had it been threatening to rain all night without me noticing? Clouds in New Orleans are always emptying out or bursting at the seams, the humidity woven into the fabric of the city as tightly as hot sauce and hospitality.

Lightning ripped through the sky, confirming my suspicions. My nerves tingled with alarm. Something in the air tasted burnt, like boiling water forgotten on the stove. Four banged-up Jeeps with hard tops and muddy tires waited for us, their engines rumbling.

"Get in where you fit in," Officer Crash said. "Hop to it!"

Xavier hesitated, eyeing the vehicles. He squeezed my hand until it hurt. "My mom wouldn't let me have a Jeep. She says they flip."

"Relax," I mumbled, pulling him along through the mud. I opened the door to the backseat of a Jeep, and we squeezed in together as the first fat raindrops started to fall. "Pretend it's a ride at Universal. Nothing here can *actually* hurt you."

Through the darkly tinted window, I saw a stranger in a Mario costume, complete with a fake mustache, racing toward us. He shouted, "Shotgun!" His friend Luigi hopped in the back beside me. I angled my knees to the right, away from him.

Princess Peach opened the door and glared at Xavier and me. "Where am I supposed to sit?" she asked us like we were the help.

"Pick another car, Princess," the driver growled. He wore a white racing jacket and aviators, despite the fact that the sun had long since gone down. His face makeup was caked on thick and carved up into a hundred tiny pinkish-white lines to emulate burn scars.

"You heard the man," Princess Peach said to Mario. "Let's go. Hurry! I'm getting wet."

Luigi laughed. "You are so whipped, dude."

Mario crossed his arms. "I got shotgun, Chrissy. The best seat. Why can't you pick another car?"

Princess Peach's eyes bulged. "Are you seriously not coming with me?"

Mario groaned. "Aw, don't be a pill, Chrissy. You didn't even wanna come 'til you heard about the money. Pick a different car and I'll catch up with you in the next realm, okay?"

"Fine!" she snapped, though I noticed the wobble in her voice, the tears trying to break through. She slammed the door.

I almost felt sorry for her trekking through the rain alone, but only an idiot dated that big of a tool. They probably deserved each other.

"That costume is in poor taste," Xavier whispered to me, interrupting the real live soap opera I'd been watching.

"Whose costume?" I asked a little too loud.

"Shhh," Xavi hissed at me. "The driver? Dale Earnhardt? Hello?"

"Who's that?"

"He's a famous race car driver. He died this year."

"Since when do you know anything about race car drivers? Xavier, are you secretly a redneck? I thought you watched wrestling for the skimpy costumes."

"And the storylines," Xavier protested.

"All right, everybody, get ready for a wild ride," the Dale Earnhardt imposter said. "Say the phrase 'buckle up' if you want out, and of course, forfeit your chance at the prize money."

I looked around for a seatbelt but couldn't find one.

Xavier dug his nails into my palm. "There are no seatbelts," he said. "Lisette, why aren't there any seatbelts? I don't like this. I don't like this at all."

Dale turned around; the burn scars on his face seemed to grow whiter against his red cheeks. "What's the matter, Mr. Powers? You scared already?"

"No," Xavier mumbled.

"Then why are you holding your sister's hand?"

"She's not my sister."

"Well, she's too young to be your mother and too hot to be your lover. Final guess: she's using you for your money. That it, boy?"

Xavier scoffed, but he didn't speak. He let go of my hand.

I tried to keep my face neutral, but one of my greatest fears had come true. Xavier thought I was using him for his money. I would never do that. Not to him. Didn't he know me at all? In that moment, it sure as hell didn't feel like it. But I didn't have much time to feel sorry for myself.

Dale pressed down on the gas and didn't let up, accelerating, then swerving so fast my knees bumped into the center console. I looked at Xavier; all the color had left his face. "It's okay," I said to him. "It's just a haunted house."

"No, it's not. I don't know what it is—but it's not *just* a haunted house. Have *you* ever been to a haunted house where, as soon as you walk in, they force you outside? Because I haven't."

"You're high," I said. "You're being paranoid."

"I am *not* high," Xavier snapped. "You were probably too busy mooning over that pretty goth boy to notice, but I didn't smoke."

I rolled my eyes. "You got a contact high, though. Don't deny it."

Xavier said nothing. But there was no denying that the Jeep was picking up speed. And though the rain beat against the windshield, making it impossible for me to see out, Dale didn't turn the wipers on. He breathed excitedly, almost hyperventilating, as he casually gripped the wheel like he was out for a joy ride.

"Where are we going, man?" Mario asked. "How can you see?"

Dale didn't answer, but his smirk said enough.

Xavier shut his eyes and made the sign of the cross. Kinda funny coming from someone who didn't believe in God ten minutes ago.

"He must know the way by heart," I whispered.

Xavier only shook his head, unwilling or unable to weigh in.

I stole a glance at Luigi, whose eyes were transfixed on

something outside the window. I opened my mouth to ask what he saw, but before the words left my lips, the Jeep slammed into something. My body jerked forward, ears assaulted by the nails-on-chalkboard sound of metal tearing at metal. My knees slammed against the center console, much harder than before. The pain at the top of my spine buzzed right below the surface, like a shock from static electricity.

"Hold on!" Xavier commanded me. Both of his hands gripped my shoulders, pulling me back. "Hold on to me!"

I threw my arms around his neck and interlaced my fingers.

Whatever we'd hit, Dale seemed completely unfazed by it. I reasoned this was all part of their plan. I loosened my grip around Xavier's neck. They must have planted something on the course to make us *think* we hit something. That had to be it.

Dale's foot pressed down on the gas pedal again. The tires squealed beneath us. The road sounded thick, gurgling like mud.

"We aren't going that fast," I said to assure Xavier. Okay, fine, and to assure me. "It only feels super-fast because we're stoned. Everything speeds up when you're high."

He didn't reply, and from his wheezing breaths, I wasn't sure he could.

I nestled into him, burying my face in the crook of his arm. He smelled like Brute deodorant and aftershave, like an old man. I wanted him to comfort me, but he said, "We're barreling toward our doom. We're on a collision course, and we need to get off before we're roadkill."

"Not if I have anything to do with it." I let go of him and directed my anger toward Dale. "Hey! You up there!" I shouted. "What's wrong with you? Slow down!"

He cupped his ear. "What was that, sweetie?"

"I said slow down!"

"Everybody hates a backseat driver," he said with a nasty

chuckle. "Let's see if you can do any better." He pressed a button, opening the Jeep's sunroof. The sky above us was blue-black, a blur of fast-moving storm clouds, until Dale hit another button, ejecting himself from the vehicle, and his body blocked out the sky.

It would have been comical if it weren't really happening —the way he soared above us, a red-and-white-striped para-chute billowing behind him like something out of a cartoon. I tried to laugh, but it came out as a squeak.

Mario screamed. He sputtered nonsense while everyone else pleaded with him to grab the wheel. Close the sunroof. Do something! His wits returned, and he climbed into the driver's seat. Shaking, he shouted, "I'm pressing the brake, but it won't slow down!"

The car splashed through a giant puddle. Then it began to spin. There was an explosion of shattering glass and Luigi shouted, "Buckle up!" He went sailing out the window as if yanked by an invisible arm. I was desperate to look, needed to know he was okay, that this was a game, but I didn't dare let go of Xavier.

At last, the spinning stopped. Then the Jeep rocked toward Xavier's side, threatening to tip. I took a chance and let go of Xavi, moving over in an attempt to balance the vehicle, but it was too late. The Jeep started to roll.

"Cover your head!" Xavier instructed me.

Obediently, I assumed the fetal position. I thought about playing "crack the egg" on Xavier's trampoline. Thought about bouncing without coming undone. *This egg isn't gonna crack.* Though the Jeep flipped—once, twice, three times—I felt grounded in my weightlessness, as though I were suspended safely in the air, cradled in the angelic embrace of some unseen guardian.

At last we stopped. There was no sound at first, then I could hear Xavier's ragged breaths. He was still right beside me. I exhaled with relief. I carefully unfolded my body and assessed the situation. The Jeep had landed on its side, where the third passenger had been. Its frame was bent, the jagged red metal reminding me of a crushed Coke can. Luigi got out in the nick of time.

I rubbed my eyes, certain what I saw couldn't be real. It had to be some elaborate set design, because if I didn't know better—which of course I did—I would have said the Jeep was dangling one-third of the way off the edge of a cliff.

Mario, still in the front seat, whimpered softly.

"Lis? Are you okay, Lis?" Xavier asked.

"Yeah, I think so. You?"

"I don't know." Xavier studied his unscathed hands. "Nothing hurts but… we flipped three times. I feel like adrenaline is holding something off. Like any moment…"

The sound of metal grating against rock interrupted him with a screech. The Jeep was sliding off the edge and into an abyss. I dared not stare into its infinite blackness for too long. If you gaze long enough into an abyss, the abyss will gaze back into you. Nietzsche would've loved this haunted house.

"Lis! What's happening!" Xavier screamed. "How are we on a *cliff*! There are no *mountains* in Louisiana!"

"Exactly," I said as calmly as I could. "It's not real." I looked at the sunroof, which was now perpendicular to the ground. The Jeep's frame caved inward, leaving only a sliver for us to escape through. "All the same, let's move slowly."

Mario either didn't hear our conversation or didn't care. "Let me out!" he yelped, fists hammering against the front passenger side door. "I'm too young to die! I've never even had a threesome!"

"Calm down!" I barked at him.

The Jeep lurched forward. It was half on solid ground and half off at this point, but Mario wasn't deterred. "Let me out! Let me out!" he howled, seemingly forgetting the safe phrase.

I didn't waste my breath admonishing him again. I squeezed through the mangled roof, then reached back in to help Xavier out. Though he was a few inches shorter than me, his shoulders were wider. He had to twist and wriggle before he freed himself.

"Wait! Help me!" Mario cried. He tried to squeeze through without assistance, but he was too broad. Xavier grabbed his arms, but I hung back, watching from a safe distance. I would have intervened if Xavier was at risk, but I wasn't about to stick my neck out for some jerk like Mario.

Xavier pulled with all his might, which wasn't much. The Jeep pulled back, skidding through the mud so it was more off the cliff than on.

"Tense up!" Xavier shouted. "I know you're scared, but you're not making this any easier by shaking, dude."

"Please!" Mario begged. "You gotta help me! Please! I'll do anything. I'll be indebted to you for life!"

"Hey man, it's okay. Don't panic. I got through and you can, too. Squeeze as tight as you can. Make yourself as small as possible."

Mario concentrated so hard that the sweat from his lip loosened his fake mustache. It flapped free and slid off his face. The fuzzy little mustache fell out of the Jeep and went sailing down into the darkness where my eyes dared not follow.

Spurred by seeing what could happen to Mario, Xavier's panic reached a fever pitch. "Hey! Little help here, Lis?"

I rolled my eyes. As if they were *really* going to fall off an imaginary cliff. "No one helped me. He needs to jump forward like I did."

The Jeep moved again, which finally gave Mario the courage to leap forward. The sides of the roof scraped his shoulders, ripping his red jumper, but at last, he was out.

The Jeep broke free, too. The sound it made as it bounced off the side of the mountain made all three of us shudder. I pricked my ears but didn't hear it land. Another trick, I was sure. No one really threw away a vehicle.

Mario sucked in air greedily. His cheeks flushed red.

"Are you okay, dude?" Xavier asked.

"Yeah, I'm fine!" Mario scrambled away from the edge of the cliff.

"You sure? Your face is super red."

"I said I'm good," Mario insisted as his whole face flushed as red as his jumpsuit.

Xavier turned to me. "This is beyond creepy. What *is* this place?"

I just shrugged. "At least it stopped raining."

Xavier stared at me as I squeezed the water from the end of my braid.

I spied a little arrow pointing down with *2nd Realm* hand-painted on it and busied myself trying to figure out how best to descend the mountain. Well, not a mountain. It couldn't be a mountain. It was a set-piece or *something*. Whatever it was, I had to climb down it to get to the next realm.

"Did you hear me, Lisette?" Xavier's tone grew agitated. "What's gotten into you? First you *stand* there while this guy nearly plummets to his death—"

"He was fine. If he really feared for his life, he could've used the safe word."

"You aren't acting like yourself." He crossed his arms. "I want to go home."

"Go home if you want," I shouted up at him as I inched down the side of the mountain. "I need that money, and I'm going to get it."

14

CAVE OF
BLUNDERS

I counted nine people from our original group of thirteen, milling around the mouth of a cave at the base of the mountain. That included me and a reluctant Xavier panting beside me. He sounded like a chain smoker after a long weekend, and I wondered how long he would last in this high-octane environment. But it didn't matter. I was doing this. I would win the haunted house—with or without him.

Mario and Princess Peach reunited, kissing sloppily as though they had been apart for months instead of minutes. She touched his scratched shoulders through his tattered costume. "Does it hurt?" she asked. "You should've come with me. Our driver didn't abandon us."

"Sorry I didn't follow you to another car, babe," Mario spoke into her plastic crown. He laced his fingers through her hair, holding her head against his chest as if to avoid making eye contact.

"Where's your precious Luigi?" Princess Peach asked with a sarcastic snort.

Mario swallowed as if suppressing the memory of our wild ride. "Got to be too much for him. He tapped out."

"In the first realm?" Peach scoffed. "And he had the nerve to call you whipped! Better to be whipped by a pussy than to *be* a pussy."

"Yeah, I agree, babe." Mario stroked her hair. "You don't have to tell me, I agree."

I shook my head. I never liked the word "pussy" being thrown around as slang—especially when used to refer to weakness. Balls are far more sensitive. Had to be tough realizing your girlfriend is stronger than your best friend. I smiled. Amusing as their reconciliation was, I doubted their relationship would survive the night. Still, I appreciated the distraction from wondering what had happened to the rest of our group.

In a way, I was glad they were gone. Fewer people meant less competition. But there was a small, compassionate side of me that worried for them. I hushed that side up. Forgot their faces so fast I couldn't have picked them out of a line-up if my prize money depended on it.

Mud dripped from my boot as I tapped my foot. At last, a man wearing a movie-quality Batman suit emerged from the shadows at the mouth of the cave.

"Welcome to the second realm!" Batman said, his arms outstretched, cape billowing behind him. "Take care not to disturb my little flying friends. They so rarely receive guests! Once they notice you've trespassed into their home, they won't want you to leave."

"Bats have rabies," Xavier hissed in my ear. "If you get bit, you have to get, like, a hundred shots in the butt."

"Okay," I said. "So don't get bit." I tried not to think about the kind of medical treatment Ruelle could afford. It would probably be worse than being bitten. She would cover me in rocks, praying to spirits while I went frothing mad. Clearly what they did to poor Bebe hadn't fixed my back, at least not entirely.

People entered the cave ahead of us. I must've missed the safe word while talking to Xavi. *No big deal*, I told myself; *Bats are actually kinda cool.*

As soon as Batman was out of sight, Xavier reached for

my hand. His palms were sweaty, but I didn't recoil. He needed me. I didn't need him, but I wasn't going to ditch him like some people would.

The ceiling of the cave pressed down on us, bringing the bats closer. Dozens and dozens of them clung to the stalactites overhead, their bony black wings folded up but their beady little eyes wide open. Watching. Like they were waiting for a signal. I giggled.

"What's so funny?" Xavier asked.

"They're waiting for a signal," I said. "Like a bat signal. Get it?"

"You're so high," he said.

"I am ru-bber and you are g-lue," I trilled, "whatever you say bounces off of *me* and sticks to *you*."

Xavier covered his mouth to keep his giggles to himself. "Be quiet," he whispered, "or you'll disturb the bats."

I rolled my eyes. "This is boring. Let them come at me. I'm not afraid of bats."

Xavier shook his head. "You love needles, too. That's why you want us to get giant tattoos on our butts."

I snickered. Getting matching tattoos on our butt cheeks had been a long-running joke. Truthfully, I thought I'd rather get one on my arm where I could look at it all the time. Besides, that would really piss Ruelle off. She had tattoos, symbols she wouldn't explain, but that didn't stop her from forbidding me from getting one.

The deeper we ventured inside the cave, the dimmer it became. Darkness pressed in from all four sides, threatening to swallow us up. A handful of flickering torches held it at bay; their flames were hardly sufficient to light our way. We shuffled along, following the sound of footsteps ahead of us as much as the path. I did my best to keep us in the middle of the pack. If something bad happened to the people in front of us, I would hear their screams, and if the bats came down behind us, they would go after the stragglers first. I was going to be fine. I had a plan.

Once my eyes adjusted, the realm was kind of beautiful. The rock formations varied from the floor to the ceiling. The clusters at our feet looked like mushrooms and those above our heads like icicles. Some of the crystals looked familiar. I paused, bending down closer near a particularly large cluster of smoky quartz, a stone Ruelle swore could cure depression. I had always assumed it was merely a placebo effect when it seemed to lift her mood, and yet, now that I was finally touching it myself, I had to admit it gave me a dopamine rush. I smiled like I'd gotten a perfect ten from a tough judge at a gymnastics meet.

"C'mon Lis," Xavier said gently, snapping me back to reality. "Everyone else is ahead of us."

Somewhat reluctantly, I left the smoky quartz and trudged after him. Before long, we reached a fork in the path where the cave split into two paths with equal wear from travel. Mario and his Princess stood at the fork in front of a row of lanterns, the bright light casting them in an eerie glow amongst the shadows. Peach's lipstick was smeared, like maybe they'd paused to make out. It was definitely dark enough in here, and fear had a strange way of making people horny.

She pointed left. "I'm telling you, Dave, I can see light coming from that side!"

"Yeah, and I'm telling *you* it's a trick! I've seen it used in haunted houses before; they hang a lantern to confuse you. Only an amateur would fall for it. Come on, Chrissy, we're going right!"

"Stop acting like a know-it-all!" Chrissy stamped her foot. "You've never been in a haunted house like this one and—"

Maybe it was the screaming. Maybe it was the stomping. Or maybe it was just time.

A single bat dropped down, the flutter of his velvety wings so soft I barely heard him gliding through the cave.

"What's that?" I whispered.

But before Xavier could venture a guess, tiny feet found purchase on my bare shoulder. Claws, as delicate and sharp as ten little needles, sunk into my skin. Maybe I didn't want a tattoo after all. The muscles in my throat constricted to strangle my scream so only a gurgle escaped.

"Don't move!" Xavier said, boldly slapping at the bat. But the bat didn't let go. It flashed its canines, as if daring him to come feel how sharp they were.

Princess Peach gasped. Mario grabbed her arm. "All right, you win!" he said. "We can go left. Let's just get out of here!"

Xavier tried to cash in on his favor. "Hey! Wait! Mario! Help us!"

But that coward Mario didn't slow down as he called over his shoulder, "Sorry, man. Gotta keep moving or they'll get us too."

Xavier steeled himself as more shadows glided toward us. "I've got you, Lis! Hold still!" He charged, both arms swinging wildly, eyes closed so if a bat did bite, at least he wouldn't suffer the terror of seeing it coming. *Bam!* He got a lucky hit, and the bat hopped down, shrieking.

"Are you okay? Did it get you?" Xavier pulled me toward him.

I twisted my neck to examine my shoulder, but I couldn't see anything in the dim lighting. Though I could hear the steady beat of wings advancing. "I'm fine," I said. My whole body shook involuntarily, as though my brain were still sending signals to dislodge the bat. "Let's go!"

"Which way?" Xavier asked. "Should we follow them or…?"

I nodded while I ran. There was no time for discussion. Hell, I didn't even tell him thank you. I don't know why.

Maybe because thanking him would acknowledge I needed him.

Xavier scrambled to keep up with me. I slowed my gait, noting his ragged breaths.

"Did you ever see Cujo?" he asked once he caught up to me. "Where the bats bite the St. Bernard and he turns into this murderous—"

"Yeah, Xavier," I patronized. "I saw Cujo with you. Remember? I hated it. Who wants to watch a movie where the dog is the bad guy?"

"He wasn't the bad guy. If anything, rabies is the bad guy."

"Speaking of bad guys, what about that Mario dude? Remember when he said he'd be indebted to you forever or something? What a joke. Should've left him in the Jeep."

"Naw," Xavier said. "We didn't know he was bad back then. Besides, pulling him out was the right thing to do."

"I knew he was bad back then," I said. "That's why I didn't—"

"Look!" Xavier pointed to a growing beam of light. "We're almost out."

"Finally! If I had to spend another minute stuck in this cave listening to you try to justify the actions of every jerk we've ever met—"

"I try to see the good in everyone," Xavier interrupted me. "Even you."

Ouch. That stung worse than the bat's claws.

"Enough yapping," I whispered. "We aren't outta here yet."

In the quiet, I found myself reflecting on the bat. Was it real? It had to be! They couldn't make a fake one shriek in my ear. But I distinctly remembered learning last year in Biology that bats weren't aggressive. Was Xavier right? Did this one have rabies?

A shudder shook my fears away. At least it didn't bite me.

This place wasn't so bad. In fact, in the right light, it was kind of beautiful. Like the golden rays of hope pouring in from outside the cave.

The closer we got to the light, the smaller my concerns shrunk until I had reduced the haunted house to one great big ruse. Everything that didn't fit into this prognosis—like the cave itself—I disregarded as easily as the waiver.

PRETTY
LITTLE
PREDATORS

Outside of the cave, a dangerously alluring woman painted like a porcelain doll greeted us. Her brightly lacquered red lips and sparkly orange eyelids reminded me of a poisonous butterfly. Her smooth skin gleaming in the moonlight made me want to hide my imperfect face. My eyes roamed to the run-down mansion behind her.

It had once been a great beauty, too, judging by its intricate scaffolding, but now the mansion was old and brooding, its windows dark behind broken shutters. The flower beds in the front yard were overrun with weeds, but a simple wooden swing hung from a magnificent oak tree as if children still resided here. The unoccupied swing rocked back and forth in the stagnant air. Unnerved, I looked away, up toward the second-floor terrace. A small, shadowy figure tiptoed past a window.

"What a treat to have so many visitors," the poisonous doll addressed the eight remaining entrants of our original thirteen. Mario and Princess Peach were still with us, his arm draped over her shoulder. She leaned into him, and I looked away to avoid vomiting in my mouth.

How did someone not make it out of that lame cave? I counted again to make sure. Eight again. Odd. But I was sure whoever we lost would catch up.

"Come along," the vacant-eyed beauty said, her hoop skirt

spinning as she turned around, "and I shall take you to the dollhouse. We have lots of toys there, and they all want to play with you." She walked ahead, her arms stiff, her movements stilted.

I blinked in disbelief when I noticed a giant brass wind-up key sticking out between her shoulder blades. The skin around the key was reddish-purple, as though healing from a deep wound. Was it makeup? How did they make it look so real? I chased after her, trying to get a better look. I expected Xavier to pull me back, but he squeezed in beside me. I raised an eyebrow at him. "What? No speech about how this place is creepy and we should leave?"

"You didn't listen the first hundred times I told you." Xavier followed me through a broken wooden gate and up wide stairs that led to a wraparound porch. "I'm starting to think I should just get this over with. Besides, what's so scary about dolls?"

"Go watch *Child's Play* and then get back to me," I said.

"I prefer *Toy Story*."

"When I was a little kid, I told myself that if my dolls came to life and tried to kill me, my stuffed animals would protect me."

"Adorable, but I don't follow. Why would dolls be evil but not other toys?"

"Because you treat your stuffed animals better." I winced, thinking of poor Bebe. "You let them sleep in your bed, take them places. You don't cut their hair off or pop off their heads. Dolls have a reason to be mad."

"Shhh." Xavier raised a finger to his lips. "I wanna hear the safe word—just in case."

The doll-woman paused in front of a door with a brass lion knocker surrounded by peeling paint. "Find the elevator key and ride up to the second floor for further instructions. If you're nice to the dolls, they'll be nice to you. If you're naughty, you better say *Playtime's Over* before they enact their own form of justice."

As we entered the foyer, a guy dressed up as a Ghostbuster —Egon, if his thick glasses were any indication—took charge. "Everybody split up and search separate rooms for the key," he barked. "We've got the kitchen." He nodded toward his buddy, a chunky fellow fittingly dressed as Slimer, his thick green face-paint extending past his double chin.

"Powers, Croft—you two check the living room," Egon said to Xavier and me.

I gave him a mock salute and a sarcastic, "Aye aye, captain." I grabbed Xavier's arm and tugged him through the center of the crowd.

"Where *is* the living room?" Xavier whispered in my ear.

"Hell if I know."

We passed a grand staircase in abysmal condition. About a third of the steps were busted, and the banister wobbled wildly, though no one was holding onto it. I froze in my tracks, spellbound, searching for what controlled it—surely there was some scientific explanation. I thought about what Kennedy had said, that this was some kind of mass hallucination. It *had* to be. Even the house itself, out in the middle of nowhere, made no sense.

"Ummm… hey, Lisette?" Xavier's voice warbled, and he gripped my arm a little too tightly for comfort.

I was annoyed at the interruption from puzzling out the mystery of the stairs. "What?"

His voice was reverent and soft. "I understand why dolls are so scary now."

I followed his wide-eyed gaze to a humongous glass curio containing fifty or more porcelain dolls. Their impish, painted-on smiles sent shivers down my spine. More unsettling, their giant eyes tracked me as I wandered closer. How could something be so *creepy* and so *magnetic* at the same time? I needed to take a closer look.

"Lis! What are you *doing*?" Xavi squeaked.

"Relax. I'm going to check this armoire next to the curio," I said. "It's a logical place to hide a key—no one wants to look so close to these freaky dolls."

"Um, okay. I'm gonna… check behind this painting." He forked a finger behind him, toward a wall that was as far as he could get from the dolls without leaving the room.

"Fine, whatever," I grumbled as I searched the armoire. It *had* to contain the key; why else did I feel so drawn to it?

Xavier's shaky voice sounded behind me. "Hey, Lis? I've been thinking—"

I didn't bother looking up from the drawer I was digging through. "Let me guess—you think we should leave?"

"Obviously. But that wasn't what I was gonna say. I was gonna say I was thinking about Charlie and the Chocolate Factory—you know, how he won."

"He cheated."

"But he still had a good heart. So maybe we should consider—"

Cheating? As if I couldn't legitimately win! I whirled around and gave him an incredulous look. "What are you doing? Are you even looking for the key?"

"It's not like I'm gonna find it," Xavier protested. "I'm the worst at finding things. Don't worry though, I'm watching your back."

"Watching for wh—" I stopped mid-sentence. "Holy tamales!" I shouted.

The curio door creaked open, and the dolls began climbing out. Their little porcelain limbs scraping against their joints made an awful screeching sound. They all had wild looks in their eyes, wicked sneers to their painted-on smiles.

"Run, Xavier! Run!" I shouted.

We darted into the next closest room, the kitchen. I scanned the space for a pantry or some place we could hide until someone else found the stupid key. There weren't any appliances or cabinets. Nothing except row after row of glass curios—every last one empty.

I found our fearless leader Egon poking around inside the pantry. "Have the dolls attacked anyone?" I asked him.

"Not yet." Egon opened a cookie jar, disappointment flashing across his face.

"Well, where are they? What are they doing?"

"Some people can hear them talking. Haven't heard it myself." He nodded at a woman in the adjacent dining room. She was dressed as Cruella De Vil, but she didn't look so tough with her hands covering her ears. "She heard them say something—must have been super weird because now she won't talk to anyone."

I approached Cruella, my curiosity running wild, but she retreated, backing into a small space between two empty curios. She closed her eyes as if only what she could see really existed. As I inched closer, I could hear Cruella singing something to herself—a song I vaguely recognized—something about living forever.

Xavier hung back near the dining room. Probably inching away from the empty curios. I had more pressing concerns—the key. Where was that the stupid key? Where would I hide a key? Ruelle always hid ours on top of door frames. With nothing else to go on, I felt along the top of each door frame. My fingers brushed over nothing special, cobwebs and occasionally an agitated spider. I pressed on, tuning out everything else going on in the house, until I heard a small voice from directly behind me.

"They want me to join them," the voice whispered. I turned, thinking it might be Cruella coming over to explain, but it was Princess Peach.

Mario tugged on her arm. "What are you talking about, Chrissy? Join who?"

"The dolls," Chrissy said, tearing away from him. "They

say I can trade *now* for *forever.* They say… they can make me one of them!"

"Stop saying stuff like that," Mario snapped. "Have you lost your mind?"

"Please. I want to join them. They can make me young and beautiful forever!" The frenzied look on her face told me she'd made up her mind.

Impolite as it was, I couldn't help staring. I'd been waiting for a moment like this all night, for these awful people to come unglued.

Mario tried to drag Princess Peach away. Her flouncy pink dress twirled as she twisted her body, desperate to free herself from his grasp. She kicked with reckless abandon, begging him to release her.

A group of dolls, a dozen or so, watched with me. Their heads were cocked at impossible angles. Their eyes were expectant, alive. I had never been so terrified of something so small. How could they be so small and still human?

The question made my pulse quicken. My sweat smelled like moldy fruit. Like fear. I tried to talk myself down.

"They're little kids… little kids in costumes," I told myself.

But even I didn't believe me. The dolls moved with such coordination, such purpose. Toddlers didn't walk like that. And how could they breathe behind a solid porcelain mask?

I thought about Bebe. Fuzzy memories of her screaming sharpened. The lines between reality and nightmare blurred. Could this be something like that? Maybe Kennedy was wrong, and this wasn't a mass hallucination. Maybe this was magic.

Princess Peach wrenched one arm free and swiped at Mario's face, leaving a significant scratch. "Let me go! I'm sick of you holding me back!"

"What the hell, Chrissy. You're nuts!" he howled, finally releasing her. She wasted no time running toward the dolls, their porcelain arms extended toward her like babies longing to be held.

"I'm ready to be one of you." Tears of joy streamed down Chrissy's cheeks as the dolls surrounded her, enveloping her with their cold little bodies.

"Chrissy!" Mario called out. "Get away from them!"

"It's okay, Dave," she said, wiping her eyes. "This is what I want."

Tiny doll hands blurred across her body, erasing her. Little by little, she ceased to exist. What did they do with her?

I gasped with the realization that Peach wasn't gone, just miniaturized. In her place stood a little doll with the same pink dress, the same glittering gold crown scaled down to fit her tiny new head. Strange as it was, I swear she looked happy.

Drool dribbled from Mario's slackened jaw. He didn't see the pack of dolls closing in until four of them were wrapped around his ankles. Until it was too late. A fifth doll shimmied up his knee, bringing him down. "Help!" he screamed. "Let me go! Somebody help me!"

I don't know why it took me so long to look for Xavier, to call for him to share in this spectacle. Surely if anyone could help me make sense of what I was seeing, it was him. But when I finally turned back toward him, the dining room was empty.

16

DOLL FACED LIES

Egon found the key. Naturally, as he was the only competent person still looking for it. I was looking for Xavier, and everyone else was looking for a way out. But I didn't see Xavi anywhere on the first floor and thought maybe he'd been so scared of the dolls that he'd found some way to scale the stairs and beat me to the second.

I squeezed into the elevator right as Slimer pressed the *close door* button. The metal doors clanked together, and Slimer muttered something to Egon.

"Wild stuff back there, huh guys?" I said, forcing myself to be friendly.

They looked at each other, but neither one acknowledged me. Awkward. This was why I didn't like people. To make myself feel better, I reasoned that they viewed the competition like Kennedy did, thought there was only one winner. I wondered when they would turn on each other. We exited the elevator, stepping uncertainly onto creaky wooden floors topped by pea-soup green rugs with faded pink flowers. Besides being hideous, the rugs made me nervous. I wouldn't be able to see a rotted board before it was too late to avoid it.

Behind us, the elevator car went back down. A part of my heart sunk with it. Another part of me hoped against hope that if Xavier was still down there, that he had the courage to come up. Together we could face anything, but alone my faith wavered. Maybe I did need him.

The second floor was as dilapidated as the first, with mold-speckled wallpaper peeling beneath dusty oil paintings in tarnished gold frames. I peered down the hallway. It seemed to go on forever; I counted at least six doors.

Within a few minutes, the elevator returned, bringing four more contestants with it—Cruella among them, grinning, appearing quite pleased with herself. But Xavier wasn't with them. I winced. What if what happened to Princess Peach happened to Xavier?

"My, what a rag-tag crew *you* are!" proclaimed a nasally voice. I didn't see where it came from, and apparently, neither did anyone else. We huddled together. *Like sheep*, I thought, and moved to the middle.

An image of a woman, opaque like a projection, material-ized out of thin air. She hovered above us, scowling. Her features were hazy, but from the way they wrinkled, I put her in her fifties. She wore an old-school black-and-white satin maid's costume, complete with a lace collar.

"A ghost," Cruella said, awestruck.

If I hadn't seen what the dolls did to Princess Peach, I might have laughed at her. As things stood, I could barely breathe for fear of inhaling more of the icy air whooshing from the ghost maid's mouth as she spoke. "I suppose *some* of you might survive the second half of this realm. I clearly didn't."

Cruella fainted. I dropped to my knees under the pretense of checking on her. Truly, I wanted to be as far away from the ghost as possible, even if it meant being closer to the gross rug. I squeezed Cruella's shoulder through her fake fur coat. "You all right?"

At first, she didn't respond. I gave her a little shake. "Hey, snap out of it!"

"Gh-gh-gh," Cruella stammered.

"It's not real," I lied to her, to myself. "Anyway, it's only talking. At least sit up and listen."

Cruella obediently sat cross-legged on the second floor of the weirdest mansion I had ever been inside. Growing up in New Orleans, I had seen my share, but this creepy dump took the cake.

Our ghost guide continued, "The spoiled child who lives here demands a souvenir from everyone she meets. Offer her what you will, but beware, if your gift displeases the little brat, she'll take a vindictive token. Make your way through the second floor until you find the room with the unlocked door leading out to the terrace. *If* you make it to the door, there is a rope ladder so that you may climb down and proceed to the next realm."

Two more people had caught up to our group now, which gave me hope for Xavier. I helped Cruella to her feet, and she followed the others into the bedrooms.

I lingered by the elevator, hoping it would bring Xavier up. The ghost maid swooped down mere inches from my face. Her breath stung like being pelted with hail. "I am sorry to inform you, but you must enter—or else say 'playtime's over' if you wish to exit the haunted house."

Up close, I couldn't deny what I saw. She wasn't a projection or a hallucination. She was *real*, whatever she was, emitting a sulfuric odor that made me retch.

"All right, back off, I'm going," I said, covering my mouth as I stumbled back from her.

I made myself stand up straight. At least I could affect an air of fearlessness. Sometimes predators left you alone if they thought someone else looked like an easier meal.

"Go!" the ghost ordered, then cocked her head. "Unless you're too afraid to continue?"

"Like I'd be afraid of a little kid," I scoffed, unable to admit, even to myself, that children horrified me. Perhaps it was the result of being an only child. Perhaps it was the fear of the unknown. In any case, children made me break out in hives. I hoped I wouldn't encounter any here.

The first room I wandered into was a study with two walls of built-in bookshelves. Four overstuffed leather chairs circled an old Victrola where a record spun. Ring a Ring o' Roses played with no lyrics, just the melody. But it didn't matter. I knew the words.

Ring a ring o' roses. Pocket full of posies.

The door leading out to the terrace was locked. I wasn't surprised. Nothing in this haunted house had been easy, and I imagined things would only get harder.

Faster. Faster. We all fall down.

The study was connected to a playroom so cluttered I struggled to navigate the obstacle course of toys. I bumped into a splintered wooden rocking horse, tripped over chipped pieces from a tea set, and fell into a pile of creepy stuffed animals with their eyes missing or otherwise dangling by threads. I scrambled to my feet, brushing off dust bunnies. But it was all for nothing; the terrace door was locked tight.

Where was everyone else? I couldn't hear their voices. A scream would have been better than silence. A scream would at least tell me where *not* to go.

"Where are you, Xavi? I miss you," I said to a baby doll propped up in a miniature rocking chair. Her hair had been cut down to the scalp, her eyelids stuck shut as if sleeping.

Right as I turned to leave, something Xavier said earlier crept to the forefront of my mind. *Charlie and the Chocolate Factory.* I turned back to the terrace door. Such a flimsy little door could be kicked down; I'd seen my mother do it before. I reared back, but a creaking floorboard behind me froze my leg mid-air.

"What are you doing in here?" a small but haughty voice asked. "That door is locked."

I lowered my leg and turned around slowly, as if she might

go away if I took too much time to look. When I did face her, what I saw made my blood freeze in my veins.

No. I told myself it wasn't real. It was a mask. A trick of the light. But no matter what angle I squinted from, the effect remained the same; the little girl before me had eye sockets with nothing inside them.

"I said, 'What are you doing in here?'" she repeated more sharply.

"Nothing. I was leaving," I muttered.

The hair on her head was wispy and blonde, but she was clutching two fistfuls of thick, bright red locks.

"You can't go," she said. "We haven't played a game yet."

"Oh, okay. What game would you like to play?" I stammered, trying not to piss myself.

"We could play dolls," the little girl said. "Have you seen mine? I can't find her."

"I've seen a lot of dolls." I gestured toward the one I'd been talking to. "Is this yours?"

"No. That doll's practically bald. *Mine* has a French braid —like you. Say, maybe you could be my new doll."

My legs were shaking, desperate to take me someplace far away, but I resisted the urge to run. The little girl would know the terrain, have the home-field advantage. What had the maid said? Was it that I had to do something for her? Or give her something? Terror had taken root in my mind, erasing my memory.

"Wh-what was your doll wearing? I saw a whole bunch of really pretty dolls downstairs." I gulped. "Have you checked down there? I could... help you look if you like?"

The little girl cocked her head curiously. "No one's ever offered to help me before."

"How sad. Is it... hard to see with... your... condition?"

"Some things, yes. But other things I see much clearer than anyone else." As she stepped forward, her powder-blue silk nightgown brushed against her dainty ankles. "I see your soul."

"Oh. Uhhh, that's cool," I managed to eke out.

The eyeless girl inched closer. I squeezed my hands together as if in prayer and was reminded of my mother's ring. The prongs holding the diamonds cut into the soft flesh between my fingers, the dull pain grounding me in reality. The girl before me had no eyes, but she saw through me. Into me. Did she see what an unholy mess I was?

"Your soul is beautiful," she said.

"Oh. Thank you." I tried not to tense up as the little girl moved closer.

"And such beautiful eyes. They're blue, aren't they? My eyes used to be blue." The girl released a sad little sigh. "I might have plucked yours out and kept them for my own—but you have been kind to me. I shall let you pass."

"But your lost doll. Would you like me to—"

"There is no doll," the little girl interjected. "Or, not yet, at least. Perhaps in the next group. Now go—before I change my mind."

I hustled by her at a speed somewhere in between a sprint and a jog. I entered the next room and—yes! The door to the terrace was already open!

The balcony air tasted like a wedding-cake snowball with condensed milk, sweet like victory. It must have been from the honeysuckle that wrapped around the columns. For a split-second, the smell whisked me back to lazy afternoons feeding the ducks in City Park, and I forgot where I was.

A trio of costumed characters lingered at the edge of the terrace, as if working up the nerve to climb down. Their apprehension reminded me this competition was far from over.

From a distance, I thought they were leaning on each other for support. Their camaraderie spurred a strange combination of jealousy and fascination inside of me. I'd never had *one* close female friend, much less two. I could never relate to other women. Maybe it was like Emma said, and it was my fault for not opening up enough.

Up close, I realized all three were dressed as different music video versions of Britney Spears. There was the schoolgirl from the Hit Me One More Time video—unmistakable with her black knee-high socks and fluffy pink hair ties—on the left. On the right was the I'm a Slave 4 U Britney, complete with a stuffed snake around her neck. These two Britneys propped up the third, who rocked a red jumpsuit like the one in the Oops I Did It Again video.

The woman in the middle, Oops Britney, was the prettiest, though her mascara was runny from crying. Her face contorted in a wail. "She cut my hair! She can't do that!"

"Snap out of it." Schoolgirl Britney gave her a rough shake. Her icy rebuke and her short plaid skirt swishing across her tan thighs instantly reminded me of Alison Smithers.

"But she cut it!" Oops Britney screamed. "I'm hideous now! I wanna go home!"

"You can't." Snake Charmer Britney shoved the rope ladder into her friend's chest. "We're *all* going to make it through, and we're going to use the money to get our boobs done and go on a cruise together. Remember? You promised. Now climb down. We aren't leaving you here."

"I don't wanna climb down. I don't wanna get my tits done. I don't wanna go on a cruise. I don't wanna go to the next realm. I wanna get out!" Oops wailed.

After a beat, I connected the dots to discern the source of Oops' anguish. Her hair, a vibrant shade of red, must have been in a high ponytail before, which would have fit with her costume. But the woman before me sported a blunt cut that grazed the bottom of her ears, giving her the appearance of a Raggedy-Ann doll. Then it clicked—I knew where those fistfuls of red hair the eyeless girl possessed had come from.

I shook my head solemnly as I imagined Oops' crowning glory being snatched away. I touched my own braid protectively, remembering what it felt like to lose a measly two inches against my will. The memory of the ritual that had created my poppet resurfaced, and I had to comfort her to keep from falling apart myself.

"Hey, don't cry," I said to Oops. "You gotta keep your head up and keep going. Otherwise, the little girl might come back and take much more—"

"Who the hell are you? Mind your own business!" Schoolgirl Britney chided me, wrapping her arm protectively around her friend.

"Can't you see she's scared enough already?" Snake Charmer Britney added.

I took a step back, confused. "I was trying to help."

"We don't want your help," Schoolgirl Britney said briskly.

My ears burned. Served me right. Every time I tried to do something kind, it blew up in my face—spraying shrapnel on those around me.

"Suit yourself," I said. "Can I at least have the ladder?"

"No." Snake Charmer Britney turned her nose up. "We're using it. Wait your turn."

"I'm not staying on this stupid terrace so someone can come along and chop *my* hair off."

Oops Britney wailed with increased gusto. "My hair! She took my hair!"

"Look what you've done!" Schoolgirl Britney brandished the rope ladder like a weapon. "No wonder you're going through alone—you probably don't have any friends."

"Only weak people need friends," I fired back. I wasted no time finding an alternate route down—a bit of lattice tacked to one side of the house.

Eager to get away from the Britneys, I hopped off a few feet before I reached the ground. My cheeks burnt with embarrassment, my ego stung by their rejection. I was so caught up in my misstep, I almost forgot that I *did* come here with a friend. A friend I never meant to leave behind.

17

WOMAN
VS
WILD

I followed a trail of sloppily painted wooden signs past an abandoned treehouse. Soft giggles sounded at my back—someone watching me—but I ignored them, swiftly trotting through the broken back gate and shutting it behind me. More signs directed me into a heavily wooded area, the path so narrow I had to bend branches back to make my way through. The trees grew thicker and thicker, crowding together until their limbs intertwined. The light of the moon slipped through the dense canopy of leaves, but I could hardly see a few feet ahead of me.

What sounded like a wolf howl echoed from too-close-for-comfort, and I broke into a jog. At least I couldn't hear anything coming for me over my own ragged breaths. A sharp, stabbing pain radiated from underneath my ribcage, forcing me to slow down. My hand flew to my side, pressing down over the stitch so hard I could feel the weight of my mother's ring.

What would Ruelle say if she were here? Probably that I should leave. That I never should've come. I was foolish to think I could match wits with witches. But hadn't she told me I came from magical stock?

"Our coven added to their number wherever they laid anchor. Magical customs muddled together on their ships until rituals blended together like delicious gumbo," Ruelle used to say when I was a child, before I asked questions that made her squirm.

Why didn't we join them on their enchanted ships? What had we done to earn this exile? She shut up fast. Ruelle could spin a good yarn, but none of her fables added up to anything useful.

What advice would Coach Karla give me? She'd tell me to inhale through my nose and exhale out of my mouth. Force enough oxygen in to ease my cramp. As I made myself relax, I thought about the money. My feet hurt; sporting the same boots every day for years had worn them down. Besides, I had grown enough that my toes pressed against the tips. If I won the haunted house, I would never have to stomach the shame of stealing a new pair.

After a few minutes of rest, my plans to spend my ensuing riches decreased the pain enough that I could hobble on, traversing through what felt like miles of forest until I finally came to the entrance of the fourth realm, marked by a stark change in the atmosphere.

The trees were sparser but brighter, their leaves a green so dazzling they appeared radioactive. The temperature had gone up by several degrees, accompanied by a stifling humidity that made me adjust the guns holstered at my hip, allowing some air to pass through where they stuck to my skin.

A muscular man in khaki cargo shorts and a matching safari hat paced in front of the entrance. When I reached him, he was alone. He stretched his thick neck to look behind me. "Lost your group, eh? Not a good look," he tutted. "Number one rule of the jungle is to stay with your group."

"Tarzan did okay on his own," I bantered back. "But since you mentioned it, did you happen to see a dude dressed up as Austin Powers come through recently?"

The safari guide shrugged. "I don't notice the costumes much."

"Maybe I could hang out for a second, see if he catches up?"

The guide grinned mischievously. "I'd love the company, but I'm not supposed to let anyone dawdle. Suppose I could bend the rules a little… if I wanted to."

The words "bend the rules" perked me up. Maybe Xavier had been right. This was a situation where cheaters prospered. Or at least, had the benefit of catching their breath.

"Pu-leeze let me hang out with you?" I said in my sweetest Southern drawl. "Just for a minute? Pretty please with sugar on top?"

"What's in it for me?" the guide asked with a cruel chuckle.

I willed my body not to tremble. With some effort, I managed to wield the same fetching smile I'd used on my teachers when my science projects were piecemeal. Not that it was my fault—what with Ruelle uninterested in assisting, much less purchasing supplies. It was a skill I'd learned to survive. How to communicate without speaking.

My tongue stayed still, but my lips said, *Please don't fail me*, parting with an affected bashfulness I prayed was endearing.

He didn't seem to soften. Maybe words would be necessary.

"Come on, man. Be cool," I said, flashing that charming grin. "I'll be outta your hair in five, ten minutes tops. Aren't you bored waiting here all by yourself?"

The guide nodded. "Fair enough. All right, I'll let you wait here—five minutes max—to see if your boyfriend catches up."

"He's not my boyfriend, just a friend," I said without thinking about how he'd interpret it.

"Maybe we *do* have ten minutes." The guide waggled his eyebrows suggestively. He stepped so close that I had to bring my hands to my face, pretending to scratch my nose to hide my disgust. He smelled like he hadn't showered in days.

"Now, how's a pretty girl like you single? Wait, don't

answer. I'd rather find out on my own. What are you doing after this? We throw a *wicked* afterparty. I could get you an invite."

I faked a cough, hopeful he'd step back—his breath reeked. "I won't feel like partying unless I win the prize money. Any tips?"

"Tips?" The guide scratched his jutting chin. "First, don't say the safe word—it's 'tiger bait' for this realm. You definitely won't win if you say the safe word."

"Well, duh!" I crossed my arms, anything to put a few precious inches between us. "Come on, you've gotta give me something better than that."

"I dunno. It's been so long since I made it through myself."

"Come on, can't you let me peek behind the curtain? Surely you know how to beat the realm you're guarding?"

"I'm afraid I've only been through once," the guard said. "You could spend a lifetime in that jungle and still never see all the wonders it contains. There's more in there I haven't seen that—"

"Please, do me a solid. One little tip. That's all."

"Well, I do know about the heavy hitters: the animals with the highest body count."

I gulped. "Go on."

The guide smiled. "Some say it's the tiger—that he's the deadliest creature hunting you. But I've never seen him myself. Maybe he stays hidden. Maybe he only hunts when he's hungry. I'd be more afraid of the snake. He kills for sport."

"Snake?" I repeated. Despite the warm air, chill bumps rose across my arms. Bats were one thing, but snakes were something else entirely. Snakes struck first and asked questions later.

"Did I stutter?" the guide teased me.

"What kind of snake?" I pressed.

"An anaconda, a real man-eater. But his length makes him

awkward on land, so it's easy enough to avoid him if you stay away from the water. The real danger in there is the mosquitos."

"Mosquitos, huh?"

"Big as birds," the guide said.

"I hate mosquitos."

The guide's eyes roamed over my skimpy costume. "They're gonna love you."

I groaned. "What do you suggest I do?"

"Hmm. Okay, tell you what—you promise you'll come to the party?"

A branch snapped in the distance. As he glanced behind me, his brow crinkled in concern. "Better make your decision quickly; I hear someone coming."

"Yes, I promise I'll come to the party," I said. "Now, what do I do about the mosquitos?"

"Don't worry, I got you, errr, what's your name? I'm Bud, by the way." He unzipped the largest pocket of his cargo shorts and produced a bottle of bug spray.

"Li—Lisa," I lied.

"Okay, Lisa. Spread your arms and legs," Bud instructed me, then sprayed my exposed skin liberally. He was fumbling to put the bottle away when someone burst through the trees.

I could hardly control my delighted squeals. "Xavier!" I wrapped him up in a hug so tight that I lifted him off the ground and cracked his back.

"Oh, thank God," Xavier said. "I thought I'd lost you. I was so close to calling it, Lisette; you have no idea. I saw some *bizarre* stuff happen back there."

I released him and turned toward Bud. "Hit him with the spray, too, please."

Bud hesitated. "Lisa, huh? Lisette is much prettier."

A sheepish smile flickered across my lips. "Aw, don't be mad. I would've come clean eventually—at the party."

Bud huffed. "Probably weren't gonna come."

"Party? What party? I'm great at parties," Xavier said. "Can we go there now? Seriously, Lis. I am *through* with this place!"

"Come on, Bud, please spray him? This is my last favor, *promise*."

"Okay, but you *owe* me one." Bud shook his head but whipped the bug spray back out, anyway. "Don't either of you dare tell anyone I did this."

"My lips are sealed," Xavier said playfully, then pressed a finger over them to illustrate as Bud made a quick pass over his face.

Bud chuckled. "All right, go on. Get out of here. And I better see you at the after-party!"

"Where is it?" Xavier asked.

"You'll find it." Bud winked. "Everyone who is meant to come finds it."

"Cool, then we'll be there. Hopefully sooner rather than later," Xavier added.

I yanked him away. "Come on! It's almost eleven. We only have an hour left until the witching hour!"

"Are you sure?" Xavier gave me that snotty, brow-furrow thing he did whenever he thought he was right about something.

"Yes, I'm sure. I have a watch." I pointed to my wrist for emphasis.

"That's not what I meant. I think the witching hour is three a.m., not midnight."

"Well, whatever," I huffed. "We're not even halfway through. So try to keep up. You're never gonna do this without me."

"*Pfft!* You need me too!" Xavier insisted. "Anyway, we have time. I kinda wanna go flirt with that dude some more—"

I laughed and pulled him deeper into the jungle. Maybe if

I turned it into a game, he'd move faster. "Very funny," I said. "Now—let's see who can get to the end first!"

Xavier stiffened, making it harder for me to pull him along. "Hold up. What's so funny? Can no one flirt with me?"

"Who cares? He smells disgusting. Watch your head." I held back a branch so it wouldn't snap back and hit him.

"So much judgment. I thought he was nice. You don't appreciate nice people like I do." Xavier sounded irritated, but he still followed me into the maze of trees.

"I appreciate *actual* nice people—I don't appreciate *fake* people who do things under the pretense of being nice when really they just want something," I said.

Xavier didn't seem to hear me. He looked everywhere but into my eyes. "This place is surreal," he said. "I wonder how much all of this cost. Trees ain't cheap, you know. One of our palms died last winter and my mom complained about the cost to replace it for months."

"I get the feeling the people who put this together have more money than your mom. Besides, how can you think about trees? It's so hot in here I can barely think at all." I ripped a palm frond off a nearby plant and fanned myself with it.

"Ugh, I know." Xavier tugged at his ruffled collar. "I'll have to shower and change before the party."

"You and me both," I said, but my voice was lost among an orchestra of sounds—monkeys screaming, birds calling, and countless insects buzzing. I scouted around, more curious than surprised. I was beginning to understand that in The Thirteenth Realm, anything was possible.

"Can we talk about that doll realm?" Xavier said. "Because I don't know what you saw back there, but I—"

"No," I said the way my mother did when the discussion was over. "Save your breath. You'll need it if we have to run."

At last, we arrived at a body of water too wide to leap

cleanly across—even for me. The water was calm, but its muddy greenish-brown hue shrouded its depths in mystery.

A rickety little boat was tied up along the shore, beckoning to us like bait. Xavier started toward it, but I grabbed his forearm. "Wait! We need to stick to the trees. There's a man-eating anaconda in here that enjoys waterfront dining."

Xavier huffed. "Says who?"

"Your little crush told me."

"Well, obviously I didn't hear that part. What's the safe word, anyway?"

I opened my mouth to say it but stopped. "I can't tell you —if I say it, they'll take me out."

"Oh right," Xavier mumbled. "Sorry. The heat's making me so dizzy I can't think straight."

"Then take your shirt off. We'll follow the river and be out of here as soon as we can."

"I can't take my shirt off!" Xavier said indignantly. "It's essential to my costume."

"You're ridiculous," I said with a well-deserved eye-roll. "I wish I were a dude. I would run through here shirtless, not caring one bit."

"Yeah, well, don't take being noticed for granted. You don't know how bad it sucks to feel invisible all the time."

I opened my mouth to say something stupid—something mean. The heat had gotten to me. But fortunately, I never got the insult out of my mouth. A cloud of massive mosquitos, each the size of a hummingbird, crashed his pity party. They steadily buzzed toward us like little heat-seeking missiles.

"What are those?" Xavier tilted his head up and pursed his lips. "Giant dragonflies?"

Thinking fast, I choked up on the branch I had been using as a fan, prepared to defend us. I snapped off a second palm frond to increase the radius of my assault.

"Grab a branch or something!" I barked at him. "We're gonna have to get them before they get us!"

Xavier stared at me as the swarm grew larger and larger, as it moved closer and closer to us. The long tubes extending from the mosquitoes' mouths were pointed like switchblades.

"Xavi! Help me!" I pleaded, waving my makeshift weapons wildly, daring those bloodsuckers to come near me.

Xavier blinked in astonishment, motionless.

"Help! Help me!" I shouted as the murder-mosquitos homed in on us. Their deafening buzzing rang in my ears, drowning out my last squeaky plea for assistance.

Xavi remained still as a statue, slack-jawed and useless. I clenched my own jaw, thinking if the mosquitoes didn't kill him, I would do it myself.

But his inaction proved inconsequential. Most of the swarm redirected and sailed over our heads. The few that didn't divert their course in time split off to the left and the right. Not a single one landed.

When the threat had passed, Xavier snapped out of his trance. "Whoa! Lisette, did you SEE that? That was some Jumanji shit right there, right? I would hate to be in here without bug spray. See, that's one benefit of being a beautiful woman; you can talk men into doing things for you."

I glared at him. "Don't try to butter me up now. What happened to you?"

"What do you mean? Nothing happened."

"Yeah, exactly. You did *nothing*. I had to defend us on my own."

"Wow. You're right. I… I'm sorry," Xavier stammered. "I don't know what happened. I guess I froze."

I winced, but not because of the mosquitos. I was caught up in the memory of another time Xavier had left me to fend for myself. The fight with Alison. The cheap shots he let me take. He was my best friend, but suddenly, I couldn't look at him without wanting to punch him. I needed to put some space between us.

Without another word, I resumed my trek through the

jungle, moving as quickly as I dared across the uneven terrain. A branch scratched my bare shoulder, but I didn't slow down to assess the damage. The small sting was nothing compared to the sick feeling in my chest, like my heart might wither up and die. I had thought the incident at school was a fluke. That Xavi regretted it. That he would never leave me to fend for myself again. Now I wasn't sure he'd learned his lesson.

I could still hear his heavy steps and panicked breath as he chased after me. Despite my recent injury, I was in far better shape, and the chasm between us grew and grew.

"Wait!" Xavier shouted, wheezing like he had no energy to spare. "Why are you running from me? I didn't freeze on purpose! Lisette, wait!"

The cat-and-mouse game invigorated me, gave me hope we'd make it through on time. I kept running, marveling at how quickly we moved through the jungle without Xavier's hesitation holding us back. I got excited, certain we couldn't have much further to go. This realm couldn't be too big. Not with the density of the trees.

I paused for a moment and looked at the rich soil beneath my feet. I shook my head in amazement. This *one* realm had so many layers, it must've taken forever to build. Digging the river alone would have been a major undertaking. They must keep the haunted house up all year; no one would put in so much effort just for one night.

"Lisette, please!" Xavier called out behind me. "I'm begging you—don't leave me! I don't know the safe word! Please don't leave me!"

I decided I was ready to face him again, that he'd been punished enough. I waited while he sprinted to catch up. As he came closer, I watched giant beads of sweat drip from his beet-red face, and it filled me with a strange kind of satisfaction. It seemed fair for him to suffer. It wasn't nearly as much pain as I had endured.

He doubled over in front of me and tore at his shirt,

popping two buttons. The sweat-drenched fabric clung to his chest. He looked as miserable as I'd ever seen him.

"Please," he said in between pitiful dry sobs. "Please don't leave me like that again. I was so scared! Those dolls... and those mosquitos... they blew my mind, Lis! I'm so sorry I froze!"

I narrowed my eyes. Of course I didn't *want* to leave him. Didn't want to punish him. But I'd made a mistake the first time he failed me. I was too easy on him. Must've been, or he wouldn't have done it again. Without consequences, he would abandon me again and again. I was doing this for his own good. For the good of our friendship.

"Enough with the boohooing," I said. "I was only a little ahead of you. I didn't leave you."

"You were so far away. Too far away to help me if... if..."

"I would've come back if you needed me. At least now you have an idea of how I feel."

"What are you talking about?" he sniffled.

"You know what I'm talking about. You always leave me when I need you."

"That's not true!" Xavier argued. "What about when the bat attacked you? I didn't leave you then, did I?"

I bit my lip. Crap on a croissant. Maybe if I was quiet for a few moments, I wouldn't have to acknowledge that he had a point.

"Lisette?" Xavier said softly. "I really am sorry I froze. This place, it's doing something to me. I don't like it. Please— let's leave. You want ten grand? I'll give you ten grand. Tell me the safe word, we can say it together and—"

I interrupted him with an incredulous *pfft*. "You think I took you here because I want *your* money? I'm not a charity case!"

"No, I never said that! I want to leave! Please, Lisette, I'm so tired."

"Come on," I said, turning away from him with my head

held high, my ego injured but still intact. "This realm isn't even scary."

"Okay, Lis," Xavier said with a weary sigh. "Whatever you want. But remember, I offered you the money. Not because I think that's what you want—I know you want to earn it—but because I want to give it to you. I promise I will. When I get access to my trust fund—"

"Even if I wanted your money, which I don't, it would be too late by then," I said. "We're getting evicted, Xavi. We're losing our apartment tomorrow unless I find a way to pay."

"Jesus, Lis. I didn't know. I—"

"Yeah, well, now you do. Come on."

I turned my back to him and jogged through the jungle. I went slower this time, let him keep up with me so he'd know I didn't want to lose him. I loved him, needed him, but I couldn't let him know. Whether or not he wanted to leave me, the universe wasn't good to people who loved me.

We traveled somberly for some time, neither of us speaking except for the occasional warning: "Watch out for that root," or "Don't lose sight of the water."

Xavier didn't look at me. I knew he was mad; he always avoided my eyes when he was mad at me. But he wouldn't admit it. He pretended to be keeping an eye out for the snake. He blamed this on every break he took. No twisted stick escaped his inspection. He kept one ear turned toward the water, too.

"I'd hear the splash of the snake dropping down from a branch before I'd see it," he reasoned out loud. "Between the murky water and the thick trees, this jungle offers perfect camouflage."

I grumbled an acknowledgment, still not in the mood to talk.

Our silence paid off. But the sound that pricked my ears wasn't a single great splash, but a series of plunks. "What was that?" I whispered.

Xavier moved closer to the noise. *Plunk. Plunk. Plunk.* He peered through the trees to see what disrupted the water's surface.

"What is it?" I asked, impatient to move on. To get the hell out of this realm. We still had such a long way to go.

Xavier's eyes grew wider as he watched the water. "Oh-em-gee! You have to see this; it's adorable!" he announced with glee.

Curious, I moved closer to the bank to join him. I should've known it would be them.

The three Britneys looked woefully out-of-place riding in the rickety little boat. Two of them dipped their oars into the water—*plunk plunk plunk*—while the third slumped over in the middle, nothing but dead weight.

"We should have coordinated our costumes," Xavi said. "You could have been a fembot."

"Me? A fembot? Have you lost your mind?"

"Aw, but they look so cute."

"Can't believe all three of them made it out," I marveled.

"You know them?"

"Not really," I said, turning away from the water. "Saw 'em in the last realm. I tried to give them some advice but..." I stopped, realizing there was no reason to tell Xavier about my mistake.

But he had already latched onto my reluctance and wouldn't let go. "What? What happened?"

"It's dumb," I answered, trying on the tone Ruelle used when she was done discussing something with me.

"But I'm your best friend. If you can't tell me dumb stuff, who can you tell?"

"Nobody."

"Aw, come on, Lisette. Are you still mad at me about the stupid mosquitoes? I'm really sorry. I don't know what happened to me back there. You know I'm always here for

you. I won't make fun of you. Tell me what happened with
those Britneys."

"It's nothing, really. They were kinda mean to me, that's
all."

"So I guess you don't want to tell them about the
snake?"

"Come on, let's go." I walked away, fighting the urge to
look at them in their deathtrap boat. "They were rude the last
time I tried to warn them about something."

"Some people have to be warned more than once," Xavier
said. "I think we should tell them. Let them decide what to do
with the information."

"You tell them then. Go ahead, get as close to the water as
you dare. I'm not walking toward a giant snake to warn some
ungrateful strangers."

Xavier frowned, but he took a hesitant step forward,
anyway. He cupped his hands and yelled, "Hey! Watch out for
the anaconda! He's in the water somewhere!"

Schoolgirl Britney looked around suspiciously. "Who said
that?"

"What's it matter?" answered Snake Charmer Britney.
"It's probably a trick. Whoever's hiding in the trees wants us
to go over there so they can get us."

The poor half-conscious Oops Britney slumped over in the
middle of the boat moaned something unintelligible.

"Pull yourself together," Schoolgirl Britney scolded her
struggling friend. "We can't keep dragging you along. Ought
to dump you out of this boat."

"We need her," Snake Charmer Britney protested. "How
else are we gonna get the friends-and-family discount on the
cruise?"

Xavier shook his head and turned back toward me. He
looked a little surprised to see me still standing there. "Hey,"
he said. "Thanks for waiting for me."

"Satisfied now?"

"Guess you were right." He sighed. "They didn't listen to me."

"Can't save everyone, may as well save yourself."

He nodded but said nothing in response.

We walked a little slower now, weighed down by our unspoken thoughts.

"Lis?" Xavier said at last.

"Yeah?"

"If something bad happens to me in here, would you carry me around or cut me loose?"

"Huh?" I bit my lip. So that was what he thought about me. Maybe I deserved it.

"We've been in here a long time. We could be going in circles. If I pass out or get hurt, and you leave me, I don't know the safe word. I could be stuck in here forever. I only wanted to know—"

His accusation embarrassed me so badly I had no choice but to laugh it off. "Jesus, Xavi. What kind of monster do you think I am?"

But Xavi didn't laugh. "I don't think you're a monster. But I know how bad you want to win this. Please, promise you won't leave me in here, okay?"

"Xavi—"

"Promise!"

I exhaled. "Okay, okay. I promise I won't leave you in here."

Xavier opened his mouth, but whatever he was going to say was interrupted by a scream. Xavier rushed toward the noise, but I lagged behind him, close enough to help him if he needed me but not close enough to get there first. I didn't owe those people anything.

"It's coming right for us! Do something!" Schoolgirl Britney yelled, the panic rising in her voice with each syllable.

"What am I supposed to do? You do something!" Snake Charmer Britney shouted back.

"You're the one with the snake around her neck! I dunno, charm it or something."

"I picked this costume to show off my stomach," Snake Charmer Britney whined. "You do something. It's on your side of the boat."

A huge splash sent Xavier racing toward the water. Where was that kind of energy when I was in trouble?

"Don't do anything stupid," I called after him. I shifted from one boot to the other, anxious to see what was happening, but unwilling to risk being sucked in by the impulse to help.

Xavier got there first. But I arrived in time to see Oops Britney splashing around, too stunned to scream.

"You threw her in!" Snake Charmer Britney gasped. "How could you?"

"It was either her or us," Schoolgirl Britney answered with righteous indignation. "Now start rowing!" She turned her body so she wouldn't have to see the enormous anaconda slithering toward her friend.

Xavier's eyes tripled in size. "Say the safe word! Get out!" he shouted.

Oops Britney didn't acknowledge if she heard him. She barely moved as the anaconda slithered around her body, as though savoring the anticipation of its meal.

"Lis, what's the safe word!" Xavier screamed at me, but I didn't dare say it.

He had a wild look in his eyes, like he might do something stupid. Like he might get in the water and try to save her himself. I clamped a hand down on his shoulder to hold him back.

"Come on," I said, pulling him away, willing myself not to look, knowing from his horrified expression that I didn't want to see what was happening in the water.

"We have to do something. We have to help her," Xavier insisted.

"I said come on!" I snapped. "You tried to warn her. She didn't listen. Her own friends ditched her. Shows what kind of people all three of them are."

"But maybe she…"

"Sharks swim with sharks. They're exactly like the 'sons.'" I walked away—I had to—had to put some distance between us and the snake. Who knew how close it might come to the shore?

Xavier wasn't letting go so easily. "Her friend threw her over. It *was* exactly like something Alison would do to Madison."

"Don't go after her, Xavi," I shouted. "Don't make me decide between saving you or saving myself."

"This isn't right, Lis." But he followed me despite his protests. Maybe he worried I'd leave him again. Couldn't blame him.

"Wait up, Lis," he panted. "Do you hear yourself? You don't sound like the Lisette I know. The Lisette I know would've at least tried to help. Something is happening to you in here. This place doesn't feel like just a haunted house, it feels like—"

A sickening snap—like the sound of bones being crushed —interrupted him.

"Come on," I barked, resuming my trek through the jungle. "It's too late for her."

Defeated, Xavi followed me. He was all talk. If it came down to it, he'd freeze. Then it would be me against the snake, and the snake would win. At least that was what I told myself. I would have latched onto any lie to avoid admitting the truth: I wasn't really the hero of the story. When it came down to it, I didn't want to rescue anyone.

18

JUNK
BOND
TRAITOR

The trees thinned out and changed species. Skinny, barren pines with boring bark replaced the lush greenery of the jungle disappearing at our backs. Little by little, the buzzing bugs and trickling river faded into nothing.

Xavier stole a glance back. What was he looking for? The boat? He didn't say, and I didn't ask—didn't want to know if the other two Britneys had survived. Couldn't bring myself to acknowledge what happened to the one who didn't. Teenage naivety permitted me to believe as long as I never spoke a word of the snake, it might slither out of my memories.

When we saw the sign for the fifth realm, Xavier blinked at it. "Wow. We did it," he whispered. "For a minute there, I didn't think we would but—we made it out of that jungle."

"Uh-huh," I muttered, envious of the relief relaxing his face. I couldn't let up, not yet. Not when there were eight realms left. I checked my watch. Eight realms and only an hour to go. I wouldn't relax until I had that prize money in my hand. Whoever built this beast had big bucks, and I was gonna get my share. And until then, nothing would make me happy.

A warehouse drifted into view. We'd come full circle. I wondered if anyone was still waiting in line, willing to try their luck zipping through this macabre maze. But my attention jumped back to the building—to the bass thumping inside, shaking the cinder-block walls. It sounded more like a night-club than a haunted house. I picked up my pace, eager to join the party.

"Slow down," Xavier said. "You said you wouldn't leave me again!"

"Sorry… I got excited." I fell into step with him, trying to hide my frown.

"How can you be so eager after everything we've seen in here? I know you said that you don't want to talk about the doll realm, but people were getting turned into—"

"Can you just stop?" I curled my fingers, holding back a curse. "You're being a buzzkill."

Xavier stopped dead in his tracks, effectively pushing me over the edge. Did he not care that we had a time limit?

"Dude!" I snapped. "What the hell is wrong with you? Do you want me to lose you again?"

Xavier winced, but at least he started walking. "I just want to make a plan first, that's all."

"Yeah, right," I snorted. "You wanna bounce—so do it, leave. Won't be the first time you've gotten scared and left me."

He blinked at me as if I were speaking another language. "Lis, what do you mean? Are you still mad about the stupid mosquitos? I said I was sorry."

"I'm talking about the fight." I pointed at my bruised nose and immediately regretted it. I never wanted to relive the worst day of my life, but it came bursting out of me anyway, like the vomit at my final gymnastics practice.

"Seriously? I didn't get scared and leave you," Xavier said, exasperated. "I went to get help! What was I supposed to do? Punch a girl?"

"You could have pulled them off me! Y'know Emma and Madison held me down, right? So Alison could wail on me."

Xavier looked at his shoes. "I didn't know that. You never told me."

"Because it didn't matter. Anyway, it still doesn't matter." I tossed my braid over my shoulder. "I don't need help from anyone. So go if you want, but stop trying to talk *me* into going with you. I've made up my mind; I'm gonna see this thing through."

"Fine, you're right. I'm scared, and I want to leave." Xavier rubbed the collar of his ridiculous frilly shirt. "I don't understand why you're doing this. We could find you a new apartment. Or you can stay with me. Let me help. I want to."

"No! It's not *just* about the apartment. It's about proving I'm not a quitter. I used to give up too easily—on gymnastics, school. But not this time."

"I don't think you're a quitter," Xavier said. "And I don't think leaving will make you one."

"Thanks, but—" I set my jaw "—I'm not letting this haunted house get the best of me, too. I'm gonna make it through. So are you with me—or not?"

He kicked at the ground, scuffing his shoes. "I'm with you," he muttered like he didn't really mean it. But I didn't have any more energy to devote to mobilizing him.

"Come on, then." I resumed the grueling pace I preferred, though it left him gasping for air. Maybe he'd have more stamina if he hadn't wasted energy arguing.

We finally made it to the warehouse.

The man posted on the front steps, behind a washed-out red velvet rope threaded through silver posts, must've fallen asleep on the job. He was slumped over, his back against the railing, greasy hair hanging in clumps around his ashen face. When I leaned down to check him out, the odor of vomit soiling his shirt made me jump back and come up gagging.

"What's the matter?" Xavier gulped. "Is he… dead?"

I held my breath, watching the stranger's ribcage rise and fall through his thin white undershirt. "Not dead. Passed out, I think." My eyes wandered over his exposed forearms—past his bright blue veins covered with vicious red wounds with purplish edges. Track marks.

"What are we gonna do?" Xavier brought his nails to his face, started to put them in his mouth, but stopped himself. "Should we try to wake him up?"

I gently prodded the man with my boot, a little cruel, but what else could I do? Primal animal instinct warned me he might grab my ankle. This might be the realm without an explanation. No safe word. Finally, something scary enough that I'd pray for an easy way out.

The man stirred. His red-lined eyes opened gradually like a clunky old garage door. He used the velvet rope to pull himself up. "That's the fifth realm." He nodded toward the door. "If I were you, I would say the safe word—rehab—but go in if you want. I don't care."

"That's it?" Xavier balked. "Aren't you supposed to tell us what we're up against or whatever? Some advice would be great."

With a hoarse laugh that morphed into a cough, the junkie guard lowered himself back down. His pale skin and dingy once-white shirt blended into the gray steps as he rested his head against the metal railing and closed his eyes. "As if anyone should be taking advice from me."

"Please?" I appealed to him. "We're cool. Are you going to the after-party? We are."

The junkie only opened one eye this time. He regarded me with cool indifference. "You bringing any heroin? Meth? Molly?"

His casual tone toward serious substances caught me off-guard. I'd never done anything harder than pot. Words stuck to the roof of my mouth, "Ummm, well…"

"Exactly what I thought," the junkie said. "The after-party is worthless. This life is worthless. This realm is worthless—it's not even that scary. It's just really hard to leave." He closed his eyes again. But even if he hadn't, I wouldn't have stuck around.

I strode toward the door. No worries about what waited behind it, only the desire to get away from this loser. From his stench. From his apathy.

"Wait!" Xavier shouted at my back. "Let's strategize before we go in."

"About what? We don't know what's in there. Anyway, the dude said it's not scary. Come on, let's get on with it." My hand raised toward the handle, fingers closing around it.

Xavier put his hand over mine. "Hold up, Lis, let's talk about this. The person guarding the door always has something to do with the realm, right?"

My grip tightened in annoyance. "Yeah, so?"

"Well, this guy's clearly an addict. So what if as soon as we walk in, they stab us with heroin needles or something?"

"Do you hear yourself?" I released the handle and threw my hands up in exasperation. "You sound like somebody's mom. People don't go around giving away free heroin. It's expensive."

"Lis, you didn't read the waiver, and to be honest, I didn't finish it, but what I *did* read was terrifying! It was all about what they *could* do and nothing about what they couldn't."

"Okay, so what's the worst thing that could happen?"

"I could get addicted to heroin. My life would be over."

My shocked laugh came out as a snort. "Doing heroin one time, which won't happen but hypothetically speaking, doing it one time won't make you an addict."

"My dad was an addict," Xavier said softly, like a confession. "What if it's in my DNA? What if one hit turns me into an addict?"

"Look at me, Xavi, you're nothing like him."

But Xavier wouldn't meet my gaze. "What if I am like him? What if something really bad happens to me and I turn into a bad person? My dad tried to get his act together. He tried rehab—"

As soon as the word "rehab" left Xavier's lips, the junkie guard sprang to his feet like a deployed jack-in-the-box. He latched onto Xavier's wrists.

"Ahhh! What are you doing? Let go of me!" Xavier yelped.

"Sorry, man. Ain't like I wanna do this," the junkie sighed, seeming put-upon. "You said the safe word. Now I gotta wait for someone to come haul your scaredy-cat ass outta here." He dug into the pocket of his soiled jeans, produced a walkie-talkie and said into it, "Code yellow at entrance five."

"But I didn't mean to say it!" Xavier's eyes widened, rapt with horror behind his clunky plastic glasses. "Oh no, Lisette! Lisette, I didn't mean to!"

A multitude of emotions competed for center stage inside of me. Fear stole the spotlight. If I tried to help him, they might yank me out too. But I needed to win. Otherwise we'd lose our apartment. No more balcony to watch the parades from. No more alley cats who needed me. No more cute neighbor or the possibility of fitting into a group who seemed to celebrate my flaws. I was so sick of getting settled in some place just to leave. Sick of losing. Damn, I wanted a win for once.

"Come with me," Xavier pleaded as I turned away from him, back toward the door. "I'll find a way to get you the money. Whatever you want, Lis. Please?"

Naturally, I felt sorry for him, but what I wanted was to stay and fight for my own victory. Winning would give my life meaning. Show my mother and everyone else I'd leveled up. What if I was the only one who made it through? I couldn't let Xavier, or anyone else, take that from me.

The door to the fifth realm flung open, and two tall men came bursting out. At first glance, I actually thought they were kinda sexy with their strong jaws and dark, slicked-back hair.

Then one of them seized Xavier roughly, breaking the spell. The other laid a light hand on my shoulder.

"Not her," the junkie guard said. "She hasn't said it—yet. How about it, sweetheart, you gonna join your friend in the loser's circle?" He grinned, exposing pale purple gums.

I shook off the disgust and straightened my shoulders. He wasn't going to get to me. I swatted the stranger's hand, refusing to look at him. "Back off! I'm going in."

"Lisette! Wait!" Xavier cried out as the guards grabbed him, one on either side. "You said you wouldn't leave me!"

Boy, did that infuriate me. How dare he have the *nerve* to act like I was the one who left him? The one who couldn't hang?

"See ya later, traitor," I called over my shoulder. It was way too harsh, and I instantly regretted saying it. Sometimes my acid tongue cut deep, my sharp words burning scars in the hearts of all who dared pay attention to me. I didn't know how to process disappointment or sadness. Didn't know how to be brave or confident. Everything came out as anger. And so I left my best friend behind with a jab he didn't deserve. And entered the fifth realm alone.

NO
GOOD
DEED

Helping people never seemed to work out well for me. My thoughts drifted back to Miss Opal. The smell in this realm—like the formaldehyde they'd used to preserve what was left of my sweet neighbor's body—reminded me of the funeral parlor. It took me back to the carpet, receding under my feet as I approached her closed casket. Her smiling face behind tasteful silver frames, photographs of a younger, happier version of Miss Opal. A woman with a husband, kids, more people than cats in her life. But then the awful vinegary smell rose over the faint scent of day-old flowers, stinging my nostrils and reminding me everybody dies.

Techno music without lyrics burst through the speakers. Nothing I would have willingly listened to, but clearly some people liked it. Two dozen or more costumed dancers clustered beneath a deejay booth on a raised platform positioned parallel to a giant spinning disco ball. Their gyrating bodies glistened with sweat as flashes of purple, green, blue, and red pulsed across their faces, illuminating their eyes, some wide with wonder and others clenched tight as if worshipping the rhythm.

Near the front of the revelers, I spied Cruella. Though she'd lost her fur coat, I recognized her black-and-white hair that stuck straight up like she'd been electrocuted. A ghost of a smile graced my lips. She'd made it through the jungle. I almost went over to see what she knew about this realm, but then I stopped. How long had she been here?

Warning sirens that weren't part of the song playing rang in my mind. Something was unnatural about the way these people were moving—all synchronized as if under a spell. When I ventured a bit closer, their eyes seemed faded too, or maybe that was all in my head. Perhaps the light show overhead made everything else dim by comparison.

Still, I dared not come any closer, afraid the dance floor might suck me in like quicksand. I skulked around the edges of the party, thinking about what the addict guarding the door had said: this place wasn't scary, just hard to leave. With every step, my boots stuck to the tar-black floor. But I trudged on.

The door behind me swung open, and two new contestants joined the party. Schoolgirl Britney sauntered in first, followed closely by her friend Snake Charmer Britney, who tugged at the stuffed snake draped over her shoulders as if she could hide behind it. I was so distracted watching them, I didn't realize someone was sneaking up on me.

A girl in her late twenties trying to look younger with rainbow streaks in her blonde pigtails enveloped me in a friendly hug, too friendly. I tried to shake her off, but she clung tight.

"Well hello Alice, welcome to Wonderland," she trilled. "I'm the Caterpillar, Cat for short, and I've got what you need. What's your poison? Uppers? Downers? In-betweeners…"

"I think you've got me confused with someone else." I spun away, but Cat caught my hand, digging her fingernails into my palm so hard I cried out in shock.

"Where do you think you're going, narc?" Cat hissed, pulling me toward her. "Only thing I hate more than a rat is a rat jumping ship at the first sign of pirates."

"Let go of me," I snarled. "I'm not a narc or a rat—I just don't want to—"

"End up like me?" Cat smiled broadly, baring teeth that were few and far between. "It's not so bad, really. The trick is to get so high you don't notice you're in the gutter."

"Glad you found something that works for you." I finally shook Cat off and fixed my iciest glare on her to keep her back. "If you touch me again, I'll punch you right in the mouth. And you don't look like you've got teeth to spare."

"Whoa! She's feisty! I like it." Cat chuckled. "I thought you were a creampuff. Maybe I judged you too fast."

"Yeah, so back off." I stretched to my full height, hoping it might scare her. Being a giant came in handy sometimes.

Judging by her pout, Cat seemed more disappointed than intimidated. "Aw, don't be mad. I'm sorry I called you a rat. Let me make it up to you?" She reached forward, much faster than I would've anticipated was possible. Before I could dodge her, she karate-chopped my upper back, not hard enough to upset a normal person, but excruciating for me. I sputtered, unable to understand how a light touch hurt so much. How did she know precisely where to strike my spine? I straightened up and tried to play it off, but Cat was pretty observant for someone so strung out.

"You're hurting bad, huh?" Her voice sounded strangely tender. "I could make that go away. I could make it go away forever. Would you like that?"

"I don't know what you're talking about," I said through gritted teeth. And yet, I couldn't fight the feeling that she knew more about me than I knew about myself.

"Are you sure?" Cat untwisted the cap on an orange pill bottle missing its label. "I'm a little surprised you don't want me to fix your back. What about your nose, then? Tell me where it hurts."

The temptation stunned me into silence. I was no great beauty before my busted nose, but with it, I was hideous. I felt like everyone being kind to me actually felt sorry for me —for the ogre with the bad acne and swollen honker. But

Cat had to be lying. How could she fix my nose? She must've meant she had a pill to make the pain recede. To help me forget about it until the next time I looked in the mirror.

"I can see that you're skeptical, and rightfully so," Cat said. "But I'm not a *drug*-dealer. I'm a *dream*-dealer. What's your dream?"

"Dream?" I laughed. "I don't have time to dream. I just wanna get through another day."

"What you really crave is belonging," Cat purred. Her rings glimmered under the light of the disco ball as she shook something shiny into her palm. "You want to be part of a group. Why not be part of ours? Why not find yourself here? It'll be a version you'll love. Don't you want that? Don't you want this?" Cat uncurled her fingers to reveal a sapphire the size of a robin's egg.

Of course I wanted it. Sapphires were my favorite stone. How did she know so much about me? Was she clairvoyant? I ached to buy the dream she was selling. My head began to nod, and my hand reached out for the beautiful, blue stone. But as Cat stretched the sapphire toward me, I caught a sudden change come over her, a glimpse beneath her facade—something so depraved it was hardly human. A villainous glee flickered in her eyes.

I pressed my lips together, tight. I took a step back and crossed my arms like a shield. "I don't know what you're sell-ing, but I'm not buying it. Why don't you go find someone stupid enough to believe you can help them?"

Cat laughed like this was all part of our witty banter. "Oh you," she said. "You're so funny. I'll talk to you later—when you come back. They all come back. At least, the smart ones do." She spun around, dancing, her movements fluid.

Before I was finished staring and marveling at her, the crowd swallowed her up. But that gave me an idea. Instead of creeping around the perimeter, I pretended to enjoy the music. I blended in by dancing like the rest of the zombies, throwing my hands up and bouncing to the beat.

I pushed through the crowd, cringing as I pivoted around their sweaty bodies. As I got closer, I could see the far wall but no sign of an exit door. Right before my eyes, a tall figure pressed his palm into the wall and pushed a secret door open. He ushered someone else ahead of him—someone wearing a plaid skirt. Before I could follow Schoolgirl Britney deeper down this rabbit hole, I felt something soft loop around my neck.

Confused, I spun around and came face to face with Snake Charmer Britney. She gave me a little wave, like we were old friends. "Hi. Remember me? From the dollhouse?"

"Umm, sure," I mumbled, reaching behind my head to remove her prop.

"I'm sorry we were mean to you," she said, eyes watery and wide with fright. "I should've just given you the ladder; it was dumb."

"Okay, apology accepted," I said. "Bye."

"Wait! Please don't go... I don't even know your name. Mine's Erika. I'm... I'm so scared. First Kitty fell in the river..."

I interrupted her with a snort. "Pretty sure your other friend pushed her."

Either Erika didn't hear me or refused to believe what we both witnessed. "I don't know where Jillian went. She's the one with the schoolgirl uniform and the pigtails. Please, you have to help me. I know you want to. You're a good person, I can tell."

I bit my lip. Not like it would hurt me to tell Erika where I'd last seen her friend. After a moment's deliberation, I sighed. "Come on, I think she went this way."

"Okay, but there's one little problem." Erika pointed to her feet, which were performing the same steps as the dancers around us. "I can't get off the dance floor. I keep trying, but as soon as I get to the edge, my feet just—dance me right back to the middle."

My eyes moved up her body, studying the way her hips quivered as if fighting the urge to give in to the rhythm. "You can't get off the dance floor? What am I supposed to do about that?" I snapped.

She fixed her eyes on me as if I were her last beacon of hope. "Help me?"

GOES
UNPUNISHED

"I don't know how to help you," I said, half lying. Of course, I could think of ways. I could grab her hand, pull her off the dance floor. But what if that didn't work? What if she dragged me back with her? Even from the edge, I could feel the center sucking at my skin.

"Please," Erika whimpered, "at least tell me how you're doing it."

I raised my hands in a beat's me gesture, and out of the corner of my eye, I saw my mother's ring—the blinding sparkle of its brilliant diamonds. Erika must've seen it, too, because her jaw dropped down to the bottom of her neck.

"A magic ring," she said, far too loud for comfort.

"Quiet," I snapped at her, shoving my hand into my pocket. I snuck a glance around, but no one seemed to watch us. "There's no such thing as magic," I said, "but that doesn't mean I want somebody to try to take—"

Her hand darted out and grabbed my wrist, squeezing it tight. "Please, just hold my hand," she said. "I know I could make it out of here if you'd only hold my hand."

She really wasn't going to quit. I sighed so hard my apprehension finally left my body, and softening, I took my hand out of my pocket and extended it to her. She latched onto me, shaking, tears rolling down her cheeks.

"Oh, thank you! Thank you—what did you say your name was?"

"Lisette," I grumbled. "Come on. I'll help you find your friend—but then the two of you are on your own. Got it?"

Erika didn't reply, and if not for her clammy hand in mine, I might not have even noticed her behind me. But when we neared the border of the dance floor, my arm ached, straining against the weight of whatever held her in place.

With a sneer of determination, I looked over my shoulder. Erika shivered like a Chihuahua who needed a sweater. "Come on," I urged her, "fight it."

"I'm trying," she insisted, her voice quivering. "Please... help me."

Gritting my teeth, I gave her a yank. She lurched forward, then back, limp as a rag doll. Her head and shoulders shook like she was having a seizure.

"Come on, Erika! I did it—why can't you? " I pulled with all my might, but she didn't budge. "You're not trying hard enough. You gotta pull your weight."

But we'd fought the dance floor for too long, drawn too much attention to ourselves to escape unseen. Now its army closed in on us, wiggling closer in lockstep. A large man dressed as a cowboy positioned himself behind me and began to thrust his pelvis toward my butt—*gross*. While he distracted me, a woman wearing a flapper dress with a matching sequined headband slipped between Erika and me.

"Help me!" Erika begged as her feet spun around on their own. Her torso followed, and only her head managed to fight the music. Her hand clung to mine and her bulging eyes stayed with me, lips moving, but I couldn't hear the words over the thump of the bass.

My heart ached. But I let her go. I had to. I was running out of time.

As soon as I released her, I went reeling backward, my arms pinwheeling. I fell on my butt, and Erika disappeared, enveloped by the crowd. It was the right choice because it was the only choice, and I didn't have time to regret it.

I jumped to my feet and dashed to the wall that had swallowed up Schoolgirl Britney—Jillian, Erika had called her, but I tried to forget her name. Couldn't afford to humanize anyone else.

There were three faint rectangular indentations in the wall —three different doors. They had no handles but were so smudged with handprints around the center it almost appeared to be an invitation. Which one would lead me out? I was fairly certain I'd seen Jillian go through the one on the left, so that's where I began.

With a shove, the door on the left opened into a long, narrow room with a row of flickering pendant lights suspended from the vaulted ceiling. Two rows of soiled mattresses, six on either side of the aisle, were spaced so closely together across the floor their tops nearly touched. One mattress was empty, but the other eleven were occupied— mostly by couples and a few with trios in various states of undress, their hands and lips roaming, enjoying the chemically heightened sensation of exploring and being explored.

Two or three of the mattresses had only one occupant, some passed out in private bliss, but most were awake and watching. If the lovers noticed their audience, they didn't care or else derived illicit pleasure from the voyeurs.

I looked past the orgy, searching for a sign this room provided more than a peep show. But there wasn't a way out, no windows and no other doors. I turned to go, but a firm hand clapped down on my shoulder.

"People in this haunted house need to stop touching me," I grumbled under my breath.

I turned back slowly, dreading having to face another drug-peddler or worse. But the man who barred my escape didn't look deranged. On the contrary, he was actually handsome. His chiseled cheekbones and dark, slicked-back hair reminded me of someone. But before I realized who exactly, I'd moved on to marveling at how tall he was, at least four or five inches taller than me. His warm copper eyes burned with an intensity I'd only seen in my own reflection.

"Hello beautiful," he said. "Is that you, Aphrodite? Goddess of love?"

I sputtered out a nervous little laugh. Beautiful? Goddess? Who was he talking to?

"It's a pleasure to meet you, Aphrodite." He took my hand, kissing it, drawing me nearer. "I'm Desmond. We should get to know each other. Would you like that?"

"Sorry, but I don't have the—" I pulled my hand back and tapped my wristwatch because the words wouldn't come. His handsomeness overwhelmed me. More than that, the way he stared, drinking me in, stirred something inside me. Did he like what he tasted? I found myself fixated on his lips.

"Let's speed things up then," Desmond said. In one fluid motion, he slipped something over my head—a necklace. Its heavy pendant landed against my chest, and the whole room changed.

The flickering lights overhead became glistening three-tier crystal chandeliers. The dirty mattress on the floor in front of us transformed into a tall canopy bed. We were all alone. He fell back onto the bed and gestured for me to sit beside him, grinning irresistibly. I swore I felt silk sheets brush against my bare legs as I obeyed.

I lifted the pendant around my neck to inspect it, but I didn't just see a brilliant cluster of stones—purple, gold, and green—I saw our entire relationship unfolding in a daydream.

For our first date, Desmond took me to see a foreign film. He spoke the language so well he didn't need subtitles. Afterward, we shared our opinions about it over coffee. He made fun of me for ordering a fancy frappe, but his rebuke was silly and not snobby.

For our second date, we drove out to a cemetery for a

picnic. He recited poetry by E.E. Cummings and served me strawberry wine he'd brewed in his bathtub. We traced our favorite tombstones with wax paper and charcoal pencils. We ended the evening picking wildflower bouquets to set beside the tiny graves marking children's final resting places.

On our third date, he told me he was in love with me by playing a song he wrote on stage at a White Stripes concert. He got down on one knee, and the crowd went wild.

Desmond took my hand so gently I barely felt it leave my side. "Do you like what you see? I can make all your dreams come true. I'll make you feel so good," he crooned. "I won't let anything hurt you. Promise you'll stay, Lisette?"

"How... how do you know my name?" I asked, but as soon as the question left my lips, it ceased to matter.

"So beautiful," he whispered, running a finger down my jaw, giving me heart palpitations. "Why don't you realize you're beautiful?"

His touch, his words, spoke to a side of me no one seemed to address. My heart clung to the hope that someone, some-day, could really see me. See past my busted-up nose and broken-out skin. See something worth saving.

My pessimistic brain fought back hard, reminding me this place contained monsters, and to trust one of them was stupider than trying to save one of their victims. I needed to turn my back on him. Even if it meant turning my back on poetry and the possibility of being understood.

"I'm sorry, but I just don't have time. The witching hour is almost here, it's—"

"Not until 3 a.m."

"Huh?" I blinked at him, feeling stupid. Xavi had been right. What else had Xavi been right about?

"The witching hour is the inverse of Christ's death," Desmond explained. "You have plenty of time. Stay awhile?" He grabbed my hand, his huge one dwarfing mine. "The next realm will contain your greatest fear. If you stay here, I can protect you."

I knew I needed to run, but his hands felt so good. So warm and comforting. His rings pressed into my fingers, intriguing me further. I'd never known a man with a penchant for jewelry. "Come with me?" I said, though it sounded stupid even in my own ears.

"But we have everything we need right here," Desmond said, and then with a roguish laugh, "All I need is you. Do you need me, too? Give me one kiss to prove you do."

I caught his contagious glee and laughed, too. "One kiss," I said, the words tumbling off my tongue before I could pull them back.

He pulled me into his arms. His kiss contained a needfulness I'd never known, as though my saliva were the antidote to a deadly disease. Like only I could end his suffering.

This wasn't my first kiss. There'd been Bert Pelletier my freshman year, for two seconds in a closet at Xavier's birthday party. Then a long, agonizing flirtation with Landon Galloway spanning my sophomore and junior years. It never progressed past two passionate make-out sessions in his truck because he'd refused to acknowledge me at school —though he'd stay up all night talking to me on AIM. I didn't care too much about whose bare cheeks had already touched his truck's bench seat, but if I was going to add mine to their number, I needed to know he wouldn't break my heart. Rejection hurts less from someone who doesn't really know you. But once you let someone inside, what if they want out? How do you brush off a burn of that degree?

"Don't worry," Desmond said. "I won't be like the others. I'll never leave you."

He knew what I was thinking—but how? He knew, but he wanted me anyway? How could that be? But it didn't matter; I couldn't stay here. Why wouldn't the words come to say I had to go? I pressed my lips together, clenched my jaw, and pulled back.

His warm copper cat-eyes lapped me up, their thirst unquenchable. I shrunk from his fiery gaze, looking past him, around the four-poster bed, plotting my escape.

"My, my. Look at you, Lisette. You're *so* beautiful! Absolutely gorgeous!" He pulled me close, pressing his body against mine as though he wanted to absorb every inch of me. Something about the way he smelled—like gasoline and burning leaves—both set me on edge and drew me in. A scent I knew I shouldn't be inhaling, but I couldn't help myself.

"I want you so bad," he whispered in my ear.

But I didn't trust him. How could he love me? No one could love me. They all wanted something from me. Especially this handsome devil—emphasis on *devil*.

"I'm not beautiful." I pushed him away. "I've got a busted-up nose, and my face has more craters than the moon. I'm so tall that—"

"Those things make you unique. No one could ever duplicate you." He reached out to close the gap between us, his fingers softly tracing the indentations of acne scars on my cheek. "I especially like this part. Reminds me of the constellation Taurus."

Lies, lies, lusty lies—too lovely to be true. "I have to go," I said.

"Not yet." Desmond stroked the nape of my neck, loosening my braid. "Lay down with me for a little while. Let me hold you. I wanna make you feel good. I promise you'll love it."

"Maybe we could meet at the after-party?" I suggested.

Desmond shook his head. "I want you now." He took my right hand, studying it. "I think this is holding you back. I'll take care of it." He tried to pull Ruelle's ring off, but it responded with a jolt of electricity so strong we both felt it.

When Desmond recoiled, the smoky smell in the air

increased. His eyes blazed, and his lips curled into a snarl. What was happening?

The sight of my mother's ring made me remember the necklace he'd given me. I lifted it off my chest, examining it. The center stone was a bright purple amethyst, an emerald fused on its left, a yellow citrine on its right. I tried to remember what Ruelle said these stones did, but my head felt fuzzy, my body tingling, begging to return to Desmond's warm embrace.

"You need to take your ring off," Desmond ordered me, his soft tone hardened.

But I held my hand. I hated being told what to do.

"Why are you scared?" Desmond raised a brow. "Oh, I understand—you're a virgin. That's all right, I'll be gentle. And then after, you'll feel like a whole different person."

I scoffed. What an antiquated concept—the notion that his dick could change who I was. Defiant, I ripped his stupid necklace off. The room transformed before my eyes. Dirty mattresses, flickering lights. The smell of sweat, snickers, and moans. What was I doing in this den of depravity? I had to escape.

I threw the necklace as hard as I could, so far down the narrow room, I didn't hear it land, and ran. My lips trembled in a prayer that he'd be more concerned with reclaiming his jewelry than chasing me. While I ran, I formed a half-baked plan—run out of this room and go straight into the next, never looking back. But then I saw something happening that I couldn't ignore.

21

KICKING
DOWN
THE
HABIT

Jillian was sprawled out on one of the mattresses—legs akimbo—pinned down by a man at least twice her size. Her eyes were wide with terror as he pulled on her plaid skirt. In what seemed like a final act of desperation, she spat in his face.

He barely paused to wipe her saliva from his chiseled cheek. "Stop fighting," he growled at her. "You'll like it once—"

Without stopping to think, I grabbed him from behind. With my hands around his waist, I brought my knee up as hard as I could into his groin. He doubled over, sputtering.

Jillian popped out from beneath him and started pummeling him, too.

"Quick! Get away!" I shouted at her.

"Grab his keys!" Jillian replied.

I followed her wide eyes to the brass ring clipped to his pants. It came loose easily—perhaps too easily—and I realized this had been her plan all along. She'd been working at the keyring, trying to swipe it when he pounced on her. Jillian might've been a disloyal shrew, but I could tell she was clever, too.

We burst out of the room, the key ring jangling in my hand. She pointed to a vague outline marking the center door, and I didn't hesitate to dip my shoulder into it. We raced to the other side together, hugging each other to steady ourselves. But as soon as Jillian got her footing, she released me, nose in the air as if I were a bag of garbage she'd been tasked with taking to the curb.

This room featured the same bland overhead lights, but in other ways it was the opposite of the last room. Stacks of black metal folding chairs were pushed against all four walls, but there weren't any people here. Something in the room, maybe a change in atmospheric pressure, gave me a splitting headache. I rubbed my temple, but the pain refused to subside.

"Who are you?" Jillian asked with a manicured brow raised. "Why did you save me?"

"I'm Lisette," I said, unsure why I needed to explain myself. "And I saved you because it was the right thing to do. What kind of monster would leave someone in that situation?"

"This place has a way of making monsters out of ordinary people."

"I'm not an ordinary person."

"Fair enough. Well, thanks, I guess. But listen—only one person wins this thing. So, I owe you one. But only one."

I rolled my eyes. What an ungrateful little—before I could tell her off, movement out of the corner of my eye drew my attention. A cockroach, the size of a mouse, crawled out from the shadows and skittered across the floor. I backed up, thinking, *That thing better not touch me.* As if privy to my innermost thoughts, the cockroach made a beeline for me.

In a flash, the roach was off the floor, crawling across the toe of my boot. I hollered and shook it off. But it didn't scamper away; it *flew.* It made an awful sound, more whine than words, but it taunted me anyway: *I can go anywhere,* its whine seemed to say. *There is no escape.*

"Ugh! Absolutely disgusting!" I yelped, covering my face as I fled from the flying roach.

"Yeah, this room is gross," Jillian agreed. "Give me the

keys. I'll figure out which one opens the door. We can both get out of here."

"Where's the door?" I asked, but before she deigned to answer, I followed her eyes to a tiny circle of light. A keyhole, maybe?

"Let me worry about the door," Jillian said. "You're on bug duty. Squash as many as you can—looks like you've got the perfect boots for it."

I crossed my arms. I did *not* save this girl so she could make cracks about my boots. "How about *I'll* find the key, and *you* can be on bug duty?"

While we were arguing, a second roach—larger than the last one—jumped off the wall and charted a flight right for my face. I ducked, hands over my mouth to stifle another shriek.

"Give me the keys," Jillian demanded.

But I shouldered past her, toward the tiny circle of light escaping from behind a stack of chairs on the back wall. Yes! A keyhole! I was right! I pumped my fist in the air triumphantly, then wiggled behind the chairs.

While I tried the keys, one after the other, I could hear the *crunch* of Jillian waging war on the roaches. Bile rose at the back of my throat, but I swallowed it; vomit would only draw more bugs. My heart pounded harder than I cared to acknowledge. *Bugs can't hurt you!* I tried to reason with myself, but it was too disgusting. I couldn't stand them touching me.

"Would you hurry up already?" Jillian snapped. "I'm covered in roach guts."

Fear flooded my brain, drowning out my usual clever retorts. I almost said something stupid, but the door behind us swung open, distracting me. I stole a glance, thinking it'd be more contestants entering, but instead it was Desmond and Cat. I crouched down low, but it was no use. I could tell by the satiated look in Desmond's hungry eyes that he'd already seen me.

"Told you she'd be in here," Cat said proudly. She stepped

toward me, ignoring Jillian. "She's a smart one. And with my help, she can be beautiful, too. So how 'bout it, Lisette? You ready to fix everything that's wrong with you?"

"Leave her alone," Desmond said. He edged closer to the stack of chairs. "She's perfect the way she is."

"Both of you leave me alone," I said, trying to focus on the door. Concentration made my hands slippery with sweat. I tightened my grip on the keys. "All I want is to get out of here."

"Simple enough," Cat said. "Say the safe word, and someone will come get you."

Jillian stepped in between them and me—assuming a confident stance with her hands on her hips. "If either of you wants to get to my friend, you'll have to go through me first."

My heart swelled; its heavy pounding slowed to a relaxed thump as I returned to the door. Only three more keys left to try—one of them had to be the right one.

Behind me, Cat laughed. "Two feisty little things. Which one do you want, Desi?"

"I want the one at the door," Desmond said.

"Of course. You love sucking down the tall drinks of water —but I'm not picky," Cat replied with a delirious cackle. Out of the corner of my eye, I caught Cat lurching forward and grabbing Jillian by one of her pigtails.

While Jillian was wrestling with Cat, the roaches skittered past her. I had the right key now—I could tell by the way it slid in—but I couldn't quite get it to turn. Something inside gummed up the works, and something, or several somethings, crawled up my legs. I yelped, batting them off with the backs of my hands, but the foul little suckers were relentless.

"This is silly, Lisette," Desmond said as I desperately wiggled the key. "Why roll around in the dirt with bugs when you could be rolling around in bed with me?"

I didn't bother answering him. I was close to finishing the

realm, the excitement building in my chest like Coke inside a shaken can.

"Lisette, wait," Desmond said, "the next realm is full of clowns."

What's the expression, the wind going out of your sails? I felt like the wind had gone out of my whole body, his revelation making it hard to breathe. There was nothing—not ghosts or bugs or dolls—I hated more than clowns. And worse, how did he know? I had never told anyone why.

"You're lying," I hissed.

Desmond's hand snaked through the stack of chairs. "Take my hand," he said. "The waking world is a miserable place. Stay with me here. I'll make your dreams come true."

My heart longed to go with him, back to a place that didn't exist. Feel good forever, even if none of it was real. Anything to stop the pounding in my head, like nails being driven into my skull.

"Lisette! Do you have the door open yet?" Jillian cried out, jolting me back into reality.

I dipped my shoulder and pushed as hard as I could. The door creaked open, allowing the faint sound of music to trickle past me. It sounded like the kind of song played beneath a Big Top, bouncy and sickly sweet.

"Almost," I tried to shout, but my voice was faint even inside my own head.

"Stay with me," Desmond repeated. He tried to squeeze in between the stacks of chairs like I had, but his shoulders were too broad. As he attempted to worm his way in, I caught the flash of purple, gold, and green—his amulet. Part of me wished it had broken into a million pieces when I threw it, yet another part of me longed to touch it. Yearned to take a break from running and fighting.

"Lisette!" Jillian shouted. "Open the door; I'm coming!"

"Don't go," Desmond said, so close I could smell him—

gasoline, dead leaves, a man who would burn the world down
to get to me.

I reared back and kicked the door as hard as I could. At
last, it flew open, and I toppled through, my momentum dragging me down. I would've fallen, but someone caught my arm.
I spun around, expecting to see Jillian. But it was Desmond.

MERRY
LITTLE
FOOL

Despite being on the other side of the door, I could still feel the sensation of something crawling up my legs. I pushed Desmond off me and shook my limbs. Strange how a moment ago I was considering staying with him forever and now I wanted to be as far away from him as possible.

"What is this?" I asked. "Wasn't that the end of the realm?"

He slammed the door shut behind us. "Wow. I never thought I was gonna get out of there." He laughed, nervous like we were on a first date. His whole demeanor was different, lighter.

I pulled my eyes off him and looked around. We were in a little alley, the gravel underfoot reminding me of the parking lot. There were no signs, but I figured I could follow the music, as much as I dreaded finding the clowns.

"What do you mean? Don't you work here?" I said, kicking gravel but not moving forward.

"No. Well, maybe," he conceded. "But it didn't start out that way. Listen, I know you think I'm a monster, but it's that realm—it changes you. Anyway, I'm out now. And I couldn't have done it without you."

I couldn't help staring at the door, waiting for it to open and Jillian to appear. But what if she never came? Though my brain told me to move on, to run. Foolish loyalty cemented my feet.

"To repay you, I'll tell you how to get past the clowns," Desmond offered.

"But what about Jillian? Where is she?"

"She wouldn't have waited for you," Desmond said. "Come on, let's walk and talk. I'm not so sure they won't send someone after me."

I straightened my shoulders; at least I didn't have a headache anymore. I trailed him closely as he approached the source of the bouncy circus music. A gust of wind shot past us, carrying the faint smell of buttery popcorn. "How did you know I was afraid of clowns?"

"When you wore my necklace, I got a glimpse into your head," Desmond explained. He grinned. "Very interesting in there. Shame we don't have more time to explore it."

I blushed. "It's rude to peep in people's heads without telling them."

"You didn't seem to mind at the time."

"So you know everything about me?" I asked with a gulp.

"Pretty much," Desmond replied. "Don't be embarrassed; it was fascinating stuff. Oh, and I'm sorry about what happened to you with the clown. That was awful."

I shrugged. "I've mostly forgotten about it."

"Good. The clowns in here will pick up on it if you're scared," Desmond said. "Those big honking noses of theirs can smell fear."

I smiled. It was sweet how he tried to calm me down with a joke. "So, what's our plan to get through?"

"*My* plan isn't to get *through*—it's to get *out*. My plan is to say the safe word the moment I hear it," Desmond said.

"But what about me?" I squeaked.

He scratched his head. "Tell you what, I'll make you a deal. I'll stay with you in the clown realm, help you get through. But then I'm leaving, okay?"

"Yeah, sure," I agreed. But it seemed too easy. "Wait, what's the catch?"

"Catch is you won't tell anyone how we met—I'm not going back there, Lisette. I can't. And if they know where I came from…" Genuine terror widened his copper eyes, and I couldn't help but feel sorry for him. I was a fool.

"Okay, I won't. Is that all?" I asked. My throat felt tight and scratchy, like the butterflies in my stomach had finally decided to fly out but couldn't escape.

"Swear it," Desmond said, desperation heightening the pitch of his voice. "Swear you'll never tell a single soul how we met. Say you'll take my secrets to your grave."

"I swear," I said, hoping it would calm him down.

He brightened instantly and grabbed my hand. "Come on, the faster we get through this realm, the faster I can leave this cursed place forever."

At least I wasn't entering the sixth realm alone.

Once Desmond and I reached the mouth of the tent, I saw five other hopefuls waiting to enter. From the way they clustered together and their matching costumes, I assumed there were two couples—one pair dressed as Roger Rabbit and Jessica and the other as a hunter with his doe. The latter had the perfect wide eyes for the look. The loner was dressed as Indiana Jones, complete with a whip that might come in useful.

I leaned into Desmond, who responded by clasping my hand in his. He probably only wanted us to look like a couple to be less suspicious, but I leaned into his embrace, anyway. His body heat relaxed me, lulled me into a false sense of security. If only I'd known then how badly he could burn.

A mustached man dressed as a ringmaster, complete with a red coat and black top hat accented in gold, explained what awaited us. I had trouble paying attention to him. The real, live lion resting at his feet was infinitely more interesting.

The lion stared back at me, still as a statue, apart from the occasional shake of his lustrous tawny mane as though agreeing with his companion. Back when Emma was my pseudo-friend, she told me about a trip to Indonesia she'd taken. Her family had visited a zoo full of drugged tigers that would pose for pictures and let you pet them. At the time, this had seemed both fantastically foolish and unbelievably sad. But in the presence of this sublime beast, I found myself clenching and unclenching my trembling hands, longing to feel his fur.

Without thinking, I raised my hand, the one with my mother's lucky ring, but before I could touch the lion, I attracted the attention of the ringmaster. He grabbed my hand, inspecting the ring curiously. "Where did you get this?" he demanded.

"None of your business." I tried to pull away, but he had me in a vice-like grip.

"You stole it," the ringmaster hissed. "As soon as I saw you, I thought, now there's a thief if I ever saw one."

"Let me go." I twisted my hand, tried to slip out of his grasp, but he clamped down harder. "I didn't steal it. Someone gave it to me."

"Who gave it to you, girl? I know who this ring belongs to."

His eyes burnt a hole through me, but it wasn't him I was afraid of. The lion pricked its golden ears too, listening. Its mouth parted slightly to reveal teeth like rows of butcher knives. I found myself trembling, thinking about the bat, the snake, and the waiver I hadn't read.

The other contestants waiting to enter stared at me too, jealously, as if I'd been given some unfair advantage. Jessica Rabbit bent down, the high slit in her red-sequined dress parting to reveal a milky-white leg marred with cuts and fresh bruises. What had she been through to make it this far? No wonder she glared at me.

Maybe I *had* been given an unfair advantage. The ring had

seemed to repel the trap on the dance floor. But it's not like I meant to cheat. Okay, so maybe I *had* asked for special treatment in the jungle. And Desmond was kind of helping me now. Ugh, this must be why people said cheaters never prospered. It was a one step forward, two steps back kind of shuffle.

"Come on then, girl," the ringmaster snarled. His grip crushed my fingers. "Out with it."

But before I could try my best lie on him, Desmond stepped forward. "It's her mother's ring," he said, "but she loaned it to her for tonight. Anyway, rings aren't against the rules. So why don't you get on with it?"

The ringmaster let me go and favored him with a sinister smile. "Now that wasn't so hard, was it? How ridiculous your little girlfriend doesn't know how to speak for herself. Now, where were we? Ah, yes, the sixth realm is—"

I clutched both hands to my chest. Though I tried to listen to the instructions, I couldn't help but hear Desmond whispering in my ear, "Are you all right? Did he hurt you?"

"No," I whispered. "I'm all right… but I'm afraid. He wants my mother's ring, doesn't he?"

Desmond's voice wrapped around me like a soft blanket. "Don't worry about him. No one can take your ring. You would have to give it to them."

"Why do they want it? What does it do?" I whispered back.

"The ring is limited only by your imagination and your faith," Desmond answered.

"Could it make everyone else in here disappear?" I asked just loud enough for him to hear.

He chuckled. "Don't worry. The clowns will take care of most of them."

My pulse quickened. "I hate clowns."

"I know you do. Don't worry." He gave my hand a little squeeze. "I'm going to help you."

Before I could ask how, the lion reared up on its hind legs. It roared, paws swiping the air around us as it drove us into the sixth realm.

Balloons in every color of the rainbow bounced around the room and floated up to the red-and-white-striped ceiling. Circus music played, and the smell of buttery popcorn filled the air. The path was boxed in with funhouse mirrors, making it nearly impossible to see the way through. I soldiered on, noting the little gaps between the mirrors where someone—or something—might hide. Desmond kept close, his copper eyes scouting out our path.

A clown wearing a bright red rubber nose and a wide grin whacked a balloon next to me with a giant mallet. I wanted to believe his mallet was a prop, an inflatable toy to scare people. The way the balloon popped suggested otherwise.

"Out of my way, Bozo!" I tried to sound tough, but my voice shook as I pushed past him.

Desmond grabbed my hand, yanking me to the left and out of the path of a tiny car I hadn't noticed. It screeched to a stop, and clowns began pouring out. They spilled from the compact car, one after the other, in a stream that seemed like it might never end.

If not for Desmond, I would've kept watching, waiting for the finale. But he pulled me away just as the hunter and his doe sprinted past, a different clown in a neon green jumpsuit with a larger mallet prancing after them, laughing. The clown brought the mallet down on the hunter's head with a sickening thud. We didn't stick around to see how the rest of the show would shake out. We ran and kept running, Desmond leading the way as we dodged clowns who seemed to come out from every direction.

"Ughhh! I *hate* clowns!" I shouted.

"Shhh," Desmond hissed. "Don't draw attention to yourself. Just keep going, we're almost there. Don't stop now!"

"What's happening! Are the clowns really hurting people?

I can't let them; I have to help." As the words left my lips, I realized I wouldn't be able to confront a clown like I had Jillian's attacker. Not without acknowledging what had happened to me.

"Don't worry about them. Focus on my voice," he whispered into my ear, relaxing me like ambient rain.

"Thank you," I said, "for staying with me."

"Don't thank me yet—quick! Hide!"

I pressed my body against a gap between the mirrors. Desmond stood in front of me, protecting me. I slunk into the shadows, barely able to see the girl dressed as a doe stumble past us. A clown wearing a wig like ramen noodles chased after her. He grabbed her by her shoulders, then sprayed her in the face with a fake daisy pinned to the lapel of his floral jumpsuit. The doe toppled over, and the clown scooped her up, cradling her like a child. He walked away with her. No one tried to stop him.

"Where is he taking her?" I asked Desmond, unable to see from my hiding spot.

"Forget about her," Desmond replied. "When I say 'go,' run straight ahead and don't look back. Ready?"

"Ready," I whispered, even though I definitely wasn't.

"On three. One, two—"

He didn't have to say it. The moment he moved out of the way, I sprang forward as if I'd heard a gun go off. My arms and legs pumped like pistons as I tore through the rest of the realm, leaving behind the popcorn smell, the carnival music punctuated by the clowns' hysterical laughter. It wasn't until I reached the door to the next realm, my heart fluttering against my ribcage like a wild bird with a broken wing, that I finally caught my breath long enough to speak. "Holy tamales, that was crazy! What now, Desmond?"

But he didn't reply. "Desmond? Desmond, where are you?" I looked back, but there was no one behind me. No one beside me. He was just gone.

"Oh no!" I gasped. My fingers massaged my temples roughly as I tried to decide what to do. What had happened to him? I knew I had to go back for him, but I couldn't stand the thought of facing killer clowns again—alone.

While I was rubbing my head, my vision was blocked, and I didn't see the terrified woman in all black barreling toward me. She knocked me through the exit door and into the beginning of the seventh realm.

"No! Desmond!" I cried.

I didn't bother getting my bearings in the dimly lit space. I pushed past the clumsy woman and grabbed the door handle. I pulled, twisted, and shoved it with my shoulder. But it didn't budge.

"What are you doing?" a voice boomed. Its authoritative tone made me cringe.

I slowly pivoted away from the door to face the stranger—emitting a tiny gasp when I saw him. He was easily a foot taller than me—seven feet tall at least—and the black cloak hanging from his broad shoulders billowed behind him in the windless room as if possessed. It might not have shocked me, except his body stopped at his shoulders, with a gaping hole where his head should rest. A swirling mist of black, like a cloud of flies, buzzed where his neck should've been. His appearance unnerved me enough that I returned to the door. If I could just find Desmond—

"You!" The deep timbre of his voice reverberated from the jack-o'-lantern clutched in one black-gloved hand. "Do you want to get out? You can leave if you want, but that's not the way."

"I have to go back!" I insisted. My fists balled up; I had to fight for him like I should've fought for Xavi. "I lost my friend—"

"There's no going back," the headless horseman thundered, the jack-o'-lantern animated with anger. "You can get out, but you can't go back."

23

STAGE
FRIGHT

I set my jaw. "I'm not trying to leave; I just want to go back."

"You go forward, or you get out." The headless horseman reached for something in his pocket. "Make your choice."

I didn't have to see it to know it was a walkie-talkie. He was gonna call someone to take me out. I backed away from the door.

"What's in the next realm?" the woman who had knocked me through asked anxiously.

I glared at her—but then my gaze softened. She had a red welt across her forehead. Yet it wasn't pity that made me look twice; there was something familiar about her heart-shaped face. Try as I might, I couldn't place her. It was too dark; the only light in the space came from the dancing flames of a tarnished brass candelabra centered on a marble mantle to the left of another door. But I didn't stop squinting at her, searching for a sign.

"Kennedy?" I whispered, only half believing it was really her.

She didn't look directly at me, so I couldn't be sure. The girl I'd joked with in the parking lot was full of bravado. This woman trembled before the headless horseman as if she thought the next head he claimed would be hers. And yet, the more I squinted, the surer I was. But if she was Kennedy—

then where was Tucker? Oh, and Hal? Had they already been taken out?

I inched closer to her, not wanting to startle her. But before I could ask her anything, the headless horseman began his speech about the next realm.

"A public speaking challenge awaits you," the headless horseman explained. "Tonight, you died. Walk up to the microphone and give your own eulogy. Minimum talking time is three minutes. If you stall or stutter, you must start over. Maximum number of attempts is six. If you want to give up before then, say 'kill me now.'"

Probably-Kennedy sighed. "I'll go first. I think my boyfriend is ahead of me, anyway."

I blinked at her. Maybe the candlelight was playing tricks on me, but... "Do I... know you from somewhere?"

She raised her hands in a beats-me gesture, and that's when I saw it—her nails.

"Kennedy! What happened to your face? I almost didn't recognize you."

"Oh! Hey Lisette. I didn't recognize you either—it's kinda dark in here." Kennedy touched her wound and tried to smile behind the pain. "Does my face look bad? One of those fucking clowns clobbered me with a mallet."

I tried to temper my excitement with an appropriate level of sympathy. "It's not *too* bad," I said. "Wow, it's so great to see you. I guess Tucker and Hal didn't make it this far?"

Kennedy shrugged. "I think they're ahead of me. Are you... by yourself?" The pity in her voice curbed my enthusiasm.

She was the one with the injury, but *she* felt sorry for *me*. Was it really so pathetic to be alone? How was my situation any different than hers?

"I'm doing okay on my own," I said, adopting a confident stance, my hand wearing Ruelle's ring brushing against my holstered guns. "What about you? Still think you can win?"

She shrugged again, tried to smile, but couldn't get her face to cooperate. Even in the dark, I could tell Kennedy had lost her spark. Maybe that was why I had trouble recognizing her before.

"Enough chit-chat," the headless horseman snapped. "Take your turn or tap out."

Kennedy started toward the door, hesitantly, like a child being called to the principal's office. "See you on the other side," she muttered.

"Good luck, Kennedy," I said.

Her spine straightened a bit. "Same to you," she said, sauntering through the door. Somehow, I doubted a public speaking challenge would eliminate her—but there was always a twist in this game, wasn't there?

About five minutes later, it was my turn. I crept with trepidation onto an empty stage. A single microphone waited on a silver stand, illuminated by a spotlight so bright it blinded me. I blinked, but the room remained black.

I couldn't see them, but I knew they were there.

"Look at her waltzing in like she's hot shit," a voice drifted up from the darkness.

"Just like her mother, all swagger and no substance," a second unseen person said.

Their words stung, but I set my jaw. They didn't know me or my mother. It was all just an attempt to pierce my armor. But I could not shake off the crushing weight of the audience's presence. I could feel their eyes watching, sizing me up. Their ears listened, waiting for me to slip up. Someone coughed. But I couldn't see a single face. Couldn't return their greedy stares with a plaintive look of my own or secretly ask them to take pity on me. To help me get through this.

What was I supposed to say about myself, anyway? It wasn't like I was some important figure. In that moment, I wasn't sure who would miss me. At least I might have some time left to change things.

"You have six tries," a high-pitched feminine voice cut through the darkness. "The timer will begin whenever you do."

"Ummm, okay, my name is ummm—"

"No stuttering. Five attempts left. Starting over," the shrill voice said. "Three more minutes on the clock."

I swallowed down the lump in my throat. It was dry and scratchy, like steel wool. "Can I have a glass of water?" I asked.

"No," the voice said. "Four attempts left. Three more minutes."

"Okay, well, here lies Lisette." The kickback from the microphone startled me. I stammered an apology, but the voice showed no mercy.

"Three attempts left," she said. "Three more minutes on the clock."

Seriously? This was *not* going to be how I got eliminated. Not after how far I'd come. I took another deep breath, but this time I meant it. No more clowning around.

"My name is Lisette Starling Colbert, and I died young, before I accomplished anything noteworthy. Though I like to think I would have done something great given enough time. I was brave and bold and smarter than anyone gave me credit for. Okay, so everyone except my best friend, he's the only one who ever believed in me. He believed me in, so naturally, I pushed him away like an anti-social idiot."

A few audience members responded with a tittering of laughter. I paused, allowing their amusement to empower me, which thankfully didn't knock off another attempt.

"Anyway, it's a real shame I died tonight because I didn't get a chance to tell my best friend how sorry I am. And because I had so much ahead of me. I don't know how I know this, but I do. I suppose only the alley cats will miss me now, and maybe my mother when she finds out how close I got to bringing home ten thousand dollars. We're embarrassingly poor. Like, I can't even talk about what my mom does to make money."

I took a breath, unsure of what else to say. More laughter —the tiniest wave at first. But it grew bigger and louder as it rippled through the crowd. They liked me. Maybe in spite of themselves, but they liked me. It gave me the encouragement I needed to keep going.

"Not so long ago, I was an accomplished gymnast. I was good, really good when I was a little kid. But then I got older, taller, and I went from being really good to just kinda there. Then I got hurt, and I went from kinda there to not there at all. Nothing that matters to me ever lasts. I tried to dust myself off, tried to focus on my grades. Do the right thing, you know? But sometimes it doesn't matter if you do the right thing. Everything goes to hell anyway. A few days ago, I was a student at one of the best private schools in the entire state of Louisiana. I worked hard, and I got good grades. Like I said, I'm smarter than I look. But none of that matters. It all got ripped away because a spoiled rich jerk wanted to prove something by picking a fight with me. So I got this—" I touched my nose "—instead of a diploma. Instead of getting into a good college. Guess it's good I died now. Before my mother finds out I got expelled."

I pretended to shade my eyes and peered into the crowd. "I don't see anyone I went to school with here, but if you know my mom, please don't tell her. Pretend like I died before reaching my potential and let her believe I had a lot of it."

Chuckles hit my ears like hype music, the kind of jams we played in the locker room before a big meet.

"She makes me mad sometimes because she won't admit when she's wrong. She'll do things differently going forward, but she won't swallow her pride and say she's sorry. Little things get under my skin like splinters, small enough they don't really hurt, but they're annoying all the same. Stuff I have to numb myself to and dig out when she's not looking."

I shifted from one foot to the other. "Now that I'm dead, I guess I'll miss her, but I'm glad I never had to face her finding out what I really am. I guess it's better to die young, with a whole lot of untapped potential, than to live a long life without ever accomplishing anything. Without ever belonging anywhere or mattering in the grand scheme of things."

A bell went off, and I jumped a little. "What happened?" I demanded. "I wasn't stuttering!"

"Your three minutes are up," the woman said curtly. "You may continue to the ninth realm."

"Okay," I looked around. "Exit stage left or…"

"Get inside the coffin," she ordered.

I followed the spotlight as it panned over an open casket surrounded by mirrors so that it looked like pictures of my horrified face were on display. Like I was already dead.

LIVING
DEAD
GIRL
INTERRUPTED

Lying down inside of the coffin, staring up at the ceiling of the packed theater, made my bowels rumble. I realized, with urgency, the only thing in my stomach was coffee. It wanted out. Did it cross my mind to yank my shorts down and ruin the red velvet liner in this port-o-potty for corpses? Yes, yes, it did. The velvet itched my exposed skin as I wondered how long I could stand being confined in this stiff, scratchy box. Then it hit me harder than the ache in my intestines: dead people don't care about comfort.

I squeezed my eyes shut, tried to make peace with the situation—my upset stomach, the unsettling tight space—by blocking it out. Miss Fenty had taught me multiple meditation techniques, and I was usually pretty good at using them. This time I disappeared to my happy place, Café du Monde. I could almost taste a beignet when—BAM! The lid slammed down hard, like someone making a point. The unmistakable *click* of a key twisting into a lock thudded in my left ear. Now I knew exactly where the lock was, and I knew how to handle locks.

While I waited for their next move, I went back to Café du Monde in my mind. Hot, sugary goodness. An indulgent sip of cafe au lait. I felt calm. At least, as calm as a *very* much alive person could feel inside a *very* cramped space meant for a *very* much *not* alive person. A very much alive person who needed to do something dead people didn't. Then the casket moved.

"Hey!" I rapped my knuckles against the wood. "Helloooo? Anyone there? Where are you taking me? When are you gonna tell me about the rules for the eighth realm? Has it started or what?"

No answer. Merely a delighted cackle muffled by the coffin between us. I shut up, if only to keep from giving whoever was out there the satisfaction of knowing I was scared. My stomach made a loud, embarrassing sound I was certain was audible to anyone listening.

So I was in a locked coffin, big deal. What were they gonna do? Toss a snake in here with me or something? Yeah, that wasn't outside the realm of possibility.

I removed a bobby pin from the back of my hair, loosening a few wild curls that hadn't submitted to the braid. The action made me feel better, like I had a weapon. A silly notion when a flimsy bobby pin couldn't smash a fly, but it was better than nothing.

At last, the coffin came to a stop. I braced myself. Prepared for swords or creepy-crawly creatures. The unexpected sensation of falling sent my brain into a tailspin. My palms pressed against my shorts as if tearing them off might help, as if voiding my bowels might end this experience.

Good news, no swords. Bad news, I was getting tossed around, jostling my already queasy stomach. My nose slammed into the coffin and throbbed with fresh pain layered on top of the old injury. My hands reached out to cup it, soothe it, which caused me to smash my elbows when the coffin hit the ground.

"Ahhh!" I groaned. The sharp pain flared through my nerves, spreading like fire.

The next noise was so soft I couldn't be sure what it was. I slowed my breath and pricked up my ears. I heard the tiniest scraping sound and then a whoosh as subtle as sand slipping into the other side of an hourglass. Though the evidence was far from comprehensive, somehow, I *sensed* what was happening. I had a premonition so clear and undeniable that my heart seemed to stop for a moment. I took a shaky breath. They were burying me.

"Welcome to the eighth realm!" a sinister voice said. Another scrape, followed by another whoosh. "Break out of the coffin and make your escape from the grave. But hurry; the higher the dirt is piled, the harder it'll be to claw your way to the surface. If you give up, the safe phrase is 'Wake me up' but really scream it." The voice laughed mischievously. "It's hard to hear you once you're good and buried."

Having my fears confirmed should have sent me down a fresh spiral of terror, but instead it calmed my nerves. I actually laughed. They had no idea how easy this was going to be for me. I'd pick the lock and presto, I'd be out. Then I'd tell whoever I saw next that I *had* to go to the bathroom.

My fingers barely shook as I felt along the edge of the coffin for the lock. The piece of wood separating the lock from the interior of the casket was so flimsy that it broke with one quick jab. Made sense—the lock was built to keep people out, not in.

The scrape of the shovel and the dirt raining down overhead faded away, and I focused on my internal voice. *Up and to the left. Yes, that's it. Give it a little wiggle. Okay, now turn. Turn harder. Little harder. Almost there—*

Snap! The tip of the bobby pin broke off inside the lock. Seriously? Crap on a croissant. Breaking into Miss Opal's had been much easier than breaking out of this casket. I tried to pinch the bobby pin with my fingernails, but I couldn't get a good enough grip to dislodge it.

The scrapes seemed to be coming in shorter intervals. I imagined the dirt piling up faster and faster. "I gotta get out NOW!" I said to myself like a rallying cry. The longer it took me to open the casket, the more dirt I'd have to dig through. And more likely, I'd be buried in a coffin with my own crap.

I tried the bobby pin one last time, aware in the back of my mind that it was a lost cause. There had to be another way out. I asked myself, *What would someone who didn't know how to pick locks do?*

Kicking frantically seemed as good an idea as any. My muscular legs slammed against the top of the coffin with as much momentum behind them as I could muster in the tight space. My back throbbed, adding its protest to the parade of pain stampeding down my spine and through my bowels.

The top of the coffin rattled, teasing me. It reminded me of that stupid locked door at the pawnshop. But I got in there with perseverance, didn't I? And I would get out of here with perseverance, too.

I squeezed my eyes shut and blocked out reality. *You're not Lisette Colbert in a coffin. You're a racehorse locked up in a stable. If you don't escape, it's the glue factory for you. You gotta get out. You gotta be free.* Holding this vision tightly in my mind, I willed my already sore legs to forget all the running they had done tonight and work like they were fresh. I kicked like my life depended on it. At last, the coffin's lid splintered.

Yes! Yes! I kicked harder and harder. The wood began to crack!

This was not, however, as much of a relief as I had anticipated it would be. I blinked in disbelief as dirt rushed through the cracks.

"Great!" I howled. "Peachy freakin' keen! Really thought that one through, didn't you, genius?" I rubbed at a sudden sharp pain in the center of my forehead. Okay, enough. I had to get the casket unlocked, then swing the top open to take some of the dirt with it.

I returned to the lock, but this time it wasn't a game. Dirt streamed through the hole at a steady rate, stinging my eyes and making me cough as I tried to wriggle the lock loose.

The thought crossed my mind that I might never get out. Maybe that was the point. I thought I could come in here and take their money, well, they showed me, didn't they?

"No. Enough. I have to get out! I have to get this money!" I shouted. I spit out the dirt in my mouth. My face screwed up in concentration, all my attention laser-focused on the lock.

No lullaby, no profession of love could have sounded as sweet as the click the lock made when it finally gave up the ghost. I pushed the lid, splintered wood tugging at my palms, but it only lifted halfway. The dirt piled on top weighed it down so that my upper body strength alone couldn't move it. I tried again to lift the lid, this time using my legs, too, and it finally swung open.

No time to celebrate. One last load of dirt clobbered me and left me sputtering. "Hey!" I called out in between attempts to spit the dirt out. "Stop shoveling, I won. I'm out of the coffin. I need to go to the bathroom like NOW."

No answer. At least my head wasn't buried. I tried to center myself. It was important to stay grateful. That was how you made it through the hard stuff, by counting your blessings and keeping your head up.

The earth felt so good under my feet I would've kissed it, if not for the image of creepy crawly things wriggling around in the soil. I spied a rope ladder dangling to my right. Bingo! Never would have seen that if I was wasting time feeling sorry for myself.

Gently, so as not to do more damage to the busted lid, I shut the coffin. I balanced precariously on top of the casket to reach the rope. Once I grabbed hold of it, climbing up was easy. I shimmied halfway up before I realized it wasn't a ladder; it was a piece of rope attached to a bell.

Bong! Bong! Bong! The bell rang, over and over, loud enough to wake the dead. The palms of my hands were rubbed raw, but I managed to climb up a few more inches, then I jumped the rest of the way out of what would have been my grave.

"Congratulations!" a voice called out from overhead, a different speaker than the one who told me the rules of the eighth realm. A good thing. But not great. I needed a person, not a machine. Someone who might bend the rules and point out a restroom. I exhaled, sending a cloud of dirt flying from my sore nose.

This voice was masculine and deep but slow and sleepy like someone roused from a nap. "You are now beginning the ninth realm. Your goal is to get behind that fence dead ahead of you."

I couldn't see the fence, couldn't look past the cemetery. My eyes got stuck on the path between graves, certain I'd walked it before. Surely, they couldn't have... *transported* me. I rubbed my eyes. Before me was the spitting image of St. Louis Cemetery.

25

**FOR WHOM
THE BELL
TOLLS**

"No. It can't be," I muttered to myself. "It's just a replica. An incredible replica."

I didn't know *how*—or why it seemed more unbelievable than a necklace that connected my brain to someone else's—but I knew I was in St. Louis Cemetery.

I stared at the familiar white mausoleums. Every feature, right down to the ivy vines creeping over cracked plaster and crumbling stone, was here. Once upon a time, I may have found the attention to detail impressive. But at this point, I only saw row after row of perfect hiding places.

My eyes roved past them, toward a twelve-foot-high chain-link fence a couple hundred feet away. I wondered what the big deal was. I could get there in five minutes if I put my mind to it. I ignored my sore legs.

"If you're ready to give up, better let us know now," the sleepy voice taunted me. "The safe phrase is, 'Living Dead,' but let's be frank, if you get bit, you won't remember it."

The word *bit* echoed in my ears like a death sentence. No monster—not vampires or werewolves or even psycho clowns —scared me quite like zombies.

There was no *reasoning* with them. One zombie, sure, that was easy enough. With stealth and smarts, you could give someone with literally no brains the shake. But there was never only one zombie. You might only see one, but soon there was a whole horde moving toward you *en masse*. That wasn't fair. That wasn't about skills or smarts. Sometimes someone got lucky. And it might not be you.

I scrambled up to the top of the closest mausoleum. The inscription CHARBONET sent an uncontrollable burst of fear gushing through my body. I felt like a plastic cup contending with the street sweepers that blasted through Bourbon Street on Sunday mornings. My knees wobbled, and I nearly fell. But I grabbed an iron cross affixed to the top and steadied myself.

Clutching the cross, I squinted into the misty horizon, searching for the enemy. I tried to strategize. Could zombies climb? In most movies they were slow, but sometimes they were fast. What about water? Could they swim? Not that it mattered because *I* couldn't swim.

I struggled to remember which rules from the movies repeated the most—I always closed my eyes through the gory parts. Then I heard a chorus of off-key groans. Zombies lumbered into view, grouped together in clusters of two and three. I counted them at first, but had to stop at thirty to regain my nerve.

Holy tamales, this was ridiculous! How was I supposed to get around this? Were they as real as they looked, or could they be some sort of hallucination? After seeing what the dolls did to Princess Peach and hearing what the snake did to Oops Britney, I didn't dare risk it.

I pulled at the front of my tank top. Suddenly I was so hot I felt like I might pass out. "Relax," I whispered to myself. "It's only scary because you can't spot the cracks in the illusion."

The moon and the stars barely pierced the thick blanket of clouds in the sky. But there was light. The entire cemetery was awash in a neon green glow from row after row of giant, luminescent mushrooms. In a different scenario, I would've been desperate to pick a bouquet of the glow-stick fungi to examine them up close, but, in that moment, all I cared about was getting out of there.

Better not leave without your poppet, a voice in my head, one I didn't recognize, whispered.

I inhaled as deeply as I dared, then exhaled as soft as a feather falls. My eyes darted around the mob of zombies, who didn't seem to have noticed me yet, trying to decide if I had time to duck inside the vault. My stomach grumbled.

"My poppet's not here because this isn't real," I spat at the voice.

No way was I ceding the higher ground. I mentally calculated the distance between the nearest mausoleum. I could jump to that one. Maybe I could jump to the next one too. What would Coach Karla do? She'd spider-woman her way around the cemetery, that's what. So that was what I was gonna do.

The first jump was easy enough, especially with my extensive experience on the uneven bars. When I landed, I steadied myself by clinging to a giant cross. A smug smile spread across my face. Piece of cake. This realm was practically designed with me in mind.

A pause would have slowed my momentum, so I jumped again. I reached my target, but the top of this mausoleum was much narrower than the last. As I scrambled to maintain my footing, stray pieces of stone came loose and sailed down to the earth below.

First, one rotting head pivoted, then another. The second one grunted, and the first nodded as if plotting. They both broke away from the pack. They shuffled toward me. Lovely. I hadn't foreseen wanting to crawl back into that casket so soon.

I tugged on the end of my braid as I tried to decide whether I should press forward or hide somewhere, throw them off my trail. I landed on a mix of the two and began to move randomly, hoping they would lose track of me.

Leaping onto the mausoleum to my left was no trouble.

Then I jumped forward, then back and to the right. All those years of plyometrics training in the gym certainly helped me, but it was by sheer luck that I didn't make enough noise to draw any further attention.

Feeling satisfied with my current position, I crouched down and scouted out the cemetery. So far, the two zombies who seemed to be after me were frozen in place. They craned their purplish-gray necks, searching. Their movements were stiff. Their snorts sounded impeded as they took short inhales. I gulped. They were trying to sniff me out. I hunched down, praying the wind wouldn't carry my scent to their rotting nostrils.

I drew my lower lip into my mouth and nibbled on it, forming a plan to make it to the fence. I couldn't help thinking these were *real* zombies, like the mallet that had smashed into Kennedy's head had formed a real gash.

Fear paralyzed me. I looked down at my boots, which were covered in chalky scuffs from the crumbling stone. My mind drifted back to gymnastics, to dusting chalk onto my hands.

Eureka! I could launch stones in the opposite direction. They had chased after the sound before. Maybe they would do it again.

I selected a piece of stone about the size of my fist and hurled it as hard as I could to my right. It struck a tombstone and exploded like grayscale fireworks. The effect it had was so immediate I had to stifle a victory whoop—both zombies began to amble erratically toward the noise. The way their bodies twisted, their strained movements, made me shiver. I was *not* going to end up like them. I had to get to that fence.

I cut my celebration short and hopped over to the next mausoleum. I didn't waste time moving back and forth now, just straight ahead, a brief pause to make sure the coast was clear, then onward until the fence was so close, I could hear the chain-link clinking softly in the breeze.

One final little stretch remained between the mausoleum where I stood and the fence, a few graves away, where I would have to drop down and run. I paused to gather more rocks; they might be useful later, though not many fit in the tiny pockets of my cut-offs. Why hadn't I opted for cargo shorts? Besides, the rocks weighed me down. I wasn't sure they were worth the trouble. While weighing the pros and cons, I caught something flesh-toned wriggling around out of the corner of my eye.

A worm? What was a worm doing way up here? No, too big to be a worm. I inched a little closer to inspect it. Dumb move. The thing—a freakishly big rat—whirled around and charged at me, its yellow teeth snapping. I backed up too far and fell, landing with a thud that seemed to send shock waves through the whole cemetery. At least I landed on my feet.

Crap on a croissant! What had I done? I looked around. I didn't see the zombies yet, but I could hear their feet dragging across the soggy earth. Their unnerving groans had a strange familiarity to them. Hunger. They were hungry.

No choice left but to run for the fence. My legs pounded the earth so furiously that my thighs quivered from the impact. Sweat beaded up on my dirty forehead and turned to mud, slipping down and stinging my eyes. I only made it a few feet before the ground beneath me gave way.

I didn't realize what was happening until I landed with an audible *whack* on top of a closed casket. Wonderful. Not only was I *not* above them anymore, worse, I was below them.

At least this grave was shallow, and I wouldn't have to stand on the coffin to climb out. Then again, that meant it wouldn't be hard for someone to climb in either. I knew they heard me fall. Did they see where I fell, too?

My instincts urged me to climb inside the casket. I figured I'd be safe—well, not safe, but safer. With no time to second guess myself, I threw the coffin open, darted in, and shut myself inside so fast I didn't take time to savor the relief of its emptiness.

In the coffin's darkness, my heart knocked against my ribcage. I placed my hand over it and willed it to be still. I closed my eyes to sharpen the rest of my senses.

The zombies were so close now I could hear not only grunts but an audible word.

"Brains, brains, brains!" they chanted like children demanding ice cream. I felt as though I might vomit. Or worse.

"Shhh, Lis, it's okay," I whispered to myself. "Don't hurl. And definitely don't crap your pants. It'll make it easier for them to smell you."

It occurred to me that I could say the safe phrase. I could scream it. I could get out before I became one of them.

No! I couldn't give up now. I didn't come this far to quit! But there was no other way out. They would keep searching, sniffing, stumbling around until one of them found me.

I patted my pockets as though searching for an answer inside. Nothing but a few random stones. Then my fingers grazed the guns in their holsters. Those wouldn't help me either. They weren't real and anyway, zombies weren't afraid of guns. They weren't afraid of anything. They felt nothing— except the need to feed.

"Brains! Brains! Brains!" they chanted.

Louder. Closer.

I tried to dissolve the lump in my throat, but my mouth was too dry for a proper swallow. Soon their brittle hands would pry open the coffin lid. Maybe one would fall in by accident like I had. My last hope was to say the safe phrase. At least that way they wouldn't bite me. At least that way I would still be me.

With a sigh of defeat, I ran my dry tongue across my cracked lips. "Living—" I croaked so softly I wasn't sure anyone could hear me, but before I could get the second part of the phrase out, a familiar *bong, bong, bong* thundered through the cemetery.

The zombies began to plod away. Their chilling refrain of "Brains! Brains! Brains!" faded as they moved toward the sound. Someone else had escaped from their coffin. My terror gave way to relief. I was saved by the bell.

FAMILIAR
FACES AND
PLACES

I silently cursed the subtle squeak of the coffin hinges as I dared to lift the lid. I popped my head up and scanned the horizon like a prairie dog. Coast was clear.

With pluck and a prayer, I oriented myself toward the fence, took a deep breath, and prepared to explode toward the finish line. Right before I took off running, an unexpected sound sent paralyzing chills up and down my spine. "Help! Help! They've got me! I want out—I—Living—ahhhhh!"

The final visceral scream echoed through the air like a fire alarm.

I couldn't pretend anymore. This was not a drill. I blasted off like a rocket. Every sprint, every suicide in every practice sprung to my mind. Memories of Coach Karla barking, "Don't let me catch you slacking," sounded in my ears like a war cry.

Counting the tombstones kept me focused. Three tombstones left between me and the fence. Two tombstones. One tombstone. None. I didn't see a gate, so I started to climb. Dear God, would that screaming ever stop? I feared it would echo through a lifetime of nightmares. That it would cut through peaceful silence like the phantom sound of my morning alarm two minutes before it actually went off.

At my back I heard crunching, slurping, and greedy

smacks. They were eating him. Devouring him. I told myself not to listen. *Don't think about what's happening behind you. Run!*

I made it about two-thirds of the way up the twelve-foot fence before the unthinkable happened. I got stuck. At first, the direness of my situation didn't register. I looked down, expecting to see my shoelace snagged on something. I never considered that it'd been caught by *someone.*

The zombie tilted his head up to look at me; the spikes on the black leather dog collar around his pale neck shimmered in the moonlight. A gust of wind blew his blood-splattered hair back, revealing gray, lifeless eyes lined in charcoal black.

For what felt like hours, we were locked in a stalemate. I frantically tried to shake him off. He was trying to shake me off, too. Off the fence. I dug my fingers into the fence, the metal scratching my palms, still tender from where the rope burned them, and I held on like a cowboy riding a bucking bronco.

The zombie gripped the heel of my boot. He dodged most of the rocks that came tumbling from my pockets, but the ones that struck him didn't faze him. One rock left. Stupid, impractical cut-offs with their stupid, shallow pockets! I thought about hurling the last rock at him, but that meant letting go. I couldn't convince myself to let go.

As the screams in the distance died down, the realization struck me like an open-handed slap: my time playing this game one-on-one was running out. Pretty soon, my adversary would have backup. There was nothing left to do now— except take a risk.

"Had fun hanging out," I said, "but I've got a prize to collect. Nothing personal."

I lifted my free boot away from the safety of the fence, and for a brief, terrifying moment, all that remained between me and being bitten was the power of my trembling hands, my arms that had blessedly spent years carrying my entire body weight. I brought my boot back down with all my might, crushing the zombie's fingers under my heel.

The zombie groaned and pulled his hand back, but he didn't retreat. I had avoided his nasty teeth for now, but I was still very much in his neck of the woods, and his pack was not far off.

I scrambled higher up the fence as quickly as I could. But the zombie had sampled victory. He wouldn't give up so easily. He lunged and barely nabbed my dangling shoelace. This time, instead of shaking the fence, he started to climb up after me. A dopey grin spread across his disgusting face, clearly pleased with his new trick.

He was faster than I'd anticipated, and his weight as he clung to my lace slowed me down. His hand inched up my ankle. He hooked his stiff fingers through the tongue of my boot. I could feel his icy touch through my sock. His grip was so desperate, so determined, that I almost yelled the safe word —*almost.*

I don't know what compelled me to look down, straight into his dead eyes. I don't know what I hoped to see. But what I saw shocked me—the tiniest glimmer of recognition. Like he knew me. Then the unthinkable happened.

The zombie let go. He grumbled something unintelligible. Just when I thought things couldn't get weirder, he winked. Was he flirting with me? Seriously? Did I know him? For a second, I lost my mind, allowed myself to linger. But I quickly shook the sentiment off. Who cared why he let me go? This was my chance to escape. Breathless, I raced up the fence.

Climbing down seemed too risky, so I jumped from the top. I stuck the landing. Not even a little disqualifying hop at the end. Total control. But my poise didn't stop the impact from smashing the arches in my feet and sending white-hot pain searing through my spine. I didn't care.

"I made it! I made it!" I pumped my fist into the air.

"What ya got to throw at me now? Take aim, fire at will, I'm bulletproof!" I taunted the zombie.

Once I realized what I was doing, I felt kinda bad about it. But the emotion in his undead face wasn't disappointment or defeat. Instead, he made googly eyes at me. He lifted a hand and waved. Then it clicked.

"Hal?" I whispered.

No, it couldn't be. He would have said if he was working here. Unless... unless... I didn't know what it meant, and I shouldn't have wasted more time trying to figure it out. But I couldn't leave him there, not like that. I cocked my head and watched him from a safe distance. "Hal, is that you?"

The zombie grunted. A thin line of saliva dribbled out of his slack jaw and down his chin. He looked at the fence long-ingly, as if he wanted to climb over but couldn't leave the realm. In a flash, a different kind of desire took over. He charged, snapping his teeth at me like a rabid wolf.

I jumped back, raising my arms to shield myself. In my terror, I forgot about the fence, until I felt a new presence hovering over my shoulder. I whirled around, ready to fight, but the sour-faced woman wearing a pristine white skirted nurse's uniform appeared to be unarmed. A little white hat was perched atop her impeccably styled victory rolls, evoking another era. The silver identification badge pinned to her lapel read *Ratched*. I frowned as I recognized the costume—the evil nurse from *One Flew Over the Cuckoo's Nest*.

"Bravo," Nurse Ratched said. "You have completed the ninth realm. Are you ready for the tenth?" She gestured toward the multi-level building behind her. "Of course you are. And the doctor is ready to see you now."

I grimaced. My last visit to a *doctor* was a bruise fresh enough to protest when prodded.

"Doctor who?" I asked.

Nurse Ratched nodded to a manila folder in her hand. "Doctor Verity."

"Oh, all right," I said, allowing myself to exhale. "Hey, first I need to go to the bathroom—"

"Sorry. No can do. Doctors hate to wait. Ironic, but true."

I blinked at her. "But I really have to—"

"Save it for the doctor. Come along now." She spun on her heel and marched toward the building.

"Um, okay." I trailed after her, watching how she kept clear of puddles. "Well, aren't you going to tell me the safe word?"

"Why? Don't you like going to the doctor?"

"Ummm… no."

"But he'll make you better."

"Whatever." I rolled my eyes. "And the safe word is…"

She turned around to glare at me. "Crazy—because that's what you'd have to be to go through life refusing treatment. People like you truly baffle me. You puff up with pride and refuse help because you think it makes you weak."

"You don't know me," I scoffed. "Get on with it."

Nurse Ratched shielded her gaze, looking into the distance. "I don't have time to take you to his office, but you'll find it easily." She pointed to the giant cement building. "Through the double doors, the elevators are straight back and on the right. Go up to the second floor, third office on the right. Don't go snooping around—you wouldn't want to *accidentally* end up in an operating room."

"Lovely. I won't."

As happy as I was to leave the nut-job nurse behind me, I still proceeded with caution. I no longer bought into Kennedy's theory about this being a mass hallucination. If the haunted house supplied someone on my mind, it would have been Tucker, not Hal. Poor Hal had *really* become part of the haunted house somehow. Maybe it was the same thing that'd happened to Desmond. And if I didn't watch my back, it could happen to me, too.

The heavy antiseptic smell inside the hospital stung my

nostrils. A few generic paintings lined the stark white walls. One directional sign pointed toward the elevators. But another sign distracted me—restrooms!

One little detour couldn't hurt.

The bathrooms were so clean I spent an extra few minutes washing out the dirt from under my fingernails. The botanical paintings were upbeat, almost chipper. Nothing here seemed to match the haunted house motif. Maybe that's why I let my guard down.

As soon as I stepped outside, strong arms grabbed me from behind. Gloved hands pressed against my mouth to stifle my scream. I tried to whip my head around, to at least face my assailant, but I smacked my cheek on something hard. A mask.

27

CRAZY
LOVES
COMPANY

"What do you want from me?" I tried to scream, but Dr. Montgomery kept his gloved hand against my mouth, muffling the sound.

"Shut up," he said. "Can't you see I'm trying to save you?"

I coughed. The rubbery taste of his gloves made me want to gag. I twisted my head out of his reach. "Save me from what?"

"We can't talk here," he said as he stole me away.

I had no choice in the matter, which unearthed the repressed memory of our last encounter. The ritual had been real, just like the magic here was real. And I was like my stuffed bear to Dr. Montgomery, my struggles unable to spark his sympathy.

He carried me inside an operating room, which only served to spike my panic.

"Please put me down. I won't try to get away," I lied. "Please, tell me what you want."

Dr. Montgomery plopped me down on the operating table. The cold metal made me jump.

"Easy now," he said, hovering over me. "Trust me, I just wanna talk."

"Kinda hard to trust a man who won't show me his face," I said, backing as far away from him as I could get without falling off the table.

He shook his head. "Neutrality is not possible without anonymity. What about you, Lisette? Whose side are you on?"

"What do you mean?" I asked. "Is that a riddle or something?"

"Spirits talk to me about you. A woman, her name is Opal, like the stone. Ring any bells? She has a message for you."

I said nothing. If he'd really heard from Miss Opal, he wouldn't need my confirmation that I knew her.

"I'll give you the message," Dr. Montgomery said, "but there's a delivery fee."

"Oh?" I raised an eyebrow.

"I want the truth from you, too." He clapped his hands, producing a puff of green smoke in the shape of twin snakes curling around each other. When the smoke cleared, he held a beaker full of bubbling blue liquid. He extended it toward me.

"I'm not drinking that." I pursed my lips.

"Fine, I don't need *you* to drink it," he relented a little too quickly for comfort.

Before I could ask what he meant, he reached into the pocket of his lab coat. I knew what he was getting before he pulled her out, could feel *his* hands on *my* neck. Bebe. He had my bear. Though her poor fur was streaked with dirt, I instantly recognized the hair sewn to her head—my hair.

"I don't want to hurt you. But I *need* the truth." Dr. Montgomery ran his fingers through Bebe's hair, working out the kinks in her curls. I could feel him gently tugging. It didn't hurt, but the realization that he *could* hurt me, that whatever he did to Bebe happened to me, was sheer torture.

"I'm surprised you're not afraid of Marie," I said. "She's immensely powerful. I paid her tribute to watch over Bebe, to keep her safe. If you hurt her—"

Dr. Montgomery chuckled. "Your piddly offerings hold no sway compared to my lifetime of sacrifice. Besides, Marie gave you the chance to get your poppet, set it right under your nose, and you passed it by."

The voice in the cemetery. I tried not to gasp. Tried to do as Ruelle had advised me if Bebe fell into the wrong hands— to question the power of the ritual.

"How do I know it's really the same bear? You could have made one that looked like mine."

Dr. Montgomery reached into his pocket again. This time he retrieved a scalpel. He held the razor-sharp blade to Bebe's throat. I shivered against the chill of the metal, the pressure against my windpipe.

"Fine," I hissed. "So it is mine. What are you going to do with her?"

"That all depends." Dr. Montgomery held out the beaker of blue liquid again. "Are you gonna drink it? Are you gonna tell me the truth?"

"The truth about what?" I asked.

"Your powers. Opal tells me your people got all kinds of powers. Now, drink."

I took the beaker, gently swirled it to watch the fizzy blue liquid spin. My powers? What powers? Did I have some sort of magical ability? It sounded nuts, but it wouldn't be the craziest thing that had happened to me tonight. Ten minutes ago, I narrowly escaped being eaten by a guy I used to think was sexy.

Even before the haunted house, strange occurrences had plagued me. The terrible thing with the clown. My neighbor's murder. Dark omens chased me like hornets whose nests I couldn't stop tripping over. And yet, I never got stung. Was magic protecting me?

I looked at the vial again. "If I drink this, will you give me my bear back?"

Dr. Montgomery nodded. "Eventually."

The blue liquid bubbled to the top of the beaker, daring me to take a swallow. I momentarily disassociated from the dirty, desperate girl who was about to make a fatal error. She was a horror movie heroine contemplating running up the stairs, and I was the baffled audience member screaming for her to run out of the house.

"Drink it," Dr. Montgomery snarled. "I will get the truth, one way or another." He pressed the tip of the scalpel against Bebe's mouth, hard enough for me to feel the prick against my lips.

I threw the beaker back. It tasted citrusy yet sweet for a second, but the aftertaste was bitter like an orange peel. The effect was immediate. My vision blurred as though a fog had descended inside the room. My brain went swampy. My tongue seemed to swell in my mouth.

"Now," Dr. Montgomery said. "Tell me about this teleportation you can do—how far can you move while holding objects?"

I scrunched up my nose. "Teleportation? Are you serious?"

"The night we met," Dr. Montgomery says slowly. "You teleported. Yes or no?"

I sputtered, unable to form complete words. *Had* I done that? It made sense when I thought about it. One moment I'd been on the ground outside Miss Opal's apartment, and then suddenly, I was in my bedroom. The image of Ruelle's shocked face hovering above me flashed in my mind.

"Answer me," Dr. Montgomery growled. "How far did you go?"

"From outside my neighbor's apartment to my own," I mumbled, doing the math in my head. "So not far, really. But I was in excruciating pain; no way did I walk."

"Have you ever traveled further than that?" Dr. Montgomery asked. As he leaned in, his mask tilted up, revealing the finely carved curve of his jaw.

"Yes, I think so," I said, but even as the words came out, I could hardly believe them. The memory tried to surface, and I fought to shove it back down. But some unseen force wrestled the words out of my mouth. "I was so young I hardly remember... but I think I went from Biloxi to New Orleans once."

"Only once?" Dr. Montgomery grabbed the empty vial from me. I'd forgotten I was holding it. He turned it upside down, as if he thought a drop of liquid might spill out. "She's telling the truth," he muttered when none did.

"Are you going to give me the message now?" I asked.

His shoulders tensed. "When you teleported from New Orleans to Biloxi—were you under a great deal of distress?"

I laughed nervously. "Sure, you could call it that. Look, I don't want to talk about it. Are you going to give me the message or—"

"Who sent you?" he bellowed.

"No one sent me. I've answered all your questions honestly. This is cr—holy tamales!" I clamped a hand over my mouth. "I almost said the safe word!"

Dr. Montgomery laughed. "Holy tamales? What are you, twelve? Okay... maybe you're telling the truth. But it doesn't make any sense. How did you find The Thirteenth Realm?"

"My neighbor told me about it. I needed the money. I didn't know... I still don't know what this place is."

"It's a competition," Dr. Montgomery said. "Hundreds of years ago, the four covens built the haunted house together, as a testing ground for young witches. But the place their magic built has its own will now. The covens all fight for control, but now the Thirteenth Realm fights back. Now tell me, who sent you?" He pressed the scalpel against Bebe's throat again. It was so close I was afraid to nod.

"Please let me go," I whispered. "I came here to win the prize. That's it. I don't... I don't know anything about covens, okay?"

"Swear it!" Dr. Montgomery shouted at me. "Swear you have no allegiance to any of the covens!"

"I swear I have no allegiance to the covens!"

He lowered his scalpel. "Then you will join me. Together, we will slay this monster."

I frowned at him. "Like I said, I need the prize money."

"You don't understand," Dr. Montgomery balked. "If you fail to complete the Thirteenth Realm, you will die. If you succeed, they will force you to choose a coven. If you do this, you will never be free again."

"No one is going to take my freedom," I insisted. A quick glance at my watch confirmed my greatest fears. I was nearly out of time. "Now please, let me leave!"

"Swear you won't join a coven," Dr. Montgomery pressed me.

"Fine. I swear I won't join," I said, the words tasting bitter and familiar. I was giving up on something, and I didn't even know what. Did I dare still ask about Miss Opal's message?

Dr. Montgomery released me, returning his scalpel to the deep pockets of his lab coat.

"What about the message?" I asked. "From Opal or whoever?"

"She said she's been watching you since she passed. Said your momma's wrong not to trust you. Wrong to clip your wings, steal your magic from you."

My heart pounded like a hummingbird, a frantic blur so loud it made my ears throb. "Is that all?"

"Her spirit was faded," Dr. Montgomery said. "You'd have to feed her to hear more. Although there was something about your accident. Said your momma tricked you with some coffee? Does that make sense to you?"

I licked my lips. I tried to understand what it could mean —those three days after the accident when Ruelle made me drink every last drop of that dark, bitter liquid. Was there some sinister meaning behind it?

Consciously, I never would've shared my concerns. The words that flowed out of my mouth weren't ones I wanted to say. "After my accident, Ruelle brought me breakfast in bed every day, up until the morning after we buried Bebe. Come to think of it, she didn't let me *bury* my bear. She told me to put her inside the mausoleum. She ruined the ritual on purpose, didn't she? But why?"

Dr. Montgomery lifted his mask—revealing a handsome face with far fewer lines in it than I had pictured. He raised my bear up to his eye level and squinted at her. "Because," he said, "she didn't want the ritual to be binding. You can reverse it. She left you the choice."

"Why would I want to undo it? Wouldn't my pain come back?"

"You'd get your pain back, sure enough. But you'd also get your powers back."

I stared at Bebe. "My powers... you mean teleportation? But it would make my back hurt again. How bad would it be?"

Dr. Montgomery slid his mask back in place. "Magic isn't an exact science. Gotta take your pain to get your power. Don't get one without the other."

"Let me guess; if I wanna know more, I have to pay for it?"

Before Dr. Montgomery could name his price, the door swung open.

28

FIT
TO
SERVE

Nurse Ratched stood in the doorway, her glare bouncing between us like she couldn't decide who'd earned more of her ire. "What did I tell you about wandering off, Lisette?"

"Sorry." I jumped down from the operating table. "I got lost. Can you show me where I'm supposed to go?"

Nurse Ratched sighed. "Yes, but Dr. Verity is going to be *furious*. He hates it when people are late. And as for you, *Doctor* Montgomery, I thought we were quite clear on which competitors you were allowed to detain. I am absolutely certain her name was not on your list."

Dr. Montgomery's expression behind his mask remained a mystery, but I swore I heard a haughtiness in his voice. "Your list is merely a suggestion. You do not control me."

She wagged a finger at him. "I know you don't *mean* that." She hooked an arm through mine. "Come along, Lisette. We've wasted quite enough time already."

She walked me briskly back to the elevators, and as we went along, her expression softened. "He didn't hurt you, did he?"

"No… he… I'm okay."

"He has a reputation for being rough. I, for one, would like to dissociate with him—with his whole ilk—but Dr. Verity thinks he's harmless. Wait until he hears about him going rogue."

I started to tell her about Bebe—to insist we go back—but something stopped me. A feeling deep in my gut said the fewer people who knew about my bear, the better.

When we reached Dr. Verity's office, Nurse Ratched gestured for me to go in first. The room was surprisingly cozy, decorated with warm brass and crisp navy. I took a seat on a leather chaise lounge with tufting that begged to be touched.

"I'm sorry we're late, Doctor," Nurse Ratched said. "Montgomery refuses to follow orders. He plucked her right—"

"That's quite enough, Nurse Ratched. I'll take things from here," Dr. Verity said.

"As you wish, Dr. Verity," Nurse Ratched huffed. She shut the door on her way out.

The white poofs of hair on either side of Verity's head reminded me of Doc, the dwarf from Snow White. He reclined behind a behemoth of a desk, the lacquered mahogany top gleaming as he adjusted his glasses. "Did Nurse Ratched explain the evaluation we are going to perform?"

"No."

"Wonderful, then—oh, did you say no? Allow me to summarize: the Thirteenth Realm was constructed by four covens. Phaelgood which was founded by the archangel Raphael, Sciella which was founded by the archangel Gabriella—"

"Don't you mean Gabriel?"

"No. I mean Gabriella. You truly expect your patriarchal religion to stick to the facts? Moving on, Micompas was founded by the archangel Michael, and Freestar was founded by the notorious Lucifer Morningstar. Each coven has a specific philosophy, principles, and qualities valued over others. So now we'll have a chat to determine which one your psychological profile is best suited for."

"So you're like the doctor version of the sorting hat?"

"I beg your pardon?"

"It's from—"

"I know what it's from. I don't appreciate the insinuation that I read those infantilized books, much less base my life philosophy on them. I am a scholar of magic, an expert on the minds of its chosen vessels. Show some respect, baby witch. Now then, each coven has a mantra of sorts. Phaelgood believes—"

"Should I be taking notes?" I said with a sarcastic giggle.

The look Dr. Verity gave me could've chilled asphalt in July. "You've already wasted too much of my time playing around with Montgomery. Let me get through this questionnaire, or I'll recommend that you're unfit to continue. Do you understand?"

I bit the mess out of my tongue and nodded. Too much was on the line.

"Phaelgood believes if it feels good, it is good. They value pleasure. Sciella believes the good of all comes above the good of anyone. They value community. Micompas believes those ordained by the gods should rule without question. They value obedience. Freestar believes each individual should aspire to be their own god. They value freedom. Any questions?"

I glanced at my watch and shook my head.

"Splendid. Now, let's get to the meat of it. What's more important: love or freedom?"

"Well, freedom, of course. But if someone really loves you—"

"Save it. I don't need love advice from someone no one loves." Dr. Verity snorted. "Moving on, which do you prefer: pain now or pain later?"

"Umm... I guess pain now..."

"Clever girl. The anticipation of pain is worse than the pain itself. Next: science or faith?"

"Science," I answered confidently.

Dr. Verity shook his head and scribbled something into his red Moleskine notebook.

"What? Did I get that one wrong?"

"There's no wrong or right. Moving on: money or friends?"

"Money. I mean, money! What's happening? Why can't I say money? FRIENDS! Why can't I say friends?"

Dr. Verity clicked on a penlight and shone it directly in my eyes. "Oh, interesting. Did Dr. Montgomery give you something to drink? Perhaps something blue?"

I drew my bottom lip into my mouth and clamped down hard.

Dr. Verity laughed. "Your facial expression can't lie either. Fascinating!" More scribbles in his stupid notebook. "Leisure or power?"

"I'm not doing this anymore."

"Oh, interesting. She can lie after all! Answer the question, Miss Colbert. A life of leisure or a life of power?"

My blood boiled. If I didn't let off some steam soon, I was going to explode. "Power. How many more questions until I can go to the next realm?"

Dr. Verity's eyes danced. "I admire your moxie. All right, I'll let you in on a little secret. I've narrowed my recommendation down to two. Two more questions. Then you can be on your way."

I gritted my teeth but choked out, "Fine."

"First question: are people, by and large, good? Or are most people bad?"

I suppressed my anger and feigned confusion. "I'm not sure I understand the question."

"Don't overthink it. Are most people you meet good or bad?"

I didn't want to say what I thought because I knew what he'd do with my answer. He'd use my prognosis, that most people were indeed bad, to prove that I was bad. Well, I wasn't falling for it. I crossed my legs in the opposite direction. "I'd like a different question."

Dr. Verity laughed. "Answer the question, and we can move on: are people generally good or bad?"

"Good," I said, as surprised as he was to hear the word come out of my mouth.

"Interesting. Very interesting," Dr. Verity said, as though his science experiment had taken on a life of its own. "You'll fit in quite nicely if you survive the rest of the realms."

To be fair, I was surprised, too. I thought I didn't trust anyone because most people were bad. But maybe the truth was more complicated than that. Maybe *I* was a bad person. Maybe I didn't want to let anyone close enough to find out. They couldn't reject me if I rejected them first.

"Final question: what's more important, action or intent?"

"Action, of course. You can intend to do something good but not do anything. Action is the only thing that really matters."

"Then would you conclude that a *good* action done with *ill* intent is superior to a bad action done by good intent?"

"Nice try, but you're out of questions."

"So I am," Dr. Verity agreed. "Well then, all that's left is your prescription." He retrieved a plastic orange cylinder from his desk and twisted off the cap. He shook out a black pill with white spots, like a reverse Dalmatian, into his palm.

I shook my head. "That wasn't part of the deal. You said I could go if I answered two more questions. I'm not taking that."

Dr. Verity scowled at me. "Sometimes the course of treatment must be corrected when new symptoms arise."

"What the hell does that mean?"

"It means you'll take your medicine, or you'll be escorted out with the rest of the losers," Dr. Verity said, extending his palm toward me. "Your choice."

I didn't want to take the stupid pill. But damn was I parched. "I can't swallow it dry. Could I have a glass of water?"

"Of course, how rude of me not to offer," Dr. Verity said. He turned to a cabinet behind him and produced a tall, darkly tinted glass. He poured water from a matching decanter on his desk. Had it been there all along? I rubbed my eyes. What else was hiding in plain sight?

I gulped down the water, not registering that it tasted *off* until my tongue tingled. My limbs grew heavy, and slowly my whole body fell asleep. I melted into the chaise, but my mind stayed present. My eyes were wide open as Dr. Verity hovered over me.

"Patient prefers *liquid* medication to pill form." He closed his joke with a wicked laugh.

I tried to speak, to ask him what he was going to do to me —to plead with him not to, whatever it was. But my tongue was as paralyzed as the rest of me.

"This is for your own good, Lisette. Sometimes you have to re-break a bone so that it sets properly. When we finish with you, you'll be stronger than you were before we broke you."

My mind tapped out. I didn't blame it. Nothing like being poisoned by a dude standing over you giving a Bond villain speech to make you welcome unconsciousness.

29

THE FLOOR IS LAVA

Sweat dripped from my forehead down the side of my nose. It tickled as it slid down the small strip of flesh above my chapped lips. Maybe this was what woke me up. Or maybe it was the oppressive heat, worse than the muggiest August afternoon. Like being trapped inside a sauna. It reminded me of the first time Alison and her little lackeys messed with me. As a demented prank, those psychotic prep-school princesses had pushed me, fully clothed, into the locker room showers with the hot water turned all the way up. Thank God I had enough sense to pull my sweater over my face; otherwise, I would've been scalded. At first, I thought I was having a nightmare about that day, because the memory resurfaced so clearly, I could feel the steam.

Without opening my eyes, I fanned myself. I pushed the air toward my sweaty face like it could push those pesky images out of my mind. The borrowed, baggy school uniform I had to wear when mine got drenched. The humiliation of walking around with wet hair the rest of the day. But I had to let it go, couldn't waste energy being angry about it now. I needed to focus on how to get out of here, wherever *here* was.

I sat up slowly, taking in my surroundings. The ceilings in this realm were much higher than in any of the others, and though the grey steel beams were masked by shadows, I got the feeling something up there was watching me.

Much to my relief, three other people—two men and one woman—started waking up around me, rubbing their eyes and gawking. I had been going through this nightmare-scape alone for long enough. It would be nice to have some company.

The men got my attention first; it was Egon and Slimer. I shouldn't have been surprised to see them, especially Egon, who seemed cool and collected. His friend, however, had long since come unglued. Slimer's green face paint had worn down into splotches smaller than the sweat beading on his brow.

It took me a moment to realize the woman on the platform across from me was Kennedy. She looked worse than the last time I'd seen her; her face was now caked with dirt and blood. I imagined I didn't look so hot myself. Except I was *so hot*, I felt like I was on fire. I tried to call out to Kennedy, desperate to ask her about Hal. Was he really a zombie? Would she even know? But a screech of static from the speakers overhead drowned me out.

An ominous voice announced, "You are now inside the eleventh realm. We call it 'Mount St. Lucifer.' You can likely already *feel* why!" The voice cackled, which felt like overkill.

Enough with the theatrics, I wanted to scream.

"Use whatever you can to move through this bubbling, boiling realm," the disembodied voice said. "If your footing feels uncertain, say 'wings of fire' as fast as you can. Once you've fallen, there's only so much we can do to treat the burns."

I knew better than to look down. Like I knew better than to sign that waiver without reading it. But knowing you shouldn't do something and actually acting on that knowledge are two entirely different things.

I looked down. My platform was about the size of a pallet, and it didn't feel like it would hold me for long. The lava beneath me flowed, an ocean of red so wide it made the muddy river in the jungle where the anaconda hunted look like a trickle. It rushed by at a speed so fantastic that the volcanic rocks and stray hunks of sandstone floating by shifted and spun.

It reminded me of the level in the Aladdin video game where he has to escape from the Cave of Wonders. But I wouldn't get a second shot at this. And I didn't have a magic carpet.

I watched, and I waited to see how the others would progress through this apocalyptic obstacle course. Slimer, being the heaviest, started to sink first.

"Get going, man!" Egon snapped at him.

"Where?" Slimer spat back hoarsely.

"Anywhere!" Egon demonstrated by leaping to a sizable stone. It dipped under his weight, and he had no choice but to dart forward. His second jump took him to a sturdier volcanic rock.

I couldn't watch him forever. My own platform had already begun to collapse. Instinct took over, propelling me into the unknown. Before I could get comfortable, my perch would become perilous, forcing me onward.

From studying Slimer and Egon, I noticed the pyramid-shaped rocks sunk more slowly, affording me extra time to survey the course. But those were the hardest to balance on, requiring arm strength I didn't have. These men had another advantage over me—each other. Whenever one started to slip, the other stayed nearby, reaching out and offering assistance.

I missed Xavier. Why hadn't I fought for him to stay? Why couldn't I swallow my pride and admit I needed help? Though I knew I couldn't afford distractions, part of me looked back, searching for Kennedy. So many big questions burned inside of me, questions I thought she could answer. But none of them were bigger than what burned beneath me.

As I followed the rocks deeper into the realm, the lava flowed just as fast and furious, but the rocks became fewer and

farther between. Egon and Slimer remained ahead of me,
though Slimer was running out of steam.

"Dude, I can't do this anymore," Slimer whined. "Go on
without me."

"No!" Egon snapped. "You can do this. We're almost
there."

"I mean it, man, I'm slipping," Slimer said.

But Egon kept barking orders as a spray of lava erupted
next to his friend. Startled, Slimer raised his hands to protect
his face. By the time his hands reached for the next rock,
fingers clawing, desperate, it was too late. He'd lost his footing.
The lava seemed to rise up, eager to receive him. His scream
as he fell was short and not nearly as terrifying as his final
gurgling cry.

I shook my head, but his death rattle wouldn't fall out of
my ears. Was Slimer dead? I was losing my tenuous grip on
reality, trying to explain it, unable to, spiraling. My body went
on strike, refusing to move until my mind supplied an
adequate explanation for this madness.

Then I heard a meek voice over my shoulder. "Hey,
Lisette? Is that you?"

"Hey, Kennedy!" I tried to sound cheerful. "Fancy seeing
you here."

Kennedy jumped onto the rock across from me, as close as
she could get. "Listen," she croaked out. "I don't think I have
much time left—"

"Did you ever find Tucker?" I interrupted her.

Kennedy huffed. "No, but I'm not sure he could help me
now, anyway. Maybe it's too late for me."

"No! Don't say that!"

"I'm hot, and I'm tired. I can't... I can't hold on much
longer. But I need to tell you I'm sorry. Sorry for dragging you
into this—"

"You... you didn't drag me—"

"I did!" Kennedy wailed. "Listen. Something is *wrong* with

Tucker. I don't know what it is, but you have to stay away from him. Promise me?"

I frowned. I didn't understand why she cared if I was friends with him. I wasn't anywhere near as pretty as Kennedy. I wasn't a threat. I scoffed at her and hurried to the next rock.

But Kennedy chased me. Her voice cracked as if she were too dehydrated to cry. "Tucker made me *lie* to lead people here—people like you. The stuff about the guy I knew who won? I lied. He told me what to say, and I said it. And then once I entered, I *lost* him—and Hal too! Do you know what happened to Hal? I saw him… in the graveyard realm… he was…"

She didn't have to say it. I knew what he'd become, but I didn't want to admit it. I slowed down enough so I could still hear her. I had my own questions that needed answers. "How do you know it was Tucker who led us here? What if *Hal* worked here, and that's why—"

"Because I've known Hal since we were kids. I met Tucker six months ago. And things with him were weird, Lisette. You have to believe me. I didn't want to admit it because I loved him, but things were weird."

"Weird how?"

"He never let me in his apartment. Never introduced me to his grandma, to anyone. Avoided the questions I asked about his past. If you don't believe me, ask him. Ask him why he won't let anyone in. Do what I was too love-drunk to!"

I stayed on my stone too late, contemplating this. By the time I realized I needed to move, I had to make an artless jump with an even uglier landing. I hit my chin first, then my nose. My poor purple nose would never heal. I would be hideous forever.

Kennedy followed me. Had to admire her tenacity. "Are you okay?" She put a hand out to steady me, and the gesture made my heart ache.

"Fine," I lied. "Let's talk about something else. I need this money bad. How about you?"

Kennedy offered something like a shrug, both hands clinging to the rock. "I thought I did. Now I just want to get out alive."

I didn't want to be alone anymore. Maybe she was lying about Tucker, but I still felt I could trust her to help me beat the realm. "We can work together. You go left, I'll go right. If we need to cross over into the center, we'll warn each other so we don't both get taken out. Okay?"

"Okay," Kennedy croaked. "I'll hang on for as long as I can."

Though it slowed my trajectory to watch Kennedy, I couldn't give up on her. It offered a wider avenue for the molten air to drift up and into my raw throat, but I gave her words of encouragement. "Stay with me. You can do this!"

The end of the realm—a pair of black doors with intricately carved silver filigree—slowly slipped into view. Gray stone stairs, half-submerged by lava, rose toward the doors. I looked to my right, hoping to steal a second to celebrate. But Kennedy did not appear in any mood to join me.

"Hey, you doing okay over there?" I called out.

"No," Kennedy said softly. "I wanna say the safe word. I'm so hot. I'm so sweaty—"

"We're almost there!"

"Hal started to say the safe word," Kennedy told me, her words a bucket of ice-water. "But they bit him, anyway. Maybe—maybe he said it too late."

"Kennedy, no. You can do this. Come on!"

"My hands are so sweaty, so slippery, I—"

I didn't accept right away that Kennedy was falling. I needed her to finish the realm with me. I needed it so badly I couldn't see anything threatening the possibility. My brain refused to process it. I told myself she only *looked* like she was falling.

That was the moment I learned telling yourself something didn't make it true.

By the time I moved toward her, desperate to save her, it was too late. My hand shot out, fingertips grazing her sweat-soaked skin, but I couldn't get a grip on her. My eyes swelled up with terror and tears as I watched her plummet toward certain death.

"Wings of fire!" Kennedy screamed.

Four gigantic birds with wings as black as shadows swooped down, moving in a synchronized blur so fast I could hardly see their individual features. They plucked Kennedy up right before she fell into the river of no return. I couldn't see her face as they whisked her away, but I hoped she was okay. I hoped she was proud of herself for how far she had come. I tried not to add the impossible birds to the unsolvable puzzle of this place.

The rock I was clinging to tilted violently to the right, knocking me off balance. I barely steadied myself before it began to sink. My eyes darted around wildly, searching for a new haven. I sprung onto another stone, but it dipped down so fast I couldn't catch my breath.

Not thinking, just reacting, I leaped to the next and the next until one rock remained between me and the door. One leap. Two leaps. And I was out. Every inch of my body, especially my overworked lungs, felt charred. I didn't save Kennedy, but I didn't turn my back on her either. It was as though part of me did fall into the lava, part of my cold exterior had melted away, and I didn't want it back.

I checked my watch. 2:30. Thirty minutes left before I ran out of time. Two more realms and I'd be out of the haunted house. Just two more, and I'd be rich. I could do this. I had to. For Kennedy. When I saw her again, I would tell her how grateful I was that she held on as long as she did. I didn't think about what I would do if I saw Tucker.

Behind the black, stone doors stretched a short corridor. I wandered down the dimly lit path until I reached the doors to a single elevator. Before I could work up the courage to press a button, the number twelve lit up on its own.

As the elevator car climbed up, my stomach lurched with it. It grumbled, reminding me I hadn't eaten all day. On the plus side, if I threw up, all I had to lose was bile. My skin stung as if sunburnt. I bent over, head dangling between my legs, taking deep breaths to snuff out the fire in my lungs.

The elevator screeched to a stop. A deep, foreboding *ding-dong* sounded, and the doors slid open. The guard of the twelfth realm—a farmer with an ax buried in his head—perched like a redneck king atop a stack of hay bales, legs splayed wide in his overalls. He spat brown liquid into a red Solo cup. "Never seen someone who looked like you make it this far."

A weak smile made a play for my lips, but it didn't stick. It was a back-handed compliment. A dig at the strength of my gender. I wished Kennedy was with me. She would've slapped him silly.

The *ding-dong* of another elevator arriving behind me made me jump. When I saw who tumbled out, I couldn't help but gasp his name. "Tucker."

He swaggered over, hardly looking worse for wear, with his plastic machine gun tucked against his chest. Not a single thread of his mobster suit seemed disturbed. It was almost as if he'd been waiting somewhere this whole time instead of dodging death like the rest of us.

"Look who it is, my favorite neighbor," Tucker said, wrapping me in a big hug. "You doin' okay, Lisette?"

"As well as can be expected," I muttered. I tried not to be too obvious as I drank in his musk—sandalwood, smoke, and sugar—like roasting s'mores at a beach bonfire.

"He with you?" the farmer inquired.

I started to shake my head, but Tucker cut me off. "I am now. So what's up with this realm? Let's get this shit show on the road."

As the farmer shook his head, blood dripped down the blade of the ax and splattered his bare feet. "You must go through the last two realms of Hell alone."

My jaw dropped. "But that's not fair!"

He climbed down from his hillbilly throne to leer at me. "We make the rules. If you don't like 'em, leave. Say the word 'slaughter', and the game will end right now."

Tucker sidled up to me, close enough for me to catch a whiff of beer on his breath. Beer? Where did he get beer in here?

"Don't worry," Tucker whispered. "I'll go in first and wait for you. You don't have to go it alone anymore."

"Thanks," I whispered back, remembering Kennedy's warning. Had Tucker really lured me here? He *was* the one who invited me...

"This isn't social hour," the farmer snapped. "One of you needs to go. And only one."

My lust-dizzy brain spun in circles. I couldn't trust myself, much less Tucker. Still, I flashed him a coy smile. "You go ahead. See you on the other side?"

He blew me a kiss. "I'll take you to a fancy dinner with my winnings."

My cheeks flushed, and my heart fluttered. He was flirting with me. But guilt swiftly followed my elation. Kennedy didn't deserve this. To be left behind while he pressed on alone. To be outside, worried about him, while he acted like she didn't exist. No wonder she had tried to warn me about him.

The farmer grunted as he pulled the shiny silver door to the twelfth realm open. As he stepped aside, delicious freezing air flowed past him. I drank it up, much to the relief of my scorched lungs. Tucker waved bye, but I ignored him. Kennedy seemed cool. I wasn't going to do her dirty, even if he would.

I retreated into my own world. Focused on my breathing the way Miss Fenty taught me, slowly inhaling and exhaling as I imagined myself ten thousand dollars richer. Nirvana hovered near the forefront of my mind, when a series of guttural screams shattered my concentration. Someone was always screaming in this godforsaken place. That was nothing new. But these struck me differently. They might belong to someone I cared about, warning or not.

In my head, I ticked off all the people I had left behind or allowed to die—Mario in the dollhouse, Oops Britney with the snake. Her friend, Erika, on the dance floor and then Jillian shortly after that. I shook my head, willing their names and faces to fall out. But then I heard the screams of the faceless stranger I heard being devoured by the horde of zombies. Weird how I had the least connection to him—never saw his face as I climbed from the casket and ran for the fence—and yet his suffering hit me the hardest. Maybe because when I thought about him, I had to admit his misfortune saved me. Would Tucker's sacrifice create the same sensation—unsteadying waves of guilt crashing into my wobbly knees?

After the screaming finally stopped, the farmer flashed me a sociopathic grin. I flinched at his tobacco-stained teeth.

"Your turn." He opened the door.

A dark premonition danced into my mind, warning me of the mortal peril waiting for me. I opened my mouth to tell him I was done—they could shove the ten grand up their spooky asses—but then I remembered all I'd been through to get here. I remembered the defeated look on Ruelle's face when I asked about the eviction notice plastered to our front door. I was so close. I couldn't give up now.

The cold air whooshed over me, but it didn't offer refreshment this time. It felt like being embraced by a ghost. Like the chilling grip of death.

"How are you gonna feel with all that money in your hand?" I whispered to myself. "You can do this. Pretend you're playing a video game and walk through the door."

My hands shook as I pantomimed moving a joystick forward. My avatar stepped through the door, and I tried not to think about the fact that I had no extra lives.

A sweet, burning smell permeated the air. Smoke filled my nostrils and cast an unearthly bluish-black fog over the room. I rubbed at my watery eyes, smearing the remnants of my mascara down the side of my face. But I didn't care anymore. I'd come too far to care.

"You're delirious. It's colored lights. Dr. Verity gave you something that's making you hallucinate," I said aloud. "It's like Kennedy said; it's all one big mirage."

Though it bled through the margins of my mind, I refused to acknowledge what happened before I met Verity: the green smoke snakes Dr. Montgomery made appear from nowhere. Everything had to have an explanation; it had to make sense. I had to logic my way through to hold on to the notion that I could logic my way out.

I didn't have long to ponder the eerie lighting before my attention was diverted to two rows of bodies swaying from meat hooks on either side of the narrow path.

"They're not real," my voice warbled. I rubbed my arms to ward off the chill. "They're dummies. Extremely lifelike dummies."

But it didn't matter what lies I spoke aloud. Perspiration popped at my brow, the sour smell of unholy fear. Those were people. Victims of the haunted house. I tried not to look at them. I couldn't see them and hold on to my sanity at the same time. The safe word raced down to the tip of my tongue. I shut my mouth and swallowed. I swallowed again and again until I had no spit left to sound out the word.

Trembling from the tips of my toes to the top of my head, I fixed my blurry eyes straight ahead. Any second, someone might spring out from a smokey shadow. One of the bodies could climb down and come after me. All I could do was walk deeper into the trap.

The farther I walked, the thicker the blue-black smoke swirled around me. A groan of sheer agony cut the silence and made goosebumps ripple across my arms. I stiffened in antici-pation of an attack but had no choice but to keep walking toward the unnerving sounds. As the groans grew louder, I became more certain it was Tucker. It felt like hearing the voice of a musician you know spilling from a stereo, but you can't name the song. Finally, I found Tucker, strung up on one of the meat hooks.

Between the smoke and the way his ankles were bound with thick rope, I couldn't tell whether the hook pierced his flesh or if he just was tied to it—and he wasn't talking.

Two pieces of silver duct tape formed an "x" across Tuck-er's mouth. His eyes bulged when he saw me. He flopped around, trying in vain to wriggle free. He reminded me of a fish, not a trophy fish, more like a minnow used for bait.

Kennedy's warning played in my mind as clear as a recording. Tucker was not to be trusted. He'd brought us all here with lies. He wasn't on our side.

Still, my mind argued with my heart. I had left so many others to their fates, and I regretted it, I really did. But how could I be sorry if I didn't help him? What good was confession without penance, without a promise not to commit the same sin?

"I don't know what to do," I said to Tucker. "I don't want to leave you here, but I'm not strong enough to get you down."

His eyes widened, and he groaned in response.

"Oh, right." I ripped the duct tape off his mouth, causing him to wince.

Then he began to scream, "Slaughter! Slaughter!"

I scowled. Though I'd considered the possibility of his betrayal, it still hurt like hell. "You ungrateful little…"

My anger softened as I realized he was yelling the safe word. Kennedy must've been wrong. He wasn't part of the madness; he just wanted to get out. He twisted around frantically, still screaming.

I wanted to look away, but my head refused to turn. My eyes bulged in disbelief. From this new angle, I could see the hook had impaled both of his feet; blood trickled down his calves. "What in God's name did they do to you?"

His lips trembled, his eyes focused on something behind me.

"Look out!" Tucker shouted.

The silver gleam of a butcher's knife sliced through the air, inches from my face. I ducked, but the black hoof wielding the weapon clipped the top of my head. That was gonna leave a bruise. I tried to run but slipped and fell to my knees. The slick floor smelled like rusty pennies.

A stocky pigheaded figure wearing a filthy apron that read *Kill the Cook* towered over me. The crusty blood baked into his apron was unnerving enough, but I couldn't take my eyes off the cleaver wedged between his black hooves.

"You really thought we were gonna let you live?" the pig butcher squealed with manic laughter. He brought the knife down in a hacking motion. I spun away, blocking my face with my forearm. He nicked me with the tip of the knife.

I don't know why I thought it wouldn't hurt. The clowns' mallets gave Kennedy a real bruise. The zombies really bit Hal. The butcher knife delivered a real blow. I could *feel* the metal clanging against my bone in the back of my teeth.

I should have read the damn waiver! Xavier was right, and I didn't listen!

My blood pulsed through my veins at a breakneck speed. I had no time to consider the severity of my injury. Adrenaline shot through my system to soften the sting. It pushed me to react. I rolled out of the way of a third assault, but the pain from the first two pulsed to the hollows of my bones. I was afraid to look, afraid to find confirmation he had cut me too deep to heal on its own. At least, as far as I could tell, he hadn't struck any major arteries.

Thinking fast, I cradled my injured arm against my chest and rolled deeper into the realm. I prayed he wouldn't be able to get down this low and still hold the knife with his hooves.

Pig Butcher tapped his foot. Though I could hardly see through the smoke, it appeared to be a hoof like those on his hands. What was he waiting for? Maybe he wasn't waiting for *something*, but *someone*. No, that couldn't be it. He must have thought I would stand up and run. Fat chance, Pig. As long as I stayed down, I thought I could make it through.

With my bad arm tucked tight to my chest, I alternated between crawling and rolling through the realm. Crawling hurt less with my injury, but rolling was faster.

The further I progressed, the thicker the smoke grew. As

my sight diminished, my other senses sharpened. The over-powering aroma of barbecue made my mouth water, a knee-jerk response. Once my mind caught up, it shut that nonsense down, reminding me that whatever was cooking wasn't cow. At last, the hazy frame of a large silver door drifted into view. The exit. I rose slowly on shaky legs. A buzzing sound—like a bug zapper—made me snap my head around. A slim creature in a cow costume with a chef's hat and apron that read *Eat More Human* stepped in front of me.

Ridiculous as she was, my vision tunneled to what was behind her—a barbecue grill lined with a human-sized ribcage and a row of hastily severed hands. I tried to peel my eyes away, because I knew I needed to watch her, to watch the electric cattle prod she held.

As I gripped my injured arm close, a fact that had served me well before surfaced: predators sometimes lose interest if you don't act like prey.

"I'm done playing defense," I snarled. I pulled one of my fake guns out of its holster and leveled it at the cow. "Back up, heifer, or I'll blow a hole through your head."

The cow chef's voice was surprisingly feminine. "That's not real."

"It's as real as the knife your pig friend cut me with." I pretended to take the safety off my gun. *Thank you, persnickety drama teacher.*

"Now back up!" I shouted. "Or Lord help me, I'll mow you down where you stand."

Cow Chef paused for a moment and cocked her head. The rubber mask inched up, exposing her creamy collarbone. "You're bluffing." She stepped forward, the cattle prod buzzing in her hand. "Your move, little girl."

I stood my ground and snarled, "You shouldn't have taken any chances with me, you dumb cow. I'm from New Orleans." I reared back to gain momentum, then kicked Cow Chef in her knee with all my might.

With a shocked yelp, she doubled over. She clutched her knee and howled.

"Who's the little girl now, cow?" I shouted as I brought the butt of the gun down into the back of her head, over and over, until she finally dropped the cattle prod to shield herself.

I dashed past her, panting. As I strained against the weight of the exit door, Cow Chef screamed at my back, "You'll never finish the final realm! No one does!"

Panic made a play for the front of my mind, but I shoved it to the ground like a defensive linebacker. No, I was not going to let her win the war, not after I had already defeated her in battle. What would anyone in her position—desperate and humiliated—say? Something cliché and obvious, which was what she did. That didn't make it true.

31

SALT
NOT OF
THE
EARTH

I was out of the twelfth realm, but not out of the metaphorical woods. Its figurative trees still pressed in around me, restricting my movements. My chest felt tight, as if constricted by an invisible corset. But whatever happened next, it wouldn't be happening for long. Soon, I would be free. Free and rich.

In the middle of this pleasant thought, I came face-to-face with a horrible sight—an oddly proportioned, bloody creature so sinister the sight of it made me sputter. Its face was mostly shades of red that darkened to purple around the center above its nostrils. Wild black hair, speckled rusty-red like the floor of the slaughterhouse, stuck out at odd angles. It matched my frantic breathing, as if mocking me.

Then I realized it wasn't a monster. It was my reflection, distorted by a funhouse mirror. It was me. I was the monster. A cryptic hand-drawn sign hung over the bright red frame: *You Are Here. You Look Like This. Get Out While You Can.*

I winced as I held my injured arm in front of me, turning it in the mirror to inspect it. My eyes flitted across my watch— 2:45! I was almost out of time!

Worse, the adrenaline had worn off, and my arm hurt so spectacularly I could hardly stand it. I had to keep it elevated to stop the steady flow of blood. Blood. I was covered in blood. How much of it was mine, and how much did I pick up rolling around on that disgusting floor?

Bone! Was that bone? It certainly looked like it, the thinnest gleam of white surrounded by blood, blood, blood. I felt woozy, not far off from fainting.

"Welcome," a thunderous voice startled me, "to the thirteenth realm of Hell!"

I turned to face the final gatekeeper. He reclined on his throne of skulls and stroked his black beard, tugging the ends into a point that touched the middle of his bare chest. Every detail of his Satan costume had been carefully considered, from his burning red eyes to his jagged yellow fingernails that curved claw-like around a gleaming golden pitchfork. He wore a deep emerald cloak and so many rings they were doubled and tripled on each long finger. And he had an aura, something no makeup kit could create, evil but alluring all the same. If he entered a costume contest, his win would be unanimous. But I didn't appreciate any of it. "Cut the crap, Satan. Pig Boy back there sliced my arm wide open. I should sue— shut this whole freak show down."

The smile on Satan's face faded. "That's not supposed to happen. Let me see it."

I knew I shouldn't trust him. Yet I couldn't stop walking toward him. Something in his voice beckoned, drew me in like metal to a magnet.

Satan reached behind his throne and produced a classic white first-aid kit. The irony of its red cross almost made me laugh. He popped it open and, after a little fumbling due to his cumbersome claws, he soaked a few cotton balls in alcohol. "Hold out your arm, please."

I could no longer contain my amusement. It escaped in raspy chuckles as he tenderly cleaned my wound. "Satan saying please, now I've literally heard everything."

He smiled at me. "It's not so bad."

"Not so bad? Are you serious! I saw bone!"

Satan shook his head. "You were imagining things. It's

pretty long, but not deep enough for stitches. Have a look for yourself."

When I pulled my arm back, the cut had all but disappeared. Even as I stared at it in wonder, it shrunk before my eyes. "You... you fixed it somehow. That dude cut me with a cleaver! It was huge! How did you..."

"Your mind plays tricks on you in here. That's kind of the idea." Satan winked at me.

I thought back to what Kennedy said while we were getting high in her van. This was all a hallucination. Somehow, as comforting as that notion may have been, I didn't buy into it anymore.

"Chin up, you're fine now," Satan said. "Ready for the thirteenth realm?"

I shifted back and forth, unable to take my eyes off the cut on my arm. It had stopped shrinking, but I wasn't convinced it had been this small five minutes ago.

"Well?" Satan asked like he was bored.

"I still don't understand what happened. I swear to you, he cut me with a butcher knife! I could *see* the bone."

"The important thing is, you're fine now. 'Tis but a flesh wound. Still, it's gonna burn like hell in the final realm— because of the salt water."

"Salt water!" I screeched. I hoped he didn't know I couldn't swim. "How 'bout you give me the prize money now and I'll agree not to sue?"

His smile spread, the corners lifting to his pointed ears. "Sweet summer child, you can't sue. You signed the waiver. But I'll admit your experience has been a bit unfair. Let's tip the scales back in your favor. How about a few tips to make it through the final realm?"

I sighed. I looked at my arm again, only the tiniest red mark remaining where the wound had been. My mind flitted back to Dr. Montgomery. Had Satan taken only my pain, or some of my power, too? "Okay, fine, whatever. Get on with your spiel."

"Gladly—the thirteenth realm is something of a sensory deprivation maze. You won't be able to see your hand if you hold it out in front of your face."

"A maze! How am I supposed to make it through a maze in fifteen minutes?" I balked.

"One right choice at a time, I suppose," Satan said.

Doubt crept into my cloudy head, but I shoved it down to my empty stomach. I feigned confidence, elongating my spine and tossing my deconstructed braid over my shoulder. "What's this realm about? Is anyone gonna chase me? Cut me? Shock me?"

Satan shook his head. "You'll be alone with the terror of your own thoughts. There's no safe word, but every twenty feet or so, you'll see a small red light above, indicating the presence of an escape hatch. Open it if you want to give up, and someone will come get you."

"How do I make it through the realm?"

Satan laughed. "If I told you, it would ruin the surprise."

"Come on, man. You said you'd help me out."

"And so I shall give you three hints. One: don't go in circles. Two: conserve your energy. If you need a break, lie on your back and let the water propel you forward. Three: when you come to an obstacle that looks like a dead end—take a leap of faith."

"So I have to jump over something?"

"I've already said too much. Are you ready?"

Then I had an idea. Maybe a stupid one, but any ditch during a tornado. I gestured toward the first aid kit. "You got any Band-Aids in there?"

"Yes," Satan said uncertainly, cracking open the kit. "But they'll just come off in the water."

"Give me all the Band-Aids you have then."

Satan gave me a fistful. He didn't ask why I shoved them

in my pockets instead of covering up what remained of my battle wound. He led me to an elevator and rode with me up to the thirteenth floor.

"What is this place, anyway?" I asked.

Satan seemed delighted by my question. "What do you think it is?"

"I don't know. Maybe it's a competition to get into a coven." I watched his face, but his red eyes didn't blink. "Maybe it's some kind of trap for desperate people."

Satan looked at me, laughed, and said, "Why can't it be both?"

An elevator chime announced our arrival. The room we stepped into was so cold it made my teeth chatter. "I th-th-thought heat was supposed to ri-ri-rise."

Satan didn't reply. He twisted open a small, circular door to reveal a tunnel about half the size of a city sewer pipe. I couldn't make sense of it. Everything else I'd seen, the aggressive bats, the living dolls, seemed grounded in some kind of nightmare I'd had before. They all seemed to spring from me, and so, like a fever dream, could have been part of my imagination.

Not this. This left me completely flabbergasted. I couldn't see where the water originated, though it smelled clean, if a little salty. It was unlike anything I had ever seen before. A sour taste, like expired milk, rose at the back of my throat.

"I am not going in there." I crossed my arms over my chest and tried to rub some warmth back into my body.

"So you're done? Pity, I thought, you would at least give it a shot. You've come so far."

I craned my neck, trying to see inside without actually getting in. "How does this work? How does any of this work?"

"Magic," Satan replied. "Why don't you climb in and see for yourself?"

I stared at the water, giving myself an internal pep talk. *Come on Lis, if you stop now it'll all have been for nothing. You'll lose the apartment. Where will you live? It can't be that bad. What about that pig, though? Was that really an accident? Of course it was. He probably cut you because you put your arm up and he couldn't stop swinging in time. Anyway, you're fine now, aren't you?*

With a heavy sigh, I crawled in.

32

A
VISION
IN BLUE

Once Satan shut the door behind me, the darkness encased me like a tomb. But this was worse than the casket. The water stoked a fear inside me so primal I couldn't hope to overcome it. I couldn't swim. Maybe I didn't need to yet, but what about when I reached wherever all this water led to?

I shook my head, then allowed the tremor to go down to my shoulders, as if I could jostle my brain just right and become someone else. Someone who loved the water.

Of course, I could always open one of the hatches. I could turn around before it got to a point where I might drown. But Tucker had said the safe word, and no one had rescued him.

The tunnel was too tight to stand up in, which made crawling the quickest mode of locomotion. I scrambled along on all fours. The salt water slapped mercilessly against my elbows, stinging what remained of my cut over and over, like the steady prick of a tattoo needle. It was tiny now, the size of a paper cut, but it was still big enough to bother me. I was down to my last shred of energy, the smallest snags threatening to destroy me.

About twenty feet into the maze, the first escape hatch popped up overhead. It was so dark I would've missed it except for the tiny red light alerting me to its location. I forced myself to look away. "Don't you dare give up," I said aloud. "Better to drown than give up now."

Time slipped away as I ventured deeper and deeper into the maze. My soaked skin shriveled. My eyelids trembled, trying to close of their own volition.

"I can't give up," I reminded myself, though my voice was weak, garbled as though already underwater. "I need that money."

The tunnel stopped abruptly. No hurdle to clear, it just ended. The saltwater hit the wall and bounced back submissively. I sighed and did the same. I retraced my path to the fork where I'd chosen wrong. I used the red light to find a spot on the ceiling suitable for a Band-Aid and slapped it on. The idea had seemed brilliant when I first thought of it, but I questioned myself while putting it into action. Someone could open the escape hatch and rip the stupid Band-Aid off the second I turned the corner. I couldn't crawl any farther—my knees were numb.

"Maybe I should conserve my energy—like Satan suggested," I said to myself, yawning.

Careful not to get any water in my mouth, I rolled over onto my back. The current sped up without the resistance of my anchored body, moving me along much faster than before. I could still see the escape hatches overhead, could still stop myself from getting stuck in the same dead ends. It was almost pleasant traveling this way. Relaxing, like a lazy river, if you could ignore the whiny kids bumping into your inner tube and forget about how much piss you were soaking in.

What would happen when I got out? If I ever got out. I sighed.

"You can't think like that," I scolded myself. "You WILL get out."

I yawned again. I was so tired. My mind kept slipping like a bad transmission.

"How did they build this realm? Why haven't I seen any tunnels before?" I wondered aloud.

But it wasn't like I'd been looking for any. Hard to observe your surroundings when you're running nonstop.

My eyes fluttered shut so gradually that I barely noticed. The maze faded away, and my apartment—the exposed brick walls, the comforting smell of gumbo cooking across the hall, the dingy denim sofa that sagged so badly only the middle seat was safe—came into view.

Its familiarity soothed me like a lullaby, unlike the sharp voice of the tall stranger that had taken over Ruelle's chair. "Do you realize how stupid you are being?" He slapped his knee for emphasis, the mug on the end table beside him wobbling.

"Come now, Wolfram. I may be stubborn, but I'm not stupid." Ruelle sunk down into the center of the sofa. "Life on a ship, it's no life for a child. Trust me, I know."

"She's not a child anymore," Wolfram countered. "By our laws, she's an adult."

"*Your* laws," Ruelle corrected him. "And she isn't bound by them. She's happy here; she has friends—a future. She could be more than a witch if she stays here."

"Oh, forgive me," Wolfram said with a sarcastic sneer. "How dare I steal her away from this life of splendor." He gestured around the apartment. "Both of you deserve better. Come back to Micompas. You would be welcomed aboard the ship with open arms, both of you."

"I appreciate the offer Wolfram, I really do, but—"

"You act as if you have a choice," Wolfram growled. "I will see to it she joins her kind. If not on my ship, under our watch, then on one of the others. Surely you would prefer she remains under your care?"

"Stop pretending you care about her. It's me you want, and you can't force me to go. Now leave," my mother said, her eyes set in that familiar way of hers. She was done talking, and yet he pressed on.

"Lisette is on her own journey. Your pride prevents you from seeing that. Everything is not about you."

Ruelle gritted her teeth. "What if I agreed to go in her place?"

He perched at the edge of his seat, leaning toward her as if he might pounce. "A trade. Interesting. How do I know you would stay?"

She wilted in response. "I will stay. As long as she has the freedom of choice, I will take my place on a ship."

A vein in Wolfram's forehead pulsed. "But not my ship?"

"No, not yours."

"There is always a catch with you. Always secrets. Tell me, did you mislead me about Lisette? Are you afraid if I became close to her, I would see the truth?"

Ruelle leaped up, striking before he had the chance. She slapped him as hard as she could; I could tell by the fury on her face. But Wolfram looked more amused than hurt as she wagged her finger at him and shouted, "You will not speak to me that way in my own home!"

"All the more reason for us to get going." He pointed at the sofa where Ruelle had been sitting; a tiny spark flew out of his finger and struck it.

At first glance, I thought he had simply destroyed the sofa, but when I looked past my poor, stunned mother, I realized it was still there. It had been reduced to about one-tenth of its original size. Okay, so his finger was basically the ray-gun from Honey I Shrunk the Kids. Pretty cool. But who was this Wolfram guy? He clearly knew who I was, but Ruelle had never mentioned him.

"Please, stop!" Ruelle begged him. "I said I'd go with you —just don't destroy my home. Lisette loves it here; this place is important to her."

But Wolfram shook his head and carried on, zapping the paintings off the wall, reducing a giant canvas to a single square inch. He was cruel, ruthless even, yet I longed to earn his approval. For a split second, a childish longing rose in my heart. He might be my father. I used to think every man I met could be my father. I would assign infinite importance to the most minute actions. The streetcar driver who let me ride when I was short on fare, the trombone player that stopped his song to acknowledge my piddly offering of spare change.

How foolish I had been.

But with Wolfram, I knew it was more than that. His aqua eyes, his frame so tall he made Ruelle's chair look like doll furniture. This could be real. He could be my father. But I didn't dwell too long on that.

He pointed his finger at the rug and zapped it, too. Ruelle covered her eyes, as if unwilling to acknowledge what he was gawking at—her graffiti on the floor.

"So *this* is how you hid from me!" Wolfram bellowed.

Ruelle didn't look up. She touched her bare finger where her ring should be. I winced. Was this my fault? After all, I had stolen her ring.

"I had no choice," Ruelle said. "You weren't the only one hunting me."

"Why did you leave my ship, Merahita? At least tell me that."

She shook her head. "That's not my name anymore."

"Please tell me." The wood floors groaned beneath the weight of his heavy boots as he stepped forward and took her hands. "Whatever did I do to drive you away?"

"It wasn't you," Ruelle—or Merahita, I'd never considered she might have another name—answered him in a whisper. "It was the lifestyle. I couldn't raise a baby on a ship."

"If you were so unhappy, why not say something?"

"What difference would it have made? You know the rules —no one leaves except by way of the plank. And you never break the rules."

He dropped her hands. "What can I do to make it up to you?"

"Give me a few days to prepare. Lisette will need guidance, a plan."

"The ships leave tonight, Mera."

"A few days. Time to get some things in order."

Wolfram shook his head. "I can give you a few hours. By the time the competition ends, you must be with your kind, or I will see to it that she is."

I awoke with a smack. At first, I was so discombobulated, I forgot where I was. I pulled myself into a sitting position and rubbed my throbbing head. Slowly, my eyes adjusted to the darkness. Wonderful, I'd hit a wall. What a weird dream.

A film had formed over my eyes. I rubbed it away and began to turn around, but stopped at the sight of the faintest glimmer. A small golden knob jutted out right above the waterline. It felt cool and inviting in my palm. I started to turn it, but then paused, drawing my hand back.

Something terrible waited on the other side. As my fingers hovered above the knob, I could feel trouble nearby, like heat wafting off a hot stove. But it didn't matter. I'd come too far to turn back now. My heart leaped up into my throat, and I gulped to keep from choking. I inhaled slowly through my nose, exhaled through my mouth, then opened the door.

33

THE
BONUS
ROUND

As the door swung open, I fell back, crouched but ready to defend myself. I drew both guns and hyped myself up. "You got this, Lis. Fake it until you make it. Give 'em that real gun swagger."

But nothing greeted me on the other side of the door. The tunnel simply ended. Water slipped over the edge without a sound, as though the bottom existed in theory alone.

"Great—you put on a show for no one, as usual."

My frustrated howls echoed across the dark abyss. Then something Satan said returned to me: *take a leap of faith.*

Was this the dead end he foretold? Only one way to find out for sure. I jumped.

For several excruciating seconds, I free fell. My arms spun, clawing at the air but striking nothing. Horrifying thoughts filled my mind. What if this was a garbage chute? I might wind up in a trash compactor or an incinerator or…

Something rubbery, like a bounce house the rich kids had at their birthday parties, broke my fall. The breath I'd been holding in whooshed out. For a moment I felt relieved, like a sailor stepping out of turbulent waters onto the platform of a steady dock. But it was only a mirage of stability. Whatever surface I had slid down ended, and gravity sent me sailing through the air again.

At last, I landed face-down onto a sticky net. With a

herculean effort, I peeled my head loose and rose unsteadily on all fours. The moment my pupils adjusted to the dim lighting, a spotlight struck me hard across the face.

My eyes squinched up. My hearing sharpened. From somewhere below I caught the rumblings of conversation, but no distinguishable words. The spotlight panned a few inches in front of me. I looked down, searching for the source of the voices, but saw nothing below me but an Olympic-sized swimming pool—three times bigger than the one at school—full of murky water.

I gulped. Why hadn't I sucked up my pride long enough to let Xavier teach me to swim? I'd given up after the first lesson like a fragile little egg baby.

"Okay, enough," I said to myself. "Regret won't save you now. Come on, think. There's gotta be a way down that doesn't involve diving to your death."

Though speaking aloud strengthened my resolve to find an alternative route, before I could put that plan into action, a more pressing problem emerged. An unusual hiss sounded over my shoulder.

A second spotlight clicked on, moving across the net until it landed on the biggest spider I had ever seen, including in nature documentaries. My heart boomed like an 808 drum.

"Holy tamales... that thing is the size of... a St. Bernard!" I sputtered.

The Cujo-spider stared back with eight hungry eyes—two large round ones in the middle as big as my own, surrounded by three smaller eyes on each side.

For the first time all night, I screamed like my life depended on it. No safe word sprang to mind. It was me against the spider. Eight legs against two.

Desperation propelled my eyes down to the pool. But unfortunately, looking harder didn't make a float appear. Right then, I would've settled for a moldy old pool noodle.

I backpedaled away from the spider until mere inches of

web remained between me and falling into the pool. I couldn't tell how high up I was—ten, maybe twelve feet. Even if I managed to jump to the perimeter of the pool, I risked bashing my head open on the concrete.

My eyes widened with hope at a thin white sliver jutting out over the deep end of the pool. It was a diving board—an island in the middle of that murderous sea. Could I reach it? If I tried and missed, I'd land in the deep end.

"Okay, then. Don't miss," I told myself.

The spider raised two spindly legs and shot a pair of silky snares straight at my face. I ducked. The webbing landed in my hair, covering both of my ears. Tiny, gooey creatures seemed to scuttle in through my ears, worming their way toward my brain.

My revolted scream reverberated through the expansive space as I swatted away the invisible attackers. I tore at the web, but it didn't break. It expanded and stretched, sticking to my hands with incredible strength despite its elasticity.

"Are you serious right now?" I said to myself. "How strong is this spider web? This is ridiculous!"

My fingers were still entangled when the spider fired again. I raised my hands to block my face. Bad idea. The webbing wrapped around my wrists like a lasso, and the spider yanked me forward. It opened its mouth, baring fangs as long as my forearms.

I fell on my knees. With all my might, I threw my body backward. Sweat streamed down my forehead and stung my eyes. I squeezed them shut as I inched blindly to the edge of the web. My feet dangled in the air, helplessly kicking and wriggling. I forced my burning eyes open, searching for a less risky way down, but only two options remained: I could stay and fight the king of all arachnids, or I could take my chances with the water.

At least the water was less likely to eat me. With each push and pull, I could see the webbing growing thinner and thinner until finally it snapped.

This is it, I thought as I plummeted to my fate. *This is how I die. I drown to avoid being sucked dry by a spider.*

My entire body tensed. I squeezed my eyes and mouth shut, covered my ears, and waited for the pool to swallow me up.

The water wasn't nearly as forgiving as I thought it would be. In fact, it was rock hard and oddly springy. I opened my eyes slowly, surprised to find that I wasn't in the water. I made it! I was on the diving board!

I ripped at the webbing binding my wrists. It fell away easily, like a regular old spider web, as though the source of its strength was the spider itself.

When I looked down at my trembling legs, I saw her right away—Bebe. Right there between my feet. Had someone thrown her up here? Used her to guide me to the diving board? Was Dr. Montgomery responsible, somehow knowing the exact moment to save me?

More lights flicked on, exposing rows of metal bleachers positioned around the perimeter of the room. I gawked slack-jawed at the spectators huddled together without a single space between them. Most wore costumes, some characters I recognized from the various realms.

Pig Butcher lifted a hoof in the air in either a wave or a one-finger salute. Dr. Verity jotted something down in his red Moleskine notebook. I looked for Desmond, but I didn't see him. Maybe he was there, but I didn't recognize him. He could have been sitting with the people in the front row wearing cloaks.

Everyone in the front row was adorned in a heavy cloak—green, blue, red, and silver—all grouped together according to their color. Hoods shrouded their faces and heavy robes obscured their figures to the point that I couldn't distinguish between males and females.

Perhaps more peculiar, most of them had various animals on their laps—cats, lizards, rats, and a few dogs posed like statues beside their masters. Crows, bats, and owls perched on shoulders or glided around, scouting out the space.

"Congratulations, competitor!" a deep voice boomed overhead. I looked up and spotted several speakers attached to the ceiling. The voice bled from the speakers, "You have completed the thirteenth realm of Hell!"

The crowd went wild, like their team had won the super bowl. Their stomping shook the bleachers. Some of them threw roses as if I were an actress after a successful show. And yet, they all stared at me so expectantly, as if anticipating an encore.

I bent down, picked up a rose that had fallen by my boots, and gave them a bashful little wave. They seemed into it. Clapping, cheering. Under the pretense of collecting the roses, I scooped up my bear and tucked her into the waistband of my shorts. I smoothed down my tank top, praying no one noticed.

I scanned the crowd for Dr. Montgomery—hoping to at least give him a smile of gratitude—but didn't see him. I would've known his mask anywhere. But even as my memories of the night of the ritual returned to me—the strange certainty I'd witnessed magic—his face still eluded me. Maybe he'd finally removed his mask and blended into the mob.

"Annnnd now!" the deep voice continued, "Welcome—to the BONUS ROUND!"

"Bonus round?" I repeated dumbly.

"That's right, the BONUS ROUND! Where our brave competitor can DOUBLE or TRIPLE her winnings!"

More applause followed, enough to drown out the hushed conversations between various audience members. Their lips moved and their eyes burned holes in me. What were they saying? I pricked my ears but couldn't catch a single word.

"Competitor," the booming voice addressed me, "if you

would please direct your attention to the pool, the home of a TERRIFYING, BLOOD-THIRSTY, MONSTER!"

A spotlight landed on the murky pool. Two yellow bulbous eyes broke the surface, blinking as they adjusted to the light. I could make out snippets of dark green scales through the algae. The creature meandered around the deep end of the pool, its fat tail slicing through the water like a boat propeller.

"Holy tamales, that alligator looks prehistoric!" I said with a sick reverence.

I reasoned that perhaps he was an old, slow alligator. Nothing that big could be very fast. He sure was moving slow when I first saw him, but maybe he was conserving energy.

"Enter the pool from the diving board and make it allll the way across to DOUBLE your winnings!" the announcer explained. "BUT WAIT, THERE'S MORE!"

Heavy metal chains clanged into action above me. A displaced bat screeched and swooped down to find a new roost. The bottom of a large metal cage crept into my view. When it stopped, it dangled above the center of the pool.

"Use the lever to your left to lower your bait into the water and buy yourself time to cross," the announcer said. "If your bait is STILL BREATHING when you exit the pool, then you, my lucky friend, have TRIPLED YOUR WINNINGS!"

The crowd roared, their screams tinged with violence and jubilation, like drunks who had not decided which raw emotions to unbridle.

I peered inside the cage. A young girl no more than six or seven years old shivered inside a sleeveless dress. The heavy chains around her neck caused her little head to dip down so that her dark wavy hair grazed her bony shoulders. Her huge blue eyes bulged with terror. She looked eerily like I had around that same age.

What was all of this? Could I walk away without playing? I bit my lip so hard I tasted the metallic tang of blood. A demon perched on my shoulder, reminding me of the money, but I swatted it away before an angel showed up to help.

No way was I doing this. I couldn't sacrifice a child. And I couldn't swim across a pool. I couldn't swim at all. Still—triple my winnings. That was thirty thousand dollars. Rent wouldn't matter; we could use that for a down payment on a house. I needed this money. There had to be a way to beat them at their own game. I needed to look harder.

My heart swollen with greed, I eyed the lever to the left of the diving board. I weighed my options. My conscience tried to speak, but I shouted it down.

"This isn't real," I lied to myself. It couldn't be real. If it were, wouldn't the girl be crying or begging? Unless she had given up. No, this had to be another trick. I reasoned that the alligator wasn't real. Or at least it couldn't really get through the cage. But the fact remained: I really couldn't swim.

The audience shuffled in their seats. By their gestures in my direction, pointing claws and shaking fists, brandishing weapons like daggers and mallets, I assumed they were talking about me. Was this how my night would end? At the mercy of this mysterious mob?

Someone complained over the fray, "She's not going to do it."

"Come on, competitor!" the announcer egged me on. "Will you sell yourself short, or WILL YOU RISE TO THE CHALLENGE!"

I gazed across the pool, mentally calculating the distance to the steps. After how far I'd come, it didn't seem like too far to go. What if I threw my poppet? That could work. It seemed to have worked with the diving board… but what if I missed and that monster gobbled her up?

"You can do this," I told myself.

I homed in on the middle of the pool, a few feet past the cage where it sloped down into the shallow end. Exactly like

Xavier's pool did. Tall as I was, I might be able to stand up where the drains caught the water in either direction.

My eyes fell on the lever again. It called to me and I obeyed. As I came closer, I noticed something familiar about its engravings. Everything else clicked into place, like solving a crucial clue in a crossword puzzle.

The sword! The lever was made from its hilt. *Perhaps*, I thought as I swallowed the tight ball in my chest, *this is a sign that I can beat it.* But how could I win without sacrificing the little girl?

I scratched my head, and the diamonds on my mother's ring bounced against the golden hilt. *Touch the sword*, whispered a voice in my head. A different voice than the one that told me to get my bear in the cemetery, but this one I would heed. I reached out, fingers tracing the fine engraving, and accidentally bumped it. The tiny tap moved the cage an inch or two. But that was all I needed. I knew exactly what to do.

The crowd watched in stunned silence as I manipulated the cage into place with one cautious tap at a time. The closer I got to the water, the wider the little girl's eyes grew. Yet she never cried. I tried to connect with her petrified gaze, to send her a message: *Everything's going to be okay, I'm not going to hurt you.*

With the top of the cage nearly even with the diving board, I stopped the lever. Any lower and the bottom of the cage would be in the water. I took a final deep breath before I ran—long, lean arms flailing—from the end of the diving board and vaulted myself onto the top of the cage.

Always a tad overzealous, I miscalculated and paid for it. I clung to the metal chain connecting the cage to the ceiling to keep from falling overboard.

Coach Karla would love this, I thought with a weak little laugh. *She would say, 'no one can accuse you of not trying hard enough, Colbert.'*

I imagined this was just a gymnastics meet, the monsters in the audience only parents, as I rode the waves of the swinging cage. My palms were sweaty, and my fingers trembled, but I didn't let go. Finally, the cage began to lose momentum, and I exhaled.

Of course, I couldn't see the little girl from my current location, but she remained my inspiration. I closed my eyes and pictured her safe and dry, not too shaken.

Oblivious to the spectacle above the water, the beast patrolled the deep end of the pool. It kept close to the space near the end of the diving board, as though it knew where its dinner would be delivered. I watched the monster, unable to tear myself away. To quell my terror, I told myself, "He's all gums and no teeth."

But the truth way down in my gut piped up, *This isn't his first meal on the go*.

"You're descended from pirate witches," I whispered. "You can best this beast."

I took a quick inventory of my person. I worried my boots might weigh me down, but chucking them would make my feet vulnerable; better keep them.

"Don't need this anymore, may as well put it to use," I mumbled, unbuckling my holster. I tossed a gun to the far right of the alligator. He sped through the water like a bullet —*oh hell no*.

My throat tightened. He wasn't as slow as I had hoped. I couldn't focus on that, not if I was going to do this. And I could. I had to. I could beat this thing.

The chain anchoring the cage to the ceiling creaked and complained.

"Crap on a croissant," I said. "This thing isn't gonna hold much longer."

I couldn't let that little girl drown. It was now or never.

The crowd probably thought I'd gone mad when I began to rock the cage again. If I'd cared to listen, I probably could've deciphered their whispers as they speculated about my plan, but I had shifted into laser focus. Nothing but me and the pool. Nothing else. Not even the beast below me.

At the precise moment when the cage was as close to the diving board as it would swing, I tossed my holster into the deep end of the pool. When the cage turned back toward the stairs, I let go, springing forward with all my might.

For a blessed minute, I was at the most important meet of my life. I could feel the audience on the edge of their seats, craning their collective necks to see the freak show fly. Would they enjoy the show? Or would they just feel sorry for me when I failed? I imagined some of the more empathetic spectators shuddering as I landed with an audible *crack*.

"All you saw were the stairs, you arrogant little fool," I scolded myself, biting back tears. The pain from crashing into the rock-hard bottom was so violent, and I was so weak, for a moment I thought it would overtake me. Part of me *wanted* to blackout again, to be taken from this world with no awareness of it.

Then the adrenaline kicked in, leaving nothing but the pulsing pain of wounded pride.

"You idiot. Didn't even consider the risk of landing in the shallow end. At least I can't feel it now," I said, trying to stay positive as my left ankle went numb.

"Hurry," I implored my broken body. "The adrenaline rush won't last. Make it count."

I pumped my arms wildly as I splashed through the pool. The water rushed into my boots, weighing me down. It felt like wading through cement. No time to take them off. Left one wouldn't budge anyway with my swollen ankle. I groaned. How could I have been so stupid?

A sprained ankle was only the tip of the iceberg threatening to sink me. The beast was smarter than I'd expected. Though it had hungrily chased the small ripple from my gun, it ignored the abandoned holster and waited for a human-sized splash. The second I touched the surface of the pool, my adversary became a single-minded green blur. I felt the water parting at my back, heard its tail sloshing back and forth at full speed. I could feel it barreling down on me.

"Don't you dare look back," I warned myself. "Lose one inch and lose it all."

I wanted to cheer but could barely whimper as I reached the first of four cement steps. With the ladder inches out of reach, my entire body quivered and threatened to collapse. I had already been through hell, and yet this final push could be the part where I faltered.

"Jump! Jump! Jump!" a small shrill voice screamed above me. Without looking, I knew the warning came from the little girl in the cage. No one else watching cared if I lived or died. Either way was as entertaining as the other for these savages.

Drawing on strength I didn't know I had, I surged out of the water, attempting to bypass the last two steps. But I tripped on my own water-logged boots and fell back down into the pool. I was done for. The creature had to be close enough to close the gap between us. No way did I have the strength to get back up, much less fight it off. But maybe I didn't need it.

In a Hail Mary attempt, I pulled Bebe from the waistband of my shorts. I hurled her out of the pool. Her cloth body skid across the concrete. Miraculously, I rose from the water as if plucked up by an invisible power, and I followed my bear to victory. To freedom. The skin on my knees shredded against the unforgiving concrete. My ankle throbbed. Even the long-forgotten wound on my forearm reopened and bled anew. But I was alive. Alive and out of the water.

FOUR
INVITATIONS,
NO
RESERVATIONS

I crawled forward and grabbed Bebe. She was damp, several of her threads torn loose, but otherwise okay. Yet, I felt uneasy as I tucked her back into the waistband of my wet shorts. Why did it feel like the worst still waited for me? An unfathomable thought flashed into my mind: what if the alligator kept coming after me? I flipped onto my back and watched the pool. Would it chase me? No, that wouldn't make any—okay, when was the last time this place made sense? After all, it wasn't as though alligators *never* came on land.

With bated breath, I trembled, ready for whatever horrible thing might happen next. What I witnessed was more bizarre than anything I could have conjured up on my own—a fuzzy orange paw punctuated by jagged black bands swiped at the air above the water. Its claws connected with a clang against the pool ladder.

My ears rang. I rubbed my eyes in astonishment. When I dared to look again, the entire animal had disappeared, nothing save fading ripples in the pool's surface to verify it had ever existed at all.

"Wow! What a performance," a deep voice boomed. "Give her a hand, everyone."

The audience in the bleachers clapped obediently. No one stomped or hooted. They were all out of roses. Out of interest. Even the animals looked bored.

They must have been rooting for the monster, I thought bitterly.

I tried to stand but lacked the strength. I stayed on my back like a winded turtle and prayed my head would stop swimming.

A tall figure loomed over me. At first, I thought maybe it was Wolfram—the tall stranger from my dream. But when he reached a hand down, I recognized his jagged yellow fingernails and stacks of glittering rings, though his opposite hand now gripped a wireless microphone instead of a pitchfork. When I didn't take his hand, Satan bent down closer. His long beard tickled my chin as he whispered in my ear, "Impressive. Risky, but impressive."

"What *is* that thing?" I pointed at the cloudy water, at nothing but algae.

Satan smirked. "What did you see?" He tipped the microphone toward my lips.

"An alligator… with tiger paws?"

Satan took the mic back. "Remarkable! A formidable opponent indeed. Let's give a round of applause to our brave competitor."

The crowd clapped a little louder than they had the last time. There seemed to be a general shift in their energy from disappointment to acceptance. The winged creatures had all settled down as though the show was over, and they were sitting through the credits to see if there were any clever bloopers at the end.

Satan cupped his mouth and hissed at me, "Stand up and take a bow; you won."

I pushed his hand away, and ignoring my poor ankle, pulled myself to my feet. I took an awkward bow to a chorus of enthusiastic cheers. They were on my side again. Even their pets joined in, howling, cawing, and screeching with excitement.

Yet I couldn't help but wonder what Satan meant. What the hell had been in that water? Was I hallucinating? No, I couldn't have been. I couldn't have cooked up something that bizarre. From my new vantage point, I scanned the pool again, but a thick fog had settled over the deep end. My heart sank as my eyes landed on something else—the cage. It still hung inches above the water, but now it was empty.

"Where is she?" I cried out. A sharp pain radiated from my chest as if my heart had been pierced with an arrow. "Where's the little girl?"

Satan feigned concern. "Little girl? What little girl? Can you tell us what she looks like?" He thrust the microphone back in my face.

"The little girl in the cage! She had dark hair and blue eyes… she looked like… like me when I was little. Why am I telling you this? You know what she looks like; you put her there!" The desperation in my voice echoed through the crowd. Some of them snickered. This was what they were waiting for, the final scene that was funnier than the whole movie.

Bile crawled up my throat, but I forced it back down. This place, these people, were making me sick, but I wouldn't give them the satisfaction of seeing me spew. "What have you done to her? Where is she?" I demanded.

A pitying smile spread across Satan's thin lips. He leaned forward and tapped a claw against the center of my forehead. "She's right where she's always been—in here."

My cheeks burned as peals of laughter broke out all around me. I knew I was the butt of the joke, but I still didn't get it. The girl was in my head? I had made her up? Was any of this real? Yes! It had to be! And yet…

"I don't understand," I choked out.

"Competitors usually see puppies or kittens," Satan answered flippantly. "I'm guessing you're not an animal person?"

"I… I am an animal person!" I insisted.

"When animals aren't inspiring enough to risk mortal

danger, the bait appears human. *Most* people care enough about strangers not to sacrifice them, but YOU are a special case. You didn't see just *any* little girl—you saw a little you. You're so selfish that the only thing worth saving to you is, well, you."

"You're lying," I snarled. "There was a little girl in that cage!"

Satan shrugged. "I don't care if you believe me. Any other questions?"

I couldn't let them have the last laugh, yet I had nothing to say. No way to refute his claims. I huffed. "Yeah, where's my money?"

"Right, of course. The other thing you care about." Satan snapped his nasty fingers, rings clinking together, and produced a black leather briefcase.

I snatched it from him. They may have stolen my sanity, but I was leaving with their money. I popped the briefcase open and counted its contents—twice, three times to be sure. Thirty thousand dollars! I'd never seen so much money in my life. And yet, there was an emptiness in my chest that hadn't been there when I entered the haunted house.

"Don't feel bad, Lisette," Satan said. "There are worse things in the world to be than selfish. In fact, some would say your greatest flaw is also your greatest asset. You made it through alive, didn't you?"

"Can I go now?" I spat.

"Wait," Satan said. "I have another gift for you." He reached into his cloak again, and this time he produced a shiny emerald-colored card folded like a party invitation.

"I don't want it." I pulled the briefcase to my chest like a shield.

"Destiny doesn't care what you want." Satan's red eyes locked onto mine until I had no choice but to look away first.

I didn't take the card, yet somehow it found a way into my hand. On the front, the words *Your Presence is Requested* appeared in eye-catching calligraphy. I opened it up to find an address I recognized, a street near the Mississippi River, above the words *We Sail at Dawn* written in the same style.

"We're always looking for clever, motivated people like you," Satan said. "You could benefit from being part of a family like ours."

I took a small step back. "Sure, I'll consider it."

"We call our coven Phaelgood. It's a very exclusive group," he said. "You would love it. Everything you crave at your fingertips, no rules, just fun."

"Great. Maybe I'll stop by sometime." I looked into the bleachers, half expecting to be mobbed, but only three people moved toward me. I couldn't see their faces, just their robes — red, blue, and silver.

"You seem nervous," Satan said. "Perhaps this will help." He slid something the size and weight of a leaf behind my ear.

I batted his hand away and grabbed the leaf. No, not a leaf. A joint. This psycho seriously just gave me a joint.

"Thanks," I mumbled. "What are they doing? What do they want?"

"Only to offer you inferior invitations." Satan rolled his eyes so hard I bet he saw his own brain. "Trust me, those three covens are terrible. The best witches are Phaelgood witches."

A man in a red cloak reached me first, or rather, his pet did. It had the body of an ocelot, but black, spindly wings like a bat. I blinked at it, unable to register such a creature—were the wings some kind of accessory, or were they fused to its spotted shoulders? As if the creature could sense my confusion, it spread its wings and fluttered them, showing off.

I was so mesmerized watching it that I hardly noticed the man until he was beside me. His hood slipped back, revealing a handsome, if unusually angular, face, like a cartoon villain's.

"Styg Pilate," he introduced himself. "I am the highest-ranking witch in Freestar. Several of our members were quite impressed with your performance tonight, but I will be the judge of your acceptance into our group. If it's a mutual fit, Freestar will be the best decision you've ever made. We can make your wildest dreams come true. We're talking complete physical reconstruction, a six-figure sign-on bonus. But unlike *some* covens, we have a process before we offer—"

Before I could ask him to go back to the part about the six-figure bonus, a woman with a commanding presence, clad in a silver cloak, used her meaty hips to bounce him out of the way. His face twisted ghoulishly, and for a split-second, he looked more corpse than human. I shuddered. He could keep his money.

"So lovely to finally meet you, Lisette! I am Celeste Honeycutt of Sciella. Surely your mother spoke of me?" the pushy woman said. "We helped her get set up in New Orleans. It's our policy to help all refugees."

I shook my head, but she didn't seem deterred. Where was her weird pet? I looked around but didn't see one.

"One of our members scouted you out in the dollhouse level," Celeste continued. "She's young, but she has a gift for reading people that many seers do not receive until the end of their lives. For the sake of all magickind, you must join Sciella. We don't have deep pockets, but we can help you tap into your potential better than anyone. The good of all above the good of anyone!"

Before I could ask this Celeste character what in the actual hell she was talking about, she swept my hair back and clasped a silver chain around my neck. The silver rocket-ship-shaped pendant was barely the size of a nickel, but it felt heavy against my breastbone.

"Welcome to Sciella!" Celeste declared. "Now if you will come with me this way—"

I was sick of people telling me where to go. There was nothing else in this nightmare-scape for me. I grabbed the pendant and yanked as hard as I could. A single link of the silver chain snapped, and the necklace slithered off. I tossed it on the ground and glared at Celeste. "The only place I'm going is home."

My vision tunneled toward Satan. "How do I get out of here?"

Satan pointed toward a red sign I had to squint to read. The light on the "e" had burnt out so only "xit" could be seen, but I got the gist.

"Excuse me, Lisette?" the man wearing the blue cloak addressed me humbly. He had a thick white beard and a charming smile that reminded me of a department store Santa Claus. A ginormous white dog, with alert ears and expressive eyes, panted at his feet. They both smelled like salt water, like freedom. I don't know why, but I instantly trusted this jolly fellow.

"My name is Joaquin Nova," the blue-cloaked Santa doppelgänger said. "I represent Micompas. You should have been raised on our ship. I will not force a conversation, as that is not our way. Leave if you wish. But your father instructed me to tell you that he would appreciate it if you would join him in Micompas."

I studied him first, and then his dog, searching for some sign their kind vibe was a front. "Ship, eh?" I repeated. "So you're pirates?"

Joaquin grinned. "We've been called worse. Haven't we, Nimbus?"

His giant white dog barked as if in agreement.

"Don't listen to him, Lisette!" Celeste, the woman who had tried to give me the necklace, warned. "Your mother escaped from Micompas when you were a baby. Surely she would not wish you to return."

Joaquin huffed. "You speak as if we held her prisoner. She joined our coven willingly."

"Yet she departed without a word to anyone," Celeste

argued. "We protected her in her time of need. She would want her daughter to join us, not you."

"Right, well, thanks for the invitations, all of you," I said. "But I can't swim. Tell my father if he wants to see me, we'll have to arrange for a meeting on dry land."

Celeste looked stunned, but Joaquin shrugged, his blue velvet cloak wrinkling across his broad shoulders. "I will pass on your message," he said.

I shuffled away as fast as my bad ankle allowed. Thankfully, none of them were undignified enough to give chase.

Of every part of me that ached, my head hurt the worst. My mind grappled with too many mysteries to process. How much of what I had experienced was real, and how much did I make up? That girl in the cage was real. She had to be. If she wasn't real, how did she warn me? And what was that whole thing at the end? Were those people actual witches or only amateurs pretending? Okay, I knew the answer to that one. These people were serious. Whoever made the Thirteenth Realm wasn't a weekend witch or whatever. If none of it was real, how the hell did they all know my name? They could have read it on the liability waiver. Or heard me say it during my eulogy. Who cared if they knew my name? They didn't know me like they thought they did.

I wasn't going to sell my soul like that Styg guy thought I would. I wasn't going to be pushed around like that Celeste woman assumed. Joaquin might have been okay, but if my father really wanted to see me, he could come tell me so himself. And most of all, I didn't agree with what Satan had said about me. I wasn't selfish; I was a survivor.

35

A
BODY
OF
EVIDENCE

Xavier looked different, taller than usual. Then it registered he was only holding himself differently, not slouching. Of course it was him. Who else could wear that goofy costume so well?

He nearly tripped over his bell-bottoms and narrowly avoided face-planting as he ran to meet me. I tried to smile at him, but my head hurt too much, even for a fake one. I was happy to see him, relieved to be reunited with my one true friend and free of all those monsters.

"Lisette! Darling, are you okay? I've been so worried about you!"

"I'm fine." I winced as he wrapped his arms around me; his hug was too tight. "Just really sore. Ouch." I withdrew from his embrace. "Feels like my bruises have bruises. Gimme some space, okay?"

"Okay," Xavier said, though his pout said it wasn't. "I'm so happy to see you. You have no idea. I was so worried."

"What time is it?" I searched the foggy sky for clues. The clouds billowed past at breakneck speed, as though they were being chased.

He plucked a piece of web out of my hair. "After three. I was about to call the cops. No one else has come out in like an hour. Did you do it?" He paused, waiting with wide-eyed wonder. "Did you make it all the way through?"

I cast a suspicious glance over my shoulder. "Come on, let's go to the car."

"Wow!" He pointed at my briefcase. "You did. You won!"

"Not here." I grabbed his forearm.

He allowed me to drag him along until he noticed the blood. "Jesus, look at your knees. What happened? They're ripped to ribbons!"

"It's nothing."

"It doesn't look like nothing." He planted his feet. "What gives, Lisette? There's something you're not telling me. How did you make it through? Did you get help?"

"What? No, of course not. I relied on my gut instinct or whatever."

"Come on, not one single person helped you?"

I narrowed my eyes at him. There was no way I was gonna get roped into talking about the other Britneys, or worse, Desmond. "Other than the one time you were there, when the safari guy helped us, no. No one helped me."

"What safari guy?"

"The one who gave us bug spray. You don't remember? You totally flirted with him."

"Aw, come on, you know I'm pulling your chain," Xavier said. "I can't believe you made it out without help. That's really something."

"Okay, well, if you must know—there was this *one* other guy who helped me."

"Was he sexy?"

"Ummm maybe?"

"That was a rhetorical question. I could tell by the way your voice went up like a gazillion octaves. We should go to the after-party. Maybe he'll be there."

I rubbed my sleepy eyes. "I'm exhausted, and I'm pretty sure I sprained my ankle. Could you please take me home?"

"That sucks about your ankle. Wait here and I'll go get the car."

"No! We should stay together. Let's hurry."

"Whatever you want." Xavier grinned at me stupidly, like I was a celebrity or something. "I can hardly believe it. My girl made it all the way through the Thirteenth Realm of Hell and lived to tell the tale."

The corners of my mouth moved upwards for a flash, then flattened. It was too soon to gloat. And I couldn't help but cringe when Xavier called me 'his girl.' I knew he didn't mean anything by it, but it still sounded weird.

My head stayed moving, eyes scanning the shadows all the way through the parking lot. As soon as we were inside Xavier's car, I locked the door. I could feel Bebe pressing against my stomach. I wanted to move her but didn't dare. Instead, I opened the briefcase again, counting the stacks with my eyes.

Nothing escaped Xavier. "Wow! You're rich. That looks like more than ten grand…"

"Oh, here you go." I peeled a hundred-dollar bill out of a band and held it toward him.

He shook his head. "I don't need it."

"Please take it." I waved the bill. "You're always paying my way."

Xavier licked his lips. "If you really wanna make us even, tell me what happened in the last realm. I'm *dying* to know."

I flinched at the memory of the little girl in the cage. She had looked so *cold*. So *real*.

"Poor choice of words." I opened the center console and shoved the bill inside. "Wound's still fresh. I'll tell you about it some other time."

Xavier's face fell. "But you'll tell me soon? When it's not so raw, of course."

"Soon, yeah," I echoed.

I didn't mean to lie.

We rode the rest of the way in somber silence, punctuated by Xavier asking me for directions.

"What gives?" I asked him. "You come here like, every day."

"Yeah, but I'm tired. And things look different at night."

As we drew closer to my apartment, I thought about how I would explain the money to Ruelle. *Oh, you know, won it playing a deadly game with some Satanists. No big deal.*

"Are you sure you wanna go home?" Xavier asked. "You can't climb through the window in the shape you're in."

"It's fine. I can go through the front door."

"You could crash at my place—my room, a guest room, wherever you're comfortable."

"Not just no, but hell no."

"Why not?"

"Because if I bleed on Karyn's fancy sheets, she'll have an aneurism. Which she would survive and then have me charged with attempted manslaughter."

Xavier laughed. "Mom's not home. She's traveling. Like usual."

I massaged my brow and tried not to roll my eyes at him. He usually called his mother Karyn. It was one of our things, referring to our mothers by their first names. I figured he must have been exhausted to abandon it in favor of something as intimate as "mom."

"It's fine," I said. "When Ruelle sees this fat stack of cash, she won't care how I got it."

"At least call me, let me know you're not grounded for life."

"Stop worrying," I groaned. "I'll be fine. I always am."

"Worrying is how I express my love," Xavier said.

I shook my head. *Poor Xavier*, I thought. *He can barely handle the problems he sees on the surface. If he knew how bad things really were, he'd run for sure.* I was so lost in my own thoughts that when we reached my building, I hopped out without saying goodbye. I thought about checking on Cali, then decided I'd better wait until morning since I was already unsteady with exhaustion.

Xavier shouted, "Call me as soon as you can."

I didn't make any promises before I shut the car door.

A sneer of sheer determination spread across my face as I stared up at the shaky iron stairwell. "All right, you *stairs*," I muttered like a slur, "before you come at me, keep in mind that I usually take two or three of you at a time, so you're not gonna defeat me one-on-one. So be cool and let me pass."

My ankle throbbed steadily as I climbed, like water dripping in the same exact spot. Even when the stairs ended, my torture wasn't over. I had to jump to grab the spare key off the top of the door frame. My fingertips brushed a cobweb. Chills danced down my spine.

That spider wasn't real, I told myself. *There's no such thing as a spider that big. At least I'm pretty sure there's not.*

I landed with a yelp. This *is real,* I assured myself, trying to ground my thoughts in this world. *This is all that matters. Well, and this money. This money better be real.*

When I jammed the key in the lock, the door creaked open before I gave it a good twist. I hesitated. Ruelle never left the door unlocked. She was obsessed with locks. I figured she must have left in a hurry. Guilt crept in as I walked into our apartment. It had a distinctly empty feeling, and I was sure she was out looking for me. I flipped on the light.

My jaw dropped. Empty. Everything from the hook in the hallway where Ruelle hung her keys to the stupid rugs. I walked across the smudged ink, wondering what it all meant. Had my dream in the sensory deprivation maze been real?

"This can't be happening," I said to the empty apartment. "Did I pass out on the stairs? This must be a nightmare. Dear God, what if I'm still floating in the dark, hallucinating this? What if I never got out?"

I pinched myself hard. "Ow," I yelped. "It's real. Everything is gone."

Still reeling in disbelief, I tugged at the blood-speckled ends of my hair until my braid came completely undone. I rushed into my bedroom. My entire room was bare, even my poster of the '96 Women's Olympics Champions had been torn off the wall for some cruel reason. Nothing remained but the residue of the duct tape I had used to hang it.

Fighting back tears, I pulled open the accordion doors to my closet. Nothing inside except my old blue backpack. I unzipped it cautiously, hands shaking like whatever had taken everything else might be waiting to jump out at me, but it only had my favorite clothes inside. I rifled through them cautiously—one pair of jeans, two concert t-shirts, my Batgirl pajamas, and a couple pairs of socks and underwear.

At the bottom of my backpack, buried beneath the clothes, I discovered an old photograph. Strange, I didn't remember sitting in the lap of that mall Santa, but the white beard framing his sour face struck me as familiar all the same.

"Has to be from when I was six; I'm missing my front teeth. Rough Christmas," I mumbled.

The dress in the picture—red velvet with ruffles—didn't look like anything I remembered owning. Then it dawned on me; we had tucked the tags in and returned it right after the picture.

I chuckled at the contrast between my wide grin and Santa's frown—like he was about to add me to the naughty list. Though I couldn't recall our interaction, I must've asked him for something sassy, like a baby reindeer and a tiny sleigh to pull me around the world or an elf to make me toys in the off-season.

When I flipped the photo over, looking for a date to jog my memory, I found a message. The handwriting was sloppy, hurried. It read: *Don't follow me.*

No signature. It didn't need one. I recognized Ruelle's careless handwriting.

"What a dirty trick!" I declared. "This makes no sense!

She loses her mind when I go somewhere without telling her first, and now she's vanished? Why? To teach me a lesson?"

My chest hitched. I could barely breathe. I wanted to cry, but I willed myself not to. I desperately struggled to flip my perspective.

"Her loss," I snapped like a steel trap closing tight. "I don't need her. I've got more money now than I've had in my entire life. No one to share it with, but also no one to hold me back."

Dazed but determined, I considered the ring on my finger, turning it so the diamonds faced me. "She must be mad about the ring. But why? She practically told me to take it."

I dropped the photograph, and it fluttered to the closet floor. I didn't bother picking it up. Panicked thoughts rushed into my weary brain. *Where am I going to sleep tonight? I bet she didn't leave me soap to take a shower. Or a towel to dry off.*

"Stop it!" I admonished myself aloud. "You gotta think big picture. What's one thing you can do to make this mess better?"

I sat down on the floor, still sniffling. I closed my eyes and tried to focus on my breathing. Tried to make it through the calming exercises, anything to pretend the sick feeling in my stomach was the usual butterflies that fluttered around inside me before executing a new routine at competition. I cleared my mind and stretched my spine. My back popped. That was when it clicked.

"I can call Xavier for help." I chewed on my lower lip. "I don't want to, but what other choice do I have?"

My ankle had gone numb. I limped toward the kitchen. My eyes watered at the sight of the empty wall where the phone should be. My lips quivered.

"Why did she take it? To spite me? To kick me while I'm down?" Hot tears stung my cheeks. "No way! Don't you dare cry right now! Suck it up!" I took deep belly breaths, filling up my ribcage until the urge to sob subsided. "You'll figure something out, but not by feeling sorry for yourself. Think, Lisette, think!"

Nothing came. I slunk back into my room and searched the backpack again, hoping there might be toiletries in one pocket. No such luck.

Something tickled my belly button. I gasped. Bebe. I took her out of my waistband and considered the way her forehead seemed to crease in a warning. We weren't safe here. She was telling me to go and go fast. I wrapped her up in a pair of underwear, shoved her inside a zippered compartment, and closed the backpack.

Where would I feel safe? A lightbulb flickered inside my brain like a candle down to its last centimeter of wax. Maybe he was still outside. Maybe if I hurried, I could catch him.

As I stumbled down the stairs, with my backpack slung over my shoulder and my briefcase full of money hooked under one arm, my legs wobbled like undercooked noodles. The pain my adrenaline had held at bay for hours finally broke through. It crashed over me and ripped me apart like the Mississippi River laying waste to an ancient levee. This was it—sink or swim.

Then there it was at the bottom of the stairs, my life raft. Xavier's vintage Thunderbird idled in the alley where he'd dropped me off.

He cranked the window down and stuck his head out. "Need help getting in?"

"You're still here," I squeaked. "How did you know to stay?"

Xavier just smiled. "Intuition, darling. You ready to go?"

"Yeah, wait a second, though. I gotta check on Cali before I go."

"Who?" Xavier killed the engine.

I waved for him to follow me. He got out of the car, and I led him to the little blanketed cardboard box I'd set up for her. Sure enough, there was Cali, her golden eyes glued to three newborn kittens—an orange one, a black one, and a calico like her—all nestled close.

"Xavi, look," I whispered. "They're so small and helpless."

He stayed in the shadows for a moment. "What do we do? We can't leave them here."

I said nothing. Bad enough that I needed a place to crash; I couldn't possibly ask him to take in four stray cats, too. When my lip trembled, I bit down on it. No, I would not allow myself the catharsis of crying. I didn't deserve it.

"Do you think she'll let me pick up the whole box?" Xavier said, breaking the silence. "Maybe you should explain to her where we're going—so she won't be scared?"

I was so stunned I could hardly speak. "Okay, yeah." I blinked back the happy tears welling in my eyes as I bent down to her level. "Hey Cali girl—remember me? You trust me, right?" I reached over and gently stroked her ears until she purred. "Okay, cool. Xavi here is gonna pick you up. We're taking you and your babies someplace safe, friend."

As Xavi scooped up the box, I shook my head slowly, in shock. Who was this person putting a dirty old cardboard box in their beloved backseat, and what had he done with Xavi?

I wanted to help, but I could barely hobble over, carrying all my stuff, and get myself in. I sat in the backseat beside Cali and her kittens, cooing to them, promising them everything would be all right. Their presence helped distract me from my pain.

"Guess your mom was pissed, huh?" Xavier threw the car into reverse and backed out of the alley. "I had this gut feeling that you needed me. It was wild. Unlike anything I've ever—"

"Yeah, I'm sure it was life-changing," I humored him. "And yeah, Ruelle was pissed. So pissed apparently that she dipped."

"Dipped?" Xavi repeated.

"Bounced. Flew the coop. She's gone." I leaned back, thinking, breathing, feeling the pain pulse through my body like waves full of jellyfish crashing into me, setting my skin on fire with their stings.

"Seriously? That's messed up," Xavier said. "Well, you know you're welcome to stay with me for as long as you need to."

"Thanks. I promise it won't be long. Same goes for the cats, too. As soon as I can, I'll find them new homes, I promise."

Xavier shrugged. "Don't worry about it. I know you will."

For the first time in a long time, I felt at peace. Quick as it came, it dissipated. Xavier was too good of a friend. I didn't deserve him. Satan had been right about me.

"Xavier?" I asked. "Do you think I'm selfish?"

"Selfish?" Xavier repeated curiously. "I wouldn't use *that* word to describe you."

"What word would you use?"

"Focused," Xavier said. "Sometimes you get so focused on what you want, you forget other people want things too."

"Okay." I drummed my fingers against the center console. "Thanks for being honest."

Xavier glanced back at me. For a split second, I was certain he would tell me to stop abusing his beloved car, but instead he said, "You're wearing Ruelle's ring. She uhhh... she left it behind?"

I drew my hand in. "How did you know it was her ring?"

"Are you kidding?" Xavier laughed a little nervously. "She wears it, like, all the time."

"Okay, yeah, but... you've only ever met my mom once or twice. How would you know it's hers?"

"You're being weird, Lisette," Xavier said. "Totally understandable, you've been through some scary shit. But I'm trying to help you, and you're jumping down my throat for every little thing."

I rubbed my aching head, as though trying to loosen the mistrust that clung to the forefront of my mind. "You're right.

I don't know what got into me. Of course you'd notice her ring; it's like, the only nice thing she wears."

Xavier smiled and nodded. "And now it's yours."

The GPS cut in, a pleasant woman's directive to turn.

"Why's your GPS on?" I asked. "You don't know the way back to your own house?" I teased him.

"Of course I do," Xavier replied, patting the device on his dash like a good luck charm. "I use it as a backup. It's late, and I'm tired. I don't wanna get mixed up and turn the wrong way into a bad neighborhood."

I opened my mouth, ready to tell him off for insulting where I lived, but then I softened. Xavi was a good friend to me. The least I could do was stop mouthing off. Besides, he wasn't wrong. Compared to where he lived, my neighborhood was rough.

My fingers absently stroked the top of Cali's head. She purred, expressing her gratitude. That alley was no place for a new mother and her family.

"Thanks for letting me bring the cats, Xavier," I said.

"You're welcome."

Maybe I wasn't totally selfish. But I could work on being more grateful.

36

THE
PERFECT
HOST

You could tell old money built the neighborhood where Xavier lived because the road deferred to the trees and not the other way around. Usually, I liked how they expressed their gratitude, dipping their branches across to create a shady canopy, but in the near dawn darkness, they only added to my sense of uneasiness.

The car slowed to a crawl. "You have reached your destination," the GPS reported.

Xavier idled in front of the massive iron gate for no reason I could figure out. I reached over and tapped the button attached to his visor.

"What were you waiting for?" I asked, but Xavier simply shrugged.

Twin topiaries trimmed into elephants greeted us as we turned onto the cobblestone driveway that circled in front of a tasteful fountain spraying tiers of water like a wedding cake.

"I still can't believe only two people live here," I said, eternally awestruck at the three-story Tudor-style behemoth.

"Three now," Xavier said. "Ford moved in."

"Karyn's new man?"

"Man-child is more like it. He's like, twenty-three, I think? Twenty-four? And he acts like a four-year-old."

"Oh dude, I'm sorry. How bad is it?"

"Not *that* bad. He only comes out of my mom's room to smoke pot and play video games. Oh, and he doesn't keep tabs on his stash, so that's cool."

"Cool," I agreed. "Hope he doesn't notice me either."

The black-and-white checkered tile garage floor was pristine, with not so much as a single spot of oil. Apparently, the Monroes kept their cars in a place nicer than I'd ever lived. I clutched my briefcase to my chest like a shield and prayed I didn't track anything inside.

Xavier brought some old blankets down, and we set up a bigger, better bed for Cali and her kittens. He raided his fridge and found some tuna salad and crackers, which she devoured.

I snuck a few crackers for myself. I had too much dignity to ask if I could share the tuna salad with the cat, but my hunger would not be tamed without a cracker or three.

"I'll have to go to the store and get her some real food," I said between crunches. "But it'll have to wait until tomorrow, I'm exhausted."

"You should sleep in my room," Xavier said. "It'll feel safer than being on your own."

"I'm fine on my own, thanks," I replied, adjusting my backpack on my shoulder.

"Suit yourself." Xavier shrugged.

As I stepped in front of him, he put a hand on my shoulder.

"Can I carry something for you?"

"Naw, I got it," I said with more confidence than I felt. In reality, I thought I might collapse at any moment, overtaken at last by my various maladies.

When we reached the guest suite, he ducked into the bathroom to check for toiletries and towels. I don't know what came over me, but I slid the briefcase under the bed. I didn't know who I was hiding it from, but I figured it was better to be paranoid than penniless.

"You're in luck, we're all stocked up," Xavi announced. "I

know you're tired, but *please* shower before you get in bed. It'll make you feel better."

"Right, and more importantly, it'll keep Karyn from murdering us. I get it. Can you help me take my boot off? It feels like it's fused to my foot."

I sat down on a tufted bench at the foot of the bed and swung my leg up onto the other end so he didn't have to bend down to reach my boot.

Xavier tugged at my soggy laces. "We're gonna have to take you to the doctor tomorrow. Your ankle might be broken."

"Don't worry about it, I'm fine." I yelped as Xavier began to wiggle my boot loose.

"Clearly, you aren't. I'm barely touching it. Besides, while you're there, they can look at your nose, too. You need to take better care of yourself, Lis. You only get one face."

"Ow! Okay, that's enough." I pulled back. The pain overwhelmed me, and I bit my lip to stifle a cry. "I've got it from here," I grumbled.

"Let me help you. I wanna see it—"

"I said I got it! Now be a good host and leave me alone."

"All right, all right." Xavier threw his hands up. "What about the ring? Do you need help taking it off?"

"What? No. Why would I take it off?"

Xavier frowned. "I dunno Lis, it looks pretty dirty."

I twisted it around, inspecting it. It didn't look dirty to me, but clearly, we had different standards of cleanliness. "So what if it's dirty? I'll wear it while I shower."

"I've got jewelry cleaning solution upstairs. Why don't you let me take it—"

"Goodnight, Xavier," I snapped.

Though I was grateful for his help, I wish he knew when to stop. I gave him a withering look to let him know the discussion was over.

"Fine," Xavier huffed. "Good night."

He looked so defeated. He didn't deserve that. Why was I always so afraid to let anyone in?

"Wait a minute, Xavi. I wanna tell you something." I inhaled deeply and exhaled slowly, mustering courage. "I wanna say that, while most people suck, you're one of the good ones. I don't tell you that enough."

He blushed. "You don't. But that's okay. It makes it special when you do."

"Cool. Okay, well, good night."

"Sweet dreams, darling."

As soon as he was gone, I locked the door. It was another silly thing to do, not like he would've busted in while I was naked or something. Not my best friend.

I plugged the fancy clawfoot tub and ran a bath, squeezing copious amounts of lavender-scented body wash into the water.

"Since when does Xavier call me darling?" I mumbled. "He sure was acting weird. I guess tonight was tough on both of us."

I eased my bruised body into the bubbles. For a moment, it was so relaxing I nearly dozed off. Then I gently lifted my giant swollen ankle up to assess the damage. I turned it in little semi-circles. It hurt like hell, but at least I could move it.

"Only a bad sprain," I assured myself. "I couldn't do this if it were broken."

I scrubbed the gore and grime from my skin, but the memories wouldn't wash off. "Was any of it real? The zombies? The lava? Did people actually die in there? What happened to Hal and Tucker and Kennedy? What in God's name was that thing in the pool?" I yawned.

My voice grew more and more incoherent with exhaustion. "Alligators don't have paws. Did I imagine it? No, I couldn't have. Well, not unless someone drugged me or…"

As I washed the blood from my hair, I racked my foggy

brain. Had the joint I smoked in the parking lot been laced with something? Angel dust? I'd heard of it but never tried it before, so no telling what effect it could have had on me.

I yawned again. Could have been Dr. Montgomery's so-called truth serum… but the zombies happened *before* I drank it…somehow… someone… must have done something… must have made me imagine… it… all…

My eyelids drooped. "Better get out of here before I drown," I muttered to myself.

But the jumbled thoughts kept unwinding in my head. How did they find a little girl who looked so much like me as a kid? Did they know I wouldn't let her die? How did they know I'd even make it to the bonus round?

Either I narrowly escaped death, or I made the whole thing up. Which was more unbelievable? Which could I live with?

I pulled the plug. Water swirled and whooshed down the drain with a thick gurgling sound. I wrapped my sopping wet hair up in a fluffy white monogrammed towel, then used a matching one to dry off. Everything in this house was so fancy. I didn't belong in a place like this. It was only a matter of time before I ruined something and they kicked me out.

With my waning strength, I hoisted myself up onto the giant bed. I pulled the cozy down comforter up to my chin. Despite how exhausted I was, my mind wouldn't rest.

"Hush up," I whispered to it. "Your work here is done."

But thoughts kept parading through, undeterred. I began the breathing exercises Miss Fenty taught me. I allowed each thought to enter my mind but refused to engage with them. If I didn't fight them, they would go away on their own.

Where did Ruelle go? Why didn't she want me to follow her? It didn't matter. If she didn't want me to go after her, I wouldn't. Not like I needed her.

Sleep evaded me. Something wasn't right. The house was

so quiet I could hear my heart pounding out a message like Morse code: S.O.S. I clutched Bebe tight to my chest. She was still a bit soggy, but that wasn't why she didn't comfort me. Something was wrong. But what? I flipped over to the other side of the huge bed, my body sinking into the soft, soothing mattress. And yet, my mind fought to stay awake.

I was somewhere between being awake and asleep when I saw her—nothing more than a hazy outline of a woman hunched over a cane. But my heart filled in the details.

"Miss Opal!" I exclaimed. I wanted to reach for her but dared not move in case it might break the spell. "I'm so happy to see you. I miss you. Who killed you? I'll make them pay, I'll—"

She shook her head. As her wispy fingers reached toward my face, a cool chill passed through me. It reminded me of the ghost on the second floor of the dollhouse, and I recoiled.

"Weak," she whispered to me. "A warning—the perfect host…" Her lips kept moving, but the rest of her words were too soft for me to make out.

"Miss Opal, I can't hear you!" I sat up, reaching out for her frantically. But her figure grew hazier and hazier right before my eyes.

"Perfect… host," she repeated.

"Perfect host?" I echoed, exasperated. "Do you mean Xavier? Because he's hosting me at his home?"

She seemed to nod yes, yet her features knitted together into a frown. For a second, she seemed to evaporate, but then with a final burst of energy, she bellowed, "Beware, darling!" as clear as the bells of St. Louis Cathedral that marked the quarter-hour.

I wanted to tell her thank you. So many things hung between us, unspoken. And so it seemed they would remain. Her image scattered like dandelion seeds carried off by the wind. Miss Opal was no more, but her message remained. *The perfect host. Beware, darling.* What did it mean?

My mind had been muddy, but suddenly it cleared. The truth walloped me like a balance beam to the groin. Xavier had never called me darling before tonight—but I knew who had.

37

SECRETS
REVEALED

Every step up the stairs hurt my heart. How could I have missed the signs? My bad ankle throbbed, reminding me how distracted I'd been by my litany of injuries. Still, I should've known my best friend would have hesitated to load a bunch of stray cats into his precious car. That should have been my first clue. And when he didn't know the way to his own house, I'd hardly questioned it. How could I have been so stupid!

I raised my hand to knock on Xavier's bedroom door, with no idea what I would say to whoever waited behind it. Rage never needs a plan, just somewhere to go, something to strike. I pounded my fist against the door, not caring it was probably four in the morning. I needed to find my friend and bring him home.

"Come in," a strange voice called. It sounded like Xavi speaking through a microphone, his vocal cords producing the sound but someone else's mind amplifying the volume, altering the cadence.

I burst through the heavy door and was startled to see whatever or whoever gazing out the window like a prince surveying his kingdom. He wore one of Xavi's thick cotton robes monogrammed with XMM, but it seemed a bit short on him, this person who didn't slouch.

My Batgirl pajamas made me self-conscious. I hadn't thought to change clothes before I came upstairs to confront him, and now I looked silly, like someone even I couldn't take seriously.

"Hello darling," the stranger said. "Couldn't sleep? Me neither. Why don't you come in? Sit and talk with me for a while?"

"Who are you?" I asked, lingering near the door.

He smiled. "You finally noticed. I was beginning to wonder if we really had the connection I felt between us in the Thirteenth Realm."

Speaking his name would acknowledge defeat. And yet, it flew from my lips, anyway. "Desmond? But how did you—"

"Xavier wanted to trade," Desmond said. "It's not a bad deal for him. I'll finish his last year of high school while he sails from coast to coast, partying with witches."

"No." I shook my head. "No, that's not possible."

Desmond turned around. The soft moonlight illuminating his silhouette gave him a ghoulish quality. There was a spark in his eyes, a fire I never noticed in Xavier. "And in exchange, I get to spend some time on the outside, living in the lap of luxury. It might be a little boring, but with you here—"

"What did you do to my friend?" I demanded.

"I told you, he's fine. He's having the time of his life right now."

"Where? In the Thirteenth Realm? Xavi would never choose that! He was terrified the whole time we were in there. I need to see him, I need to—"

"Relax. The haunted house is only one night a year. He's at the afterparty, enjoying every indulgence known to man. Let the dude live a little."

I chewed on my lip and fiddled with my mother's ring. *Don't trust him*, an authoritative voice whispered. I nodded, mainly because it didn't jive with me either. Would the Xavier I knew really volunteer to trade places with a stranger? I couldn't picture it.

"Take me to him," I said.

Desmond shrugged. "all right, but before we go, I should clarify—you agreed to keep all my secrets. In case it wasn't already clear, this is one of them. No one else can know I'm not Xavier, understand?"

Words wouldn't come. I balked at him until he stepped forward and touched my shoulders. "Do you understand?" he asked.

I stumbled back, gritting my teeth. "I never agreed to this," I whispered. What had I said in the haunted house? Had I sold my soul without knowing what I was signing?

Desmond frowned. "You swore you'd keep my secrets. If you break your vow, I won't be responsible for the fate the spirits decide for you."

His threats of spirits would have made me laugh earlier that evening, waiting in line to enter the haunted house. Wild how fast things could change.

"I won't tell anyone," I said. "Take me to him."

*B*efore we left, I quickly changed out of my pajamas and into the only dress I knew Karyn wouldn't mind me wearing—the black sheath I'd borrowed for Miss Opal's funeral. In a way it seemed fitting, like I was back to where I started, before I believed in magic. This was the mindset that would keep me from falling apart when faced with whatever awaited me in the witches' lair.

My beloved black boots were too wet to put back on, so I borrowed a pair of Karyn's black sandals. Despite being two sizes too small, my toes barely hung over the edges. I grabbed a black satin clutch too, something so plain I prayed she wouldn't miss it. I missed my shorts, particularly the pockets, as I shoved Bebe into the bag.

"You look great," Desmond said as I stepped out into the hall. "You ready?"

I nodded, gritting my teeth against the pain radiating from my ankle. It was so swollen now I couldn't have pulled my boots on even if they had been dry. I managed to make it to the garage without complaint.

Inside the car, Desmond plugged the address into the GPS fixed on the dash, and I realized I didn't need him to get there. Satan had given me my own invitation. I wasn't eager to accept, couldn't even recall where the fancy little card was anymore. Besides, as uncertain as I was about Desmond, I couldn't stand the thought of being alone.

"These things are really cool," Desmond said, nodding at the GPS Xavier had installed into the dash of the antique car. "I've heard about them, but never seen one before."

"How long have you been in that haunted house?" I asked.

Desmond frowned. "Long enough."

Our drive took us downtown, past the World War II Museum headed toward the Mississippi River. I squirmed around in my seat, wondering if he knew I couldn't swim. How good of a look had he gotten inside my head?

Desmond said little, mostly marveling at Xavier's sound system, how smoothly the car handled. I wanted to ask him how old he was or press the matter of the last time he'd left the haunted house, but I was afraid of the answers.

"You have reached your destination," the GPS announced.

"No way," I whispered. We were at the Port of Orleans, where the cruise ships departed. I sometimes hung out in the parking garage, picking the pockets of tipsy tourists. But instead of cruise ships docked along the departures deck, there were four elegant wooden ships. In my eagerness to get closer, I scrambled out of the car the moment Desmond braked.

The ships varied greatly in size and were docked in order from smallest to largest. Their individual designs were similar, but each had its own distinct sails—two green snakes twisting around each other like bisecting pieces of a rollercoaster, a silver rocket ship floating beside a full moon so vivid I could count its craters, an enormous glittering diamond against a backdrop as black as a starless night, and a golden star bathed in the red glow of a rising sun.

While I stood there staring, Desmond jogged up behind me. "They might not let me on board," he said. "But I'll come as far as I can."

I winced. "Why wouldn't they…"

"You might decide to go with them," Desmond said. "I won't. But I'll take care of your cats for you, okay?"

Despite the pre-dawn darkness, I could see fear in his eyes. But I had to press on. Had to make sure Xavier was safe. I nodded my agreement. "Which ship do you think he's on?" I asked.

"Let's hope it's not Freestar," Desmond grumbled, which meant little to me. Though the name rang an ominous bell, I couldn't name the tune.

The ship with the snake sails was closest to us. As we approached, I noticed people dancing on the deck, but their movements had a frenzied independence I welcomed after witnessing the creepy coordinated dancers in the addiction realm.

Satan stood on the deck, waving to us. I recognized his ringed fingers instantly, though he'd changed into jeans and no longer wore his costume save the red contacts. Surely, they were contacts. No one really had red eyes, right?

I threw my shoulders back, adopting a confident stance. Never let Satan see you sweat.

"Ah, Lisette, welcome to the after-party," Satan shouted down. "We've been expecting you."

"Who is we?" I replied, planting my feet where I stood.

"You've got a short memory, kid," Satan answered.

"Phaelgood. We're the coven that likes to party. Who's your friend?"

"I was just leaving," Desmond said, turning on his heel. "Good luck, Lisette. I'll... I'll wait for you in the car—until the ships sail."

Did I dare go forward? Running away like Desmond had no longer seemed like a choice. I spied a rope ladder on the side of Satan's ship. I took a steadying breath as I neared it, resolved not to turn around.

38

A COVEN
CALLED
PHAELGOOD

Near the top of the rope ladder, one of my too-small sandals popped off and went spiraling down. It landed with a *plunk* into the water. The sound bothered me more than my bare foot because it reminded me of a certain jungle. The green sails with their twin serpents rippling in the wind jogged my memory in the worst way. But before I could turn back, a strong arm wrapped around me and pulled me up to the deck.

Satan smirked, his red eyes glowing. "Welcome, Lisette! Are you hungry? Thirsty?"

Of course I was; I'd shared my last meal with a stray cat. My apprehension kept me from opening my mouth, but I nodded anyway.

"Follow me to the banquet hall," Satan said. He gestured toward the center of the boat with a golden goblet in his hand. A tiny bit of red liquid sloshed over the brim and trickled down the side. "We have all of your favorites—crab cakes, king cakes, and non-cake stuff, too, of course."

"King cakes? But it's not Carnival season," I said, so taken aback by the blasphemy my vocal cords cracked.

Satan laughed. "You're a distrustful little thing, aren't you? We always have whatever you want to eat here. Do you think I'm lying? Do you think I'm the real devil?"

"No, of course not," I scoffed.

"My name's Fabian." He leaned in so close I caught a

whiff of his musk. It reminded me of the sweet smoke curling off the blunt we'd passed around in Kennedy's van. "I'm not a bad guy. The whole devil costume is meant to be ironic."

"Oh, okay," I answered, hardly trying to hide my skepticism.

Fabian ignored my reservations, slipping an arm around my shoulder. "I'm the unofficial leader of our little group," he said. "Usually, people warm up to me immediately. But not you. Why? What's your deal? Are you afraid of me?"

I tried to smile but couldn't make my mouth move. At least I managed to shrug, worming out of his overly familiar embrace.

His arms crashed against his sides. "Don't you remember how I helped you? I healed your cut," Fabian said, his expectant look slowly fading into sadness.

Was he truly hurt that I didn't trust him? His puppy-dog eyes were too hard to look into, so I let my gaze fall to my feet. The deck was dirty, green grime spotted with black marring the peeling wooden boards. He touched my chin, raising my eyes to his.

"Don't judge us so quickly," he said. Then he held a joint to my lips, and with one fluid motion, lit the tip.

My ankle was killing me. My whole body felt like I'd been inside a rock tumbler. Just one little puff would take away the pain. And yet, I turned my head away as if he were some sloppy high school boy trying to kiss me.

"Sorry, but I can't afford any distractions right now. I'm looking for someone," I said. "His name is Desmond. Have you seen him?"

"Desmond… Desmond…" Fabian tugged at the tip of his long beard. "The name doesn't ring a bell. Of course, I've met so many new people tonight… you know Lisette, I really can't get over the whole you not trusting me thing. What would it take to change your mind?"

I said nothing, but he must have been psychic because he

dropped down, his jeans brushing against the filthy deck, and wrapped both hands around my bad ankle. His rings were cool against my skin. I yelped in surprise, but it didn't actually hurt as he dug his fingertips into my skin, massaging the ligaments, pushing them back into place.

"It's only a sprain," Fabian said. "Might be a little sore tomorrow, but that's all."

I opened my mouth to argue—it would hurt more tomorrow, not less. I'd suffered enough rough landings in gymnastics to know how my body behaved. But when I looked down at my ankle, my tongue wouldn't move to form words. The swelling was gone. All that remained of the horrible, throbbing pain was a faint tingle like an icepack being applied to an old injury.

"What did you do to it?" I stammered.

"Healed it," Fabian answered simply. He reached up toward me, and I held out my hand reflexively, helping him to his feet.

"But how? How did you heal it?" I asked, gulping, thinking about what Dr. Montgomery had told me about the relationship between pain and power.

"There is no pain in Phaelgood," Fabian said. "All we do here is have fun. Even the Thirteenth Realm is a low-effort event for us. We show up, work a few realms, grab a few new members and go back out to sea. You would be so happy with us. We even have a place in the city if you'd rather stick to land. That's why our ship is a bit smaller than the rest; we like having options."

I looked back up, skipping over his eyes and seeing past him. The party was in full swing. Everyone was dancing and laughing, letting the good times roll. I counted at least a dozen Carnival costumes, women with feather boas draped over their sleeveless shoulders and men in color-blocked silk suits of green and purple with matching glittery top hats. But amongst the fray, a ceramic mask stuck out to me, particularly because the man wearing it also wore a familiar white lab coat.

"You're a very skilled healer," I said to Fabian. "Is that common in your coven?"

The word *coven* seemed to throw him off. Perhaps they called themselves something different. Or maybe he just didn't like the word coming out of my mouth.

"Phaelgood has only one defining principle, a motto if you will: *If it feels good, it is good.* What do you think, Lisette? Think you can get down with that?"

I sucked in a deep breath, and though I didn't say no, I didn't need to. Fabian must've read my mind again because his hopeful expression disappeared. Or perhaps Dr. Montgomery chased it away.

"Hello Lisette," Dr. Montgomery said in a scolding tone. I could feel the chill of his icy glare through the slits in his mask. "I'm surprised to see you here."

"I'm looking for someone," I said. "Guy named Desmond. Do you know him?"

Dr. Montgomery nodded, or at least his mask moved an inch or two. "Tall fellow? Dark hair?"

"That's him."

"He's on Freestar's ship, I believe," Dr. Montgomery said. "Come on, I'll take you."

I trusted Montgomery a tiny bit more than Satan, especially after he'd given me Bebe and helped me win the bonus round. So when he moved toward the ladder, I stepped forward, too.

Fabian's hand shot out so fast I didn't even see it until it landed on my wrist. "Wait! Phaelgood is more than witches who practice magic together. We're a family. You've never had a real family before, have you, Lisette?"

Tough as I believed myself to be, this cut me right to the core. I opened my mouth, praying for an insult to come rescue me, but I couldn't even eke out a sarcastic reply. Damn, the truth hurt. I looked down at the ring, the only thing I had left of my mother. Both of my parents had abandoned me.

"Oh please," Dr. Montgomery huffed. "You speak of family, yet you stand here and torment her with half-truths about her life? Let her go, Fabian."

"This is where she belongs," Fabian insisted, then, turning to me, continued, "None of the other covens will understand you. They will all work to make you into something you are not."

Though I was hungry and exhausted, with the pain from my ankle gone, I felt a surge of energy. I twisted away from him easily. "I don't belong here," I said. "Let me go."

Fabian frowned, but he released me. "You'll regret this," he grumbled.

I chased after Dr. Montgomery, cringing as something slimy squished between my toes. Silly as I felt with one shoe on, I dared not take it off. At least one of my feet would be protected against this gross sludge. But it was too hard to climb down with uneven footing, so I kicked off the second too-small sandal the moment I reached the ladder.

Montgomery gestured for me to climb down first. "Go ahead," he said. "I'll keep watch."

At first, I didn't understand what he meant, but when I looked over his shoulder, I saw it. Fabian had rallied troops— the race-car driver who'd parachuted out of the Jeep in the first realm, the headless horseman who guarded the public speaking challenge, and the flirty safari guide from the jungle round. What was his name? Bob or Bud or Bill? I had a feeling he remembered mine.

"Hurry, but watch your step," Dr. Montgomery said.

The rough rope cut into my bare feet and I prayed I wouldn't fall. Above me, I heard a scuffle, then Dr. Montgomery arguing with them. By the time I'd reached the platform below, their voices had blended into an angry buzz. I held the clutch I'd borrowed from Karyn against my chest.

Even with the satin fabric of the purse between us, Bebe comforted me.

After a few minutes, Dr. Montgomery finally came shooting down. I tensed up, ready to run in case he was being followed. But when he landed beside me, he only seemed annoyed, shaking his head. "I told you not to come here," he said. "Why didn't you listen to me?"

"Like I already told you, I'm looking for someone. Besides, if the ships are so terrible, why are you here?"

Montgomery laughed, a deep boom that echoed behind his mask. "A gambling addict goes to a casino, but he wouldn't recommend it. Did you have anything to eat or drink when you were on board?"

"No, why?" I asked.

"You consume their pleasures; they consume your soul. That's how Phaelgood operates," Dr. Montgomery said. "I visit, but I never stay long. Come on, let's find your friend before your mother sees us and tears me a new—"

Someone shouting his name stopped him from finishing. But it wasn't my mother. It was the tall stranger who had destroyed our apartment.

LET
MICOMPAS
BE YOUR
GUIDE

Wolfram and I locked eyes, and it quickly turned into a staring contest neither of us could bear to lose. His eyes were blue, but not dark and foreboding like my mother's. Instead, they were light and piercing like my own. He was tall like me too, someone whose arms I would fit into. Someone who might've rocked me like I was a child, found the strength to catch up on all we'd lost.

He squared his shoulders, regal as royalty atop the most glorious ship I had ever seen. The mahogany hull gleamed so brilliantly it reflected the blue-black waves below, their crests too subtle to sway the vessel. My eyes climbed up, past three elaborate crow's nests, to rows of taut flags featuring giant diamonds on pitch-black backdrops.

Wolfram grabbed a rope and swung down from the ship. He landed a few feet away and made up the difference strutting. His long legs quickly closed the gap.

As strange as it was to finally meet him, this man who might be my father, I appreciated his showmanship. For a moment, everything was exactly as I had always pictured it.

"Lisette," Wolfram said, grasping my hands as if he'd never let them go. "I am so glad you made it. Come up, come up. I must introduce you to everyone. Your cousins, your aunts and uncles, your grandmother—they are all here."

My heart leaped. Was this it? The moment I had longed

for my whole life. I would finally meet my family, the people who would love me unconditionally.

Dr. Montgomery clapped a hand down on my shoulder. "Do you still wish to find Desmond? The end of the party is approaching. Whichever ship you are on when the sun—"

"You have a friend here?" Wolfram asked me. He pulled me close, turning me away from Dr. Montgomery. "Come, we will discuss it on my ship. You must be careful befriending witches from other covens. None are so noble as Micompas. If you do not watch your back—"

Dr. Montgomery materialized in front of us, blocking the way, though I didn't understand how he'd gotten ahead. His mask hid his expression, but I detected a snarl in his voice as he said, "Whichever ship you are on when the sun rises is where you shall remain until next Halloween. If you wish to find your friend, you must hurry."

I nodded and started to tell Wolfram the family reunion would have to wait—as much as I wanted to meet everyone, to *finally* meet everyone, I had to talk to Xavier—I needed to remember to call him Desmond—first. Did *he* realize he'd be stuck on a ship for a whole year? But before I could explain my mission, Wolfram gave Dr. Montgomery a shove.

It wasn't a hard shove. Dr. Montgomery only stumbled. But my father's sudden violent outburst frightened me all the same. Was this why Ruelle had kept us apart?

"Back off, Montgomery," Wolfram barked. "This is a family matter."

"I'm more her family than you are," Dr. Montgomery said. "At least I care about her well-being. You don't even know her."

"Know her? Of course I know her! I am her father!" Wolfram shouted, raising his hands as if to strike again.

But Dr. Montgomery was prepared this time. He clapped his hands, sending forth a gust of wind so strong it knocked Wolfram flat on his back. Dr. Montgomery stepped forward, looking down at him. "A father is someone who raises a child, not someone who shows up and makes demands once the child is grown. You aren't a father. You're an opportunist."

I didn't know what to do. I wanted a relationship with my father, even if he wasn't perfect. He was my key to other family members, and surely some of them, or at least one of them, would understand me. No one had ever really understood me. Not even Xavier.

Suddenly I realized it didn't matter that Xavi didn't always get me. He loved me anyway. If the shoe was on the other foot, he wouldn't have gone on a side quest. He would've gotten straight to saving me. What was I doing?

Wolfram scrambled to his feet, but he eyed Montgomery with caution now. "Do not listen to him, Lisette," he said. "I am your father. Of course I care for you. I am sorry your mother kept us apart all these years. Give me a chance to make it up to you. Come with me." He extended his hand, and my own fingers trembled, desperate to take it.

I swallowed. If only I could tell him how long I'd waited for this. How many daydreams he'd starred in, fantasies where he would show up and whisk me away, especially during the worst times, when we'd slept beneath the bridge. I had looked for his face behind the driver's wheel of every passing car on those dark nights. Stayed awake until burning headlights shut my eyes. But he didn't show up to save me then. Why was he here now?

"Y'know, Mom couldn't watch me all the time," I said, choosing my words, trying to keep my voice steady, though my throat threatened to close. "I was alone a lot. Bad things happened to me. Because I was alone."

"Lisette, I am so sorry," Wolfram said, but he didn't sound sorry. He sounded angry. Maybe at Ruelle for allowing me to be in harm's way. Maybe at Dr. Montgomery for interfering. Maybe at me for not jumping at the opportunity to join him on his beautiful ship.

I didn't have to board it to know it was fantastic on the inside. His fancy clothes and polished boots told me everything I needed to know about the lifestyle he lived. Yet it spoke volumes that he hadn't noticed my cold toes. Surely if he could zap all our furniture and shrink it, he could find me a pair of shoes. But he hadn't noticed my plight. Dr. Montgomery had been right—he didn't really care about me. Probably never had.

Then I looked past Wolfram, up to the deck, and saw the man with the white beard. The revelation of who he was—the Micompas representative at the end of the haunted house and the Santa Claus in the picture my mother had left behind—made me gasp. *Don't follow me.* Ruelle wasn't mad at me. She had meant it as a warning.

"Thanks for the invitation," I muttered, turning away from Wolfram and walking past his ship. "But I have to find my friend. Maybe I'll come back."

"You are making a huge mistake," he said. "You are not thinking for yourself right now. You are allowing Montgomery and your mother to speak for you. They are telling you to run away from me. But fine, so be it. Run, Lisette. Do exactly what she did. I will tell you what I told her—whenever you are ready to return, I will be here."

"Thank you," I said, afraid anything else might set him off again.

It was a terrible feeling, finally meeting him and wanting to run from him. Finally getting to see him in the flesh only to find out he was a monster. But I'd seen enough evil beasts tonight to recognize their kind. Maybe that was why fate finally allowed us to collide—I knew what he was well enough to run.

I glanced over my shoulder only once, back at the diamond sails. My fingers brushed over my mother's ring, wondering if it were a family heirloom from his side. Wondering what I was missing because of the gatekeeper.

You are better off without him, a voice as gentle as the breeze whispered, and I closed my eyes, accepting the words of comfort.

Dr. Montgomery fell in step beside me, his hand landing lightly on my shoulder. From the side, I could see a good bit of his face; it drooped as though he was depressed. "I have something for you. A gift, a real one. I won't accept payment, so don't offer."

I laughed, surprising myself. Something about him was so funny. That alone should've told me he was all right. "What is it?"

He stopped, so I stood still, too. He reached into the pocket of his lab coat and produced three stones. "Promise you won't lose them," he said as he placed the stones into my out-turned palm. One gleamed a pale heavenly blue across its smooth rectangular surface, the second sparkled vibrant purple with three rounded edges, and the third stone was charcoal-black with jagged tips.

"What are these for?" I asked, my mind bouncing back to Ruelle and her rocks.

"The blue is angelite to keep your spirit guides close," Dr. Montgomery explained. "The purple garnet has the power to heal your body and strengthen your manifestations. The black is tourmaline to block negative influence and tether you to the earth."

"Do they actually work?" I asked.

He scoffed. "Do they work? Have faith, Lisette. Faith is free. And so is this gift. Do you want it or not?"

"Yes," I stammered, still hesitant. "Sorry, I have trouble trusting people."

Dr. Montgomery nodded. "I get it. My father abandoned me, too. I'm not perfect myself, but at least I know it. I'm trying to do better. Can't do better if you don't show up and admit you aren't perfect."

I smiled as well as I could manage, tucking his stones inside my clutch alongside Bebe. "Thank you," I said.

"You seem tired, Lisette. I know everyone hates hearing that, but you do. Are you sure you're up to boarding Freestar? They're a rough crowd."

"It doesn't matter," I said. "I have to see Desmond."

"Very well," Dr. Montgomery said. "Luckily, you have Ruelle's ring; it will afford you some protection. Do you know how it works?"

The million-dollar question. So many times tonight, it seemed the ring had helped me out of a jam, and yet I couldn't have explained how if I had a gun pointed at my head.

"It just works," I said at last. "I wish I knew how."

Dr. Montgomery pointed toward the third ship, its silver sails with rocket ships and shimmering moons fluttered in the wind. "We could always take a quick detour and ask your mother."

40

SCIENCE
WITHOUT
SENSE

"No one told me she was here," I said, eyes glued on the deck as if perhaps she'd be hanging over the edge, waiting for me. What would she say if she saw me?

I held my own hand, rubbing the diamonds as if ensuring their prongs hadn't loosened. What if she asked for the ring back?

Go to her, the encouraging voice said. *Receive your blessing.*

"She's here," Dr. Montgomery said. "I saw her not an hour ago. She asked me about you. I told her you won the money, and she seemed quite relieved."

I gulped. "Did she ask if I was here?"

"Of course she did. But I hadn't seen you yet, so I told her what I knew—that you left the Thirteenth Realm without joining any of the covens. Lisette, it's not too late to make that choice again. It's the one Ruelle would want for you. The one I think is safest for you. What do *you* want?"

What did I want?

My eyes drifted past the ships to the blue-black water. A pelican swooped down from the clouds and dove into the river. When it emerged, the fin of a dying fish wriggled in its bill.

Pelicans are fascinating birds; we studied them in biology. The mothers are so devoted that if proper nourishment cannot be located, they will pierce their breasts with their beaks to feed their young. It put a new spin on the whole "blood, sweat, and tears" thing.

So many scientists studied how animals in the wild would fight to the death for the survival of their young. But no one seemed to care about the way newborns needed their mothers, about the magnetic pull that could last a lifetime. Yes, most mothers loved their children without condition or limitation. But all children loved their mothers; their lives depended on it.

"I need to see Ruelle," I said.

Montgomery's hand fluttered up to the back of his neck. I didn't realize what he was doing until his mask fell from his face and clattered to the platform. "I will not go where I am not wanted," Dr. Montgomery said. "As such, I cannot board her ship. You may go on without me if you like, or you may come with me."

"Come with you?" I repeated uncertainly, staring at his naked face. Though I'd seen it once before briefly when he studied Bebe, it still struck me as a novelty—the small crinkles at the edges of his eyes, the sadness pooling in his deep brown irises.

"Why do you think I still participate in this Halloween madness?" Dr. Montgomery said, laughing a little too long, as if nervous to proceed. "I'm looking for an apprentice, Lisette. Go, seek your mother's blessing. I think she would agree the work would suit you—and you could stay in the city you love."

Subconsciously, my fingers brushed over my bruised nose. How could someone as reckless as me be a healer like him? "I'll think about it," I muttered, hurrying off toward the ship with the silver sails.

The closer I came to the deck, my bare feet thankful for the smooth metal ladder, the clearer I could see the sails—the glowing moon next to the rocket ship, the craters reminding me of the divots on my face.

I expected my mother to greet me, or maybe Celeste Honeycutt, the pushy witch who tried to claim me with another necklace. What was with these witches and jewelry? But never in a million years would I have imagined my own Miss Fenty to reach down and help me onto the ship.

"Welcome, Miss Colbert," she said, her milk-glass green eyes twinkling. "Everyone on the ship has been talking about you."

I gasped. "Miss Fenty? You're a witch?"

She nodded. "Official liaison to refugee witches, that's me. I met your mother the moment she left Freestar. I set her up in New Orleans. Or didn't she tell you?"

"No," I whispered, leaving the ladder to stand beside her. "She never spoke a word of it."

Miss Fenty took me in, a small frown on her lips. "Lisette, where are your shoes?"

My toes suddenly felt ten degrees colder. A shiver moved up my legs, prickling my skin. "It's a long story," I said.

"Well, I can't take you to see your mother like that," Miss Fenty said, pushing back the sleeves of her silver cloak. I noticed the hood bunched up around her shoulders and wondered if she had been in the crowd, if maybe she'd seen me outsmart that mythical creature in the pool.

Before I could ask her what she knew of the Thirteenth Realm, she directed an inky black mist toward my feet. Black droplets swirled around my anklets and solidified, turning into supple leather molded to my exact measurements.

I tapped each foot in turn, marveling at the way the soles supported my arches. "Holy tamales," I said. "These are incredible!"

"You're welcome," Miss Fenty said, clearing her throat. "But I must admit I'm quite tired now. The ship will be sailing soon, and I will be returning to my home."

"Already? But I just got here."

"You're welcome to come with me," Miss Fenty said. "I understand your situation has changed, but I can help you get established again. Help you put your winnings into a proper savings account so when college starts—"

"I need to see my mother," I interrupted her, remembering the ring and why I'd stopped here at all. Why did everyone seem so hellbent on diverting me?

"Follow me," Miss Fenty said, hurrying off toward the back of the ship much faster than I'd assumed she could go.

The cleanliness of the ship struck me as we climbed down a long flight of interior steps. Almost everything was made of metal, with gemstones encrusted here and there. There were splendid arrangements of sapphires, amethysts, pearls, and unidentifiable stones, including some I'd never seen before.

At last, Miss Fenty rapped on a wooden door that looked like all the others we had passed, and a small figure opened it. When I saw her, my palm shot over my mouth as if to hide my stunned expression. I'd thought I'd never see her again—the little girl with no eyes.

"Lisette is here, isn't she?" the eyeless girl asked excitedly. "I can sense her energy."

After a beat, Miss Fenty answered for me. "Yes, she's come to see her mother."

"Come in, but you must be quick. Ruelle is weak," the eyeless girl explained. "She's drained from healing Kennedy."

"My Kennedy?" I asked. "Pretty face? Purple fingernails? Is she okay?"

The eyeless girl's tiny chin trembled. "She was badly burned, but Ruelle is optimistic about her recovery."

My stomach knotted up like a pretzel. The lava *was* real. Even though Kennedy hadn't fallen in, even though she'd said the safe word, it had hurt her all the same.

"Step lightly," the girl said, moving back so we could enter the room. "If they are asleep, I will have to escort you back out. The sun will be up soon."

Miss Fenty frowned. "I am afraid I must depart before the ship sails. My work is in New Orleans."

The girl scoffed. "You can go whenever you wish. But Lisette is going to stay. Won't you, Lisette? We would all love you to sail with us."

I started to apologize for my lackluster feelings about the ship. But instead, I decided to give honesty a try. "I really must speak to my mother," I said, omitting the part about needing to know how the ring worked.

The little girl seemed sad, and I realized as she took us deeper into the ship, to a room protected by two locked doors, I didn't even know her name. Somehow, she appeared to read my mind.

"How kind of you to concern yourself with me," the little girl said, brightening. "Please call me Starla—and not *Starla the Spoiled,* as some do."

Miss Fenty pretended to cough to disguise a laugh. But Starla seemed to catch her intent, anyway. "I've spent years trying to shake that nickname," Starla said. "You know it isn't fair."

"I know, I know," Miss Fenty said, holding up her hands defensively. "I don't call you that."

"Not to my face anyway," Starla mumbled.

I didn't know quite what to say, but I didn't have to say anything. Starla held her finger to her lips to signal we were entering a quiet zone. She tiptoed in, and I followed, squinting in the darkness, zeroing in on the shimmying flames of a single candelabra. My mother rested in a chair beside a small bed, where Kennedy lay sleeping. I recognized her by her hands folded over her chest, her bright purple fingernails, but not by her face, which had been wrapped in white gauze secured by tiny purple crystals, amethysts if I had to guess.

"What is it now, Starla?" Ruelle asked, her voice low so as not to wake Kennedy.

"I apologize for disturbing you, but your daughter is here," Starla answered.

A shadow crossed over the candelabra as Ruelle rose to

her feet and walked toward me. "As happy as I am to see you, you shouldn't be here," she said, her tone frantic. "The ship will set sail soon. You will be stuck here."

"I know, I know," I said, annoyed at the redundant warning. "I came to ask about the ring."

"What about the ring?" Ruelle took my hand, twisting my finger so the diamonds faced out, creating little rainbows that played off the candelabra's flames.

I took a deep breath, prolonging the question. "Do you want it back?"

"No," Ruelle said without hesitation. "I want you to have it."

"Well, that's uncharacteristically generous," I said with a shaky laugh. "Especially since I stole it. Are you sure you don't want to lecture me?"

Ruelle shook her head. "I raised a thief. How could I be surprised when you took the ring without asking? Besides, you need it more than I do. Now hurry, go with Miss Fenty."

"Wait! I don't know how to use it."

She smiled at me, touching the ring again, tapping each of the four diamonds in turn. "Each stone contains the wisdom of one of the witches who wore it before—my great-grandmother, grandmother, my mother, and now me. Any time you ask the ring for guidance or protection—and sometimes even if you don't—our spirits will heed your call."

Part of me wanted to scream that was impossible—but for once, I could hush my skeptical side up. I needed to believe in magic now. I still had to save Xavier.

"I have to go," I said, swallowing hard. "I have to go to the Freestar ship, my friend—"

Ruelle took a step back as if I had struck her. "Please go with Miss Fenty, Lisette. She will make sure you are well taken care of. It is not safe on the Freestar ship, ring or no ring."

"I have to go," I said, trying on the steady tone she always used to signal finality.

"You don't have enough time," Ruelle argued. "It's nearly sunrise. You'll be stuck there for the next year."

"Then I'll get stuck," I said. "I can't leave Xavier—not again."

Once she heard his name, Ruelle seemed to soften. Perhaps she finally understood what he meant to me. "Do you still have your poppet?"

I looked down at the clutch, confused. "Yes, why?"

"As long as you have your poppet, you'll be able to teleport back to New Orleans…" she trailed off, then sighed. "I should have explained your powers to you a long time ago. My pride got in the way, and now I'm afraid time is up. But as long as you keep hold of your poppet and focus on the place you want to be, it will take you there."

"Why did you take my power from me?" I demanded, forgetting Kennedy was asleep. The poor girl stirred slightly, whimpering.

Ruelle shot a hard look at me. "I did it to protect you," she whisper-hissed. "Everything I did, I did to protect you. I'm sorry I couldn't do a better job. I did the best I could."

I didn't know how to respond to that—who wants to hear their best wasn't enough? Besides, it wasn't as if we could go back. I only hoped we were lucky enough to go forward—that I might see her again.

Without a word, I kissed her cheek, something we never did, but it felt right. She must've thought so too, because she kissed mine in return.

Ruelle glanced at my clutch again. "I thought you won. What did you do with your winnings?"

I gasped, realizing the briefcase was still stowed beneath the bed. After all I'd been through to get that money, I couldn't believe I'd forgotten it so easily. "I left it at Xavier's," I admitted, hanging my head and waiting for her to chastise me for my recklessness. "I'm sorry. I was just so worried about him..." I stopped making excuses. Apologetic words only served to spike her anger.

But when Ruelle gently tipped my chin up to meet her gaze, she didn't look mad. Or even disappointed. Her eyes glistened and chest puffed up. "I'm proud of you," she said. "You learned the value of friendship much faster than I did."

I blushed but said nothing. Her praise was too new for me to trust it. I looked around the cabin, desperate to change the subject."I knew her," I said, nodding at Kennedy. "Will she be all right?"

"Eventually," Ruelle said with a weary sigh. "She may have some scars, but she'll recover. She told me you tried to help her. That was very brave, Lisette. I know I didn't want you to go, but I'm proud of you for making it out."

"Thanks," I muttered, rocking back in my new boots. They were much more comfortable than my old pair.

"I love you, Lisette," my mother said, and in the flickering light of the candelabra, I could see the glimmer of tears in her deep blue eyes.

"Love you, too," I replied. Then I turned away before she saw her heartbroken expression mirrored on my face. We would mend the broken fence between us someday, learn to take down our walls and rebuild together. But we didn't have time now.

"Ten minutes until sunrise," Starla said, and my mind skipped down a dark path, wondering when she'd last seen orange rays pushing against a gray fog.

Ruelle handed me a single stone. A ruby that symbolized luck and family ties. So many times she'd tried to teach me about this kind of magic, but I had rolled my eyes, dismissed her. Now I smiled, adding it to the others in my bag. "Thank you," I said. "I'm sorry it took me so long to appreciate it."

"Until we meet again," Ruelle said.

Then I left before regret anchored me in place.

41

A
FRESH
START

Ruelle escorted Miss Fenty and me off the Sciella ship. As we ran, Ruelle explained how I could visualize where I wanted to go and teleport there in seconds with the aid of my poppet.

After one last hug, we left the ship. The sun was nothing but a threat. Still, Miss Fenty frowned into the horizon, her eyes avoiding the red sails with the shooting star. "Why are you so set on boarding that wicked ship?" she asked me.

I looked past her, my gaze lingering on the last and largest ship of the four. The mermaid carved into the hull—her golden gilded hair adorned with iridescent conch shells and huge, glowing pearls—took my breath away. And suddenly I knew. This was the majestic ship where my mother was born.

"Because I have to find my friend," I said. "I have to make sure he's all right—that he wants to be here."

"And if he doesn't?"

"Then I'll help him escape," I said as if it were obvious. But Miss Fenty's silent shifting, the deep frown marring her delicate features, told me I was woefully underestimating the challenges of my mission.

The Freestar vessel was fantastic and glamorous, a fairy tale made to travel from coast to coast. Yet even as I admired this unlikely union of sleekness and whimsy, I could sense it had something else in common with fairy tales. This ship carried dark secrets.

Miss Fenty stood at my shoulder, half a step behind me. "Your gifts will aid you; use them wisely," she said. "But don't get cocky. Pride proceeds the fall. And don't dare dawdle. The longer you stay, the harder it will be to leave."

I turned to give her a hug, a proper goodbye. But she was gone. Guess I wasn't the only one who could teleport. But that was okay; I was used to handling my problems alone.

As I drew nearer to the Freestar ship, the unmistakable melody of celebration—fast tempo music, laughter, the constant clink of glasses—grew louder. The ladder to ascend this ship was not a temporary addition like on the others I'd boarded, but permanent grooves cut into the side of the boat itself. A bold move, leaving the ship perpetually exposed. It led me to surmise the people partying weren't afraid of anyone.

I was afraid, though. Afraid to encounter my best friend's soul inside the body of someone I had kissed. Thank God nothing else had happened. Still, it was enough to distract me from the race against the sun coming up; no one had mentioned exactly how high in the sky it had to be before the ships would sail.

A six-piece band with a voluptuous lead singer, whose auburn curls snaked around her hourglass waist, loomed over the crowd on a stage with psychedelic lighting. Colors exploded and faded, sizzling across their golden instruments like fireworks.

Out of the corner of my eye, I saw someone with slicked-back hair slinking toward me. I thought I'd gotten lucky. He'd found me before I even started looking. But a second glance deflated me. It wasn't Xavier in Desmond's body—it was Tucker.

Aside from some ripped pant seams where he'd been hung from the meat hook, Tucker had escaped without a scratch. "Congratulations," he said. "Where are you taking me with your winnings? Commander's Palace? Galatoires?"

He tried to hug me, but I pushed him off, surprising us

both. The light show on the stage behind us made the luster of my mother's—no, my—diamond ring too spectacular to ignore.

Tucker shrank at my power. But he didn't back off. "What's gotten into you, baby?"

"Don't call me that. Do you even know where your girl-friend is?" I crossed my arms to create space between us, my satin clutch pressed against my heart.

"She's fine. She's alive, isn't she?" Tucker countered with a wicked laugh.

"What about Hal? He's a—"

"Sacrifice, yes, I know. The Thirteenth Realm of Hell demands a few every year," Tucker said.

My jaw went slack. "How can you say that so casually? You know what, never mind, I don't care. I'm here to see Xa—Desmond. Do you know where he is?"

Tucker waved a hand around. "Somewhere. Good luck."

He sulked off, and I was devastated for a totally different reason. The sky had gone from dark gray to light purple. How much time did I have left?

"Congratulations," a familiar voice said at my back.

I whirled around, surprised to see Mr. Amos. Was there anyone in my life who *wasn't* a witch? Then again, I'd known he was connected to my mother. There had to be a reason she trusted him to move our stolen goods.

"Thanks," I mumbled. "Say, do you know where a guy named Desmond is?"

"Look up," Mr. Amos said, nodding toward the sky. "But before you run off, you better thank me."

"For what?"

"Spotting you the twenty bucks to get in," Mr. Amos replied with a chuckle.

"Actually, it was thirty. So you cut it kinda close, huh?"

He rubbed his bald head. "The oracle only told me to give you a twenty. She's never wrong. I wonder why—"

"I know why," I said, looking into the sky, up at the crow's nest where I spied a familiar head of slicked-back hair.

Before Mr. Amos could ask me to stay and tell the story, I bolted. Xavier needed me to rescue him. Why else would he be all alone so high up? Clearly, he was plotting his escape. Was he thinking about jumping? I had to hurry.

I climbed after him with one arm and squeezed my satin clutch tight with the other. I would need every advantage to get us out of here—ruby for luck and family ties, amplified by my diamond ring; angelite to keep my spirit guides close—its pale blue the color of Miss Opal's hair; tourmaline to block negative influences; garnet to strengthen my manifestations, and most importantly, my break-glass-in-case-of-emergency move, Bebe.

By the time I reached Xavier, panting near the point of breathlessness, I was too tired to worry about what he was doing up there. Much less what he looked like.

His eyebrows rose to his hairline as he spotted me. "Lisette! You have to leave—now! Before the sun—"

"Rises, yes, I know. But that doesn't exactly apply to me because—"

Xavier cut me off with a snort. "The rules never apply to you."

For a second, I was so stunned I could've let go of the ladder and plummeted to my death. Xavier must have seen my lips quivering because he rushed forward, pulling me into the tiny crow's nest with him, our faces so close I could taste the sweet smoke on his breath when he spoke. "I'm tired of being your sidekick."

I flinched, my toes curling up in my boots. For the first time since I'd worn them, discomfort radiated down to the soles of my feet. "Xavi, I'm so sorry. I've been a terrible friend to you. Through this horrible experience, that twisted haunted house, I realized you're the only person who really cares about me."

Three tears fell in quick succession, chasing each other down the side of his face. "I know you mean well, trying to save me," he said, "but I'm sick of it. Let me have this adventure on my own."

My knees buckled, but he held me upright. Perhaps he was stronger in this body, or maybe I'd just never trusted him enough to hold me when I needed it.

"You really want to leave your whole life behind?" I asked. "Why? You're rich; your life is perfect."

But Xavi shook his head. "I've tried to tell you before that it's not. But your problems are always bigger. I don't say that to be cruel, Lis. They truly are. But I have problems, too. And the opportunity to take a year away from them sounded too good to pass up."

"I'll miss you," I squeaked. "And of course you don't have to, but if you could ever find it in your heart to forgive me—"

He hugged me so tight it gave me strength, hope that someday we'd be okay. "I forgave you the moment you hurt me. I know you didn't mean to." He took a deep breath. "I wish we could do this together. But I want to be in charge of my own story."

Below us, I heard shouts, then all at once, the ship lurched forward. We were moving. Moving away from the platform and I couldn't swim. Panicked, I spun away from Xavier, searching the sky. I sucked in a shaky breath. The sun had snuck up on me. I could escape by using my poppet, but I had no idea if I could take Xavier with me. More importantly, it didn't sound like he wanted to leave.

Absently, my fingers stroked my ring, and I whispered, "What do I do?"

Two different voices sprang up at once—including one I thought I remembered from the haunted house. *Give him the tourmaline*, the voice said. *He'll need it to stay grounded in this ship of sea monsters.*

The ruby, too, bade a second voice, similar to the first, if only a bit softer. *He is your family. Show him.*

My hands trembled, and I nearly dropped the clutch. But with a steeling breath, I managed to present him with the stones. "Please, take these gifts," I said, giving him the ruby first and then the tourmaline. "The red stone symbolizes luck and family ties. I want you to have it because you're my family. No matter where you are, we'll always have that bond."

"Thank you," Xavier said, squeezing the tiny gem. "What's the black one mean?"

"It blocks negative influence," I said.

"Why would I need that?" he asked, frowning.

"All the witches I have encountered say this ship is danger-ous," I explained. "And I want you to be safe."

Xavier shook his head. "You're doing it again, Lis. You're making me feel—"

"Sorry." I swallowed and smiled, hoping we wouldn't have to leave things on a bad note. "But even the hero needs a sword, doesn't he?"

He returned my smile, and I couldn't believe how good it felt. Better than winning thirty thousand dollars. "You better be waiting at the dock next Halloween."

"I will—I might even surprise you and learn how to swim."

He didn't say goodbye, so I didn't either. We weren't goodbye people. We were people who always knew there'd be a next time.

I took one last look at the early morning sun yawning over the four boats. As they split into different directions, I felt a pull to go my own way, to let Xavier go his. I pressed Bebe to my chest, and I thought about the home I'd always wanted. Not a balcony where I could watch parades or original wood floors ruined with graffiti. But a place where I was wanted and needed. I trusted Desmond to take care of my cats.

Gold bugs blinked in front of my eyes, but I didn't try to

swat them away. I didn't fear them anymore. Everything went black for a moment, but when I woke, I was on Sciella's ship. The room smelled like Ruelle. It must have been her chambers, her silver satin sheets twisting as I rose. The room could have been torn from a glossy page in a picture book. A gleaming white shark jaw jutted out from the wall, its teeth like gargantuan arrowheads. Secured to one corner with thick rope, a golden birdcage soaked up the candlelight from the swaying chandelier above.

What appeared to be a parrot blinked at me and squawked, "Stowaway."

Ruelle hovered over me. She didn't look surprised or angry as I had expected. In fact, an unfamiliar expression, something happy and hopeful, warmed her face.

"You're back," she said. "After you left, Miss Fenty returned. We had a long conversation."

"Oh? Did you two decide what's wrong with me?" I asked, sitting up in the bed, blinking as I absorbed the strange room.

"No. We scratched the surface regarding what's wrong with *me*. Too much self-doubt, not enough self-control, a strong tendency to self-medicate." She ticked her ailments off on her fingers. "But I'm sober now. And I'm going to keep digging, keep discovering my own scar tissue so I can heal. You deserve that. You deserve more, but this is what I have to give you."

"I'll take it," I said.

I couldn't go back, but why would I want to? I went forward into her arms, which finally opened to me. Fate had found us fit for a fresh start, a new adventure.

Acknowledgments

This is my first time acknowledging all of the people who helped me achieve my dream of publishing a book. I know I will probably mess up, say the wrong thing or not say enough. But if I'm lucky, I hope I get to do this again. And again and again, until I get good at it.

To my mom, the recorder of my very first story—a retelling of Little Red Riding Hood where the wolf ate everyone. Thank you for indulging my obsessions with villains and happily ever afters for every animal, no matter how wild.

To my dad, who fostered my love of writing stories by bringing me figurine animals. Your love language of gifting has truly helped me appreciate the thought behind the object.

To my sister Cassandra—if I could only bring one person into the 13th Realm with me I would choose you. I know we would make it out alive, at least ten thousand dollars richer, with some wild stories to tell. Thank you for championing all of my creative pursuits.

To my brother Troy, who gave me my first Stephen King novel and more importantly, discussed characters with me like they were real people. Thank you for nurturing my love of all things horror, especially books.

To the family I inherited when I married, thank you for celebrating all my successes with me. Kub, Belle, Grandma, Grandpa—your support and enthusiasm never ceases to amaze me. I'm so lucky to have you all in my life.

To all my relatives—so many aunts, uncles, grandparents, and cousins—thank you for appreciating my love of writing and sharing your stories with me. Thank you for shaping my sense of humor, my moral convictions, and my work ethic.

To my found family, especially those of you (Jan and Jaime) that kept teenage me in line, thanks for always being there for me. You might recognize a little bit of me in Lisette, though I was lucky to never struggle as hard as she did. I want you both to know I owe at least some of my wholesomeness to your wonderful influences.

To Jackstar, my first editor. Thank you for teaching me about deadlines and dancing on makeshift stages with me. Here's to many more decades of realizing our dreams.

To my literary family, MIND LIKE A DIAMOND wouldn't be what it is without you. I especially want to thank everyone at my publisher Sword & Silk. To Laynie and MB, who believed in me enough to invest in my book and assured me from our first conversation that they understood this story.

To Nicole who pulled my manuscript out of the slush pile and saw something worth sharing. To Jennia whose editorial skills have vastly improved my writing. To Kristin and Jenna who do an amazing job marketing and getting books in the hands of readers—you are all amazing and I'm so lucky to work with you. Much love to all my Sword & Silk publishing siblings too—such a talented, uplifting group of people!

Huge shoutout to my cover designer, Alessia of AC Graphics. Thank you for making my book look so beautiful!

To all of my critique partners—whether you saw multiple versions of MLAD like my soul sister Britney or just a few chapters like my dear friends Carrie and Emily—your input was so valuable throughout this process and I appreciate you all so much.

All my love to my carnival coworkers: Jena my therapist, Matt with his unique insight into teens, and Bethany who has provided so many resources both to me and the writing community. How lucky am I to have found friends who will critique my writing, pick me up at the airport, or help me move a body. (One of these is hypothetical, I'll let you guess which of the three.)

To my gifted friends Jordan and Nadi, our late night conversations and shared critiques have truly improved my writing. Thank you for trusting me with your words and helping shape my stories.

To Jim, who I was so lucky to be paired with during Camp Revpit, thank you for your insight and your encouragement.

Finally to my first CP, Ash, who encouraged me to write this story in first person. Thank you for guiding me outside of my comfort zone.

I saved the best for last—to the three people whose love lifts me everyday—my wonderful husband Matt and our darling little readers, Del and Kasi. First, thank you for putting up with me even when I'm being a moody artist. Second, thank you for giving me the time and space to write. But most of all, thank you for loving me so much it gave me the confidence to pursue publication.

God gave me the gift of story-telling, but my family gave me the courage to share my stories.

About the Author

Amanda Pavlov started performing stand-up over a decade ago in her hometown of New Orleans. Prior to finding her voice on stage, she imitated Kurt Vonnegut Jr. and Miranda July, much to the amusement of her Creative Writing professors. She believes in Science, kindness, and crossing the street to pet every dog she sees.

A Special Thank You to our Kickstarter Backers

Alexa James, Mary Beth Case, Jasmine, Morgan, Elayorna, Brynn, Lane R, Rhiannon Raphael, Sara Collins, Tabitha Clancy, Erica L Frank, Jen Schultz, Tao Neuendorffer, Kyle "kaz409" Kelly, Patrick Lofgren, Rebecca Fischer, Bridh Blanchard, William Spreadbury, Wm Chamberlainq, Adam Bertocci, Susan Hamm, Paula Rosenberg, Morgan Rider, Elizabeth Sargent, Greg Jayson, Jamie Kramer, Karen Gemin, Jonathan Rice, Bonnie Lechner, Katherine Pocock, Mary Anne Hinkle, Marlena Frank, Melissa Goldman, Stacy Psaros, Meghan Sommers, Marisa Greenfield, Anne-Sophie Sicotte, S. L. Puma, Jenn Thresher, Caley, Jim Cox, Kris McCormick, Jamie Provencher, Melody Hall, Ara James, Leigh W. Stuart, Sarah Lampkin, Stuart Chaplin, Amanda Le, Rae Alley, Arec Rain, Megan Van Dyke, Hannah Clement, Kathleen MacKinnon, Paul Senatillaka, Christine Kayser, Jennifer Crymes, Christa McDonald, Debra Goelz, Amber Hodges, Thuy M Nguyen, Jess Scott, Ella Burt, Sarah Ziemer, Mel Young, and Claire Jenkins.

Coming Soon from Sword and Silk

Coming February 2022

Unravel

By: Amelia Loken

Coming June 2022

Beneath the Starlit Sea

By: Nicole Bea

Coming August 2022

A Heartbeat Away From You

By: Ann M. Miller

CPSIA information can be obtained
at www.ICGtesting.com
Printed in the USA
BVHW070409161221
624023BV00011B/1078